The Oslo Affair

CW Browning

Copyright © 2020 by Clare Wroblewski

All rights reserved.

Cover design by Dissect Designs / www.dissectdesigns.com
Book design by Clare Wroblewski

No part of this publication may be reproduced, stored in or introduced into a retrieval system, or transmitted, in any form or by any means (electronic, mechanical, photocopying, recording or otherwise), without the prior written permission of the copyright owner, except by a reviewer who may quote brief passages in a review.

This is a work of fiction. All of the characters, organizations, and events portrayed in this novel are either products of the author's imagination or are used fictitiously. Any resemblance to actual persons, living or dead, or events is entirely coincidental.

CW Browning
Visit my website at www.cwbrowning.com

First Printing: 2020

ISBN-13: 9798639017926

Author's Note:

Throughout the fall of 1939, England and France were in the midst of what is known as the Phony War. After advancing through Poland in four weeks, the German and Soviet forces had stopped, victorious. Many believed that they would not go any further and that their objectives had been completed. The Phony War only served to reinforce that belief.

Others, however, knew that Hitler would not stop now. Training and rearmament became a priority, as did the need for information. While the rest of the world watched and waited, England and France reluctantly mobilized their forces, all the while hoping that further bloodshed could be averted.

The Oslo Affair

"It is evil things we shall be fighting against, brute force, bad faith, injustice, oppression and persecution."
~ *Neville Chamberlain, 1939*

Prologue

Bern, Switzerland
September 21, 1939

The door to the hotel swung open and a tall, lean man entered, glancing around the busy lobby as he shook off the rain. The sun was just sinking outside, casting light shadows over the city as patrons came and went through the ornately crafted entrance. After studying the people around him for a moment, the man turned to stride towards the counter. As he approached, the manager looked up and a smile crossed his face as he moved to the end of the counter to greet him.

"Welcome back, Herr Lyakhov! It's been a long time!"

"Thank you, Herr Denzler. It's nice to be back." Vladimir Lyakhov set his traveling case down by his feet. "I see it's very busy this evening."

"It's that time of year." Herr Denzler pulled a pad of check-in cards from beneath the counter, turning it so that Vladimir could fill one out. "How long will you be staying with us?"

"I'm here only for the weekend," Vladimir said, picking up the offered pen and scrawling his name onto the card. "I'm meeting an old friend while I'm here. Can you tell me if he's checked in yet?"

"Yes, of course. What's his name?"

Vladimir finished filling out the card and set the pen down, looking up. "Robert Ainsworth."

The manager frowned thoughtfully for a moment.
"I don't believe I've seen Herr Ainsworth recently," he said. "However, let me check. He may have come in earlier. Just a moment."

Vladimir nodded and watched as Herr Denzler moved away to the far end of the counter where he proceeded to flip through a catalog of cards identical to the one Vladimir had just filled out. While he waited, he turned and scanned the faces in the lobby once again.

"I'm afraid Herr Ainsworth has not checked in yet." Herr Denzler was back, shaking his head apologetically. "Would you like me to inform you when he arrives?"

"Yes, thank you." Vladimir turned back with a smile. "I only have a limited amount of time this trip and it would be disappointing to miss him."

"I understand." Herr Denzler turned to retrieve a room key. "I'll send a messenger up as soon as he arrives. Here is your room key. You're on the third floor. Do you need assistance with your bags?"

"No, that's quite all right. I've only got one." He took the key with a nod. "Thank you."

"Enjoy your stay, Herr Lyakhov."

"I'm sure I will."

Vladimir picked up his bag and turned away from the desk, moving towards the caged lift at the back of the lobby. He moved past a group of chattering young people and glanced over his shoulder, his eyes searching out the man in the black overcoat whom he'd noticed when he first entered the hotel. The man was still in the corner near the door, watching everyone who entered the hotel. As he looked back, the man turned his head towards him, his expression inscrutable. Vladimir's lips tightened faintly and he turned his head, continuing to the lift.

The sooner Robert arrived, the better for everyone. Vladimir had known he was being watched as soon as he got off the train. There was nothing new in that. But that man…he was different. He didn't work for the NKVD. He had the stamp of the German SD all over him.

And if the Germans were here, things were about to get ugly.

Chapter One

Lancashire, England
October 4, 1939

Evelyn Ainsworth stood before the grave as the last rites and prayers were read over the coffin of her father, Robert Ainsworth II. Her mother stood beside her, gripping a handkerchief in one hand and a rose in the other. Her shoulders were rigid, and Evelyn knew it was taking everything she had to stand there calmly while they buried her husband. At least the ordeal was almost over. The vicar would be finished soon, and then they could start the long walk back to the house.

Evelyn hated funerals. She always had. They were an ostentatious tradition, spread over death to disguise the gruesome fact that a body was now going to rot into ashes and mingle with the earth. They were preformed to comfort the grieving family and friends, and make them believe that their loved ones weren't really decaying, but were somewhere else. Somewhere better. They were a chance for people to say goodbye, but as far as she was concerned, there was no one to say goodbye to. The deceased was already gone, and Evelyn could never quite reconcile herself to the fact that a funeral was, at its core, nothing more than a facade.

Turning her attention back to the large coffin before them, Evelyn swallowed with difficulty. She still couldn't believe he was gone. She'd had dinner with him in London just before he left for that fateful trip to Poland. He had been leaving the next day for Warsaw, and even though Evelyn urged him to be careful, he had laughed and told her not to worry so much. That was at the end of August. It was a week later that the German army invaded Poland. For days, they were frantic for news of him. Finally, her mother received a telegram from Zürich: he was safe and on his way to Bern. He would be home shortly.

That was the last telegram he sent. He arrived at the Bellevue Palace Hotel in Bern, where he passed away in the night. They were told it was a heart attack, likely brought on by the stress of fleeing Poland ahead of the German forces.

When she received the news at her training post in Scotland, Evelyn had thought there must be some mistake. It was only the second telegram from London that convinced her the report was real. William Buckley, a family friend and close associate of her father, had sent it to confirm the news. In the past year working with Bill, she had never known him to be wrong. And this was no exception. He'd arranged for compassionate leave and transportation back to Lancashire for her immediately.

Evelyn glanced over her shoulder to where he stood now with his wife, Marguerite. Marguerite had been a god-send to her mother over the past few days. A Frenchwoman herself, she had been a great companion and comfort to Madeleine Ainsworth while she waited for her children to make it home from their respective postings. For that alone, Evelyn would always be grateful to the Buckleys.

Her brother Rob stood on her mother's other side, tall and immaculate in his RAF uniform. He'd arrived home yesterday, a few hours before her, and had gone to meet her at the station. The joy of seeing him for the first time in months was tempered by their sorrow. Now, looking at his profile, Evelyn swallowed again. This was just as hard for him as it was for her. His squadron had been training heavily since the summer, even before the outbreak of war, and he'd only been able to make it home to see their father a handful of times.

Now he was gone.

The vicar finished his prayers and stepped back, drawing her attention back to the proceedings before her. Four men stepped forward to lower the casket into the ground, and Evelyn took a deep, ragged breath. It was almost over.

A soft sob escaped from her mother as they struggled to lower the coffin, and Evelyn put an arm around her shoulders, squeezing gently. She met her brother's gaze over her head and smiled reassuringly. He looked concerned. Rob had never done well with tears, especially where his mother and sister were concerned. She turned her eyes back to the casket descending into the ground. Luckily for him, her mother was as determined not to make a scene as she was herself. Their tears would be reserved for when they were out of sight and alone.

A large crowd had gathered to say their final farewells to Robert Ainsworth. Many of them she didn't recognize, most likely

The Oslo Affair

associates from London who had worked with him in the Foreign Diplomatic Office. Several were neighbors and villagers who had known the family for decades. As Evelyn looked around the gathering, she sighed inwardly. It would be ages before they could politely leave and get back to the house.

As the men stepped away from the grave, the vicar motioned to her mother. She stepped forward, bowed her head briefly, then straightened her shoulders and lifted her chin resolutely as she kissed the bud of the rose in her hand before dropping it into the open grave. Rob glanced at her and Evelyn sighed, following her mother to drop her own flower into the grave. Standing before the gaping hole and seeing the shiny casket in its final resting place was almost too much for her, and hot tears pricked the back of her eyelids.

Blinking them away quickly, Evelyn reached up to touch the garnet necklace hanging around her neck. Her father had brought it back from Prague last year. As soon as her fingers touched the warm stones, she calmed, taking a deep breath. She reached out her other hand and dropped her rose into the opening, turning away from the grave quickly. Her eyes caught Rob's as he came up behind her and she swallowed again. He reached out and squeezed her shoulder gently in support as she paused and their eyes met.

"It's almost over," he whispered.

She nodded, smiling tremulously, and turned to follow their mother. He was right. It was almost over. She could make it.

Evelyn looked up as yet another stranger approached her, intent on expressing their condolences. She felt as if the smile on her face was permanently fixed into place, and she held out her hand automatically as the man stopped before her. Instead of taking her hand, he pressed something into it. Looking down in surprise, she found herself holding a business card.

"Miss Ainsworth, I'm very sorry for your loss," the man said. His voice was deep and low. "My name is Jasper Montclair and I was an associate of your fathers. He spoke often of you."

Evelyn looked at him more closely. Jasper wasn't a tall man, but what he lacked in height he more than made up for in charisma. His eyebrows were thick and dark, but his eyes were what really caught her attention. They were sharp and bright, giving the impression that he rarely missed anything.

"Thank you," she murmured, dropping her gaze to the card in her hand.

"I know this is a very difficult time for you and your family, but I would very much like to speak with you. I understand from William Buckley that you are stationed in Scotland?"

"Yes. I'm in the WAAFs."

"I know you've only been given a limited amount of leave," Jasper continued. "I'm terribly sorry to intrude on you at such a time, but it really is quite urgent. Can you come to London tomorrow? The address is on the card."

"Go to London?" Evelyn repeated, staring at him. "What on earth for?"

"I know it's very inconvenient, and believe me when I say that I would not ask it if it weren't of the utmost importance." Jasper smiled apologetically. "Buckley will vouch for me."

Evelyn frowned and looked more closely at the card in her hand. The address was in London, but it wasn't one she recognized. The crest on the card, however, she *did* recognize and she looked up, startled.

"Are you—" she began but he cut her off.

"I'll see you tomorrow then?" he asked, the smile still on his face. "Shall we say one o'clock?"

"I suppose so, if I must," Evelyn said in bemusement, slipping the card into her small clutch purse.

"I'd be very grateful," he said, holding out his hand. "Again, my sincerest condolence. Your father was an amazing man."

Evelyn shook his hand and nodded, then he moved away, mingling back into the crowds. Her brows came together in consternation, but the look disappeared as Rob joined her.

"If I have to hear that someone is sorry for my loss one more time, I think I'll do something altogether shocking," he announced, slipping his arm through hers and turning her towards the lane that ran past the churchyard. "Come on. Let's start off home."

"What about Mum?" Evelyn looked around. "Where is she?"

"Mrs. Buckley is collecting her; they'll be along directly. I think we've all had enough." He glanced down at her. "Who was that man just now?"

"Someone who worked with Dad, I think."

"Didn't he introduce himself?"

"Yes. His name is—"

"Jasper Montclair." A new voice spoke behind them. They turned and William Buckley smiled apologetically. "Sorry. Didn't mean

The Oslo Affair

to eavesdrop, but I couldn't help overhearing."

Evelyn smiled and held out her hand to him.

"You can eavesdrop all you like, Bill," she said warmly. "I appreciate everything you and Marguerite have done."

"Yes, thank you," Rob added, shaking his hand when Evelyn had finished. "I understand you've been a great help to my mother through all of this."

"It's the least we can do," Bill said, falling into step beside them. "I didn't know you were acquainted with Jasper, Evelyn."

"I'm not. I've just met him. He says he was an associate of Dad's."

"In a way, I suppose he was," Bill said obscurely.

"He wants me to go to London tomorrow," Evelyn said after a moment. "He wants to meet with me. Do you have any idea why?"

Bill looked at her, clearly surprised. "To London?"

"Yes."

"Then you'd better go," he said bluntly, shooting her a sharp look. "It's not often that Montclair requests a meeting."

Evelyn caught his sharp glance and nodded imperceptibly. If Bill said she was to go, she supposed she was going to London tomorrow.

"Why would he want to meet with Evie?" Rob demanded with a frown.

"I wouldn't worry too much about it," Bill said reassuringly. "More than likely, he just wants to make sure that you both know you have allies in London should you ever need them. It's our way of taking care of our own, you see."

Rob continued to frown. "I don't see, but if you vouch for him, I don't suppose I can say anything to stop it."

"I'll be fine," Evelyn said with a quick smile. "I'll take the train down in the morning and be back after dinner."

"William!" a voice called from behind them. "Come tell Madeleine about when you and Robert got stranded in Marseilles!"

Bill grinned apologetically and turned to join his wife and Madeleine, walking quite a way behind. Evelyn tucked her arm through her brothers again as they walked along the lane.

"I think I want to know what happened when they got stranded in Marseilles," she said. "Can you imagine Dad stranded anywhere?"

"No," he admitted. "I feel sorry for whoever was ultimately responsible for it."

They walked along in silence ahead of the others. The day was crisp and cool, with the sun shining brightly above. They went up the main road of the village, thanking those who stopped and called out their condolences. Then they were in the countryside, the road lined with thick hedgerows and tall trees. Surrounded by the comfortable smell of boxwood that Evelyn would always associate with home, she took a deep breath of fresh, clean air and looked up at Rob.

"How's the flying?"

He looked down at her with a smile. "Fantastic. How's the top-secret training?"

Evelyn couldn't stop the grin that crossed her face. When the RAF resurrected the WAAFs over the summer, they had unwittingly provided the perfect cover story for her. Bill had quickly arranged for her to be assigned to a WAAF training base in Scotland. No one in her family knew what she did there, nor would they ever know. All she told them was that the work was classified. Her parents had accepted the story readily enough, but Rob never missed an opportunity to tease her.

"Top-secret," she replied dryly. "Is it true you've been training non-stop since July?"

"More like August," he said with a shrug. "I fly every day, and three nights a week. When Jerry comes, we'll be ready."

"I imagine you'll be one of the first to know, flying Spitfires," she said absently, her eyes darting to the left. Movement through the trees caught her attention and she frowned. "How do you like being at Duxford? Is it everything you thought it would be?"

"More," he answered promptly. "The Spit's a fantastic kite! Handles like a dream."

They passed another hedgerow and Evelyn glanced through the trees again. The speck she had glimpsed before was on the other side of the field, moving quickly. Her eyes narrowed and her frown grew. Someone was riding a horse across the field towards Ainsworth Manor. She picked up her pace slightly.

"And your new CO? Do you like him?" she asked.

"He's strict and keeps us in line, but he's a bloody good pilot. I can't ask for better than that." Rob hesitated, then looked down at her. "And you? How do you like Scotland?"

"It's cold," she said promptly, drawing a laugh from him. "I'm doing something that makes me feel like I can contribute to this war, so I'm content."

"I don't know if this war is ever going to get off the ground, but if it does, the WAAFs are lucky to have you," Rob said after a long moment.

Evelyn tore her gaze away from the speck in the field to look

The Oslo Affair

at him in surprise.

"Why do you say that?"

He grinned.

"Because you're the type who never backs down, no matter what happens. You're bloody-minded and stubborn, and God help any Jerry who gets within range!"

She laughed. "Speak for yourself! I feel sorry for the pilot who has to go up against you!"

Rob grinned, then sobered.

"We're going to get through this just fine, Evie," he said suddenly, his blue eyes meeting hers. "You'll see. We'll all be home by Christmas."

The horse and rider came to an abrupt halt just outside the perimeter of the sprawling gardens stretching endlessly before the back of Ainsworth Manor. The original structure had been built in stone over three centuries before. Over the years, four separate wings were added and modern upgrades made, resulting in a massive labyrinth of corridors and stairwells. Two of the wings had been closed off twenty years before, after the last war had taken most of the servants from the estate. When the war ended and life returned to normal, Robert Ainsworth had left them closed, happy to occupy the remaining two wings and the original structure. They afforded more than enough room for his small family.

After giving the closed off sections a cursory glance, the rider directed his attention to a window on the lower floor, to the right of the stone patio facing him. He controlled his horse with a firm hand and they were both still. After studying the side of the house and the surrounding gardens, he slowly dismounted and tethered his horse, moving quietly through the immaculate lawns towards the house. The family would be back from the funeral soon, and it was now or never, as the saying went.

He slipped behind a large group of boxwoods and reached into his coat, extracting a battered old hunting cap and setting it on his head. He was under strict orders not arouse suspicion in the locals. After satisfying himself that he probably looked like a country squire out for a walk, he moved out from the shelter of the bushes, continuing through the maze of well-tended gardens until he was near the house.

The funeral would be just finishing up, and then there would be the condolences from the villagers. Silly things, funerals, arranged for the mourners to say goodbye to their loved ones. As if one could say goodbye to a corpse. Damned silly.

A sharp crack under one foot made the rider pause and look down with a frown. A thick branch had snapped in two under his boot. He should have been watching where he put his foot. Hopefully there wasn't an over-eager gardener lurking around. After listening for a moment, he moved on.

Evelyn slipped past the stables where four horses were settled comfortably in their stalls. A quick check inside assured her that all were present and accounted for. The mysterious rider was not one of the grooms then, taking a horse out for exercise.

Crossing the stable yard, she moved around the east wing and scanned the scene before her. The South lawns were immaculate and still, the breeze barely disturbing the rows of flowers and artfully arranged hedges and bushes. Even the fountain at the bottom of the first lawn was still, water not pouring from the spout of the fanciful leaping unicorn. Everything was still and quiet. Too quiet.

She had left Rob and her mother in the house with the explanation that she wanted to go upstairs and splash water on her face. Once out of sight, she slipped out the door and went around to the side of the house facing the field. Looking around slowly, Evelyn moved forward. She didn't know what she expected to find, but she knew that something wasn't right. No one with any business being here would cut across the field on horseback when there was a funeral taking place in the village. It just wasn't done.

A sharp pop from a branch brought her up short and she scanned the hedgerows nearby. Everything was silent for a moment, then she heard the unmistakable sound of a person moving through the garden towards the house.

She moved around the corner to conceal herself behind the wall of the terrace that stretched the entire length of the house. A few seconds later, she heard someone vault lightly over the balustrade and land on the flagged stones on the other side. Only two rooms faced the south lawn and opened onto the terrace on this side of the drawing room. One was the billiard room, and the other was her father's study.

The click of the window casing caused Evelyn to reach down for a large rock near her feet. Her intention was to throw the rock into

The Oslo Affair

the garden behind the terrace and make the intruder think someone was there. When he turned back towards the railing, she could intercept him.

Before her fingers touched the rock, a chorus of barking erupted from the right and her father's three hunting dogs came bounding from the direction of the woods. Evelyn stared at them, then stood up quickly. It was too late. She saw only the back of a tall man dressed in a long black coat as he disappeared into the trees on the left side of the terrace.

The dogs caught sight of her and lost interest in the man whom they had first sighted. Tom, Dick and Harry swarmed around Evelyn, barking joyfully in greeting. Dick held something clamped between his teeth and she bent to pull it away from him. Evelyn straightened up slowly and glanced towards the trees. It was a brown leather strip and, unless she was very much mistaken, it was part of a bridle.

Chapter Two

"Well, I'm glad that's over, at any rate," Mrs. Ainsworth said, standing. "I'm going to check on luncheon. I'm sure everyone is getting hungry."

The family solicitor had just left after going over the will. There had been no surprises and Evelyn looked at Rob, who had got up and was standing near the window of the study, staring out.

"I can take care of that for you, if you'd rather go and rest," she said, standing. While she was loathe to leave her brother when he was clearly feeling overwhelmed, her mother looked exhausted.

Mrs. Ainsworth smiled tiredly and reached out to take her hand.

"Thank you, dear, but it helps me to keep busy."

She turned and left the study, allowing Evelyn to turn her attention back to her brother.

"Are you all right?" she asked, walking over to join him at the window. Her gaze lingered for a moment on the window casing. There was no sign of it having been forced earlier. Someone must have found the window ajar and closed it before they gathered for the reading of the will.

Rob turned his head and glanced down at her.

"Never better."

She raised an eyebrow dubiously. "You can't lie to me, Robbie. You never could."

He let out a short laugh and turned away from the window, one hand in his pocket.

"Not for lack of trying." He pulled out a cigarette case and opened it, offering her one. She shook her head. "I suppose I've just realized that he's really gone. Nothing drives it home quite like being presented with my entire estate and birthright in a twenty-minute conversation with the family solicitor."

The Oslo Affair

"Would you rather it had been drawn out into an hour?" she asked with a quick grin.

He made a face at her and pulled a lighter out of his pocket.

"Heaven forbid! Twenty minutes was quite long enough." He turned to go to the heavy wooden desk where their father spent so many hours. "I have to go down to London tomorrow to meet with him and go over all the papers, then I have to meet with the manager at the bank. And I have to try to get Damien Stevenson up here to go over the steward accounts before I go back to Duxford. How in blazes am I going to get everything sorted? Don't they know there's a war on?"

He dropped into their father's chair behind the desk and stared glumly at the polished surface. Evelyn watched him for a second, then went over to perch on the arm of the chair, putting an arm around his shoulders.

"Damien is here now for the luncheon. Ask him to remain afterwards and fill you in on anything pressing. You're already familiar with most of it. You were starting to take it over anyway. As for the solicitor and the bank, go to London tomorrow and do what you can. I'm sure anything that isn't able to be done tomorrow can be done through the post. It will have to be. As you say, there's a war on." She leaned down and rested her cheek next to his. "Don't worry. We'll get through this. I don't know how, but we will."

Rob put his arm around her waist and squeezed, tapping ash off his cigarette into the heavy glass ashtray on the desk.

"Knowing you, you'll just throw yourself into work," he said. "What *is* work, anyway?"

Evelyn slid off the arm of the chair and went over to the side board where their father always kept decanters of brandy, scotch and sherry.

"You know I can't tell you anything," she said, picking up the brandy decanter. She held it up questioningly and Rob shook his head.

"I'll take some of the scotch, though." She nodded and poured herself a glass of brandy before reaching for the scotch. "I can't image what they have you doing up there. What's in Scotland except a bunch of haggis? Is that it? Are you on a secret haggis mission?"

Evelyn bit back a laugh and turned to carry the scotch over to him.

"If I am, I'm not telling you."

He took the drink and studied her for a moment.

"Why did you join the WAAFs, Evie?" he asked, sobering. "In all seriousness? You didn't have to. You could have gone to University.

With your language skills, you would have done well. Why the WAAFs?"

Evelyn sipped her brandy and sank into the chair across from the desk, fighting the sudden wave of guilt that washed over her. Rob had no idea what she really did, nor could he ever know. It was too dangerous. No one in her family had any clue that she wasn't really a WAAF. Once or twice, she thought her father suspected that she was up to something, but when the Women's Auxiliary Air Force was instituted over the summer, he seemed to accept her involvement without question. Now, here was Robbie looking for answers; answers she was unable to give.

"Why not?" she countered calmly. "I have to do my bit, so it might as well be in support of pilots like you. And anyway, what else would you suggest? Can you see me as a nurse?"

Rob looked comically horrified. "A nurse? Good God no!"

"Well then."

"Aren't you bored?" he asked bluntly, staring at her hard. "I love flying, but I don't see pushing papers around a desk in Scotland as being all that stimulating for you. You're as much of a daredevil as I am, if not more."

Evelyn thought of the rigorous training she'd been undergoing for months, training the likes of which would undoubtedly horrify her brother if he knew. She managed a nonchalant shrug and buried her nose in her brandy glass.

"I'm managing," she murmured. "There's some awfully good hunting up there."

His eyebrows soared into his forehead. "Hunting?"

"Yes. There's a group of us that go out once in a while on our days off."

"So you push papers during the day and hunt on your time off?" He sat back in the chair and grinned. "I suppose you have it better off than I thought."

Evelyn laughed and stood up.

"Stop worrying about me and worry about you and your airplanes," she said with a grin, setting her glass down on the side board. "I'm going to check on Mum. Are you coming to lunch?"

"I'll be along. I want to go over some of these papers before I come out and put on a good face for everyone."

"Fair enough." Evelyn turned to go to the door. She glanced over her shoulder. "Don't worry, Robbie. You'll be fine. Dad groomed you for this."

The Oslo Affair

"He may have groomed me for it, but it doesn't mean I'll be good at it," he retorted. "Put me in a cockpit and I'm sure enough of myself. This is a whole different kettle of fish."

"Rest assured, we won't let you bankrupt us. If you really start to muck everything up, we'll take over and force you out."

He let out a choked laugh.

"Thanks for that."

She winked. "Don't mention it."

Evelyn was crossing the main hall some time later when the butler opened the door to a tall man in an RAF uniform. Catching a glimpse of the familiar blue, she paused to look curiously. After a low-voiced inquiry, the butler stood aside to allow the visitor into the hall and Evelyn's eyes widened. She swallowed and resisted the urge to smooth her hair as a tall, broad-shouldered man stepped inside.

"If you'd care to follow me to the drawing room, sir, I'll let Mr. Ainsworth know you're here."

The butler closed the door and held out his hand to take the visitor's hat. The man handed it over and turned, stopping dead at the sight of her standing in the hall.

"It's quite all right, Thomas," Evelyn said smoothly, moving forward with a smile. "I'll show him to the drawing room. I believe you'll find Robbie on the terrace."

Thomas inclined his head, betraying only the mildest surprise at her intervention, and turned to leave the hall. Evelyn turned her smile on the tall man before her.

"I'm Evelyn Ainsworth," she introduced herself, holding out her hand, "Rob's sister."

A smile curved full lips and a dent appeared in one cheek as he reached out a broad, strong hand.

"It's a pleasure to meet you, Miss Ainsworth," he said. "My name's Lacey, Miles Lacey. I'm a friend of your brother's. We fly together."

Looking up into his face, Evelyn swallowed again. Handsome was a wholly inadequate word to describe the man standing before her. Miles Lacey stood well over six feet tall with thick brown hair that fell over his forehead in a careless wave. His eyes were a startling color of green, set above high cheekbones, a straight nose and a strong, firm chin. Only a faint scar near his right eyebrow saved his countenance from being flawless, giving him an air of rakish recklessness that Evelyn found irresistible.

"You're a pilot as well?" She pulled her hand away and turned to walk across the hall towards the drawing room, taking a deep breath and hoping that he didn't detect the faint tremor in her voice.

"Yes." He fell into step beside her and glanced down. "I'm very sorry to intrude at a time like this. I'm on my way to Catterick to get a plane and fly it back to Duxford. The CO asked me to drop something by for Rob on my way."

"I think he'll be grateful for the distraction," she said, opening the door to the drawing room and going in. "It's been a difficult day."

"I can only imagine." Miles followed her into the room. "I understand it was very sudden."

"Yes, it was." She walked over to a chair and sank down, motioning him into a seat. "We're still adjusting, I think. Do you fly Spitfires as well?"

"Yes." Miles seated himself in the chair opposite. "Rob and I are in the same squadron."

"And do you love flying as much as he does?" she asked with a grin. "It's all Robbie could talk about when he joined up."

Miles shrugged and smiled nonchalantly, but she saw the gleam that entered his eyes. Oh yes. He loved flying.

"I suppose I do," he admitted. "There's nothing quite like it. And you? I seem to remember Rob saying you're in the WAAFs?"

"That's right."

He was looking at her with a smile in his eyes, and she felt her lips curving in response.

"Good for you. If you girls give a good show, you'll be a lot of help." He tilted his head to study her. "Where's your station?"

"I'm posted in Scotland."

Miles gave an exaggerated grimace. "I'm terribly sorry!"

She laughed. "It's quite all right. I've got used to it."

"I went up to Turnhouse for training in the spring. I was glad to come away at the end of it. The training officer was an absolute tartar. I felt sure I was going to get run through with a sword if I missed something."

"I haven't seen one sword," she assured him. "Although, I've heard that one of the CO's has an axe in his office."

"Who has an axe in his office?" Rob spoke behind her and she turned in her chair with a laugh.

"One of the COs on my station."

"Tread carefully, then. Don't let him hear your sass," Rob said

The Oslo Affair

with a grin. He looked across the room at Miles and walked forward with his hand out. "Miles! What are you doing here? Did you desert?"

Miles stood up and gripped his hand with a laugh.

"Hardly, old man. I've been sent up to Catterick to pick up a kite. Ashmore asked me to stop by and bring you something from the station. It's in the car outside."

"Have you been waiting long?"

"Not at all. Your sister's been keeping me company."

"Well, stay for a drink. You've missed lunch, I'm afraid, but there's an excellent brandy I can offer you."

"I stopped for a bite at a pub on my way, but I'll take some brandy if it's going."

"Of course! Come into the study." Rob turned towards the door. "Are you coming, Evie?"

Evelyn stood up with a smile.

"I'm not, dearest. I'm off to check on Mother and then I'm going to hide in peace somewhere for a few minutes." She looked at Miles. "Not that it wasn't wonderful meeting you, Mr. Lacey," she added. "I hope you don't mind. I'll join you another time for a drink."

His eyes met hers and he smiled.

"Not at all. I'm sure you're just about fed up with visitors," he said, holding out his hand. "I'll hold you to that drink though, Miss Ainsworth."

She took his hand with a smile and felt his long fingers close around hers.

"Please call my Evelyn."

"Only if you'll call me Miles."

"Very well," she agreed, pulling her hand away. "I'll look forward to that drink."

"As will I," he murmured, watching her as she left.

Rob shook his head and clapped Miles on the shoulder as soon as Evelyn had disappeared out the door.

"Don't get your hopes up, old man," he advised with a grin. "It'll never happen."

Miles looked at him.

"Are you really going to play the defensive big brother?" he demanded.

"Good Lord, no! She can defend herself without any help from me." Rob led him out of the drawing room and down the corridor towards the study. "But many have come before you and crashed in flames. I'd hate to see you go down burning."

"You've seen me fly," Miles said with a grin. "I'll take my

chances."

Chapter Three

Evelyn looked up as a woman dressed in a smart, gray suit with a silk blouse came across the small waiting area.

"Miss Ainsworth?"

Evelyn stood up. "Yes."

The woman swept an assessing look over her before her sharp gaze settled on her face.

"I'll escort you to Montclair's office. Did you receive a visitors pass?"

Evelyn held it out and the woman looked at it cursorily. Even though the glance was brief, Evelyn got the distinct impression that she had examined it thoroughly.

"Right. Follow me."

She spun on her heel and Evelyn followed, her lips tightening faintly in irritation. She had no idea who the woman was or why she was being so abrupt with her. She was here because of a borderline command from William Buckley, but this woman seemed to think they were doing her a favor by allowing her into the shabby, nondescript building situated on Broadway, near St. James Park Underground. Although it was only a few blocks from Westminster, the neighborhood had absolutely nothing to recommend itself, much less the building. She had stood on the pavement with the business card in her hand for a moment, staring at the number above the door and wondering if she had somehow got it wrong.

Following the woman down the corridor, Evelyn glanced at her watch. She was a few minutes late, due solely to the fact that the young man at the desk had taken an inordinately long time to process her visitor's pass from the military ID she'd shown him. Perhaps that's why this woman was so cold. Perhaps she disapproved of tardiness.

They reached the end of the corridor and went up a flight of stairs. A man in uniform stood at the top and, as they approached, he moved forward. The woman held up an identity card and he nodded before turning his attention to Evelyn. She held out her pass and he took it, examining it carefully before raising his eyes to her face. After studying her for a moment, he nodded.

"Thank you," he said, passing it back.

She nodded and followed the woman down another long corridor lined on either side with closed doors. At the end of the hallway, she opened the last door on the left and motioned her inside.

Evelyn walked through and found herself in a large, well-appointed office with a polished mahogany desk set between two narrow windows flanked with blackout curtains. As she entered, Jasper Montclair rose from his seat behind the desk, a welcoming smile creasing his face. Bill turned in the chair before the desk and also stood as she entered. She smiled, surprised to see him there.

"Ah, Miss Ainsworth!" Jasper exclaimed, coming out from behind the desk and advancing towards her. "I'm glad you were able to come."

Evelyn smiled and held out her hand. "Of course."

"You know William Buckley, of course," he said, releasing her hand and nodding towards Bill.

"Yes." Evelyn smiled and nodded to him. "It's good to see you again."

"I trust you had an uneventful trip down?" Bill asked with a smile. "Did you take the train in?"

"No, actually. I drove down with my brother. He has some business to take care of with our solicitor before he rejoins his squadron."

"Oh yes. He's a pilot in 66 squadron, stationed at Duxford, isn't he?" Jasper asked, motioning her to the other chair before the desk. "Please, have a seat."

Evelyn thanked him and sank down into the chair opposite Bill. Once she had, the other two took their seats.

"And how are you and your family doing? Is there anything you need?" Jasper asked, sitting back in his chair behind the desk. "I know this must be a difficult time."

"Thank you. It is, but we will be fine."

"I knew your father well. He was a great man." Jasper shook his head sadly. "He spoke very highly of you. I wish we didn't have to meet for the first time under these circumstances."

Evelyn looked from one man to the other.

"With all due respect," she said slowly, "why *are* we meeting today?"

Jasper glanced at Bill with a faint smile.

"You were right," he said dryly. "She isn't much for chit-chat."

The Oslo Affair

"No, she isn't," Evelyn said a bit more sharply than she intended. "Not when I've come some distance to a meeting with a man who says he worked with my father, but whom I'd never heard of it until yesterday."

To her surprise, Jasper chuckled.

"Quite right, my dear. My apologies for that." He opened a drawer and pulled out a folder, setting it on the desk before him. "I understand you've been training in Scotland? Bill here has only good things to say about your progress."

Evelyn looked at Bill, startled, and he nodded reassuringly.

"It's quite all right," he told her. "Jasper knows everything."

"Yes, yes, I know all about you," Jasper said, glancing up from the folder before him. "Do you really speak seven languages fluently?"

"Yes."

"And they are?"

"French, German, Italian, Cantonese, Spanish, Portuguese and Russian." Evelyn smiled faintly. "Although, I'm fairly certain they're probably listed in that folder."

Another chuckle emanated from Jasper. "Yes, they are. It's quite an impressive list. Are there any others in which you are not fluent?"

"I'm learning Japanese, but it's very slow. I haven't had much time lately to concentrate on it as I'd like," she admitted.

Jasper looked at Bill.

"She's learning Japanese," he said dryly. "Just as casual as you please. As if the Cantonese and Russian weren't enough."

Bill grinned. "I did tell you she was something special."

"You know, your father told me you were very talented, but I'm afraid I wrote it off as the doting of a fond parent. It seems he wasn't exaggerating." Jasper shook his head and bent it back over the folder on the desk. "I see here that you've almost finished the MI6 training. High scores all around. Good." He looked up sharply. "How about Norwegian? Do you speak that at all?"

Evelyn shook her head. "I'm afraid not."

"Pity."

He went back to the file and continued reading, falling silent. Evelyn looked at Bill with a frown and he shrugged. He was either as much in the dark is she was regarding why they were here, or he was content to allow Jasper to get to it in his own good time. What on earth was she doing here? That Jasper Montclair was someone fairly high up in the MI6 organization was clear, especially given Bill's deference to him, but who was he, exactly? And what did he want with her? And why did she have to come the day immediately following her father's funeral?

The questions were still rolling through her mind when he looked up a few moments later.

"Well, I suppose you're wondering what this is all about," he said, sitting back in his chair. "Tell me what you know about your father's work."

Evelyn stared at him.

"Not much," she finally said. "I know he worked with the foreign office, and they relied on him to maintain precarious relationships between ambassadors and foreign dignitaries."

"And when he unfortunately passed away?"

Evelyn flinched. "We were told he had a massive heart attack, most likely brought on from the stress of fleeing Poland ahead of the Germans. He died in his hotel room in Bern."

"And that's all you know?"

"That's it, I'm afraid. Dad was very close about his work and rarely spoke about it. The circumstances of his death were no different. We were told only what someone determined we should be told."

"You sound as if you question the cause of your father's death," Jasper stated rather than asked. "Do you doubt that he had a heart attack?"

Evelyn shook her head. "No. As far as I can understand, the medical report was conclusive. What has me confused is that he was at the Bellevue Palace Hotel, in Bern. But when I saw him in London before his trip, he told me he would be staying in Zürich. I'm not sure why he would have changed cities, but I suppose he had his reasons."

"And what did he tell you about this last trip?"

She frowned.

"Only that he was going to Warsaw for a few days. He mentioned the possibility of stopping in Vienna on his way back, but he was unsure if that would be possible. Of course, then Hitler decided to invade Poland, making a stop in Vienna impossible."

"Tell me, did Robert ever mention to you what the purpose of these trips were?"

"Never. As I said, he rarely spoke about his work."

Jasper studied her pensively for a moment, then glanced at Bill. As if coming to a decision, he nodded and sat forward in his seat.

"What I'm going to say cannot leave this room. The moment you walked through that door, you became bound by the Official Secrets Act. Do you understand?"

"Yes."

The Oslo Affair

"Good. You're mostly correct about your father. Robert was invaluable to the foreign office. However, what you don't know, is that he was also invaluable to us. His loss is a great blow to MI6. He had made contacts all over Europe and in the Far East, and was able to funnel an inordinately large amount of information to us through them."

Evelyn felt as though the floor was dropping out from under her and she gripped the arms of her chair as she stared speechlessly at Jasper. He stared back stoically, waiting for her to respond.

"I...I don't understand," she stammered, glancing at Bill in confusion. "My father worked for MI6? But...that's impossible!"

"Why do you think it's impossible?" Jasper asked. "Haven't you been in a training course with us for the past six months? Why would you think it was impossible for your father to do the same?"

"Well, to begin with, because he was my father!" Evelyn exclaimed. "I mean, that's not something one thinks of when one thinks of their father. He was a family man, and one of the most forthcoming and honest men I've ever known. Why, we would have known!"

"Would you?" Bill asked softly. "He didn't have any idea that you were working for me. Does your brother know? Your mother? You've managed to hide your association with me and with MI6 from your family for over a year now. What makes you think your father wouldn't do the same?"

Evelyn stared at him, her mind spinning. He was right of course. For her to think that they would have known anything about their father if he didn't want them to was absurd. But a spy? Her father?

Suddenly, a whole new rash of questions began to fill her mind. If he had been gathering intelligence for MI6, who were his contacts? How many of them could be trusted? He was in Poland when the German army invaded. Was that intentional? Had one of his contacts cleverly planned that?

"I can see you're starting to realize the complexity of Robert's death," Jasper said, watching her face. "Before you get too carried away, let me make one thing very clear. Robert's trip to Warsaw was arranged by the foreign office, no one else. It's just bad luck that that's when Hitler decided to invade."

Evelyn looked at him, her cheeks flushing. "How did you know —"

"My dear, it was written all over your face," he replied. "You'll have to learn to guard your expressions much more carefully."

She swallowed and rubbed a hand across her forehead.

"I'm sorry. It's just such a shock."

"Believe it or not, I do understand." Jasper's voice softened and he stood up, moving to a tall wooden cabinet on the side wall. "To learn that someone you've known all your life wasn't exactly what you thought they were is never an easy thing."

He opened the cabinet to reveal a shelf with a variety of bottles and glasses. Lifting a decanter with a light amber liquid inside, he poured two fingers into a glass and turned to carry it over to her.

"Here. Have some brandy. It'll help."

Evelyn took the glass thankfully. It was a superior brandy indeed, and as it burned a path down her throat, she felt herself begin to relax.

"Evie, you mustn't think that Robert didn't want to tell you," Bill said slowly. "While he didn't know that you were working for me, I think he began to suspect in the spring that you were involved with something. He remarked to me once that he wouldn't be at all surprised if you were recruited because of your linguistic skills, and he wished he could advise you and tell you what he'd been doing for the past few years. I think it troubled him greatly that he couldn't tell anyone."

"You don't have to explain. I understand," Evelyn said. "For the same reason my brother has no idea that I'm not really a bona fide WAAF, Dad had to keep this from me. From us all."

"Precisely." Jasper went back to his seat behind the desk. "No one must ever know, not about your father and most definitely not about you. Especially now, it's far too dangerous."

"Why have you told me?" Evelyn asked, looking up from her glass of brandy. "Why tell me this now?"

Jasper and Bill shared a look and the silence was almost deafening. Evelyn looked from one to the other with a growing sense of apprehension.

"While your father was in Poland, he met with one of his regular contacts. It's a man who's been feeding us a steady stream of reliable intelligence over the course of the past three years," Jasper began. "For the first two years, he was known as Shustov."

"A Russian?" Evelyn asked, startled.

"Yes. Last year, he finally agreed to allow your father to share his true identity with us, on condition that it not be revealed in any official documents. His name is Vladimir Lyakhov, and he's an NVKD agent. The information he's been able to pass us about Moscow has been invaluable. Vladimir made contact shortly before Robert went to Poland, saying that he had urgent intelligence that he had to get out of

The Oslo Affair

Russia as soon as possible. Robert arranged to meet him in Warsaw while he was there. As far as we know, Vladimir gave him the information before your father fled the German invasion."

Evelyn raised her eyebrow. "And?"

"We had one of our men go through Robert's hotel room after his death. We found no trace of anything from Vladimir, nor was any of the information he had collected in Warsaw in his rooms. All of his diplomatic papers were intact, as were his personal effects. Only the intelligence he gathered from Russia and Poland was gone."

Evelyn swallowed heavily and lifted her glass of brandy to her lips, taking a healthy swig.

"What was the information?" she whispered.

"We have no idea," Bill said, pulling a cigarette case from his jacket. "We've managed to make contact with Vladimir since, but he refuses to meet with anyone but your father."

"But that's impossible," she pointed out with a frown. "Didn't you tell him he's dead?"

Bill opened his cigarette case and got up, offering her one. She took it gratefully and waited while he fished for a lighter in his other pocket.

"Of course we did," Jasper said, sitting back in his chair. "It makes no difference. He refuses to meet with any other contact."

"Then it would appear that you've lost your source within the Kremlin," Evelyn murmured, bending her head to light her cigarette with the offered lighter.

"Not quite," Jasper said.

Evelyn looked up with raised eyebrows. Once again, a feeling of apprehension rolled over her and she looked at Jasper almost with misgiving.

"What do you mean?"

"Robert and Shustov got to know each other quite well over the years," Jasper told her. "In relationships like these, trust must be built and, over time, many sources and contacts become rather close friends. Vladimir shared anecdotes about his family with Robert and, of course, Robert reciprocated."

Evelyn sucked in her breath, suddenly realizing why she was here.

"Dad told him that I could speak Russian."

"Among other things," Bill said, returning to his seat. He lit a cigarette for himself and looked at Jasper. "That's why we're all here today. Jasper approached me and requested your assistance. I told him that it was entirely up to you."

"Shustov will only meet with you," Jasper told her bluntly. "He knows what you look like, knows stories from when you were a girl, and knows that you speak Russian. He advised that any attempt to send an impostor would result in all communication immediately ceasing. If we try to send someone else, we'll lose one of our most important sources within Moscow."

"I don't understand," Evelyn said, lifting her cigarette to her lips. She inhaled and blew a stream of smoke up into the air. "If he already gave whatever it was to my father, and it has subsequently disappeared, why meet with me?"

Bill and Jasper exchanged another look and she frowned.

"He's willing to try again, with you."

Evelyn looked from one man to the other, her mind spinning.

"How? I can't go to Poland. It's already fallen." She hesitated, then gasped. "You don't honestly expect me to go to Moscow!"

"No."

Evelyn breathed a sigh of relief. Over the past six months, it had slowly been born upon her that, at the end of the training, she would be expected to go back into France, and even possibly as far as Belgium and Denmark. While she was fully prepared to traipse across the continent, she drew the line at going into enemy territory. The idea of starting her career with MI6 by going straight to Moscow frankly terrified her.

"Shustov suggested Oslo," Jasper said. "He's scheduled to go in November and has agreed to meet you there."

"That's why you wanted to know if I spoke Norwegian."

Jasper shrugged. "It would have made it a bit easier if you did, but we have someone at the embassy there who can put you in contact with a translator."

Evelyn stared at him. "You want me to go to Norway in November?"

Bill grinned.

"Might I suggest that very warm clothing may be in order?"

Chapter Four

Evelyn climbed out of the taxi in front of the Savoy. Darkness had fallen, and with it, the blackout that had engulfed London every night since war was declared. She squinted up at the familiar facade of the hotel before turning to collect two garment boxes from the back seat. After leaving the drab yet enlightening house on Broadway, she had felt decidedly out of her element and particularly overwhelmed. With plenty of time before she was due to meet Rob for dinner, she did the one thing that always cheered her up and made everything better: she went shopping.

Closing the taxi door, she turned towards the entrance as the doorman came forward to help her with the boxes.

"I'm dining in the restaurant. Would you mind carrying them to the coat check?" she asked with a smile as he took the boxes.

"Of course, miss."

"Thank you."

Back on familiar territory, and looking forward to dinner in her favorite restaurant, Evelyn felt herself begin to relax. The revelations of the past few hours slid to the back of her consciousness, as did the sudden and irrevocable realization that there could be no turning back now. She was on her way to Norway in a few weeks, and nothing could stop the course she had chosen, or her role in this war. For better or worse, she had agreed to be a spy for MI6. While she had been shaken to her core to find that her father wasn't exactly who she had always thought he was, learning that he was a spy before her only strengthened her resolve. If he could do it, then so could she.

"Evie!"

A voice called across the lobby and Evelyn turned to find a tall woman in evening dress coming towards her on the arm of a handsome man in tails. She smiled in greeting and lifted a hand in a half wave.

"Maryanne!" she exclaimed. "Lord Gilhurst!"

The doorman stepped back to wait, bowing his head in deference as the couple to drew near. Leaning forward, Maryanne kissed the air beside her cheek and Evelyn was engulfed in the strong, French scent that the woman was partial to.

"Evelyn, it's been an absolute age since I've seen you!" she exclaimed. "Wherever have you been?" She turned to the man at her side. "Tony, hasn't it been it ages?"

"It has indeed," Lord Antony Gilhurst agreed with a smile. "How are you, Evie? I was sorry to hear about your father."

"Yes, absolutely shocking and terrible news," Maryanne said with a vigorous nod. "When was the funeral?"

"It was yesterday."

"I'm so sorry to have missed it. But what are you doing here?"

"I'm meeting Robbie for dinner. He had to come down on some business with the solicitors, so I came along to do some shopping. I had absolutely nothing appropriate to wear for mourning. We're dining in the Grill."

"Rob's here as well? And we're on our way to the theatre! Of all the rotten luck!"

"Yes, and we have to get moving if we're going to make it," Tony interjected. "With this ridiculous blackout, it takes forever to get anywhere now."

"Really, Tony!" Maryanne exclaimed in exasperation. "Evie, don't mind my brother. You know we'd stay and say hello to Rob if we had the time."

Evelyn laughed. "Of course I do! Go!"

"We really must arrange to go out soon. I miss you dreadfully!"

"We'll arrange something, I promise," Evelyn assured her with a smile, accepting another kiss next to her cheek.

"Evie, give Robbie my best," Tony said, holding out his hand to her as his sister settled her gloved hand on his arm. "Tell him to make us proud up there in his fighter plane."

"I will."

Evelyn watched them turn and move towards the entrance before continuing to the restaurant. Maryanne Gilhurst and she had become fast friends shortly after she returned from Hong Kong, and Lord Gilhurst was like another brother to her. She never considered the fact that they were peers of the realm, only that they were dear friends. Many of her acquaintances had a title before their name, but it never seemed to make a difference. Evelyn's own family was one of the oldest and most distinguished in England, and that was all that really mattered when it came to London society. Where breeding and lineage were concerned, the Ainsworth's were right up there with the cream of nobility.

The Oslo Affair

She entered the alcove of the restaurant and turned to go to the coat check desk, the doorman following with her packages. The Grill was one of two restaurants in the famous hotel, and more relaxed than its exclusive and formal cousin. Catering more to the cosmopolitan and modern crowd, The Grill Room nonetheless still adhered to the excellent standards of both cuisine and service to which the patrons of the Savoy had grown accustomed.

"Good evening, miss," a young woman greeted her as she approached the desk.

"Good evening." The doorman set the boxes on the counter and Evelyn passed him a coin with a smile of thanks. He bent his head, wished her a good evening, and returned to his post. "I'd like to check these, please."

"Of course, miss."

The woman took the boxes and turned to carry them into a long, narrow room behind her. She returned a moment later and handed Evelyn a ticket.

"Thank you."

Turning, Evelyn slipped the ticket into her purse as she went to the entrance of the restaurant. Before she could step inside, however, a voice called out gaily behind her.

"I'm here, Evie!"

She turned to find Rob striding across the foyer towards her with Miles Lacey beside him. Evelyn's pulse leapt at the sight of the tall pilot and she had to force her breathing to remain steady.

"Sorry I'm late! I ran into Miles and convinced him to join us."

"In all honesty, I didn't need much convincing," Miles told her with a smile, holding out his hand as his green eyes met hers. "I hope you don't mind my crashing your dinner."

Evelyn took his hand, her lips curving into a smile.

"Of course not!" she said. "I thought you were picking up a plane in Catterick?"

"Oh, that's a story and a half!" Rob said with a laugh. "Let's get to our table and he can tell you all about it over a drink. Have you been waiting long?"

"No. I've just arrived. I ran into Maryanne and Tony in the lobby. They send their love."

"Tony's here? Good Lord, I haven't seen him in an age! Why didn't they come along as well?"

"They were on their way to the theatre, or I'm sure they would have."

Rob gave his name to the host standing behind the podium at the door. The man nodded, his demeanor becoming significantly warmer as he checked in the large book before him.

"Ah yes, Mr. Ainsworth. Here you are." He made no mention of the extra guest. "If you would care to follow me?"

They followed him across the restaurant to a table in the corner and Evelyn smiled in thanks as he held a chair out for her.

"I'll send someone over from the bar," he said as Miles and Rob seated themselves. "Enjoy your meal, sir."

"Thank you." Rob waited until the man had retreated back to the entrance, then looked at Evelyn. "You look refreshed. What did you get up to while I was being put to sleep by stodgy old lawyers and bankers?"

"I went shopping," she said with a laugh. "How did you know?"

"You have a gleam in your eye. I'm glad. Did you buy yourself something pretty?"

Evelyn thought of the warm pull-overs and woolen skirts that she had bought to combat the temperature of Oslo in November and repressed a laugh.

"Not pretty, no, but practical." She looked up as a server approached the table to take their drink orders. "Dad would be proud of me."

"And Mum will tell you that you should have bought yourself something nice," Rob retorted. "What will you drink?"

"I think I'd like a sidecar," she said after a moment of thought.

Rob ordered for her and he and Miles ordered pints. Once the server had gone away towards the bar, Evelyn looked at Miles.

"What happened with the plane?" she asked, pulling a cigarette case from her purse. "Was it misplaced?"

He shook his head and pulled out a lighter for her.

"Hardly. I arrived and they said it was all ready to go, but instead of flying it back to Duxford, I was to take it down to Biggin Hill instead. Well, I was halfway there when the instruments went berserk and I started losing altitude."

Evelyn gasped and stared at him. "Oh my goodness! What did you do?"

He held out the lighter and she bent her head to the flame.

"What any sensible pilot would do; I made an emergency landing at Northolt." He tucked the lighter away again as she lifted her head. "I called our CO and told him what happened. He said to check

The Oslo Affair

in again in the morning. I was on my way to a hotel when Rob caught sight of me outside Piccadilly."

"Do they know what caused it?" she asked.

"Some ground crew mucked something up, more than likely," Rob said. "It happens more than you'd think. Remember when Hadmire's wheel wouldn't come down? Some fool had left a wrench in there!"

Miles grimaced. "Didn't he end up putting up the other wheel and landing on his belly after the fourth pass?"

Rob nodded. "Yes. Bloody good landing, that was."

"Someone had to land without wheels?" Evelyn looked from one to the other. "How on earth do you do that?"

"Very carefully, m'dear," Rob said with a laugh. "It usually doesn't end well, or so I've heard."

"What will you do in the morning if the plane isn't fixed?" Evelyn asked Miles. "How will you get back?"

He shrugged. "The CO made it sound as if I'm staying here until it's fixed. But the ground chief I spoke to didn't seem confident they'd have it ready tomorrow."

The server returned with their drinks and set them down and Rob picked up his pint.

"Well, here's to an unexpected couple of days leave!" he toasted to Miles. "Enjoy it while you can!"

Miles grinned and picked up his glass. "I already am," he said, glancing at Evelyn.

She smiled and sipped her cocktail, casting an eye over the menu.

"Oh, I wouldn't speak too soon, if I were you," she said cheerfully. "You have no idea what dull company we Ainsworth's can be. We don't come from the fun branch of the family."

"Lord no," Rob agreed.

"And who's the fun branch?" Miles asked, glancing from one to the other.

"My cousins in France have that honor," Rob told him. "A more jolly pair you've never met. They're twins, you know."

"You have family in France?" Miles looked interested. "So do I. What part?"

"The family seat isn't far from Toulouse, but they spend a lot of time at their house in Paris," Rob said. "Isn't that right, Evie? She was there last summer, and went back again this spring."

Miles glanced at her. "I can see you in Paris," he said thoughtfully. "It would suit you."

She laughed lightly. "Really? I do love it there, but I'm always glad to come home again."

"My family is near Pau. I haven't been in a few years. It's beautiful country there." Miles set his menu aside and pulled out his cigarette case. "Are your cousins concerned about the war?"

"Of course, but they're very realistic about the whole thing. The French tend to think about things differently than we do."

"No point in getting upset yet," Rob interjected. "The whole thing will be over by Christmas if it keeps on like this. So far, this has been a most anti-climactic start to a war."

Evelyn looked across the table at her brother and blew smoke into the air. It was true that the nothing much had happened since Germany invaded Poland at the beginning of September, but she was very much afraid that it wouldn't last. Hitler wouldn't stop now; there was no reason to.

"I think we need to be careful about getting too complacent," Miles said slowly, lighting his cigarette. "I don't think Hitler is finished just yet."

"Well, I wish he'd hurry up and get on with it. The hours of relentless training and waiting are killing me." Rob motioned to the server hovering nearby. "Let's order. I'm starving."

After they had given their orders, Miles looked at Evelyn.

"And you? What do you think about this war?" he asked.

She put her cigarette out in the cut-glass ashtray on the table and pursed her lips thoughtfully.

"I think it was inevitable," she said slowly. "I know people are saying it will all be over in a few months, but I'm not so sure. I think Germany was allowed to build up their military to such an extent that now they're feeling very confident. Why should Hitler stop? Look at what they did in Poland. They reached Warsaw in three weeks and decimated the Polish Air Force and Army. They were unstoppable, and worse, now they know it."

"The Poles also sent men on horseback to meet tanks," Rob pointed out. "Of course they were unstoppable. A horse can't stop a tank. And the Germans did have help from the Russians in the end."

"Yes, but the German army was more than capable of carving through Poland, regardless. Anyone who thinks otherwise is a fool."

"Your father was there, wasn't he?" Miles asked after a moment. "When they invaded?"

Evelyn and Rob looked at each other, then she nodded.

The Oslo Affair

"Yes. He was in Warsaw on the 1st when they began their invasion. He evacuated on the 7th and escaped to Switzerland before the troops reached the city."

"Didn't do him much good, in the end," Rob said glumly, picking up his glass. "Still, I suppose we can't pick our time to go."

"Lord, I'm sorry," Miles said. "I didn't mean to bring it up."

"Never mind," Evelyn said, standing and holding her hand out to him. "Come dance with me and make me forget about it."

Miles grinned and pushed his chair back. "How do you know I dance?"

She raised an eyebrow and twinkled up at him. "Women's intuition."

"And is that ever wrong?" he asked, taking her hand.

"We're about to find out."

◉

The figure moved carefully through the pitch black streets, murmuring apologies as he bumped into others in the darkness. The blackout really was a nuisance. By law, there could be no light at all after nightfall. Thick black curtains shrouded windows in businesses and homes alike, and street lamps were doused. Even headlights on cars were covered to direct their beams downward so as to minimize light as much as possible.

It fell to the neighborhood wardens to enforce the strict blackout, and they did so with enthusiasm, checking each window for even the minutest gleam of light. The result was that moving around in London was decidedly tricky after dark, and the rate of accidental deaths had skyrocketed as people were hit by cars or fell and injured themselves in the darkness. If something wasn't done soon, there would be no need for the Germans to attack England. The blackout would take care of it for them.

With that thought, the figure looked both ways before jogging across a side street and going towards a telephone box on the other side. He opened the door and stepped inside, closing it firmly behind him. Picking up the receiver, he unscrewed the mouthpiece. It came away easily and he tipped the handset over his other hand. A rolled strip of microfilm dropped into his hand and he quickly replaced the mouthpiece before tucking the film into the inside pocket of his coat. Replacing the receiver in its cradle, he turned to leave the booth, closing the door again behind him. By the pre-arranged signal, if the door was left open, it meant that he had left something in turn to be picked up. By closing the door, he signaled that he needed more time. As the man walked away from the booth and headed to the corner of the dark street, his lips thinned into a line. His handler would be unhappy with the delay, but there was really no help for it.

When Robert Ainsworth had unceremoniously passed away in Bern, he hadn't had the package with him. If he had, the man would have not only heard about it, but would have it in his possession. Not surprising, really. It wasn't the sort of thing one would carry when traipsing across Europe in the twilight of another bloody war. It was far too dangerous. No. Robert had undoubtedly left it at his home in Lancashire, and that was where he would find it. The problem was retrieving it. His attempt yesterday had been a useless exercise. He would have to try again, and that meant his associates would have to wait.

The man crossed the road and turned down another street, heading towards Waterloo Station. He wasn't worried about finding the package; he had no doubt that he would. What concerned him was that in doing so, the likelihood of his being uncovered increased ten-fold. Right now, he was above suspicion in all respects. That wouldn't last if he continued to poke around in Robert Ainsworth's affairs.

His lips tightened and he buried his hands in his coat pockets. There had already been a round-up of the others. They'd been uncovered and detained practically as soon as war was declared. The only thing that saved his own identity was his strict insistence that no one ever knew of his existence. In the beginning, his superiors had thought him overly cautious. In light of the recent arrests, however, they had been forced to admit that he had been right to keep himself firmly in the shadows. Now he was the only one left.

And he had no intention of being caught.

Chapter Five

Evelyn lifted a hand to shade her eyes from the sun and peered across the south lawn at the driveway in the distance. A black, low-slung Lagonda was speeding towards the house and she felt her pulse give a little leap. Rob was back from collecting Miles at the train station.

"Your Tante Adele seems to be recovering from her bout with influenza," her mother said, looking up from a letter in her hand. "She writes that they hope to be able to travel soon and come to visit."

"Oh good!" Evelyn turned her eyes to her mother. "That will be nice company for you. How are Gisele and Nicolas?"

"Fine. Up to their usual pranks, I gather." Her mother folded the letter and slid it back into the envelope. "I do wish they had been able to make it to the funeral."

"They could hardly travel when she was so ill. At least they will be visiting soon."

"Yes, but you and Robbie will have returned to your stations." She sighed. "I don't know what I'll do when you leave. How will I keep myself busy?"

Evelyn reached across the table and squeezed her mother's hand, a gentle breeze blowing a long strand of hair into her eyes.

"You'll manage, I'm sure. Have you heard from Auntie Agatha? I thought she was considering coming to stay with you for a few months."

"I haven't had a letter from her yet, but you know your aunt. I'll receive the letter a day before she arrives." Mrs. Ainsworth set aside her correspondence. "Isn't there any possibility of your getting assigned to a posting closer to home?"

"We've been over this, Mum. I can't change stations just yet. Perhaps after Christmas I can apply for something closer."

Before Mrs. Ainsworth could reply, the butler emerged from the house, stepping onto the flagged stone patio and clearing his throat.

"Mr. Mansbridge, ma'am," he announced.

Evelyn looked up in surprise as a tall, dark haired man dressed in a charcoal gray suit followed the butler outside.

"Stephen!" Mrs. Ainsworth exclaimed, standing and moving forward to greet him. "What a surprise!"

"Hallo! I've come with my tail between my legs to beg your forgiveness for missing the funeral the other day," Stephen Mansbridge said, taking her hands in a light clasp. "I couldn't get away from London. I'm so very sorry."

"I understand," she said with a smile. "Your mother explained everything. Come, have a seat. Can I offer you tea?"

"Thank you." Stephen followed her to the table and smiled warmly at Evelyn. "Hello, Evie. How are you holding up?"

"As well as can be expected, I suppose," she replied, taking his outstretched hand. "Did you come on the train?"

"No, I drove up. I'm on my way to Wales." Stephen seated himself next to her. "Is Rob still on leave, or has he returned to his Spitfire already?"

"He's still here. He's just gone to the station to pick up a friend of his," Mrs. Ainsworth said. "He'll be returning to Duxford tomorrow."

"He's actually just arrived back," Evelyn said. "I saw the car drive up."

"Jolly good, I'll see him after all. I was afraid I'd miss him." He looked from one woman to the other. "How was the funeral? Were you inundated with all the distant relatives you'd forgotten about?"

Evelyn couldn't repress the chuckle that bubbled up.

"How did you know?" she demanded.

"Call it a hunch," he said with a grin.

"Now Evelyn, don't be impertinent," Mrs. Ainsworth admonished. "It was kind of them to come."

"I'm sorry, Mum. Of course it was." Evelyn smiled sheepishly.

"I *am* sorry I couldn't make it up," Stephen said. "I did try. If there was any way I could have been here for you, Evelyn, you know that I would have."

"Is that Stephen Mansbridge I hear?" a voice called from the other side of the patio.

They turned to watch as Rob rounded the corner of the house with Miles close behind. Evelyn caught her breath as her pulse leapt again at the sight of the tall, handsome pilot with her brother. Good grief. Why couldn't she get a hold of herself when she saw him? He was just a man, after all. A very good-looking man, but just a man.

The Oslo Affair

"Good Lord, it is!" Rob crowed, vaulting over the low balustrade that encircled the patio. "I haven't seen you in what seems like years! How *are* you?"

"Robbie!" His mother exclaimed in exasperation. "Really! There's an entrance right over there!"

Stephen grinned and went over to ring Rob's hand.

"Never better, old man, never better," he said. "I'm sorry I didn't make it for the funeral. I couldn't get away, I'm afraid."

"So we heard. You mother explained everything." Rob turned as Miles circled around the patio to come through the opening a few feet away. "Don't let it worry you. The whole day is something of a blur, to be honest. I doubt if I remember who *did* show up. Miles! This is Stephen Mansbridge. We've known him for years. Practically grew up with him. This is Miles Lacey, a mate from Duxford."

Miles grinned and shook Stephen's hand. "Hello."

"Hallo."

"You know Evie already," Rob said, continuing the introductions. "This is my mother. I don't think you met her when you were here the other day."

"No, indeed." Miles smiled and held his hand out to Mrs. Ainsworth. "It's a pleasure to meet you. Thank you for having me. I'm sure the last thing you want is a house guest right now."

"It's no trouble," she answered graciously, motioning him into the seat Stephen had vacated. "Rob explained the situation. Did you really have to land in London?"

"I'm afraid so. It doesn't look as though they'll have the plane fixed by tomorrow, so I'm to go back with Rob. I was all set to stay in the hotel another night when Rob suggested I stay here."

"Of course! You're more than welcome," Mrs. Ainsworth said warmly. "We've plenty of room."

"Have you had tea yet?" Rob asked. "I'm starving."

"Thomas is just bringing it."

"I gather from that conversation that you're a pilot as well?" Stephen asked Miles, pulling out a cigarette case.

"Yes."

"You wouldn't happen to be related to the Laceys in York, would you?" he asked, his brows creased thoughtfully. "I could swear you look familiar."

Evelyn thought she heard a very faint sigh beside her.

"Yes, I am. I believe we met last year at Lord Sandringham's masquerade," Miles said.

Stephen snapped his fingers and his face cleared.

"Of course! I knew I recognized you! And now you're flying airplanes."

"Oh, I was flying airplanes then, as well."

Evelyn looked at him and raised an eyebrow.

"I'm fairly positive you failed to mention that you were one of the Yorkshire Laceys," she said, tilting her head.

"You didn't ask," he replied with a quick grin.

"Stephen, how long are you staying?" Rob asked.

"Only for tea. I just stopped in on my way to Wales." Stephen lit a cigarette and glanced at him. "I'm glad I was able to catch you, though. It's been a long time."

"So it has. Are you still with the diplomatic service?"

"As long as they'll keep me."

Miles looked at Evelyn as Stephen and Rob moved away to the other end of the patio.

"How much longer is your leave?" he asked.

"I have to go back tomorrow, the same as Robbie."

"Doesn't seem fair, does it?" he asked. "It's hardly enough time to wrap your mind around everything."

"That's what I was saying this morning," Mrs. Ainsworth agreed.

"There *is* a war on," Evelyn pointed out. "We're lucky we got the three days that we did."

"I know," her mother sighed. "I'm grateful for the time you had. I just wish you had more of it to relax before going back. Why don't you show Mr. Lacey the stables after tea?"

"Please call me Miles," he said. "When you say Mr. Lacey, I feel I ought to look round for my father."

"Very well, Miles." Mrs. Ainsworth smiled. "Do you ride?"

"I do."

"Wonderful! Evelyn can take you out this afternoon. The fresh air will be good for her."

"And what about you?" Evelyn asked fondly. "What will you do for fresh air?"

Her mother waved a hand vaguely. "This is as much fresh air as I can stand today. Don't you worry about me."

Miles looked at Evelyn and his green eyes met hers. He smiled slowly.

"It looks like you're stuck with me."

Evelyn grinned. "I'm sure I'll find a way to manage."

The Oslo Affair

Evelyn studied her reflection in the mirror critically. She wore a simple dress in her favorite shade of blue that was more than appropriate for an evening meal at home. She'd purchased the gown in Paris in the spring during an impulsive afternoon of shopping and this was only the second time she'd worn it. The color brought out the blue of her eyes, and her cheeks were still flushed from her ride with Miles earlier. Her mother had been right. The fresh air had done her a world of good.

Well, that and the company of Miles Lacey.

Evelyn turned from the mirror and went across her room to the door. There was no denying her attraction to the pilot. From the first moment she laid eyes on him, she had felt irresistibly drawn to him. The ever-present twinkle in his green eyes filled her with warmth, and when he smiled, she felt it clear through to her toes. There was something about Miles that was altogether different from any other man of her acquaintance, and Evelyn was uncomfortably aware that this was a man she could easily fall in love with.

And they both had to return to their respective stations, and the war, in the morning. He would go back to flying his Spitfires, and she would return to Scotland to prepare for Oslo.

Evelyn opened the door and stepped into the hallway. It was only pure chance that brought him here today. If the plane he'd been flying hadn't developed mechanical issues, she probably would never have seen him again. The thought sent a dart of dismay through her and she frowned in reaction. It was just her luck. She finally met a man who was interesting and worth getting to know better, and they were in the middle of a bloody war. It was really quite impossible.

She reached the end of the thickly carpeted hallway and started down wide shallow steps. It was probably just as well. She didn't have time for any kind of relationship, and neither did he. Never mind that they had spent the entire afternoon laughing, or that he had the same sense of humor as herself. It didn't matter that when she was with him she felt perfectly at ease and comfortable. Tomorrow she had to return to Scotland and he would go back to Duxford. And that was an end to it.

"Hallo." A voice spoke behind her and Evelyn turned to see the man himself coming down the stairs behind her. He was dressed in his RAF uniform, a navy and white spotted silk neckerchief tied at his throat. "I'm not late, am I?"

"If you are, then so am I," she said with a smile, pausing to wait for him.

"It's very kind of your mother to entertain me like this," Miles said, joining her. "It can't be easy for her."

"I think it might be the best thing for her, to be honest. She's always loved having people to stay. Even though it's only for one night, it's a distraction for her, and a welcome one at that."

"That's a relief, at any rate." He glanced at her as they went down the steps. "And you? Do you mind having your brother's reckless friend hanging about?"

"Are you reckless?"

"'Course I am. I'm a pilot. Stands to reason I must be. No one with any sense would choose to go up when you can remain with your feet planted safely on the ground."

"I must be reckless myself, then. I can think of nothing I'd like more!" Evelyn said with a laugh.

Miles grinned and his eyes met hers. "Really?"

"Oh yes. I've always wanted to fly. It just never came to be. And so I content myself with driving my car very fast and associating with people like you."

"Touché," he laughed. "Is that why you joined the WAAFs?"

They reached the ground floor and Evelyn turned towards the drawing room.

"Of course! Why else?"

"Do you know, Evelyn, I think I'm really starting to like you."

She shot him a look full of mischief.

"Oh, I wouldn't do that, if I were you," she warned teasingly. "I'm dreadfully dull when you get to know me. I *am* an Assistant Section Officer, after all."

He raised his eyebrows and looked horrified. "Good God, are you really? That sounds jolly official."

"It does, doesn't it?" Evelyn laughed. "And jolly ugly, too. Don't get too comfortable with me. I fully expect to start growing warts soon."

Miles held open the door to the drawing room for her.

"I think I'll take my chances," he murmured as she passed through.

"There you are!" Rob exclaimed from the other side of the room, a drink in his hand. "We were about to send out a search party!"

"Sorry I'm late down," Evelyn apologized, moving forward to kiss her mother's cheek. "I was reading and lost track of the time."

"I have no such excuse, unfortunately," Miles said behind her.

The Oslo Affair

"I'm afraid I might have dozed off."

"We're very informal here," Mrs. Ainsworth assured him with a smile. "Never mind Rob. He's just teasing."

"What are you drinking, Miles?" Rob asked, setting down his glass and moving over to the sideboard where an array of bottles was set out.

"I'll take a sherry, thanks."

"And you, Evie?"

"I'll have the same." Evelyn sank down onto the love seat next to her mother. "Have you both been waiting long?"

"Not at all," her mother said. "How was your ride this afternoon?"

"It was lovely. You were right. The fresh air was just what I needed."

"Of course I was. You were looking quite strained, but you seem much better now."

Evelyn looked up to accept a glass of sherry from her brother.

"Did you know that Miles hunts?" she asked him. "You should bring him round at Christmas and we'll go out on Boxing Day."

"Hunting on Boxing Day?" Miles asked, seating himself in a chair across from her.

"It's a bit of a family tradition," Rob explained, leaning against the mantle. "Been doing it for years. Course, now with Dad gone…"

His voice trailed off and Evelyn swallowed.

"We really must keep it going," Mrs. Ainsworth said after a moment. "You know it's what he would have wanted. It was always such fun."

"And he wouldn't want us to mope around," Evelyn agreed. "We all know that."

"This is all assuming that we'll be able to celebrate Christmas this year," Rob said. "Lord knows where any of us will be."

"They're saying in town that the war won't last that long," Mrs. Ainsworth said. "It may be all over by Christmas."

"I wouldn't bank on that, if I were you," Evelyn said. "But that doesn't mean we won't be able to come home."

"I hope you can," her mother exclaimed. "I can't bear the thought of spending Christmas alone."

"But you won't be alone, will you?" Rob asked. "Auntie Agatha is coming to stay. If we can't get back, I'm sure she'll stay on."

"Oh, did you hear from her?" Evelyn looked at her mother.

"Yes. A letter came by the afternoon post. She'll be arriving at the end of the week."

"Oh good. That does make me feel better! Now I don't have to worry about you rattling around in the house all alone."

"Yes, but Agatha is such an old goat sometimes," her mother grumbled. "I just know we're going to rub against each other like wire wool."

"At least you're going into it with the right mind set," Rob said with a grin. "Less disillusionment that way."

Evelyn was surprised into a gurgle of laughter and she grinned at her mother.

"She'll be good company for you, and you know it," she said. "The last time she came to stay you both had a wonderful time."

"Right up until she offended the vicar," Mrs. Ainsworth retorted. "But I suppose you're right. It will probably do me a world of good. Your father wouldn't want me to be all alone."

"And neither do we," Rob said, finishing his drink. He set the empty glass on the mantle. "Especially if this war goes on for any amount of time. Shall we go into dinner? I'm hungry enough to eat a horse."

"You're always hungry," Evelyn said, standing. "Don't they feed you at that airfield of yours?"

"Oh they feed us, but I don't think there's a cook in the county that can keep up with your brother's appetite," Miles said.

"Can I help it if flying makes me hungry?" Rob demanded.

"Flying? Is that what you call it?" Miles retorted. "Never would have guessed it!"

Chapter Six

"Do you think Mum will be all right when we leave tomorrow?" Rob asked, handing Evelyn a glass of wine.

The three had retreated to the study when Mrs. Ainsworth went up to bed. Evelyn kicked off her shoes and tucked her feet up under her, leaning her head back on the worn leather of a comfortable armchair.

"I think so," she said thoughtfully. "She's stronger than she looks. And she's got Thomas and Millie to keep an eye on her."

"When is her sister coming?" Miles asked, accepting a glass of brandy and settling in the other armchair.

"At the end of the week. I think she'll be fine until then."

"I wish we weren't going back already," Rob said. "There's still so much to be done with the estate, and she won't have the faintest idea how to cope with it all."

"She won't have to. You're taking care of it," Evelyn pointed out. "And there's always Mr. Ritter, the solicitor."

"Oh blast! I completely forgot!" he exclaimed, slapping his palm against his forehead. "I have a stack of papers he needs sent back. Lord knows I won't have time to do them once I get back with the squadron tomorrow. Miles, you don't mind if I bugger off and leave you, do you?"

"Not a'tall," Miles said. "Take care of your affairs. I'm sure Evie and I will find something to talk about."

Rob glanced her sheepishly.

"Sorry, sis," he said. "You don't mind?"

"Of course not!" She got up and went over to him to give him a hug. "I'll see you in the morning."

Rob nodded, tossed his drink back and turned towards the door.

"I'll see you in the morning, Miles. Behave yourself," he threw over his shoulder.

"I always do!" Miles protested.

"I was talking to my sister."

And on that outrageous remark, Rob disappeared out the door, closing it firmly behind him. Evelyn laughed as she settled herself in her seat again.

"Should I be worried?" Miles asked with a grin.

"I have no idea what he's talking about," she replied with a devilish twinkle.

"Mm-hmm." Miles sipped his brandy and studied her over the rim of the glass. "Do you know what I've been wondering ever since I met you?" he asked.

"I couldn't guess."

"What on earth it is that you do in the WAAF."

Evelyn grinned. "I warn my girls to stay away from officers like you."

Miles laughed and held up on hand, acknowledging a hit. "Fair enough."

"I'm a training officer at the moment," she said finally.

Miles set down his glass and pulled out a cigarette case. He offered it to her, taking one for himself when she shook her head.

"Who do you train?"

"WAAFs," came the dry answer, "and don't ask me anymore. I can't tell you what I train them to do. It's classified, even from wealthy flying officers like yourself."

"Ah. You're the one teaching them to take over the world," he said, nodding wisely.

"Perhaps."

He lit his cigarette and tucked the case away.

"I expect you're training them to be plotters in the Ops Centers," he said. "We've heard rumors that the men who plot and guide aircraft in battle are going to be replaced by women. All terribly hush-hush, of course."

Evelyn was silent, watching him with faint interest and he grinned.

"Don't be afraid of me, if that *is* what you're doing. I'm not going to bite the hand that guides me, so to speak."

"I'll keep that in mind," she murmured, sipping her wine.

"In all seriousness, why did you join the WAAFs?"

"Why did you join the RAF?"

"To fly airplanes, of course," he answered. "I've always wanted to fly, since I was a boy. If I'm going to have to do my part in defense of King and Country, then I'll do so by doing something I love. Now

The Oslo Affair

it's your turn. Why did you join the WAAFs? You certainly didn't have to."

"No, but I wanted to do something," she said slowly, picking her words carefully. She suddenly found that she didn't want to lie to the man sitting across from her. She wanted to tell him as much of the truth as she could, even though it would never be nearly enough. "I couldn't sit by and watch as my brother prepared to fight for his country and not do anything."

Miles considered her thoughtfully for a long moment.

"Rob mentioned that you were in Hong Kong for a few years. I suppose coming back to England and going back into society was rather a bore after that."

She looked at him in surprise.

"It was, but you're the first one to recognize it."

"I'm just thinking of how I would feel if I spent time in another culture, another life, and then had to come back to the everyday world in Lancashire. I imagine it's rather like how I feel when I can't fly and have to do the familial rounds."

She couldn't answer him. What would she say? That she missed the excitement of practicing her Kung Fu with the local masters? That she had always yearned for more excitement than a well-bred young lady had any right to expect? Yet, when her eyes met his, Evelyn got the distinct impression that she didn't need to say anything. He completely understood.

"Of course, then you ended up in Scotland," Miles continued, the twinkle back in his eyes. "So much for a life of excitement."

Evelyn laughed. "Don't underestimate the Scots."

"Or the thrill of teaching your girls to plot," he said with a wink. "I think I'll miss you, Assistant Section Officer Ainsworth. I hope I shall hear from you."

Evelyn raised her eyebrows. "Would you like me to write to you?"

"Every pilot likes to get letters from beautiful women. Bragging rights, y'know." He finished his brandy and set the glass on the table next to the chair. "And I'd like to know how you get on in Scotland."

"Then I'll write," she said easily. "But the first time you fail to answer, I'll stop."

"That's a fair trade, in any event."

Evelyn finished her wine, suddenly loathe to finish the evening and go up to bed. She was enjoying the easy companionship between them. But they both had an early start in the morning, and the reality of what they were both going back to settled over her.

"I don't think I've ever been so happy to have an airplane malfunction on me," Miles said, his voice quiet.

Her heart thumped and she met his eyes. "Me too."

He smiled slowly and stood, holding his hand out to her.

"Perhaps I'll find a reason to go to Scotland," he said, helping her to her feet.

"I'd like that."

Evelyn slipped her shoes back on and looked up at his handsome face. The gleam was back in his bright green eyes and his lips curved faintly.

"Would you?"

"Of course I would. If I can't fly, reckless fighter pilots are the next best thing!"

Miles let out a bark of laughter. "In that case, I'll make it a priority."

She grinned and drank in the sight of him with his eyes alight with laughter and the attractive dent in his cheek. This was how she wanted to remember him: laughing at her with his eyes gleaming in that peculiar way that made her knees go weak. This was the memory she wanted to keep her warm at night in the coming weeks when there was no other warmth.

The laugh faded and Miles exhaled, his eyes meeting hers.

"You'll be sure to write?"

She smiled and nodded. "I will."

His eyes held hers and she felt something very like sorrow well up inside her. With a shock, she realized that the last thing in the world she wanted was to turn and walk out of the room and out of his life. But she knew that she must.

Turning, she went towards the door. What was she doing? She couldn't just leave without saying goodbye, yet goodbye seemed so final. As if she would never see him again. Evelyn knew she would never be able to say it. But she couldn't just walk away, either. She'd regret that more than anything.

She turned at the door and took a long, last look, memorizing every feature. She looked once again into his eyes and smiled wistfully.

"Take care of yourself, Miles."

He nodded and then she was gone, closing the door softly behind her.

The Oslo Affair

Aberdeen, Scotland
November 1, 1939

Evelyn watched as Bill shouldered his way through the people thronging the narrow, dockside street. She was seated in the back of a black Vauxhall, waiting to board a ship bound for Oslo. If there were nerves, she was trying very hard to ignore them. Instead, she was concentrating on the fact that the trip had been moved up unexpectedly, resulting in her leaving directly from Scotland rather than London as originally planned.

When her liaison officer on the RAF base in Scotland had come into her office yesterday morning, Evelyn had been expecting instructions to go to London. Instead, she was handed a train ticket to Aberdeen. When she'd arrived at the station an hour ago, Bill was waiting for her. Aside from saying that the timetable had been moved up, he'd been unusually quiet on the ride to the docks. Now, watching him make his way back to the car with a paper-wrapped package under his arm, she chewed her bottom lip thoughtfully. What had happened to make it imperative that she go to Norway a full two-weeks ahead of schedule?

He reached the car and climbed into the backseat next to her, handing her the paper-wrapped package.

"This is all your identification and press credentials," he told her, closing the door. "You'll be staying in a boarding house run by one of our agents, but you may need those to verify your identity while you're going about the city."

"Are we still going with Maggie Richardson?" she asked, opening the package and pulling out a bill-fold. Opening it, she found identification papers, press credentials for the *Daily Mail* in London, and over five hundred pounds in krone notes.

"Yes. That identity is established, and will work well in Oslo." Bill glanced at his watch. "We have a few minutes before it's time to board. I suppose you're feeling rather confused."

"A bit, yes." Evelyn tucked the billfold into her bag. "Why the sudden rush?"

"Shustov contacted us through the embassy in Helsinki. His scheduled trip to Oslo was changed. He's there now." He passed her a business card. "When you arrive, you'll check in with this contact at the embassy. Daniel Carew. He will let Shustov know that you're in Oslo with a pre-arranged signal. Beyond that, Shustov refuses any and all other contact, so the assumption is that he will find you."

"He'll find me?" Evelyn stared at him. "I don't even know what he looks like! How am I supposed to know it's him?"

"That's an excellent question, and he's already provided the answer. When he does make contact with you, he'll ask you how the weather was in London when you left." He reached into the inside pocket of his coat and pulled out a small notebook. Flipping it open, he thumbed through until he reached a particular page. "Your reply should be the following, word for word: 'I carried an umbrella because it looked like rain, but left it on the train.' Got it?"

"Yes."

"Good." Bill tucked the notebook away again and looked at her. "Once you have the package, let Carew know and he'll arrange for your return trip."

"That's it?"

"That's it. You should be back home in no time at all."

Evelyn exhaled and nodded. It certainly seemed straightforward enough. Check into her rooms, contact the embassy, wait for Vladimir to find her, and then go home. Her mind inadvertently went back to Strasbourg last summer. That had also been an easy and straightforward plan, and look at what a fiasco it had turned out to be.

"And everything's arranged with my posting in Scotland?" she asked. "In case anything comes up? They know what to do?"

Something like a smile passed over Bill's face.

"This isn't our first time out, m'dear," he assured her. "Believe me when I say that your liaison officer there is more than capable of taking care of any surprise visitors or family emergencies. You left your pre-written letters to be sent if you're delayed for some reason? Good. Then there's nothing to worry about. Should Rob or anyone else drop in, they'll be told you're away on a two-day training exercise."

They were silent for a moment and then he looked at her.

"It's time. Are you ready?"

Evelyn took a deep breath and nodded, raising her blue eyes to his. "It doesn't matter if I'm ready or not, does it?" she asked humorously. "I have to get my feet wet sooner or later."

"The nerves will pass," he told her. "You'll be just fine. I've told you before that you're a natural. Some people were made for this kind of work, and you're one of them. Keep it simple and remember your training. You'll be on your way home in no time."

The Oslo Affair

RAF Duxford
November, 1939

Miles let out a jaw-cracking yawn and looked around as a fresh burst of laughter erupted behind him. He and a few of the other pilots had come down to the pub for a drink after a long day in the air. Rob was at the end of the bar with two others, teasing the barmaid, but Miles had chosen to keep the new pilot company. Given the amount of raucous laughter coming from the other end, it appeared to be the quieter of the options, if not the most amusing. The Yank was busy reading a letter from his sister back in the States, and a long day being cramped in the cockpit was catching up with Miles.

"She's out of her mind." Flying Officer Chris Field muttered, looking up from the letter in his hand. "She says she's going to marry that Casanova I told you about. The one with the flashy car. She says she wants to be a millionairess."

"There's nothing wrong with that, is there?"

"Not at all." Chris folded the letter and shoved it back into its envelope. "Our family's got enough dough ourselves. But that's no reason to go and get hitched to the guy."

Miles sipped his pint and glanced at the man beside him.

"It's quite possible that she loves him, old boy."

Chris let out a jaded laugh and motioned to the pub landlord for another pint.

"Not Elizabeth, *old boy*. She's my sister and I love her, but she's got a heart of stone."

"Hallo Lacey! Come and bear me up!" A voice called down the bar, interrupting them. They turned to look at the pilot standing next to Rob. "Rob has the gall to suggest that I don't know a thing about women!"

Miles raised an eyebrow. "Well how should I know, Slippy?" he demanded. "Do I look like a bird to you?"

More laughter erupted from the end of the bar as Slippy protested loudly.

"Oh I say, that's jolly unfair! You've known me longer than anybody! What about that time in London at that delightful club? You remember? The one with the excellent brandy?"

"All I remember is that you spilled brandy down my best jacket and then stood on the table to recite the opening stanza of Macbeth!"

Slippy grinned, unabashed. "Did I? Well, ladies love poetry, don't they?"

"Good Lord, Slippy, you're worse than I thought!" Rob exclaimed, handing him a full pint. "Clearly you're beyond my assistance. I wash my hands of you!"

A smiling landlord set a full pint before Chris and took the coin that he handed him. He looked at Miles' glass.

"You all right, lad?"

"Yes, thanks."

He nodded and turned to make change for Chris.

"Have you heard from your WAAF?" Chris asked, lighting a cigarette.

"Got a letter from her just today, as a matter of fact," Miles said with a nod. "She's been sent to a base in Northumberland for a training course. Can't tell me where exactly. It's all terribly hush-hush."

"Where is she normally?"

"Scotland."

Chris frowned. "I didn't know we had bases in Scotland."

"Coming from the colonies as you do, I'm not very surprised," Miles said, pulling out his cigarette case.

"Hey, I'm helping you poor slugs out, aren't I?" Chris pointed out good-naturedly.

"So very kind, I'm sure." Miles lit a cigarette. "She writes that it's bound to be gloomy. She says there's a hospital nearby for pilots and for me to drop in if I get in a jam."

"Very hospitable of her."

"Yes, isn't it?"

Before Chris could answer, a bread roll hit him on the back of the head. Getting up quickly, he picked it up from the bar and chucked it back towards the group at the other end. It bounced off Slippy's shoulder and Miles grabbed his pint, diving out of the way as another roll flew by. The barmaid squealed and ducked behind the counter as bread began to fly and bodies began to crash into each other. Miles swallowed the rest of his bitter and ducked out of the way as Chris flew past his shoulder to catch another bread roll. Three pilots charged after him, turning the food fight into an impromptu game of rugby in the nearly deserted pub.

He waited until Rob was almost on top of Chris, then stuck his foot out in front of him. Rob went down and the other two pilots lost their balance and piled on top of him. Abandoning his empty glass on the bar, Miles held his hands up with a cigarette hanging out of his mouth. Chris grinned and threw the roll to him.

The Oslo Affair

Grabbing it, Miles began running in the opposite direction as the others pulled themselves up from the pile and charged after him.

Chapter Seven

Oslo, Norway
November 4, 1939

Evelyn looked up at the tall building before her and then moved towards the door on the ground floor. She was in a fairly quiet street, just a block from the busy Bygdøy Allé. Located in Olso's West End, the area was quiet and exclusive, setting her nerves at ease. If nothing else went according to plan on her first visit to Norway, at least her temporary living quarters appeared to be in a neighborhood like what she was used to.

Before she reached the door, it opened and a stocky man of medium height stared at her from under bushy brows.

"Du er yngre enn jeg trodde du ville være. Og du er sen," he said without ceremony, pinning her with a fierce look.

Evelyn swallowed. She had no idea what he was saying, or if he was even someone she had to be concerned about. She was just opening her mouth to ask if he spoke English or perhaps German when an older woman emerged from behind him, clucking in apparent disgust.

"La henne være i fred, Josef. Du vet at hun ikke skjønner norsk!" she rebuked him. Then, smiling at Evelyn, she wiped her hands on the apron covering her skirt and held out her hand. "Don't mind my husband," she said in halting English. "Welcome. You must be the journalist from London. Come in! We've been expecting you."

The woman ushered her into the house, past her husband, and showed her into a small parlor.

"My name is Else and this is my husband, Josef," she said, motioning to the man who followed them in. "We run this boarding house."

"I'm Maggie Richardson," Evelyn introduced herself. "I'm sorry I don't speak Norwegian. Does your husband speak German? I'm quite fluent."

"He does indeed, and he also speaks a little English. He was being contrary just now," the woman told her, shooting her husband another reproachful look. "He means nothing by it. He's been waiting for you and was surprised at how young you are, that is all."

Evelyn wasn't sure how to respond to that, so she nodded, smiled and offered the man a sheepish shrug.

"Never mind, dear. Is this your only luggage? Josef will take it up to your room. Come. We show you."

Else turned to bustle out of the parlor and towards a flight of stairs across from the entranceway while Josef picked up Evelyn's two bags and waited for her to follow his wife.

"How was your trip? You come by boat, yes?" the woman asked conversationally as she led the way up the old wooden stairs. Though aged, they were spotless and the walls were painted a bright and cheerful white.

"Yes. We hit a bit of a storm on the crossing, which set us behind a bit, but nothing serious."

"Do you suffer from sea sickness?"

"No, thank goodness."

"You're very lucky. The North Sea can be very rough. I don't mind it, but Josef gets ill."

They reached the top of the stairs and Else led her down a wide hallway to a door on the left. She opened it and went inside.

"Here you are. I hope you find everything comfortable."

Evelyn stepped into a large, well-appointed room with a four-poster bed and large bay window overlooking the street. One wall was dominated by a large hearth and she was grateful to see a fire blazing, casting heat and soft light into the room.

"Oh, it's lovely!" she exclaimed, turning around and taking in the floral bedspread and cheerful wallpaper. A desk stood near the window, and a chair was placed near the fire. While the room was sparsely furnished, it was clean and welcoming.

Else glowed with pleasure.

"I'm glad you like it. We started the fire for you so you would be comfortable. Josef will keep wood in the bin and there are matches on the mantle." She watched as Josef set the bags on the floor near the wardrobe. "You'll want to freshen up, and so we leave you now. Come down when you are settled and I'll give you directions around the city. It's quite simple, and the tram will take you most places you need to go."

"Thank you."

Else nodded and gave a final smile before herding her husband out of the room. Once the door closed behind them, Evelyn removed her hat and tossed it onto the bed, undoing the buttons on her coat.

Her gloves joined the hat and she took off the heavy, warm coat, draping it across the foot of the bed. She crossed the floor to stand before the roaring fire, holding her hands out to the warmth while she looked around the room.

She would be comfortable here, she decided. It was clean and overlooked the street. Else seemed nice and friendly, even if her husband was unusually quiet.

Yes. This would do nicely.

⊙

A man in a long dark coat looked up from his perusal of a selection of newspapers and glanced out the storefront window. A tram rolled by the small shop and he checked his watch before turning to pay for the newspaper in his hand. After a halting conversation with the young man behind the counter, he turned to leave with the paper tucked under his arm. Stepping into the street, he pulled on his gloves and turned the collar of his coat up against the brisk, cold blast of wind that howled down the street.

He turned to walk along the pavement, following the path of the tram car. A few minutes later, he emerged onto Thomas Heftyes Gate, a road that had the honor of hosting several different foreign powers, of which the British Embassy was one. He looked at his watch again and crossed the road to the opposite side of the embassy. It was coming up for the dinner hour and soon many of the staff would be departing for the day. His own embassy was a few blocks away, closer to the water, and he'd spent most of his morning there. He had gone out to stretch his legs after lunch and had no intention of returning that day. He had other business to attend to.

After looking over his shoulder to make sure no one was behind him, the man moved into the shadows of the fence that surrounded the Finnish Embassy. He quickened his pace and strode to the end of the block where a side street intersected the road. A moment later, he disappeared around the corner. After going a few feet, he crossed the street and went into the garden of a large, private residence. The house was a sprawling three-story affair surrounded by heavily landscaped gardens and trees.

After pausing behind an ancient, thick-trunked tree, the man cast a look around and moved to his left, staying along the outer perimeter of the property. Completely concealed from the street by the trees, he moved freely to the corner of the garden before turning to

The Oslo Affair

move along the far side. After another few moments, he came to a stop and cast another look around. Finding himself completely alone, he moved forward until he had a clear view of the British Embassy across the street.

Checking his watch yet again, he settled in to wait.

◉

Evelyn nodded in thanks to the young man holding the door open for her and walked into a small but cheerful office. A man rose from behind a cluttered desk and came around with a smile, holding out his hand.

"Miss Richardson? I'm Daniel Carew. It's a pleasure to make your acquaintance!"

"Hello!" She took the offered hand. "Thank you for seeing me without an appointment," she added for the benefit of the assistant who had escorted her through the labyrinth corridors.

"Not a'tall! Not a'tall!" Daniel motioned her to a comfortable leather seat across from his desk. "May I offer you some tea?"

"No thank you. I won't stay long. I know you're a busy man. I don't want to take up too much of your time."

Daniel nodded a dismissal to the young man and he withdrew, closing the door silently. Once he was gone, Daniel turned his attention to Evelyn, eyeing her curiously.

"So you're Bill's newest recruit," he said, going back to the seat behind his desk. "How was the trip here? Not too unpleasant, I hope?"

"No," Evelyn said, setting her purse on the chair next to her. "We hit some rough weather, but in all it was an uneventful crossing."

"And how are you finding Oslo?"

She gave a short laugh. "Very different," she admitted. "And very cold."

That drew a laugh from him and he sat back in his chair.

"The cold takes some getting used to," he said. "You'll just start to adjust and it will be time for you to leave again. Did you find the boarding house all right? Are you all settled in?"

"I did, thank you. The Kolstad's are very kind."

He nodded. "We send quite a bit of business their way, with one thing and another. A word of warning, though: they rent rooms to a number of people from various backgrounds. Don't get too comfortable, and for God's sake don't talk freely to anyone. I wouldn't trust most of their boarders as far as I could throw them."

Evelyn nodded. "I'll remember that."

"Now that's not to say you can't trust *them*," Daniel continued. "Else and Josef are firmly in our camp, but they do rent rooms to those who are not. If you run into trouble, have no hesitation in reaching out to them for help. They'll assist you in any way they can."

"Even Josef?" Evelyn asked with a grin.

Daniel chuckled.

"Don't let his bark frighten you. He's as reliable as they come." He sat forward and opened the top drawer of his desk, pulling out a long envelope. "Now then, I know Bill gave you press credentials and identification before you left. I have some additional temporary passes here. They will allow you access to some of the press spots here in Oslo that are reserved for foreign correspondents. Something I think you should be aware of is that there are several German correspondents here. There's a conference at one of the firms in the city and, as a result, there are quite a few scientists that have come from around Europe. Several of them are from Berlin, and so we also have an increased presence from the Goebbels Propaganda Ministry. I understand you speak German?"

"Yes."

"Good. You'll want to go where you are in the best position to overhear what you can. These will place you there." He passed the envelope across the desk to her. "As far as any of them will be concerned, you are just another face in the constantly rotating carousel of foreign journalists. Your appearance will help you. All the newspapermen love an attractive young woman."

"But I'm not here to mix with the Germans," she objected, taking the envelope. "I'm here to—"

"Yes, yes, I know." Daniel sat back again and waved her budding concerns away. "And I shall pass on your arrival to Comrade Shustov. Until he makes contact, though, why not see what you can pick up from the foreign correspondents? It certainly won't hurt."

Evelyn nodded slowly. He was right. If she was able to glean any information from the Germans, it could only help.

"How long do you think it will be before Shustov makes contact?"

He shrugged. "I have not the faintest idea. It could be tomorrow; it could be next week. I think we're all hoping for the former. As soon as he does, and you get the package, you can bring it here to me for safe keeping, if you like. After losing it once, we don't want to run the risk of one of Else's boarders taking it from your room."

The Oslo Affair

Evelyn's lips tightened imperceptibly. While she knew Daniel probably had no idea that it was her father who had lost the package, the reminder of the failure struck a bitter note with her.

"And, of course, that goes also for anything you may pick up from the Nazis," he continued, oblivious to her discomfort. "If all goes well, you'll have quite a packet to take back with you."

"And how shall I get it to you? If all goes well?"

"Oh, we'll set up an appointment. If you have something to bring me, send a messenger over in the morning. Then come at lunchtime when most of the building is away. Say, twelve-thirty?"

"And no one will think that strange?"

"My dear, this is Oslo, not Moscow. We're not skulking around in the shadows just yet," he said humorously.

Evelyn felt her cheeks go warm.

"I'm sorry. The last time I did anything like this, I ran head-first into a Nazi Untersturmführer of the Security Service," she told him. "I suppose I'm rather expecting more of the same."

"Good Lord, did you really?" Daniel raised his eyebrows. "Where?"

"In Strasbourg."

"Well, I'm fairly sure you won't run into any here. At least, not the Security Service. Nazis, yes. Abwehr, most definitely. But you're highly unlikely to encounter any SS or SD."

"That's a relief, in any event," she said with a smile. "It's not an experience I'm in a hurry to repeat."

"No, I don't suppose you are." Daniel studied her for a moment. "If you do run into any unpleasantness, let me know, but I really don't think you have anything to worry about."

Evelyn nodded and stood, tucking the envelope into her purse. He stood with her and came around the corner of the desk.

"I'll alert your Russian friend that you've arrived," he said. "Beyond that, let me know when you have something and I'll arrange for your return trip. Remember, if you get something you can't conceal easily, bring it here for safekeeping."

She nodded and held out her hand. "I will."

"Best of luck to you, Miss Richardson."

◉

When the blonde woman exited the embassy, the man in the garden across the street straightened up. She was wearing a long, thick navy coat with a matching hat that was made for the cold weather. Even so, the outerwear had the stamp of high quality and appeared to be in the latest fashion. He watched as she stood on the pavement and pulled on her gloves before turning to walk down the street, her purse hooked over her arm.

The man pressed his lips together thoughtfully, waiting until she reached the corner before emerging from the garden. The woman was nothing like what he'd been expecting. She was young and pretty, and obviously accustomed to moving in greater circles than the agents he was used to seeing.

She turned the corner a block away, disappearing from view, and the man crossed the road to follow. How on earth had she ended up here? She looked like she would be more suited to hosting dinners for a diplomatic husband than to visiting Oslo and meeting with the likes of Daniel Carew. The whole situation was very intriguing. He picked up his pace, rounding the corner a moment later.

She had already crossed the next side street and was on her way to Drammensveien, the busier road in the distance. Undoubtedly, she was heading for the bus stop there. He had plenty of time. The next bus wasn't due for ten minutes. She would reach the stop well ahead of it, and there was no fear of him losing her on the bus.

Turning his collar up against the wind, he pulled his hat down low over his face and lowered his head. The temperature, not very high to begin with, was dropping rapidly. Oslo in November was not his favorite place, but it couldn't be helped. He had to follow the Englishwoman, winter or not.

As the light faded, she turned onto Drammensveien. A moment later, he turned the corner and saw her up ahead, standing at the bus stop with three other passengers. He slowed his pace and lowered his head again, glancing at his watch. He didn't want to reach the small group gathered on the pavement too soon and risk her noticing him. It was imperative that she not have the faintest inkling that he was there.

Looking up, he saw a bus in the distance coming towards them. A moment later, he joined the crowd at the back as the bus pulled to a halt at the curb. A few minutes after that, he was seated four rows behind the blonde woman in blue as the bus swayed and jerked into motion.

The Oslo Affair

Chapter Eight

Evelyn poked her head into the kitchen at the back of the house. Else was standing at a large square wooden island, chopping vegetables. She looked up when the door opened and raised her eyebrows in surprise.

"Miss Richardson!" she exclaimed, setting down her knife and wiping her hands on her apron. "I thought you went out."

"I did. I've just returned." Evelyn stepped into the kitchen and let the door close behind her. "Am I interrupting?"

"Not at all, my dear." Else waved a hand, motioning to a stool. "I'm cutting vegetables for soup. Sit and keep this old woman company."

Evelyn smiled and dragged the stool over to island, perching on it while Else resumed chopping. The kitchen was a large and cheerful room with a window overlooking a small, neat garden. Afternoon sun poured through the glass, slicing across the work surface where piles of turnips, carrots and potatoes were waiting to be cut into chunks and thrown into the pot simmering on the stove.

"Did you have any trouble finding the embassy?" Else asked, glancing at her.

"No. Your directions were perfect. It was very simple." Evelyn hesitated, then took a deep breath. "I wonder if I could bother you for more assistance?"

"If I can help, I'm happy to."

"I was told you know of someone who would be able to translate for me?"

Else nodded. "Yes, there are a few different people we can contact for you. What did you have in mind?"

"I have to go out and about this evening," Evelyn said slowly. "I may need to go to a few different restaurants and would feel more comfortable if I had someone with me who spoke the language."

Else shot her a look under her eyebrows.

"Restaurants? What are you looking for?"

"Not what, who. I'm told there are a lot of Germans in the city."

Else thought for a moment. "Well, you could try the Hotel Bristol. They have a very popular restaurant and dance floor. There is also a cocktail lounge very close to it that is popular. They would be good places to start. The Hotel especially is a favorite of most visitors to Oslo. I can think of one person in particular who might be willing to go with you. She is about your age and works as a secretary for a law firm."

"How do I contact her?"

"You don't. I will send Josef with a message and he will get it to her." Else set the knife down and went to the back door. Opening it, she called out and waited for a second until she heard a muffled response. "Josef is her god-father," she added, coming back to the island. "She will come after work if he asks. She knows the city well and would also be a good guide."

"She speaks English?"

"Yes. Her mother insisted all the children learn, along with the German." Else shrugged. "She felt it would be useful for them."

The door to the garden opened and Josef came into the kitchen.

"Tørk av de støvlene før du søler til hele gulvet mitt!" Else exclaimed as he stepped into the house.

Evelyn hid a smile as Josef comically stepped back and proceeded to wipe his feet on the straw mat outside the door.

"What are you doing here?" he asked in German, re-entering the house and pinning Evelyn with a stare. "I thought you went out."

"She's been and come back, Josef." Else also switched to German, her knife slicing steadily through the pile of carrots. "She'll be going out this evening. I thought Anna could accompany her."

Josef went to the long counter adjacent to the sink and picked up a glass from the drying board. He filled it with water and turned to look across the kitchen at Evelyn.

"She would be a good choice," he agreed, sipping the water. "They're of a same age. Where are you going?"

"Else suggested the restaurant at Hotel Bristol," Evelyn said easily, glancing at the other woman. "And a cocktail lounge nearby."

Josef nodded. "I'll go send a message to her and ask her to come around when she is finished working for the day."

"Thank you."

The Oslo Affair

He finished his drink and set the glass down, turning to leave the kitchen again. When he reached the door, he glanced over his shoulder.

"If you're going to the Hotel Bristol, you'll want to be careful," he said. "It's a popular hotel with travelers, particularly the Germans."

Evelyn felt her lips curve in a faint smile.

"That's what I'm hoping for."

RAF Duxford

"All right gentlemen, that's enough."

An authoritative voice rose above the din in the pilots briefing room and Miles stubbed out his cigarette, sitting back on the two seater couch in the corner. The briefing room was unlike any other briefing room in England. The pilots of 66 Squadron were known throughout the RAF, somewhat notoriously, as Corinthian Squadron. Most of them, with the exception of the Yank, were reservists from the Auxiliary Air Force, or the weekend fliers as they were called. Chris was the only American in the squadron, having gone to Canada to join the RAF, and the only pilot without a number at the end of his name. By and large, they came from wealthy families and were accustomed to a certain standard of living. When the RAF accommodations fell short of that standard, they took it upon themselves to remedy it. Whispers of champagne with their dinner and oriental rugs in their mess halls ran rampant on other airfields, providing considerable amusement for the pilots in question. While most of the rumors were completely untrue, there was no disputing the fact that Corinthian Squadron had the most lavishly furnished briefing rooms, bedrooms and recreation rooms. There was even an old shed that they had converted into a squash court.

"Thank you."

A stocky man of medium height stood before the twelve pilots dressed in uniform with a heavy leather flight jacket tossed over his shoulders. His name was Boyd Ashmore, and he was their Squadron Leader. As the room fell quiet, he cleared his throat.

"First of all, it has been brought to my attention that there was something of a ruckus down at the pub again last night. That's the third time in the past two weeks. I'd appreciate it if you'd not upset the locals. Remember that you are officers in the Royal Air Force, and please act like it. I'm getting tired of having the pub landlord in my office." He looked around the room sternly. "We *are* at war, gentlemen, even if it doesn't seem like it. Let's try to maintain some semblance of decorum when we're out and about."

Several of the men in the room shifted in their seats uncomfortably and, after sending another glare around the room, Ashmore nodded.

"Second order of business. Once again, it has been brought to my attention that several complaints have been made about low-level flying over farmers' fields. It's disturbing the livestock, or so I'm told." He glanced up from the sheet in his hand and paused, then lowered his eyes again. "Right. I've addressed that, then," he muttered.

Miles couldn't stop the grin that stretched over his face and he looked at Rob beside him to find him shaking his head. This wasn't the first time they'd heard complaints from the farmers, and it wouldn't be last. For some reason, they seemed to think they could get through this war without having the inconvenience of planes flying overhead.

"Third, whoever pinched the tub of propeller grease from the hangars, please return it." Ashmore looked up again and this time there was a decided twinkle in his eyes. "I can't imagine what you would want with the wretched stuff, but I've a few angry ground-crew sergeants in my office. We can't get any more until the end of the month, so be considerate and return it from whence it came, please."

After some quick scanning and shuffling of the papers in his hands, Ashmore tossed them aside.

"Right. The rest is rubbish."

"And that wasn't?" Rob muttered loud enough to draw several grins from around the room.

Ashmore leaned against the desk behind him and crossed his arms over his chest.

"We have a long day ahead of us," he said. "Low-level formation flying, away from the farmers' fields if we can help it." Groans rose up and he was betrayed into a chuckle. "I know, I know. However, an end is in sight. Tomorrow we'll be rotating out sections and practicing night-flying. Today, A flight will go up first, then B flight. C flight will go after lunch, then we'll start over. You know the routine." Ashmore reached behind him and picked up his notes again. "Oh! Before we go, just one more thing. HQ sent down some papers. They're Polish phrases you have to memorize."

"Polish phrases?" Andrew "Mother" Hampton drawled from the back of the room. "What the bloody hell for?"

"We're getting some Polish refugees who were in the air force

The Oslo Affair

over there. May be helpful in communications. It would also be helpful if you end up bailing out over Poland," Ashmore added dryly.

"If I ditch in Poland, they should bloody well speak English," Mother muttered and Miles grinned.

"That's a bit much, Hampton," Ashmore said, unperturbed. "It's their country, after all. But I don't think you'll have to worry about that for quite some time. Not unless you plan on transferring over to bombers."

"Good Lord, no!"

"Well then, read these over and you'll be tested tomorrow morning. And it *is* classified, so no blabbing at the pub if you don't mind. I know it's a nuisance, but do your best." Ashmore threw the papers back down on the desk and picked up his flying gloves. "Right. Off we go."

Miles and Rob got up and ambled out of the briefing room to where a truck waited. They climbed into the back and held on to the sides as it ground into gear and began jostling and bouncing across the field to the dispersal hut that served as the 'ready' room, where the pilots spent their time between flights. Taking a deep breath, Miles inhaled the cool, morning air and gazed out across the expanse of grass. They bumped along, passing the rows of Spitfires lined up along the landing strip. The sight of the fighters never ceased to fill him with an overwhelming excitement and anticipation. This was where he felt alive.

After about five minutes of bone-jarring bumping, the truck rumbled to a stop outside the wooden hut. Inside were a few chairs and a desk where the adjutant sat with a phone, ready to dispatch fighters to meet enemy threats at a moment's notice. It was a standard set up that had been proven to work. Except the enemy wasn't showing any signs of threat, and the only time that phone rang was to inform them that tea was up.

Miles and Rob climbed down and strolled over to the deck chairs scattered about outside. They were in B flight and they watched as A flight went out to their planes and started their engines.

"Gorgeous day, isn't it?" Slippy remarked, flopping onto the grass and squinting up at the sky. "Not a cloud up there."

"Could do with a few more degrees on the temperature," Chris said, burying his hands in his jacket pockets and pulling up the leather and wool collar of his flight jacket.

Slippy squinted at him. "I thought all you Americans got mountains of snow in the colonies."

Chris ignored the reference to the colonies. Everyone mentioned it at least half a dozen times a day. They hadn't figured out yet that it didn't bother him to be called a Yank from the Colonies.

"Only after Christmas where I come from," he said easily. "Of course, I don't expect someone from the Mother Country to understand, but America is much bigger than you realize."

"Can't be bothered to realize," Slippy replied, undisturbed. "I don't normally associate with rabble rousers and war-makers."

"You know, for such a sophisticated and upper-crust society, it's amazing how you dwell on ancient history," Chris said with a good-natured laugh.

Miles settled in a wooden chair next to a small card table and stretched.

"It's unlikely Slippy dwells on anything," he remarked, tapping his forehead significantly. "Runs in the family, y'know."

Everyone laughed, including Slippy.

"Now, now, none of that, if you please." A new voice said cheerfully. "Don't you know there's a war on? We can't have laughing at the ready, now can we?"

Miles turned to look at the newcomer carrying a clipboard in his hand. Bertram Rodford, or Bertie as they all called him, was the intelligence officer. His easy sense of humor and brutal honesty had made him a favorite with the pilots. He had been a professor of history at the university before the war broke out, commanding the respect of pilots who were not known for their affinity of the written word, historical or otherwise. His primary duty was de-briefing the pilots after every sortie. If this 'Phoney War' ever got off the ground, Bertie would be the one who sorted fact from fiction, using the pilots' views of the air battles.

"A flight's only just gone up," Rob said, pulling out a pack of playing cards. "What are you doing down here already?"

"I came to give you your Polish papers, of course," Bertie replied, flourishing a handful of pamphlets.

"Well, you can jolly well take them back to wherever you got them," Slippy muttered.

Bertie clucked his tongue.

"That's no way to treat Top Secret government documents," he said, handing Rob a pamphlet. "Not that I can take them back to London, although I'd enjoy the trip if I could."

"Would you visit your sweetheart, Bertie?" Miles asked, taking his pamphlet with one hand and picking up the cards Rob had dealt with the other.

"I don't have a sweetheart," he replied cheerfully. "I'd visit the university, of course."

The Oslo Affair

"Do you mean to tell me that you really miss your stuffy old books?" Slippy demanded, sitting up. Bertie raised an eyebrow.

"Much can be learned from my stuffy old books," he murmured. "Manners, for one thing."

"Bravo!" Chris caroled, accepting his pamphlet and glancing at cursorily.

"If anyone needs to learn manners and etiquette, the Lord knows it's you Yanks," Slippy retorted. "No sense of tact or subtlety. None a'tall."

"It's bloody Swedish!"

The exclamation was made with disgust dripping from every word, and they all turned to stare. Miles very rarely was moved to any show of emotion beyond the bare minimum, and the outburst was met with a short, stunned silence.

"Hmm. So you noticed." Bertie glanced at him. "I thought you might."

"What's Swedish?" Rob asked, looking up from his cards.

"The damned pamphlets." Miles tossed the paper in question on the table disgustedly. "It's all bloody Swedish. 'Got morgan.' 'Tak'. It's Swedish, not Polish." He lit a cigarette and picked up his cards again. "Bloody RAF can't even get its languages straight."

"Is it really Swedish?" Chris examined his pamphlet. "Isn't that where the women are all tall and blonde?"

"If it is, learning the language won't do you any good," Slippy said.

"Some of it's Polish, but very little," Bertie said with a shrug. "You're being tested on it tomorrow, whatever it is. I know acquiring additional mental capacity and higher learning is not your forte, but do try."

"If it's not even Polish, I say bugger it," Slippy announced cheerfully.

Rob turned to look at him, raising an eyebrow. "And if it was Polish?"

Slippy shrugged with a grin. "Bugger it."

"Eloquent, our friend Slippy, isn't he?" Miles asked, looking at Rob across the table. "It's your go."

"It *is* a bit much, though," Rob said with a grin, turning back to the cards. "Expecting us to learn Polish or Swedish or whatever it is. I was under the impression that our job was to fly the airplanes, not learn a foreign language. That's my sister's department, not mine."

Miles looked up at that. "Really? What do you mean?"

73

"Oh Evie's been learning foreign languages for as long as I can remember. She speaks several. The last one was Russian, I believe. She's quite the linguist."

"Does she know Polish?" Chris asked, joining them at the table and motioning for Rob to deal him in. "Maybe she can come down and teach us."

"If she does, she'd be appalled at what those papers are," Miles said. "They could have come up with something better than that. The Polish refugees won't have any idea what we're saying."

"Mother was right," Slippy said. "Let the sods learn our language if they want to migrate to our country."

"In all fairness, I don't believe they had much of a choice," Rob pointed out.

"They should have seen which way the wind was blowing." Slippy parked himself in the last vacant chair. "Everyone else could."

"Sometimes I really believe that your skull was filled with jelly in utero," Miles said, throwing his cards down with a wide yawn. "Lord I'm tired. I wonder if I have time for a short kip."

"Not likely." Chris glanced at his watch. "They'll be back soon."

Miles stretched out and tilted his head back, tipping his hat across his eyes.

"Give me a shove when they do arrive," he muttered.

Chris sighed in mock despair. "A country at war and the noble pilot sleeps at his post."

"Not much of a war," Slippy said. "It will all be over and done before Christmas. Mark my words."

"Wouldn't that be a lark!" Rob crowed.

"Won't be much of a lark for you lot if you don't be quiet," Miles growled.

They all laughed and went back to their card game, the sun shining brightly in a cloudless sky.

The Oslo Affair

Chapter Nine

Oslo, Norway

Evelyn looked around as she followed the host to a table. The crowded restaurant reminded her forcibly of one of her favorite ones in Paris, glittering with light reflecting between cocktail glasses and mirrored columns. Laughter and the light chatter of patrons out to enjoy themselves surrounded her, and she felt very much at home in the gaiety. As they moved through the restaurant, she noted which tables had diners who appeared to be there for something other than food and dancing. Those were the ones she had to focus on tonight.

The host stopped at a small table and pulled the chair out for Evelyn with a smile.

"Thank you," she murmured automatically. Even if he didn't understand English, Evelyn supposed the meaning would be obvious.

She seated herself and watched as he moved to hold the chair for the tall woman with her. Anna Salvesen had hair the color of dark, rich mahogany and large brown eyes that seemed to sparkle constantly with some unshared joke. Evelyn had liked her immediately, drawn to the sense of careless enjoyment that she seemed to exude with every movement.

"You must try the Gravlax," Anna said as the host moved away and she settled herself in her seat. "It is exceptional here."

"Gravlax?"

"Smoked salmon. Trust me. You won't regret it."

"And this is why I wanted to have a local guide," Evelyn said with a smile. "I would never have known what anything was, otherwise."

Anna laughed. "I'll take care of you," she promised. "How long are you in Oslo?"

"Only a few days. I'm here to gather information for an article I'm writing. Unless my source gets delayed, it will be a quick trip." Evelyn stuck to her cover story for her trip to Oslo. "I'm meeting someone in the city who has exclusive information for me."

Anna smiled faintly.

"Then I'll have to show you as much of Oslo as possible while you are here," she said decidedly as a waiter approached the table. "We'll start with a drink. Since this is your first time in Norway, shall I order for you?"

"Why not?" Evelyn said with a laugh. "I'm always ready for an adventure."

Anna grinned and turned to the waiter, ordering their drinks swiftly. Evelyn gave up trying to understand what she was saying after the first few words and instead turned her attention to the other patrons in the restaurant. A single man sat at a table nearby, his head bent over a book while he waited for his dinner. She watched him for a moment, noting the cut of his jacket and the way he squinted at his book. He was a man used to spending more time with books than with people, she thought, and one who either didn't know or didn't care that his jacket was two seasons out of date.

"Now, tell me what it is you're looking for?" Anna said once the waiter had departed for the bar.

Evelyn brought her gaze back to the woman across from her. "Pardon?"

Anna smiled and her eyes seemed to look right through her.

"I know you're not just looking for a news story," she said calmly. "And I know you didn't come out tonight for our exciting nightlife. So what are you looking for? Perhaps I can help."

Evelyn stared at her for a moment, her heart pounding. Was it that obvious? Had she made some kind of terrible mistake? How did Anna, who had been in her company for all of an hour, know that she wasn't a journalist from London meeting a newspaper source?

"Don't look so startled," Anna said with a laugh, "and don't worry. You didn't give yourself away. Daniel Carew did. He sent me a message before Josef did."

Evelyn felt her mouth drop open and she sat back in her chair, stunned.

"You...how do you know Mr. Carew?"

Anna eyeballed her for a second and then pulled a cigarette case out of her bag.

"Do you smoke?"

Evelyn nodded mutely and Anna held out the open case.

"I suppose we haven't been very fair to you," she said. "I work as a secretary at a law firm."

"Yes, Else told me."

"Yes, well what she didn't tell you was that the law firm works closely with the French and the English embassies." Anna tucked the

The Oslo Affair

cigarette case back into her bag and watched as Evelyn lit her cigarette. "I've known Mr. Carew for almost a year now. When he needs a translator, or a courier, I've been known to assist from time to time."

"Then you know who I really am?"

"I know you're not a journalist, and I don't think your name is Maggie, is it?" Anna held up her hand. "Don't tell me your real name. We'll stick with Maggie. There are some things I don't need to know."

Evelyn couldn't stop the short laugh that escaped.

"No, it's not Maggie. I don't look much like a Maggie, do I?"

"Not very." Anna tilted her head to the side and considered her. "You don't look anything like other agents Daniel's had to visit either. I'm hoping you're not like them. They were all rather stupid, to be honest. At least, the ones I met."

"Have you met many?" Evelyn was getting over the shock now, and she even managed a smile for the server who came to the table with their drinks. "Oh lovely!" she added as a glass was set before her. "What is this?"

"Aquavit with lime cordial," Anna said, smiling in thanks as a glass of wine was set in front of her. "Aquavit is Norway's specialty. You really must try it while you're here. I think you'll like it. I'm partial to it with the lime cordial."

"What is it?"

"It's like a schnapps." Anna held up her glass and smiled brightly. "Here's to new friends and many adventures!"

Evelyn held up her glass and took a sip. Her eyes widened as the strong liquor hit the back of her throat and Anna grinned.

"It's got a kick to it," she said. "I forgot to warn you about that."

"Forgot?" Evelyn repeated, her eyes watering.

Anna laughed. "Perhaps not," she admitted, her eyes dancing. "Are you very angry?"

"Not in the slightest." Evelyn set the glass down. "It's very good. And I'm definitely more alert now."

"Fantastic! Now tell me what we're doing here tonight."

Evelyn took a deep breath and looked across the table. It was clear that Anna knew much more than she'd been led to believe. Whether or not she could be trusted was another story. However, there could be no harm in telling her what she'd probably already guessed.

"Daniel said that there is some kind of convention in Oslo," she said slowly. "He thought I might be able to gather some information from some of the visitors."

Anna nodded briskly. "Ah yes. The Germans."

She lowered her voice as she said the word and cast a quick glance around. Evelyn nodded, following her gaze. No one was paying them the least amount of attention and she exhaled.

"You say it as if it's common knowledge," she said, putting out her cigarette.

"Oh but it is! They make sure their presence is well-known, I assure you." Anna took a sip of her wine. "They are not known for their humility, the Germans. The conference is a scientific symposium. It's drawn scientists not only from Germany, but also from Sweden, France, the United States and Russia. It's become something of a competition this week, almost like the Olympics but for smart people. It's all in the newspapers."

"The Soviets are here too?" Evelyn asked. "How intriguing."

Anna grinned. "I'm glad you think so. Do you know anything about science?"

"Only what I learned at school. It wasn't my best subject."

"Nor mine. Pity. If one of us knew more about what it was they're discussing all day, we'd perhaps be able to glean something really useful." Anna drummed her fingers on the white tablecloth thoughtfully. "What does Daniel want you to discover, I wonder?"

"I don't think he had anything specific in mind," Evelyn said with a shrug. "I'm really just hoping for a bit of luck."

The waiter came to the table then to take their order and Anna ordered dinner for them both, assuring Evelyn with a twinkle that the dinner would pack less of a punch than the drinks.

While she spoke with the waiter, Evelyn's attention was caught by the table with the solitary bookworm. A tall, angular man had arrived and was in the process of taking the seat across from him. He appeared happy to see the newcomer and closed his book readily, a smile on his face. Interesting. She had received the distinct impression that the man was dining alone, but he must have simply arrived earlier than his companion. As she watched, he set the book aside and she noted the title on the spine. It was a worn copy of a scientific text and looked as though it had been read quite a few times. Evelyn's lips curved imperceptibly.

The title was in German.

◉

Evelyn laughed along with her new acquaintances, Hans and Alrick, as the latter finished sharing a particularly amusing joke. Anna

The Oslo Affair

had somehow managed to finagle an invitation from Alrick to join them for drinks after dinner, although Evelyn still wasn't clear how. One minute she was finishing her dinner and the next she was joining them in the cocktail lounge. Anna really was turning out to be invaluable.

"It's so nice to meet two such lovely ladies who can speak German so well," Alrick said, reaching for his drink. "Don't you think so, Hans?"

"What? Oh yes. Yes of course."

Hans smiled and bobbed his head while still managing to avoid looking directly at either Evelyn or Anna. He looked as if he would much rather go back to his book, but manners forbade him.

"Miss Richardson, you said you're a writer?" he asked. "What do you write?"

"Oh everything," she said gaily. "Right now I'm writing for the *Daily Mail* in London. I've also done some poetry and a few short stories. I'm working on one right now, as a matter of fact."

"Are you really? What's it about?" Anna demanded. "Something exciting?"

"It's about a girl in France who falls in love with an Austrian. I haven't decided yet if she goes back to Austria with him."

"Have you been to Austria?" Alrick asked, pulling out a cigarette case.

"Yes, but it was quite a few years ago and I was very young." Evelyn smiled and declined the proffered cigarette.

"I'm afraid you'd find it very much changed," Hans said, glancing at her. "When does your story take place?"

"In the present day."

"How romantic," Anna breathed, accepting the cigarette. "I've always wanted to visit Vienna. To see the opera there and walk where Schubert walked. Or to go to the Philharmonic and listen to Mendelssohn. It must be lovely!"

"You'll no longer hear Mendelssohn in Austria, or anywhere," Hans advised her sadly. "His music is forbidden by the Nazis, as is the work of so many others."

"Forbidden? Why?"

"Because they were Jews, of course," Aldrick said, lighting her cigarette for her. "Anything Jewish is banned."

"How utterly ridiculous!" Anna exclaimed. "What happens if you have a record in your house?"

"You'll be arrested for anti-party behavior," Hans muttered. "They've seized all the books and records that they can get their hands on and destroyed them. I'd be very surprised if any still exist, at least in Germany."

Evelyn took a sip of her drink and glanced at Hans. Whereas Aldrick had stated very matter-factly that Jewish music had been banned, Hans sounded as if he was disgusted by it.

"Do you mean to say you can be arrested simply for owning a record?" she asked.

"Yes. The Nazis are very adamant about only pure German art being celebrated. It is the same with the science. Many brilliant theories and discoveries have been discarded and ignored because the Nazis call it Jewry."

"How terrible," Anna said, gazing from one man to the other. "I'm not Jewish, but I don't see why their work should be destroyed."

Aldrick shrugged. "It's just the way it is." He looked at Evelyn and lowered his voice. "Hans is right. You'd find Austria very much changed. Unless your story is about a pure Aryan, I'd leave him in France with the French girl."

"Why are you whispering?" she asked, lowering her own voice.

"Because you never know who is listening," he replied seriously.

Anna laughed. "But we're in a bar in Oslo!"

"You don't think the Gestapo can travel?" he retorted. "They do, you know."

Throughout the conversation, Hans had been becoming more and more uneasy. Evelyn watched as he shifted in his seat, but with Aldrick's words, he suddenly leaned forward.

"It's not just their work," he said, his voice just as low as Aldrick's. "They are not allowed to have jobs, and most have had their homes taken from them. I know a researcher who was arrested because he allowed one to stay in his house overnight. He was accused of being a traitor because he was harboring a Jew."

"What happened to him?" Evelyn whispered, remembering vividly the man in Strasbourg who had given her the first hint of Nazi cruelty.

"No one knows," Hans said after a moment. "He just disappeared into a camp."

"Well, this is all very lowering," Anna said, breaking the sudden silence that had fallen over the table. "Let's talk about something fun. Or better yet, let's dance!"

Aldrick grinned and got up promptly, holding his hand out to her.

"Your wish is my command," he said with a flourish.

The Oslo Affair

Anna laughed and got up, glancing at Evelyn. "You don't mind, do you?"

"Not in the least!" she replied, waving her hand with a smile.

Anna and Aldrick went off happily, leaving Evelyn alone with Hans.

"I'm sorry for your friend," she said after a moment. "I had no idea it was like that for the Jews."

"Many don't, or don't think anything of it if they do know," he replied with a shrug. "They're inferior, you see."

Catching the sharp note of censure in his tone, Evelyn shot him a look under her lashes. However, his face was void of any emotion and when he spoke again, his tone was even.

"You said you write for a newspaper?" he asked, reaching for his drink. "Are you here on business?"

"Yes." Evelyn nodded and sipped her cocktail. "I'm covering the symposium."

Hans brightened. "Are you?"

"Yes. I'm not much of a scientist myself, but my editor wanted a piece on the people rather than the science, so here I am. Oh! I've just thought! You're a scientist, aren't you? Would you mind if I interviewed you?"

Hans looked startled. "Me? Why?"

Evelyn laughed and tossed her head. "Silly boy! Because you're here and you seem very nice and why not?"

He laughed a little uneasily. "I suppose so. What kind of questions will you ask?"

"Well, I'll start with the basics, and then see where it goes from there. As I said, my editor is more interested in the people angle than the science. He says the science will be covered well enough by other papers. When are you free tomorrow?"

Hans blinked. "Well, I'm not sure. I'm in two panels, and then there's a workshop in the afternoon."

She tilted her head and smiled at him. "You'll have to eat, won't you? Why don't we meet for dinner? Where are you staying?"

"Right here, actually. In this hotel."

"Perfect! I'll meet you in the restaurant! What time shall we say?"

"What time for what? What are you two cooking up?" Anna demanded playfully, returning to the table with Aldrick close behind.

"Herr Mayer has agreed to allow me to interview him," Evelyn said. "We're just arranging when to meet."

"That's a stroke of luck, isn't it?" Anna dropped into her seat and reached for her drink. "You have an interview for your article and you weren't even trying!"

"Article?" Aldrick looked interested. "For your newspaper?"

"Yes."

"Look at that, Hans. You'll be famous in London!" he said with a laugh, slapping him on the shoulder.

Hans looked decidedly uncomfortable, but he managed a weak smile.

"Seven o'clock?" he asked Evelyn.

She nodded. "Perfect!"

Hans nodded and stood up. "Until then," he said, bowing slightly. "I'm sorry to excuse myself, but it's getting late and I have a long day tomorrow."

Aldrick looked at his watch in surprise. "God, is that the time?" he exclaimed. "I must be off as well. I'm on the first panel tomorrow."

The two men made their farewells and went off towards the lounge doors, leaving Evelyn and Anna at the table. As soon as they were out of sight, Anna held up her cocktail.

"Well done, dear," she toasted. "Don't be late tomorrow night. I'm not sure I trust him not to scamper away if you're a minute late."

Evelyn nodded and lifted her glass. "He seemed very unsettled, didn't he?"

"I think he prefers his work to socializing," Anna said, finishing her drink. "I'm rather surprised you got him to agree to meet with you."

"So was I, actually," Evelyn admitted. "Now I just have to come up with a list of questions to ask him."

"Check with Carew in the morning," Anna advised, standing. "He'll know just what he wants to know."

Evelyn nodded and stood, turning towards the door with her new friend.

"I think I'll do that."

Chapter Ten

Evelyn waved goodbye to Anna and turned to walk down the street, turning the collar on her coat up against the bitter wind. She had waved goodbye to Anna three blocks from the boarding house after assuring her that it was an easy walk back. Used to walking for miles across English countryside, it wasn't the distance that had Evelyn gritting her teeth, but the cold. She couldn't feel her toes, and her face had gone numb a few minutes after stepping outside. Bending her head against the wind, she lowered her eyes and forged into the night. She would be very grateful to get into her nice, warm room with a roaring fire.

She turned the corner and the wind shifted to her back. Lifting her head, Evelyn cast a quick look around the dark street. The street lights were widely spaced apart and there were few cars on the road at this time of night. Aside from a couple walking hand in hand ahead on the other side of the road, she appeared to be the only person hurrying along the sidewalk. *The only person foolish enough to come out in this cold*, she thought to herself as a shiver racked her body.

Her shoes echoed on the pavement as she walked quickly along the walkway. Out of nowhere, Miles popped into her head and Evelyn wondered what he was doing. Had he gone to the pub with Robbie? Or was he in bed asleep? Her lips curved despite the cold. Somehow, she couldn't imagine Miles going to bed early unless he was ill. He seemed much more likely to be getting into trouble somehow. Then again, so did all the pilots she'd met. Strange breed, pilots. They all seemed to be a bit crazy.

Evelyn smiled faintly, recognizing the irony of that thought as she made her way through a foreign city in the dark. At least Rob and Miles were on English soil doing what was expected of them. She, on the other hand, was skulking around Oslo trying to pump information out of German scientists while waiting for a Soviet agent to make contact with her. Without a doubt, she took the prize for being the most insane out of all them.

CW Browning

A sudden gust of wind howled down the street, smacking her in the face and pushing against her with gale-like force. Gasping, Evelyn caught her breath as the collar on her coat blew back and a streak of icy air went down her back. With a violent shiver, she yanked the collar back up and turned so the gust was hitting her back and not her exposed face.

That's when she saw him, a tall shadow was just ducking into an alcove about half a block behind her. If she hadn't turned right when she did, she would have missed him completely.

The chill that streaked down her spine had nothing to do with the cold now, and Evelyn turned back into the wind, picking up her pace.

It could be anyone. It could be someone who lived in that building she'd passed and they were just going home. That gust of wind was enough to make even someone used to it duck out of its path. It was probably nothing.

Except that every hair on the back of her neck and arms told her otherwise. No one was out tonight, and the figure had moved as soon as she turned around. Resisting the urge to turn her head and look, Evelyn paused at the cross street, looking both ways. The boarding house was on the next block. She was almost there.

Stepping into the road and out from under the light of a street lamp, she glanced behind her and her heart thumped. He was still there. She could barely make him out. He was walking close to the buildings, partially concealed by their dark shadow, but he was definitely still there. And he was gaining ground.

Turning her head, she increased her pace even more and jogged across the side street, gaining the other side in seconds. Her fingers closed around the key in her pocket and she gripped it firmly, ready to pull it out and open the door of the boarding house as soon as she reached it. Only a few more feet.

A loud bang shattered the stillness of the night and Evelyn jumped, her heart surging into her throat. The sound was almost deafening, like a gun shot, and she whirled around, her eyes wide and her chest pounding. An older model car had rattled up the side street she'd just crossed and, as she watched, a lesser bang exploded from its tail pipe.

Gasping, she turned and threw caution to the wind, running the last few steps to the door of the boarding house. Pulling the key from her pocket, her hand trembled as she tried to get it into the latch. On the second try, it slid in and she turned to look over her shoulder. The man was at the corner, staring directly at her.

The Oslo Affair

Evelyn pushed the door open and slipped inside, closing it and throwing the bolt with shaking fingers. She moved away from the door and was halfway up the dark stairs before her knees began to shake uncontrollably. Sinking to sit on a step in the shadows, she leaned against the wall and stared at the front door below. There was no sound from the street beyond and no banging on the door to demand entrance. She was in, and she was safe.

For now.

Who was he? And why was he following her? Was it Vladimir? But if so, why not simply approach her? Was it someone from the hotel? Her head snapped up and she stared at the door again, her breath shallow and fast. Was it the Gestapo again? Just because Daniel Carew didn't think they were in Oslo didn't mean that they weren't. She knew first-hand just how freely they moved around outside of their Fatherland.

God, please don't let it be them again, she thought with a near groan.

After sitting for another moment, Evelyn forced her shaking legs to push her up and she gripped the railing as she made her way up the rest of the stairs. It had been so close! When she looked back at the door, he was only a few feet away. If she had fumbled any longer with the key, he would have been beside her. And if that car hadn't backfired, she wouldn't have run the last few feet.

Fear streaked down her spine again as she moved quietly down the hallway towards her room. In Scotland, they had tried to train them on how to react if they were in danger, but there was no way to prepare anyone for the sudden onslaught of adrenaline and pure fear that had crashed over her in the street. She was being followed in a strange city, with a foreign language that she didn't speak, on unfamiliar streets at night. Of course she was terrified! She'd be a fool not to be.

She unlocked her door and went in, relocking it quickly behind her. A cheerful fire burned low in the hearth, casting a welcoming glow over the room, and Evelyn went over to stand before it, holding her hands out to its warmth. She didn't remove her coat, but stood and let the warmth of the flames comfort her. Staring down into the fire, Evelyn took a deep breath and tried to think clearly.

Who was he? And what did he want with her? She hadn't done anything yet that would arouse suspicion in anyone, even a nefarious Gestapo agent. All she did was go to dinner and then have drinks with two men who were sitting at the table next to her. Hardly the stuff of spies.

After a long moment, she turned away and removed her coat, carrying it over to the wardrobe. Now that she was warm and safe, she had to take the time to think, to evaluate the situation. She had panicked in the street. That couldn't happen again. If she didn't find a way to keep her wits about her when things went wrong, she wasn't going to make it very far at all in this war.

Evelyn pressed her lips together and went over to sink into the chair near the fire. Raising shaking hands to her face, she massaged her temples and forced herself to relax. What could she have done differently? Her hands fell away from her head and she sat back tiredly.

I could have noticed him sooner, for starters, she thought disgustedly. Instead of daydreaming about a pair of green eyes back in England, she should have been paying attention to her surroundings. That was lesson number one. When she was in enemy territory, and they had been very clear that she *would* go across enemy lines, a mistake like tonight would get her killed. She had to be aware of her surroundings and who was in them at all times, even when thoughts of Miles Lacey intruded as they had tonight.

Evelyn stretched her feet towards the fire and leaned her head back. She would have to be more careful going forward. Just because this was a friendly city didn't mean that it was safe. Daniel had made it seem as if it was just like London, but it wasn't. Tonight had illustrated that very clearly. There were obviously people moving in the shadows just like her, and they wanted information as well. How someone had discovered her already she had no idea, but obviously someone had. Clearly she had to be much more alert, and much more careful.

Or she wouldn't last the week.

London, England

Jasper looked up as a shadow fell across his table. He was seated at his usual table in the Grill at the Savoy at the height of the lunch rush. Everyone knew not to intrude upon his hour of solitude, and his eyebrows crooked in surprise at the sight of William Buckley standing next to his table.

"Bill!" he exclaimed, setting down his knife and fork. "What are you doing here? I thought you had gone back to Paris with Marguerite."

"She left this morning and I'll follow tomorrow," Bill replied,

The Oslo Affair

motioning to a chair at the table questioningly.

"Please do." Jasper waved to the seat and picked up his knife and fork. "Have you eaten?"

"Actually, no. I just came from Waterloo Station." Bill seated himself with a sigh. "I was called into the War Cabinet to give a report, for all the good it will do."

He couldn't disguise the bitterness in his tone and Jasper shot him a sharp look.

"France?"

"Among other things." An attentive waiter came to the table and Bill nodded to him in greeting, taking the proffered menu. "Are you sure you don't mind my joining you? I know you're protective of your lunch break."

"That doesn't extend to you," Jasper assured him, guiding a forkful of potatoes to his mouth. "You don't inundate me with meaningless drivel. When is your meeting?"

"In an hour. I came for a quick bite before going in." Bill set the menu aside after a cursory glance. "I'm not sure why I was called, to be honest. They never listen to a word I say."

"I know why." Jasper looked at him. "Chamberlain is under tremendous pressure over how he's responding to this war. The Commons are demanding action at the same time that the Lords are demanding caution. He's caught in rather uncomfortable situation."

"Of his own making," Bill pointed out, then sighed and ran a hand through his hair. "I understand the difficulty, but I can't help but think that what we need now is to take a strong and decisive stand against Hitler."

Jasper made a sound close to a snort. "You've been listening to Churchill."

"The man makes a point." The waiter returned and Bill ordered his lunch of poached fish and potatoes. Once the man had retreated, he looked at Jasper. "I know you're close with Winston. Don't try to tell me that he's not one of the few who are taking this war seriously."

Jasper shook his head. "On the contrary," he said. "I think he speaks a lot of wisdom. I also think he speaks with a lot of heart, and that is something we can do without. However, regardless of my own thoughts on the subject, this country needs a leader. And we don't have one."

"On that, at least, we can agree." Bill nodded in thanks as a pint of ale was set beside him. He waiting until the waiter had disappeared again, then looked at Jasper. "Can we speak frankly,

Jasper?"

"You know I'll always speak frankly, Bill, even to the detriment of my political well-being. What's on your mind?"

"I've received a message from the embassy in Oslo," he said, lowering his voice. "There seems to be a slight issue."

Jasper looked up from his meal sharply, his eyes narrowing.

"What kind of issue?" he demanded.

"The kind that exposes agents," Bill said grimly. "I think Jian may have been compromised."

"In what way?"

"She was followed last night. Now, it could be nothing. Daniel Carew seems to think she's overreacting and that it *is* nothing. Simply another pedestrian out on the streets late at night."

"And you? What do you think?"

"I've known her for most of her life, and have worked with her for well over a year now. I'd be very surprised if she's overreacting. I've never known her to do so before. In fact, quite the opposite."

Jasper considered him for a long moment, then carefully set down his utensils.

"Go on."

"There's no way she could have compromised herself already. She arrived late in the afternoon and didn't leave the boarding house. The next morning, she went to the embassy and met with Carew before going straight back to the house. She stayed there until evening, when she went to the Hotel Bristol with one of our interpreters where she engaged in making contact with a German scientist who was also dining there. She was followed leaving the hotel."

"That's it?"

"That's it. As you can see, she could hardly have been more careful."

Jasper studied him for a long, silent moment.

"You have a lot more to say, Buckley. Just spit it out, will you?"

Bill sipped his ale and raised somber eyes to the man across the table.

"If I didn't know the agent as well as I do, I'd probably agree with Carew and say it was nerves on her first assignment and there was nothing there. But I do know her, and I know that unsteady nerves have never been one of her faults. She faced down two Security Service agents in Strasbourg without blinking. She does not overreact."

Jasper sat back in his chair slowly, his eyes never leaving Bill's face.

The Oslo Affair

"You think someone leaked her location overseas," he stated rather than asked.

"It's the only thing that makes sense."

Jasper exhaled, shaking his head.

"You realize what you're saying?" he demanded, his voice low. "The number of people who know our agents' identities is so limited that what you're suggesting is—"

"Someone in London is passing information on," Bill finished calmly, reaching for his pint again. "Yes. That's precisely what I'm suggesting."

Jasper was silent for a long time before he reached for the whiskey and soda near his plate.

"You realize that's damn near impossible?" he finally asked.

"Unlikely, but far from impossible," Bill corrected him.

"Impossible," Jasper repeated with more force. "Damn it, man, we've rounded up all the German agents in London. You know this! They were all interned within a month of war being declared, with the exception of one, who is working with us."

"I realize that."

Jasper stared at him, his face grim. "You'd better think very carefully about what you say next," he warned softly.

Bill made a face and opened his mouth, then closed it abruptly as the waiter came into view carrying a tray with his lunch. An uneasy silence fell over the table as the two men waited for the food to be placed before Bill.

"Put your hackles down, Jasper," Bill said as soon as the waiter had gone. "There are other possibilities besides a mole in Whitehall, although I think it would be a gross misjudgment on our part to dismiss that out of hand."

"What other possibilities?" he asked, ignoring the latter part of the statement.

Bill picked up his knife and fork and began to cut into his fish.

"Have you forgotten why Jian was sent to Oslo in the first place?" he asked, glancing up. "It wasn't to meet with German scientists."

Jasper's lips tightened.

"You think there are Soviet agents in London?"

"It's not beyond the realm of possibility. MI6 went after known German sympathizers and uncovered cells of German agents throughout London. What about the Soviets?"

"We haven't found any indication that—"

"Yes, yes, I know," Bill cut him off hastily. "I know the facts.

All I'm saying is that someone knows we have an agent in Oslo, and they know exactly who it is. That information came from somewhere, and I'm willing to stake my career that it wasn't from something Jian did herself."

"And if it wasn't, then we have a bigger problem on our hands," Jasper finished for him.

Bill was silent and Jasper exhaled again, pushing his half-eaten lunch away.

"You have one hell of a way of disrupting a perfect good afternoon, Bill." He rubbed his forehead and reached for his drink again. "What do you suggest? Pull her back?"

"Absolutely not. Shustov won't meet with anyone else. Besides, she wouldn't come."

"What makes you say that? If she's ordered back…"

"She made it clear in the message Carew forwarded this morning." Bill looked up from his lunch and something close to a grin was on his lips. "She says she has the situation under control."

"It means she has a plan. And I can say with some confidence that that plan does not include coming back just yet."

Oslo, Norway

The bell above the door jingled as the man went into the tobacconist's shop and the owner looked up from where he was helping another gentleman, nodding with a smile.

"I'll be right with you, sir."

The man nodded back and went over to stand near the counter, picking up a newspaper. He flipped through it while he waited, looking up occasionally to glance out the store front window. It was early, and he was wasting some time before going to the embassy. The English agent hadn't left the boarding house this morning and, after waiting for over an hour, he determined that she wasn't going to. At least, not before he had to go in and give his report. He had left his post across the street from the house, confident in the knowledge that he would catch up with her later in the day.

The shop owner finished up with his customer and turned to the man. "And what can I get for you today?" he asked cheerfully.

"I'd like a can of the original blend," the man said, moving over to the counter and setting the paper down. "And the newspaper,

The Oslo Affair

please."

"Of course." The shop owner turned to pull down a can of tobacco from a shelf behind the counter. "It's a lovely day outside, isn't it?"

"Yes, it is. Very nice."

The owner rang up the tobacco and reached under the counter to pull something out.

"I think you'll enjoy this," he said, putting the can into a bag and taking the money the man held out. "It's a particularly smooth blend."

"Yes. I've had it before."

The shop owner made change, passing it back along with an additional slip of paper.

"Enjoy your day."

The man palmed the paper and change and turned away from the counter with a nod. A moment later, the bell jingled again and he stepped out into the sunshine. After glancing to his left, he turned and walked to his right along the street until he reached the top where it intersected with Drammensveien. Turning left, he started down the road, reaching into his coat pocket to pull out the slip of paper. He unfolded it and scanned the message inside, pausing next to a trashcan on the pavement. After reading the message, he crumpled it in his hand and tossed it into the can before continuing down the street.

He never once looked back. A moment later, a few yards behind him, a woman reached into the trashcan as she passed, plucking the crumpled paper out and shoving it into her coat pocket without breaking stride.

The man continued down the long road, oblivious to what had happened behind him, his stride steady. The sun shone brightly over the city and the temperature was surprisingly mild for November in Norway. He took a deep breath and felt his spirits lift somewhat. The message had been a welcome one. It looked as if his time here may be coming to an end, provided the Englishwoman was indeed who they believed. Soon, he would have all the proof he needed and could return home. And that lifted his spirits considerably.

His step slowed as he approached a large building set back from the road and surrounded by a black, wrought-iron fence. He reached into the inside pocket of his coat and pulled out a leather billfold. Approaching the gate, he opened the billfold, holding his identification up for inspection. The soldier snapped to attention as soon as he saw the name and raised his hand in a salute as the man passed through the gate and went up the walkway to the building.

Behind him, the soldier closed the gate and returned to his post just inside the perimeter of the property, glancing after him with a look of fear mixed with awe.

Neither of them noticed the woman who walked past the fence, her stride long and steady. She glanced at the plaque fixed onto the gate as she passed, her lips tightening slightly. Turning her gaze forward again, she continued on her way, leaving the Russian Embassy behind her.

The Oslo Affair

Chapter Eleven

Evelyn stood up as the bus swayed to a stop at the side of the busy road. It was almost lunch time and, as she made her way down the aisle to the front of the bus, several people were getting on. She reached the front and pressed herself against the side of a seat as a woman carrying several packages tried to squeeze by her. Behind her, an older gentleman fumbled with a walking stick as he also navigated past Evelyn.

She waited until all the boarding passengers had passed her, then nodded cheerfully to the driver before disembarking quickly. Stepping onto the sidewalk, she turned and began to walk up the street, her heels clicking on the paving stones. All in all, it had been an extremely productive morning, and now she was decidedly hungry. Deciding to stop in a cafe for something, she turned down a side street and headed towards the only eatery that she knew of close by.

Ten minutes later, she was removing her coat and preparing to sit at a small table in the back of the restaurant. As she laid the coat over the back of one of the chairs, something crinkled in the pocket and a frown crossed her face. Reaching into the left pocket, her fingers touched something that hadn't been there earlier. The frown intensified and she pulled out a folded piece of crumpled paper.

Before she could look at it, a waitress came over to greet her. Seating herself at the table, Evelyn attempted to make herself understood. After a few minutes of gesticulating with their hands, she successfully managed to order a cup of coffee and a sandwich.

As soon as she was alone again, she looked down at the paper in her hand and opened it. Her eyebrows snapped together at the sight of Russian script scrawled across the paper.

Market on Frognerveien. Three-thirty. Look for a blue scarf with white trim. If all is well, carry handbag on right arm. If followed, carry handbag on left.

Evelyn's heart thumped and she caught her breath, staring at the words. It had to be Shustov. But when did he slip the note into her pocket? She must have passed him, but when? And how did he know where she would be?

She folded the note with shaking fingers and slid it into her purse. Somehow she hadn't thought that he would actually make contact with her. It had all seemed so far-fetched when she came on this trip, but now she could see that it wasn't at all. A Russian agent had slipped her a note without her knowledge and now it was up to her to meet with him. She was going to meet with Vladimir Lyakhov, the Soviet spy who had known her father so well.

Lifting her hands, she rubbed her temples for a moment. This was it. This was why she was here. This was what she had been training for in Scotland for months. But now that she was here and it was happening, Evelyn had the strangest feeling that she was living in some kind of dream.

"Hello!" A voice interrupted her thoughts cheerfully and she looked up with a start.

Anna stood before her, a wide grin on her face.

"Anna!" Evelyn exclaimed in surprise. "What are you doing here?"

"I came for lunch!" The other woman dropped into a chair across from her with a laugh. "I didn't expect to meet anyone. I always eat alone. Do you mind if I join you?"

"Please do!" Evelyn moved her purse off the table and set it on the chair with her coat. "I welcome the company."

"Wonderful!" Anna shrugged out of her coat and motioned to the waitress. "I'm glad to see you, actually. I was a little worried when I left you last night."

Evelyn felt her spine stiffen and she shot a look at the other woman under her eyelashes.

"Worried? What on earth for?"

"I didn't think of it at the time, of course, but on my way home I realized that you're not familiar with the city and it was late. By the time I reached home, I'd convinced myself that you had got hopelessly lost and were being accosted by strange men."

Anna smiled at the waitress and ordered something quickly. Once the waitress had gone, she looked at Evelyn.

"You didn't, did you?"

"Get lost? No. I made it home quite without incident," Evelyn lied.

"That's good to hear." Anna tilted her head and studied her for a moment. "You don't look like you slept well."

"Well thank you very much!" she exclaimed and Anna laughed.

"That didn't come out very well, did it?" she asked sheepishly. "I hope you're not offended."

The Oslo Affair

"It takes more than that to offend me, I assure you. You're right. I didn't sleep very well. It's the new surroundings, I expect."

"Understandable."

The waitress returned with both their lunches, and they fell silent as she laid the dishes on the table before them. She said something in Norwegian and Anna answered automatically. With a smile, the waitress left them again.

"What do you do at the law firm?" Evelyn asked, reaching for her sandwich.

"Take dictation and translate incoming mail and messages from the German and English clients," came the ready answer. "Occasionally I accompany one of the solicitors when they need a translator, but I stay mostly in the office."

"Do you enjoy the work?"

Anna shrugged. "It's a job," she said, uncommitted. "Nothing more."

Evelyn's gaze was sharp and swift across the table. The tone in the other woman's voice held an edge that she herself knew well. It was the sound of someone who wanted to do more in life than what they were currently doing. It was the same tone she'd had last year, before her father asked a favor and Bill recruited her to pick up a package in Strasbourg.

"Perhaps one day it will be more," she said.

Anna shot her a guarded look and a small smile curved her lips. "Perhaps."

"Do you come here for lunch every day?" Evelyn asked.

"Most days. My office is on the next block. I like the soup here, and it is inexpensive compared to other cafes." Anna glanced up from the soup in question. "Are you going to meet with that scientist for dinner? What was his name again?"

"Herr Mayer. I plan to. Daniel gave me some ideas of where to start with him."

"I told you he would. I hope you get somewhere with Mayer. He seemed very skittish to me last night."

Evelyn thought of the nervous man and nodded in agreement. He had seemed very uncomfortable. Yet he had agreed to meet with her, so that was a huge step in the right direction. With any luck, she'd learn something about what the Germans were focusing their scientific energies on.

And then she could focus on Vladimir Lysokov.

CW Browning

6th November, 1939

Dear Evelyn,
    I received your letter last week. It gave me a good laugh, but I haven't had another from you, despite sending you a response promptly. Have you changed your mind and decided not to write after all? As you see, I'm holding up my end of our bargain. I'll give you one more chance. Consider yourself issued fair warning.
    How's the training coming on your end? We're training day and night. I rarely get more than four hours of sleep. The RAF seems to think that we'll be having a horrific air battle soon. We did have some excitement the other day. Unfortunately, it wasn't with the Germans. C flight was called up to intercept a squadron of German planes coming in over the Thames Estuary area. Three squadrons from other bases joined them. They sighted the enemy and dove at him, guns blazing. Had a few terrific hits and one of the enemy was shot down. They came back, triumphant and flushed with success. Then our Intel Officer Bertie got a hold of them. It was one of our planes the sods shot down. Jerry wasn't even there! HQ had seen what looked like an enemy formation coming in, but it was really a formation of British bombers on exercise. Talk about one incredible cock-up. We'd better do better than that if Jerry really does come calling. It's an embarrassment!
    In between flights, they're keeping us busy with foreign language lessons. They handed out some Polish papers and tests the other day. Seem to think we need to know Polish in order to fly Spitfires. So we were told to memorize these Polish phrases and be prepared to test on them the following day. All right and above board, except that it wasn't Polish. The papers they gave us were Swedish phrases! The Intel Officer and I are one in agreeing that this, too, is a cock-up.
    I may be receiving a few days leave for Christmas. Have you heard if you will? If so, perhaps we could meet? I haven't forgotten the invitation to hunt on Boxing Day if we all manage to get some time off.
    I'm sending you a little something through one of my flight mechanics in a few days. He has to go up to Scotland to

The Oslo Affair

pick up some parts. I hope you don't mind. I saw it and thought you'd like it.

By the way, what I wrote about the Polish papers is highly confidential. Top Secret. I'm trusting you not to blab to the Germans that they're teaching us Swedish here.

Yours,

FO Miles Lacey

◉

Evelyn entered the open-air market on Frognerveien and looked around. The market was fairly busy for late afternoon and she took a deep breath, moving past the bustling stalls of produce, meat, cheese, and baked goods. As she made her way through the maze of vendors, her eyes scanned the crowds, searching for a man wearing a blue scarf with white trim.

Her purse was hooked on her right arm confidently. When she left the cafe after lunch, she had circled the block where her temporary housing was located, looking for her tail. Sure enough, he had returned and was settled across the street, waiting for her to make an appearance. After watching him watching the house for a moment, she went back around the block and climbed through an opening in the fence at the back of the small garden outside the kitchen. Josef had nodded to her as she passed him before returning to his task of chopping wood. Not by the flicker of an eyelid or twitch of his lips did he show any surprise at her climbing through the fence instead of entering through the front door. Perhaps he had already spotted the man loitering across the street.

When she had followed her tail to the Russian Embassy this morning, she had thought perhaps it was Vladimir himself that was watching her every move. But when the man held his identification out and the guard snapped to instant attention, she discarded the idea. While Shustov was, by all accounts, an NKVD agent, he didn't hold a rank worthy of that instant fear and respect. No. Lyakhov would warrant a respectful salute, perhaps, but that was it. The stranger following her had to be a member of the senior commanding staff at the very least, perhaps a Captain or a Major. She didn't think he was a Commissioner. She couldn't imagine one reason why a Commissioner would be interested in her. They were at the very top of the NKVD, one of the top commanding staff. She bit her lip now and frowned.

Whoever he was, he was still very high up in the food chain, which begged the question: why was he stalking her himself?

Admittedly, she didn't know very much about the inner workings of the Soviet agency, but it seemed to her that the higher they climbed up the military ladder, the less footwork they did themselves. So why was someone of obvious rank wasting his time observing *her*? And how on earth was she going to avoid him tonight when she went to meet Hans?

Evelyn had Bill to thank for her newfound expertise on Soviet rankings. He had been insistent that she study them thoroughly on the crossing over from England. If she didn't know better, she would have suspected that he was worried about her meeting with a Soviet agent. Instead, she decided that he was just being overly cautious. Whatever the reason, Evelyn had become an expert on Soviet rankings, insignias, and military dress on the rough North Sea crossing. But she never once thought it would come into play so quickly.

She stopped at a stall selling fruit and selected a couple of apples. After a few moments of trying to make herself understood, she finally came to an understanding with the vendor and passed over some coins. With a smile and nod of thanks, she slid the apples into an empty cloth shopping bag she had brought along and turned away from the booth. As she did so, someone bumped into her from behind and she gasped, stumbling forward and colliding with a solid body.

Strong hands steadied her and Evelyn lifted her face to stare into a pair of dark gray eyes set deeply into a square face with harsh cheekbones. Dark hair was cropped neatly and precisely and a dark mustache perched above thin lips, almost unreal in its perfection. Not a hair was out of place and the hard, unemotional face staring back at her seemed completely undisturbed by her plowing into him.

In that instant, Evelyn knew she was staring at Vladimir Lyakhov.

Dropping her eyes from his face, the navy blue scarf with white piping tied around his neck confirmed her suspicion.

Before she could speak, the hands dropped away from her arms and he nodded politely.

"My apologies. I wasn't looking where I was going," he said in heavily accented English.

"It's my fault. I lost my balance," she replied. "I'm very sorry."

"You are English?"

"Yes."

"How was the weather in London when you were there?"

The Oslo Affair

Evelyn swallowed, trying to ignore her pounding heart.

"I carried an umbrella because it looked like rain, but left it on the train."

He bowed his head in acknowledgment and turned to continue past her. As he did so, she felt something slide into her coat pocket. Resisting the urge to turn and watch him, she forced her legs to move her forward, in the opposite direction. Gripping the bag with her apples in one hand, she moved through the market, not looking back.

Her heart was pounding and her palms were damp, she realized with a start a moment later. It was really happening. A Soviet agent had really just slipped something into her pocket, and there was no turning back now.

She waited until she was on the other side of the market to reach her hand into her pocket and extract the paper. Opening it, she read the message quickly. It was a single line, an address. There were no other instructions or times. Just the address.

Evelyn pressed her lips together and crumpled the note in her hand, shoving it back into her pocket. Passing a trash receptacle, she thought of the man this morning and the message she had pulled out of the trash can. Her lips twitched. Certainly she wasn't about to make the same mistake. She'd wait until she was back in her room and then she would dispose of the messages from Shustov properly. There would be no trace by the time she was finished.

Turning out of the opposite end of the market, Evelyn glanced at her watch and started down the street. She'd find a shop where she could ask for directions to the address on the paper.

And then she'd continue this strange and unnerving scavenger hunt. She tried not to consider that it was a Soviet agent waiting at the end of it, and instead focused on the fact that her father had trusted Lyakhov enough to meet him in Warsaw as the German Army advanced into Poland. If Vladimir had gained her father's trust, the least she could do was meet with him and collect what it was that he was trying so desperately to get to London.

And in that, at least, she could finish the last task her father had been unable to complete.

Chapter Twelve

Evelyn stared up at the imposing facade of the public library and shook her head. Another library. She started up the steps, glancing behind her and scanning the street. There was no sign either of Vladimir or of her mysterious stalker. However, she knew from experience that that didn't mean anything.

Entering the library, she crossed the tiled floor to pass the circulation desk, nodding with a smile to the librarian seated behind the counter. The woman nodded back and Evelyn continued past the desk, looking around the first floor. There were a few patrons, but none of them were Vladimir.

She pursed her lips and hesitated before glancing over her shoulder again. Her eyes fell on the card catalog and she turned suddenly to go towards it. On a hunch, she moved along the neatly labeled drawers until she came to one that was only partially closed. Something like a surge of excitement went through her and she opened it to find a card sticking up, preventing it from closing all the way. She pulled out the card and scanned the title and call number on it, committing it to memory before inserting the card back into place correctly and pushing the drawer closed.

Then, after a swift look around, she turned and strode across the floor to a wide staircase leading to the upper levels. This library was larger than the one in Strasbourg had been, with at least four levels. At the foot of the steps, Evelyn glanced up, her hand on the railing. She was just in time to see a shadow disappear to the left at the top of the stairs.

Catching her breath, her heart thumped against her ribs and her stomach dropped. Was it Vladimir or someone else? She inhaled, forcing herself to calm down. She was simply a journalist from London, visiting the library. There was absolutely no reason for her to be afraid. She wasn't picking up a package, or dropping one off. There was nothing about her visit that could be construed as remotely suspect.

As long as you ignored who was most likely waiting to meet her.

The Oslo Affair

Evelyn reached the top of the steps and checked the sign on the nearest bookcase. She turned left, moving along the aisle, searching for the row that contained the book from the card. If Shustov was here, in the library, he had picked a perfect spot to meet her and not be seen. Every row that she passed was empty, and the hushed silence was almost deafening.

Her gaze caught the label on the next bookcase and she turned down the row, scanning the spines of books, looking for the one in question. She was halfway down the aisle when a deep voice spoke behind her, making her jump.

"You came faster than I expected," a man said in Russian.

Evelyn swung around to find Vladimir pulling a book out of the shelf a few feet away.

"I didn't see any point in wasting time," she replied.

"Your Russian is very good."

"Thank you."

"I'm not surprised. Your father said you had an ear for it." He didn't look in her direction but flipped open the book instead. "You speak Norwegian as well?"

"No."

"Ah. That explains the interpreter."

Evelyn raised her eyebrows in surprise. "How do you know about that?"

He finally turned his head towards her, his lips curving faintly.

"It's my job to know." He studied her for a long moment. "You look different from your photograph. Older."

"Losing your father suddenly does that sometimes," she retorted, unable to keep the sharpness out of her voice. To her surprise, a laugh leapt into his eyes and he flashed a grin.

"Of course. That was rude of me. I apologize."

Evelyn exhaled and inclined her head in acknowledgment.

"Do you know why you are here?" he asked after a moment, turning his attention back to the book in his hands.

Feeling as if she should appear to be busy as well, Evelyn pulled a random book from the shelf closest to her and opened it.

"I was told that you would meet with no one else," she said in a low voice.

"Your father and I used to have wonderful conversations over whiskey," he said, turning the page in his book. "He told me about your stay in Hong Kong. Did you like it there?"

"It was exciting for a child," she said carefully, her eyebrows draw together. What was he driving at? "I had no complaints."

"He told me an amusing story about a childhood friend of yours. He said the two of you were often inseparable and, one day, you ran away from your governess and went to the other side of the town to watch a play. Your friend carried the tale to your father, but instead of punishing you, he bought you ice cream."

Evelyn's brows smoothed. He was testing her.

"It wasn't a play," she said calmly. "And the ice cream was because I had given my friend a black eye when he tried to stop me from going again the next day." Her face softened as a smile crossed her lips. "My father said I should never let another person intimidate me. I got ice cream for standing up for myself, then was grounded for three days for disobeying him and leaving the property."

Vladimir closed the book and slid it back onto the shelf. He turned to look at her, his face softening slightly.

"Your father was an unusual man," he said. "With unusual ways of raising a daughter. Tell me, do you still practice Wing Chun?"

"Not as much as I would like, but yes."

"It's a formidable skill. I fear you will need it more than you think for the times ahead."

He held out his arm, motioning for her to walk with him. After a moment's hesitation, Evelyn slid the book onto the shelf and turned to walk with him to the opposite end of the aisle.

"This war is not something that either me or your father wanted to happen," he said slowly. "Our countries are now enemies. I will be killed if my government discovers that I am talking to you."

"Wasn't that the same with my father?"

He shot her a look. "Ah. So you know. Good. That makes things easier."

"How did you and my father meet?" she asked, glancing at him.

"We met in Zürich three years ago. I was there, well, on business for my government and he was doing the same. As fate would have it, we were both after the same thing: information about the new Führer and his National Socialist Germany. Our paths crossed. I made sure they crossed again a few months later."

"Why?"

He paused at the end of the aisle and was silent for a long moment.

"That is a much more complicated answer and one that we don't have time for today." He looked at her, his gray eyes considering. "Perhaps we save that for another time, yes? For now, just know that I respected your father and, I hope, one day you will learn to trust me."

The Oslo Affair

"I don't know if that's possible," Evelyn said softly, shaking her head. "Especially given the current situation between our two countries."

"And that is why I say one day." Vladimir turned the corner and she followed him to the next aisle. "I have something for you. Consider it a gesture of good faith."

She raised an eyebrow and shot him a look from under her lashes. "Oh?"

"What do you know of Finland?" he asked, pausing next to the shelves and reaching out to pull another book out.

"I know that Stalin has been trying to get them to cede a large portion of their border land over to him so that he can set up military protection there for Leningrad, and that Finland has refused."

"Yes. Moscow has grown tired of their refusal to allow us to protect our cities."

Evelyn looked at him sharply. "How tired?"

Gray eyes met hers. "Very tired."

She was silent, her lips tightening. If the Soviet Union invaded Finland, that could potentially spell disaster for both Norway and Sweden, both of whose neutrality was firmly established.

"Why tell me this?"

"As I said, consider it a gesture of good faith. I'm sure you're aware of the precarious situation in Finland. Should my country gain what they are seeking, then Finland will need military support. Whichever country gives it to them will have a side door into the Soviet Union."

"Why would you support that?" Evelyn asked, her brows coming together in a frown. "That can only mean war for your country."

"My country is already at war. It has been for ten years." He shrugged and closed the book, sliding it back onto the shelf. "Not everyone shares in the belief that we are better off now than we have been in the past."

Evelyn was silent. She supposed her father would have known and understood all the political nuances of the situation, and would have known what to say to that. She was not her father, however, and she had no idea what response was expected of her, if any. As if sensing her uncertainty, Vladimir glanced at her.

"In Turku, there is someone who knows the details and intricacies of what hangs in the balance. His name is Risto Niva. He has worked undercover in Turku for the NKVD for over five years. If anyone can help you understand, he can."

She stared at him. "I can't go to Finland!" she hissed.

"You don't have to. He is in Stockholm right now. I can arrange a meeting, but only if you go soon. He will be leaving in a few days to travel to Leningrad before returning to Finland." Vladimir turned and moved a few feet away, looking at the book spines. "He is staying at the Strand. He has only one weakness, from what I have observed."

"And what's that?"

He turned to smile at her. "Beautiful women, especially blondes."

Evelyn exhaled and gave him a look close to a glare. "You can't be serious."

"Of course I'm serious. I'm Russian. We don't joke about matters of security. We can't afford to."

"I thought I was here to pick up the same information you gave my father."

"The information your government managed to lose?" Vladimir made a disgusted sound in the back of his throat. "I must be mad for risking it again, but yes. It's here, in the book you looked at in the card catalog downstairs. Don't lose it again. I won't be trying a third time."

"I didn't lose it the first time," Evelyn muttered. "Why did you take the chance on smuggling it out again?"

"I believe it holds significant value for your government and the safety of your agents, both in Europe and abroad. Guard it well, for there are many who would kill to get their hands on it, and some who already have." He looked at his watch. "We've been together too long. I must go. If you will meet Niva, light the candle in your window at midnight tonight and I will make the necessary arrangements. If not, then I wish you a safe journey back to England."

He turned to leave and Evelyn watched him go, chewing her bottom lip. His back was straight as he strode to end of the aisle and turned the corner without once looking back.

And there goes Vladimir Lyakhov, Soviet agent, she thought.

Shaking her head, she turned to retrace their steps until she was back in front of the bookshelf housing the book from card downstairs. It was a slim volume and she plucked it from its place between two fat tomes. As she opened it, an envelope slid into her hand. After replacing the book, she opened the envelope to find several strips of microfilm. She tucked the envelope into her purse and turned to leave. At least this was something she was familiar with. She was no stranger to retrieving microfilm, or to concealing it.

The Oslo Affair

As Evelyn stepped out from between the tall bookshelves, she glanced at her watch. The meeting had taken longer than she thought and now she would have to hurry to make her appointment with Hans at the Hotel Bristol.

Her heels clicked rapidly across the tiled floor as she hurried to the stairs. There was no sign of Shustov. In fact, there was no sign of anyone. A shiver went through her and she hurried down the steps to the first floor, thankful to see several patrons moving through the lobby.

As she reached the ground floor and started towards the door, one thought popped into her mind and she pressed her lips together grimly.

Why did Vladimir *really* want her to go to Stockholm?

⊙

When Evelyn arrived at the Hotel Bristol exactly at seven, there was no sign of Herr Mayer waiting out front. She frowned and went in, looking around the crowded restaurant. As she was scanning the tables, the host approached her.

"Miss Richardson?" he asked.

She looked at him in surprise. "Yes?"

"This was left for you."

He handed her a folded note with a smile and retreated to his domain near the door. Evelyn looked down at the paper in her hand and opened it. As she had suspected, it was from Hans, written in a very precise hand.

> *Dear Miss Richardson,*
> *I apologize but I will be unable to meet you for dinner. Upon further consideration I have decided that it would be unwise for me to meet with a member of a foreign press without the prior approval of the Ministry of Propaganda. I hope you understand. I wish you the best of luck with your article.*
> *Sincerely,*
> *Hans Ferdinand Mayer*

Evelyn folded the note again. That was that, then. So much for her gently plying the physicist for information about Nazi controlled Germany. She wasn't surprised. He had seemed very uncomfortable with the idea last night when she proposed it. Now she understood why. He was afraid he would be punished for talking to a member of the press that wasn't controlled by the Goebbels ministry of propaganda. She really couldn't blame him. Not if the whispers coming out of Germany were true.

Turning to leave the restaurant, she gasped as she walked into a tall, solid figure.

"Oh!" she exclaimed, glancing up into an angular face. "I'm sorry!"

She spoke in German automatically, reverting to a language that she had learned was more easily understood in Oslo than English.

"It's quite all right, Fraulein," the man said easily, his brown eyes sweeping over her as his hands steadied her. "Are you hurt?"

"Not at all. Perhaps just my pride," Evelyn said with a laugh. "I wasn't paying attention. My apologies."

"None are needed, Fraulein...?"

"Richardson."

"I am Herr Renner," he said, dropping his hands from her arms. "How nice to meet a fellow German! Are you staying at the hotel?"

"I...no, I'm not." Evelyn glanced at her watch and smiled apologetically. "I'm sorry. I'm late for an appointment."

Herr Renner bowed his head politely.

"What a pity, but I understand. Have a nice evening, Fraulein."

Evelyn nodded and moved past him to leave the restaurant. As she went through the door, she looked back over her shoulder to find him watching her. She forced a bright smile and continued on her way, emerging onto the street a moment later.

Turning to walk away from the hotel, Evelyn exhaled. She was seeing nefarious intentions everywhere now. Herr Renner was probably simply another scientist staying at the hotel for the conference. There was no reason for her to think he had any interest in her other than that of a passing curiosity. After all, she had bumped into him, not the other way around.

Yet, something inside her was sending a warning all through her.

Shaking her head, her heels tapped quickly along the pavement as she headed back towards the boarding house. She must be imagining things, and no wonder! She was being followed by a mysterious Russian agent, and she had met with a member of the Soviet NKVD just that afternoon. It was hardly surprising that she was suspicious of a man who spoke German and wore a long black coat over a dark gray suit. She was seeing shadows everywhere.

The Oslo Affair

Even so, she was conscious of profound sense of gratitude for every step that put distance between Herr Renner and herself.

⦿

The man looked up impatiently at the knock on his door. He wasn't in a good mood. The Englishwoman hadn't appeared all day and he had no idea where she was or where she had gone. By the time he realized that she must have slipped out while he was at the embassy that morning, it was too late to hunt her down. Giving up, he returned to his room after a brief supper in the hotel dining room. Now he was pouring over what little information he had on her, which wasn't much, looking for clues as to where she might go tomorrow. He wasn't in the mood for visitors.

"Come!"

The door opened and small, slight man slid in.

"Comrade Grigori," he wheezed, closing the door silently.

The man threw down his pen and sat back in his chair, eyeing the newcomer. "Comrade Yakov."

"My apologies for disturbing you this late." Yakov moved further into the room. "You wanted to know if I observed any movement on the agent."

"I did."

"He is booked onto a train leaving Oslo at two in the morning."

"Where is he going?"

"Stockholm."

Comrade Grigori stared at the little man for a moment, then nodded once.

"Very well. Get yourself on the same train and follow him. Report back with any updates."

"Yes, comrade." Yakov nodded and turned to leave the room. At the door, he paused. "Do you still want to know if he meets with anyone?"

"Yes."

Yakov nodded once more and disappeared silently out the door. Grigori watched him go and lowered his gaze to the papers on the desk before him. He stared at them for a moment, lost in thought, then got up and went over to where his coat was draped over the back of a chair. Reaching into the pocket, he extracted a packet of cigarettes and pulled one out.

So Lyakhov was going to Sweden on an overnight train. Now why would he leave so suddenly? If his work here was done, why not catch a train that left at a more reasonable time? Why the rush to get to Stockholm?

He lit his cigarette and turned to pace across the room to the window. It was true that the easiest route to the Soviet Union was through Stockholm. The agent could simply have finished his assignment and be eager to get back to Moscow. And who would blame him? Oslo had little in the way of amusement, and Lyakhov had been here for three weeks already. It could simply be that he was tired of Norway and longing for home.

Grigori stared out the window thoughtfully, sucking on his cigarette. On the other hand, if he had met with someone secretly, he could be going to Sweden for an entirely different purpose. And if that was the case, Comrade Yakov would be absolutely useless. He was a snake, that one, and could extract the most interesting pieces of information from nothing, but as far as anything else went, he would be of no use at all.

If Lyakhov was indeed the traitor, Yakov would be no match for him.

And Moscow was convinced there was a traitor. Select pieces of classified intelligence had been steadily making their way into Europe, and into the hands of the English for a few years now. At first, they thought there were multiple traitors at work because the information was varied by so many different levels and departments. There was no way one person would have access to all of it. But, as the months went by and they began investigating each and every section, it ceased to look like the work of multiple people and began to appear to be the result of just one. How they were gaining access to the information was a mystery yet to be solved, but one thing had been exposed: their connection to the English agent who died in Bern in September.

Shaking his head, Grigori blew out a line of smoke. They had got there too late. The man was dead and there was no sign of Soviet intelligence on him, nor any hint as to the identity of the traitor. The trail had gone cold. Unwilling to give up, Beria had ordered that all intelligence agents be investigated. In addition, any and all communication with British agents, even accidental, carried with it the penalty of death.

Stubbing his cigarette out on the window sill, Grigori sighed and turned away from the window. And so here he was in Oslo, watching a known British agent while Yakov watched Lyakhov. And

The Oslo Affair

between them, they had nothing. As far as he could see, there was no connection.

But Beria would want more than his assumption. He would want evidence of innocence. And so Grigori would go back to watching the Englishwoman. When she left Norway, he would return home and make his report. As it stood right now, his report would be that there was no connection observed. Lyakhov's fate was his own from then on, provided Yakov didn't observe anything out of the ordinary in Stockholm.

But first, the Englishwoman.

Chapter Thirteen

"Stockholm!" Daniel Carew stared at Evelyn. "What on earth for?"

"I've heard the weather's lovely this time of year," she said dryly, seating herself in a chair across from his desk as she began to pull her gloves off.

Daniel let out a snort and sat down, his eyes fixed on her face. He was dressed in evening clothes, having come to the embassy directly from a dinner party after receiving her message. When he arrived, he had looked distinctly annoyed at having to come back to the office at such a late hour. Now he looked bemused.

"All right. Start from the beginning. Am I to gather that you've met with Shustov?"

"Yes. He gave me a rather interesting tip about the situation between Finland and the Soviet Union." Evelyn finished removing her gloves and folded her hands over them in her lap. "His exact words were, 'Moscow has grown tired of their refusal to allow us to protect our cities.'"

Daniel's brows snapped together. "How tired?"

"That's precisely what I said," she said with a laugh. "His response was that there was someone in Stockholm who could give me more detail. He lives in Turku, but is in Sweden for a few days. He will arrange a meeting for me, but only if I go immediately. I'm to let him know tonight. I thought I'd better check with London before I do anything."

Daniel blinked and ran a hand through his hair.

"Yes, of course." He shook his head and leaned forward to pull a pad of paper towards him. "I can send a message, but it may be some time before we receive an answer."

"Then the sooner you send it, the better," Evelyn said briskly.

"Who is this person in Stockholm?"

"I believe he's another Soviet agent."

Daniel looked up sharply. "NKVD?"

"I think so."

The Oslo Affair

"What's his name?"

"I wasn't given one," Evelyn lied smoothly.

"Then how are you to know who he is?"

Evelyn shrugged. "I've no idea. I presume Shustov will let me know somehow."

Daniel paused, tapping his chin thoughtfully with the end of the pen.

"If you make contact with a second Soviet agent and make a favorable impression, that will give us two sources of information out of Russia. Do you have any idea how difficult it is to get just one?"

"Yes, which is why I think it best that I go to Stockholm without delay." She pursed her lips thoughtfully. "I don't speak a word of Swedish. Perhaps I should take a translator. Do they speak English at all?"

"Many do, actually," he said, lowering his pen to his pad once more. "However, I think it would be advisable for you to take someone along. Not as much for the language barrier, but more to avoid undue interest. Were you thinking of Miss Salvesen?"

"I was, yes."

"I think that would be a perfect choice. She is familiar with Scandinavian customs and there would be nothing unusual about two women taking a holiday together." Daniel looked up. "Not that you draw suspicion," he added with a faint smile.

"Well, someone is following me, so I must draw some."

"And that I still don't understand," he said, tearing the paper off the pad and pushing his chair back. "No one aside from myself was even aware of your arrival here."

"Not to put too fine a point on it, but obviously someone was."

He walked around the desk and headed for the door to his office.

"I'll go send this message off to London. Won't be a moment. Can I get you anything? I think I could probably scrounge some tea."

"No thank you."

Evelyn waited until he'd left the office, closing the door behind him, then got up quickly and went around the desk. She had no idea how much time she had, but she was sure it wasn't going to be long. It was best to move quickly.

Starting with the top drawer, she swiftly and methodically went through Carew's desk, searching for anything that would shed some light on the fact that she had a Russian agent watching her every move. While she wanted to believe that the leak of her presence and identity hadn't come from this embassy, Evelyn knew that nothing was certain. If she wanted to survive for more than a few weeks, she couldn't fully trust anyone. That much was clear. She may be new to this whole cloak and dagger business, but even she knew that there was no way anyone could have known enough to follow her unless they had been told. It was the very fact that she *was* so new to this world that convinced her that someone had betrayed her. Who and where was another question, but there was no doubt in her mind that someone was feeding information to the Russians.

Once she had gone through all the desk drawers without finding anything, Evelyn turned to the tall filing cabinet along the wall. Vladimir hadn't asked her to keep Risto Niva's name secret, but she saw no reason to extend the risk to him as well. If no one knew his name, real or not, then there could be no leak. And she would do everything she could to keep a potential contact safe.

The filing cabinet was locked, but a few seconds with a hairpin overcame that difficulty. Opening the top drawer, she felt a rush of satisfaction at the sight of rows of neatly labeled files. Her heart was beating a steady, rapid tattoo against her chest and she glanced at the closed office door, listening. There was no sound and she turned her attention back to the files. Flipping through them quickly, she paused when she came to a name she recognized. Raising an eyebrow, she pulled it out and opened the file, scanning through the documents inside quickly.

Anna Salvesen not only spoke English, Swedish and German, but also some French. She had been to university, where she completed a secretarial course before coming to work in Oslo. Her family was originally from an area near Trollheimen, but she had come to live in Oslo two years before. Her family was still near Trollheimen, with the exception of her brother. He was a lieutenant in the army, stationed in the north. Anna was considered a class B asset, whatever that meant.

Evelyn tucked the file back into the drawer, moving on. She went through the rest quickly, looking for any that would indicate a traitor in their midst. Finding nothing, she moved on to the next drawer. She checked at her watch and her heart pounded faster. She had to be running out of time. Daniel had been gone for over ten minutes. While she had no idea how long it would take to make contact with London, Evelyn had to assume it wouldn't be long.

It was towards the back of the drawer that her fingers paused. They had landed on a file marked EISENJAGER. Her lips tightened and she pulled the file out, glancing towards the door. All the files were labeled in English, except for this one. Eisenjager translated as Iron

The Oslo Affair

Hunter. It was obviously a codename, but for whom? She flipped the folder open and found herself looking at a single sheet of paper. Scanning it quickly, her frown grew. It seemed that Daniel Carew didn't know much at all about Eisenjager. There was no known description or location. All they had were a handful of references within other communications, and one verbal confirmation by an agent in Munich named Spider. That was it.

Yet at the top was a red stamp that read High Priority.

Looking at her watch once more, Evelyn slid the file back into its spot and closed the drawer, going back to her seat across from the desk. She dared not search any longer in case Daniel came back. She pulled out a cigarette and lit it with shaking fingers, crossing her legs as she sat back in her chair, her mind spinning.

Who was Eisenjager? And why was he a high priority when they knew so little about him?

She was still considering the question a moment later when the door behind her opened and Daniel strode in.

"You're in luck, Miss Richardson," he announced, closing the door. "I made contact immediately. The radio operator was on when I transmitted. He hopes to have a response shortly."

He went around his desk and glanced at his watch.

"When is your deadline?"

"Midnight. Will we hear in time?"

He frowned thoughtfully and sat down.

"I honestly don't know," he confessed.

They were silent for a long moment, then Evelyn got up and put her cigarette out in the ashtray on his desk.

"I'll tell Shustov that I'll go," she decided. "Regardless of what the response is, I think it's the only option at this point, don't you?"

He nodded slowly, his lips pressed together.

"Yes. I think it's an opportunity that can't be missed. Furthermore, I think London will give the all clear to go ahead. As you say, it's really the only option. And it may lead to greater things in the future."

"It's settled then." She turned and picked up her purse and gloves from the chair. "I suppose I'm off to Stockholm."

"Come by first thing in the morning," he said, standing as she began to pull on her gloves. "I'll make the travel arrangements. I should definitely have a response by morning, as well as any further instructions."

"Thank you."

Daniel nodded and held out his hand.

"It's my pleasure. I'll summon my car and have it take you home."

"That's really not necessary," she protested, but he shook his head.

"I insist," he said firmly. "It's late and we don't know if your constant companion is out and about."

Evelyn hesitated, then nodded. He was right. If he was offering the safety of a diplomatic car to take her home, she'd be a fool not to accept. At her nod, he smiled.

"Good. After all, we don't want to lose you on the eve of a new mission, do we?"

◉

Josef came in through the kitchen door just as dawn was lighting the sky. The smell of coffee greeted him and he breathed deeply.

"That smells good," he said, setting the milk bottles on the counter and walking over to get a cup from the shelf.

Else turned from where she was slicing a loaf of bread on the kitchen island. She set her knife down, wiping her hands on her apron.

"You went out early," she said.

"I went to check on Alistair," he said, pouring strong black coffee into his mug. "I didn't like the look of his hoof yesterday."

"And?"

"It's much better today. I was afraid I'd have to have Karl come and look at him, but I think he'll be all right."

"Maybe that will teach him not to try to climb through the fence to the pasture."

Josef grunted and sipped his coffee, falling silent as he watched her go back to slicing the bread.

"Our visitor is back again this morning," he said after a moment.

She glanced at him sharply. "Where?"

"Across the street, down by the Nikols old place." He frowned thoughtfully. "He's changed sides. Yesterday he was up the other end."

"I suppose he thinks he's being clever. Who is he watching? Is it the gypsy in room 4?"

"I think it's the Englishwoman. She came through the back fence yesterday when I was out there."

"She's just arrived!"

The Oslo Affair

"I know."

Else shook her head and clucked her tongue. "She's a sweet girl. I don't like the idea of her being followed by a strange man."

"She'll take care of herself," he said with a surprising amount of compassion in his voice. "She has a good head on her shoulders. He stood out there all day yesterday and she'd already gone. She knows he's there, and how to avoid him."

Else was quiet as she finished cutting her loaf and turned to wipe off the knife. Once she'd placed it back in the block on the counter, she looked at her husband.

"Do you think Anna is also being watched?"

He shrugged. "He seems to be only interested in Miss Richardson."

"She came home last night in a black car. It dropped her right out front."

"You see? There's nothing for you worry over. Carew is obviously taking additional precautions with her."

"I suppose so," she said grudgingly. "Will you carry the dishes through to the dining room? The guests will be down soon."

Josef gulped down the rest his coffee and set the mug down. He looked at her and gave a rare smile, laying a hand on her shoulder.

"You care too much, Else," he said gruffly. "Don't ever change."

She laughed and patted his hand. "I'm not likely to this late in my life."

He turned away and was just lifting a tray piled with plates and cups when there was a light knock on the door from the hallway.

"Miss Richardson!" Else exclaimed as the object of their conversation poked her head into the kitchen. "God morgen! Good morning!"

"God morgen!" Evelyn repeated, stepping into the kitchen. "Am I disturbing you?"

"Not in the least. Josef was just taking the dishes through to the dining room," Else said cheerfully. "Come in. Would you like some coffee?"

"That would be lovely, if you don't mind."

"Sit down over there, then." Else took a mug from the shelf as Josef disappeared through the door with the tray. "Did you sleep well?"

"Yes, thank you. I'm sorry to be down so early. I thought I'd try to get out before...well, it doesn't matter."

Else shot her a look under her lashes as she poured coffee into the mug.

"Sugar?"

"Please."

"I suppose you're referring to the man lurking across the street," Else said a moment later, handing her the mug of coffee.

Evelyn started, almost sloshing hot liquid out of the mug. "You know?"

Else nodded and turned to get blocks of cheese from the sideboard, carrying them over to the island and beginning to prepare a second tray with the chunks of yellow and brown cheeses.

"Josef noticed him the first day. He thought he was watching you. Who is he?"

"I...I'm not sure," Evelyn said, sipping her coffee. "I was hoping to make it out today before he came. How long has he been there?"

"You'd have to ask Josef." The older woman looked at her. "He's the one who saw him. I don't think he's been there long. He must be determined to be out there this early."

"Yes."

"If you leave through the back, he won't see you. I understand you came in that way the other day."

Evelyn nodded sheepishly. "Yes. I got the impression Josef didn't approve."

Else snorted a short laugh. "Josef approves more than you realize," she said with a flash of a grin. "When will you be back?"

"This afternoon or early evening."

"Good. I will be in here preparing dinner or clearing up from it. Come back the same way if he is still there. The door will be open."

Evelyn nodded. "Thank you. I appreciate that, Mrs. Kolstad."

"No need to thank me. Just take care of yourself. You're too nice a girl to be doing what you're doing, but I know you have your reasons. One day soon, we might all have reasons to do the same. Until then, we just have to go on as we always have and hope the world rights itself." Else finished arranging her cheese tray and looked at her with a smile. "And now I've got to take this into the other room. Sit and drink your coffee, my dear. Take as long as you need."

She picked up the tray and turned to disappear through the door into the hallway. Evelyn watched her go and felt a wave of warmth go through her. Despite everything occurring around her and all the uncertainty of who she could trust, Evelyn felt instinctively that Else Kolstad was a true ally.

Sipping her coffee, she just hoped that one day she could return the kindness.

The Oslo Affair

Evelyn looked up as a shadow fell across her small corner table in the cafe.

"Good morning," Daniel greeted her, unbuttoning his coat. "You look well, all things considered."

She smiled and watched as he seated himself across from her. "Thank you."

"Any sign of your shadow today?"

"Yes. He was outside the house this morning. As far as I know, he's still there. Have we heard anything from London?"

"Yes. You've been given the all clear to pursue all possible avenues." Daniel reached into the inside pocket of his coat and pulled out an envelope, sliding it across the table. "In here are two train tickets to Stockholm and two thousand kronor. That should cover any expenses while you're in Sweden. The train leaves tonight, and the tickets are for a sleeper car."

She looked at the envelope for a moment, then raised bemused eyes to his face.

"Tickets and money? Just like that?"

He chuckled. "Just like that. This is how it works, my dear. They want to make sure there is nothing to prevent you from doing what you need to do."

Evelyn shook her head and picked up the envelope, placing it in her purse.

"I have an additional message from William Buckley for you," Daniel continued, making a motion with his hand to indicate to the waitress heading their way that he didn't want any coffee. She nodded and turned away to go to another table. "He wants to know when you arrive in Stockholm. He said to send a telegram to your newspaper."

She nodded. "Very well. Anything else?"

"Yes. When you arrive at the Strand Hotel, send a message to Horace Manchester at the embassy. Tell him that I send my regards. That will alert him to your presence in Stockholm and instruct him to provide any assistance you may require while you're there. He is very limited in his resources, but he will be able to assist in travel arrangements, among other things, if needed."

"Thank you."

Daniel looked at her for a moment, then leaned forward.

"Where is the package from Shustov?" he asked, lowering his

voice.

"It is safe."

"Perhaps you should leave it with me until you return," he said slowly. "It might not be the safest thing to carry with you when you are being followed by a Soviet agent."

"Don't worry. It won't be found," Evelyn assured him with a faint smile.

He studied her for a moment, then nodded. "Have you spoken with Anna yet?"

"No. I'll speak with her this afternoon."

"If she cannot accompany you, what will you do?"

"I'll go on my own," she said promptly. "While I agree that two women traveling together will garner less attention, I must go regardless."

"Agreed. If she seems on the fence about it, tell her that I can arrange the time with her employer. She need only call me."

"I'll pass the message on."

Daniel nodded, picked up his hat, and got up.

"Very well. I'll see you when you return." He held out his hand and Evelyn stood to grasp it. "Take very good care of yourself, Miss Richardson."

"I will."

He nodded once more and turned to leave the cafe, buttoning his coat as he went towards the door. Evelyn watched him go, then sank back into her seat and reached for her cup of coffee.

She felt rather dazed with the speed at which everything was happening. Yesterday morning, she was concerned about meeting with Lyakhov, and today she was preparing to depart for Stockholm with the equivalent of over two hundred pounds in Swedish currency in her purse. Her lips curved faintly. Bill had tried to warn her that things would move quickly once her training was over. He hadn't been exaggerating. Although, she supposed she should have been prepared for this after her maiden mission in Strasbourg last summer. That also had not gone as planned.

She pressed her lips together and cradled her cup in her hands, considering her options. If Anna agreed to accompany her, it would make things easier. Not only did she know the language, but she could help allay suspicion if anyone began to question an English journalist traveling through Scandinavia. If she declined, Evelyn would have to go alone. While that made her nervous in the same way she had been nervous when her ship departed Scotland for its journey across the North Sea a few days ago, she prosaically accepted that this was

The Oslo Affair

something that had to be done. The potential benefits of meeting Niva far outweighed any lingering discomfort she might feel at traveling to a country she'd never visited before in her life.

She finished her coffee and set the empty mug down. There was nothing for it. Whether she was ready for this or not, tonight she would board a train bound for Sweden and an unknown Soviet agent who might or might not be an ally. Evelyn stood up and gathered her purse and gloves. She couldn't think of what could happen, but could only focus on what she had to do.

And right now, that was to make preparations for another journey.

Chapter Fourteen

"I hope you don't mind having a window that faces the back. It overlooks the kitchen garden." Else said over her shoulder, leading the way up the stairs to the second floor. "It's the last available room at the moment. Now, I do have a room becoming available in two days if you'd like to switch then. We can certainly arrange it."

"I'm sure this will be fine, Frau Kolstad," the man behind her said pleasantly. "I prefer a quiet room."

"That works out nicely, then." She reached the top of the stairs and turned right. "There is very little noise from the road in the back of the house. You almost forget you're in the middle of Oslo."

She led him down the hallway to the last door on the left and opened it, standing aside so that he could enter.

"Now, I do provide toast and cheese for breakfast, along with coffee. If you prefer tea, let me know and I will provide that as well," she said as he set his suitcase down on the floor next to the bed. "The front door is locked at ten, but you may take a key if you will be out late."

"Thank you." He went over to glance out the small window that overlooked the back. "This will do nicely. It's a very nice room."

Else smiled. "I'm glad you like it, Herr Renner. I'll leave you now. If you need anything, we're just downstairs."

"Thank you again."

She departed, closing the door quietly. The congenial smile left his face as soon as the door closed and he went back to the window, peering out. The kitchen garden was small, surrounded by a fence that could be easily circumvented. A shed at the bottom of the garden drew his attention and he considered it for a moment, noting the open door. As he watched, the landlord came out and closed the door, locking it behind him. Renner watched him pocket the key and turn towards the house.

He turned away from the window and went over to his suitcase, lifting it onto the bed and unlatching it. Tossing it open, he

The Oslo Affair

moved a stack of neatly folded shirts and trousers to reveal a false bottom, which he lifted out of the case. Underneath was a square, portable radio. He pulled it out of the case and carried it over to the small desk near the window. It was time to contact Berlin.

He was in position.

◉

Evelyn stepped in the small restaurant and looked around. Towards the back, a lone woman sat at a table, eating an open sandwich. When Evelyn approached, she looked up in surprise and a smile of welcome crossed her face.

"Maggie!" she exclaimed. "What are you doing here?"

"Looking for you," Evelyn said with a smile, seating herself across from Anna. "I'm glad I caught you."

"You're lucky you did. I almost didn't come out today. Have you eaten?"

"I had toast and cheese earlier."

"If you're hungry, I recommend the smoked salmon. It's particularly good today."

"I think I'll pass. I'm not very hungry at the moment." Evelyn removed her gloves and looked up as a waitress approached. "Perhaps some coffee, though."

Anna nodded and ordered coffee, then looked across the table.

"What can I do for you? Do you need a translator?" she asked with a cheerful grin. "Or just another companion for dinner?"

"I need a translator," Evelyn said slowly, "but it's rather more involved than dinner."

"Why does that not surprise me?" Anna asked with a short laugh. "What is it?"

"How's your Swedish?"

Anna's eyebrows flew into her forehead and she blinked. "My Swedish?" she repeated. "Sufficient, I'd say. Why?"

"I find myself heading to Stockholm," Evelyn answered, smiling in thanks as a cup of coffee was set down before her. The waitress went away again and she turned her gaze to Anna's face. "I was hoping you'd consider coming with me."

"To Stockholm?" Anna stared at her. "When?"

"Tonight."

The other woman sat back in her chair, a look of astonishment on her face.

"Tonight? What on earth for?"

"I completely understand if you're unable to come," Evelyn said, ignoring the question. "I know it's very short notice. I don't know any Swedish, but I'm sure I'll be able to figure it out. There must be travel language books that will suffice."

Anna frowned and leaned forward. "How long do you expect to be gone?"

"Only a few days."

Anna was silent for a long time, finishing her lunch as Evelyn sipped her coffee.

"I need more information before I can consider this properly," she finally said. "Why the sudden jaunt to Sweden?"

"There's someone there I need to speak with," Evelyn said, lowering her voice. "They're only there for a few days, so timing is of the essence. I have tickets on a train leaving tonight."

Anna studied her for a long moment. "Is Carew aware of this?"

"He's the one who made the arrangements."

She exhaled and nodded.

"Of course he was," she muttered. "I must say, you're turning out to be a very interesting and extraordinary woman, Maggie Richardson."

Evelyn grinned. "Why is that?"

"I can't think of a single other woman of my acquaintance who would be quite this sanguine about going to a country where she doesn't speak the language, only to find that she now has to go another country where she also doesn't speak the language." Anna tilted her head and considered her. "Aren't you the least bit intimidated?"

"Would it do any good to be?" Evelyn countered. "I am here, and this must be done. So I must do it."

Anna pursed her lips thoughtfully and was silent for a long time.

"You'll go whether I accompany you or not, won't you?"

"Yes."

The other woman shook her head. "As I said, you're turning out to be an extraordinary woman."

"If you're not comfortable with coming..." Evelyn's voice trailed off when Anna waved a hand impatiently.

"It's not that I'm uncomfortable," she said, "far from it. I think it's all rather exciting, and I'd rather enjoy a little holiday into Sweden. That's not what's causing my hesitation. I don't know that I can take the time from work."

The Oslo Affair

"Daniel thought of that," Evelyn told her. "He said he can arrange it if you decide to come with me. Just let him know and he'll take care of it."

Anna raised her eyebrows, clearly surprised. "He said that? How on earth will he manage it, I wonder?"

"I have no idea."

"Well, I suppose I'm out of objections, then," she said after another moment of consideration. "If he will arrange my time from work, it must be fairly important, this trip of yours."

Evelyn was silent for a moment, then she raised her eyes to Anna's.

"I think it is," she said slowly, "but it's not without risk. I don't know how much risk, but I feel it only fair to warn you."

Anna smiled slowly, a glint coming into her eyes.

"When do we leave?"

◉

Evelyn finished folding the last blouse and laid it in the suitcase before looking around the room to see if there was anything she'd missed. She had never fully unpacked, not knowing how quickly Vladimir would contact her, so there wasn't much to re-pack. Not seeing any forgotten objects lurking in the corners, she closed the case, doing up the leather straps.

The sun had set outside and a fire blazed cheerfully in the hearth, throwing warmth out into the room. Turning, she went to stand before it, staring down into the flames thoughtfully. She had no idea how long she would be gone. It all depended upon how quickly this Risto Niva would meet with her, or even if he *would* meet with her.

Bill had anticipated that she would only be away from Scotland for a week or two, but it could very well be longer now. Evelyn frowned as a thought came into her head. She had only written enough letters to cover an absence of three weeks at most. Anything longer than that and her mother would start to wonder why she wasn't hearing from her.

And Miles would think she wasn't writing after all.

Her lips twisted and she sighed, staring into the fire. And why did that bother her so much? He was just a pilot who flew with her brother, after all. A very handsome pilot, it was true, and one whom she found interesting and fun to talk to, but an acquaintance just the same. If he thought she wasn't returning his letters, it really shouldn't matter to her.

And yet it did. For some reason that she couldn't understand, Evelyn desperately wanted to extend their acquaintance and get to know him better. It didn't matter that they were a country at war, or that his job ensured that he was in the first line of defense should Hitler attempt to invade England. It didn't matter that he thought she was a WAAF in Scotland training other WAAFs to work in the plotting stations, which was perfect really. She hadn't had to say very much at all regarding what she supposedly did in Scotland. He had made an assumption and run with it, leaving any further prevarication on her part unnecessary.

If she had an ounce of sense, she would stop writing to him and make it clear that she wasn't interested. This was a doomed friendship, all things considered. She lived a life he could never know about, and he went up in a Spitfire everyday with no guarantee that he would return.

Evelyn pressed her lips together. Of course, there was no guarantee that she would return either. There were no guarantees for anyone anymore, except that they all would have to do things they never dreamt of in order to get through each day and, with a bit of luck, the war. That was becoming increasingly obvious.

Sighing, she turned away from the fire and went over to the desk near the window where her toiletries case sat. Opening it, she removed the insert and ran her fingers along the inside lining until she came to the small tab concealed in the folds. The inside of the case lifted out to reveal a compartment in the bottom where the microfilm Vladimir had passed her was concealed.

Evelyn stared at it thoughtfully for a long moment. She could leave it there and it would be perfectly safe, or she could remove it and leave it here, ready to be collected when she returned. If she left it here, there would be no risk of anyone discovering it with her while she traveled to Sweden. While there was no reason any border agent would search her belongings so thoroughly, there was also no reason to take the added risk of carrying the microfilm to Stockholm with her.

Especially if she was to be meeting another Soviet agent. For all she knew, Risto could be a trap for the Soviets to ensnare her. Did she really want to be carrying stolen secrets from Moscow with her if that was the case?

Turning, she slowly looked around the room. She could probably conceal the microfilm easily enough in this room, ensuring its safety. Daniel had warned against it, but if she hid it well where could be the harm? She was sure she could convince Else and Josef to reserve

The Oslo Affair

the room for her and not allow another guest to stay there. Perhaps that would be the wiser course of action.

Biting her bottom lip, Evelyn hesitated. Regardless of the dangers of being caught by a Soviet NKVD agent with stolen Soviet documents, the thought of leaving that information behind made her uncomfortable. No one knew what happened when her father had the same information. Had he done this very thing? Left it somewhere? Was that how it had been lost? Or had he kept it with him and it was stolen after he died?

At the thought of her father, Evelyn felt her chest grow tight and she blinked back sudden tears. The wave of sorrow took her by surprise and she sank into the chair next to the desk, taking a deep breath. What if he hadn't died in Switzerland? She wouldn't be here, worrying over the best course of action to take with secret Soviet documents.

After taking a few deep breaths, forcing the grief aside, Evelyn glanced into the case on the desk. After another long moment of indecision, she stood up and replaced the insert, concealing the compartment with the microfilm once again. She would carry them with her. They had been lost once, as Vladimir had so coldly pointed out. They wouldn't be lost again.

◉

Evelyn watched as Josef picked up her suitcase and turned to carry it out of her room. He had offered in halting English to take the toiletries case as well, but she refused. She would carry it with her. As soon as he left the room, she turned to make one last check, ensuring that she had gathered everything. It was done more out of nervousness than anything else, for she knew she hadn't left anything behind. She was far too thorough for that.

The car would be arriving any minute to take her to the station, where Anna would meet her. There was really no reason to tarry, but Evelyn couldn't seem to make her legs move to carry her downstairs. She was comfortable here, in this room and under this roof with Else and Josef keeping an eye out for her. She had no idea what awaited her in Stockholm, and therein lay the nerves.

After taking a moment to compose herself, she pulled her coat on and picked up her shoulder bag from the desk. As her fingers closed around the handle of the toiletry case, she felt herself calm down and she turned towards the door.

In the case lay the reason she was here. No matter what Sweden held in store for her, at least she knew she had succeeded in her primary mission.

A moment later, she was striding down the hallway towards the stairs. When she was almost there, a tall figure emerged from the flight of steps, almost running into her. She let out a soft gasp and stopped mid-stride, narrowly avoiding a collision.

"Oh!"

Looking up, Evelyn felt her heart thud and her breath stopped for a moment as she stared into a face she remembered clearly.

"Fraulein!" A wide smile broke over the angular face. "Are you all right? We seem to keep running into each other."

Herr Renner stood before her, a long black coat covering his dark suit. He had obviously just returned to the house and, as he spoke, he began pulling off his black leather gloves.

"Oh hallo!" Evelyn forced a light cheerfulness into her voice as her heart pounded against her chest. "Yes, we do, don't we?"

"Now don't tell me that you're not staying here either, because I won't believe it!" he said with a laugh, dropping his gloves into his hat and tucking it under his arm.

"No. I'm staying here," she said with a perfunctory laugh.

"How wonderful. I'm glad there is a fellow German in the house. The landlord speaks a passable German, but it's nice to hear a familiar Berlin accent." Herr Renner smiled down at her. "Say you'll have a drink with me."

Evelyn swallowed. "I'd love to, Herr Renner, but I'm late for an appointment at the moment. Perhaps another time?"

"Alas, another appointment," he mourned. "I suppose it can't be helped. Perhaps tomorrow."

He bowed slightly and stepped back to allow her to pass.

"I'll look forward to it," Evelyn assured him with another forced smile. "Goodbye!"

She went past him and started down the stairs, her mind clamoring to find a reason why he would be staying in the same nondescript lodging house as herself. When she'd run into him the night before at the Hotel Bristol, she had received the distinct impression that he was staying there. Yet, here he was.

She forced herself to maintain a steady pace down the stairs even as her breath was coming fast. She didn't know who he was or what he was doing here, but she knew one thing for certain.

This was not a coincidence.

The Oslo Affair

Chapter Fifteen

Hearing a soft click, Herr Renner tucked the metal tools into his pocket and eased open the door, slipping inside. He closed it softly behind him and looked around the empty room. A fire still burned in the hearth, casting a soft glow through the darkness. Moving forward, he went to the desk before the window and switched on the lamp. Immediately, the shadows in the room dispersed and he turned to survey the space thoughtfully.

The bed was made neatly, the pillows placed perfectly, while the chair before the desk was pushed in. The Englishwoman had a penchant for precise neatness which he could appreciate. Everything had a place, and it was placed accordingly. He bent down to open the drawer of the desk. It was empty save the notepad and pencil provided by the landlord. He had the same notepad and pencil in his room.

Renner pulled out the pad and held it under the lamp, looking for signs of it having been used recently. After examining it carefully, he replaced it in the drawer. There were no indentations on the top sheet. The woman hadn't jotted down any notes, at least not on that pad. Closing the drawer, he turned to look around for a moment, then went to work.

Moving methodically around the room, he began with the bed. Bending down, he lifted the bed skirt and peered underneath. The wooden floor was bare and nothing appeared to be tucked between the wooden slats holding the mattress. Straightening, he flipped the covers away from the side of the mattress and lifted it, scanning underneath. After checking one side thoroughly, he went to the other side and did the same thing. Satisfied that nothing had been slipped under the mattress or behind the pillows, he replaced everything and smoothed the cover back. When he was finished, it looked as if the bed hadn't been touched.

Renner then moved to the side table, searching under it and leafing through the Bible resting on the surface. Systematically, he made his way around the room, going through furniture, checking behind paintings on the wall, and even inspecting the cracks in the floor. At

The Oslo Affair

one point he thought he had something when he spied a slip of paper peeking from behind the armoire, but further investigation revealed a receipt from a bookshop dated four months prior.

He had just slipped it back into the crevice between the wardrobe and the wall when he straightened up and looked around again. The room was clean, almost too clean. It was as if no one had been staying there. Renner's eyebrows came together as his eyes narrowed suddenly. There was no clutter anywhere, no sign of occupancy. Not even a hairbrush sat out on the dressing table.

With a frown, he moved to the front of the wardrobe and opened the door. The frown swiftly turned into a scowl. It was completely empty.

"Verdammt!" he swore, closing the door.

His lips pressed together unpleasantly and he strode to the window, glancing outside. The room overlooked the street and as he glowered into the night, he suddenly remembered her in the hallway. She had been carrying a square case. A toiletries or jewelry case.

"Dummkopf!" he muttered disgustedly, turning away from the window.

She had been leaving, not going out to dinner as he had assumed. The rest of her luggage must have already been downstairs when he ran into her.

Herr Renner switched off the lamp on the desk and strode across the room, pausing inside the door to listen. Hearing nothing in the hallway, he eased open the door and slipped into the empty hallway. He would have to report back to Berlin, then try to determine where she had gone. If she'd returned to England, he was out of luck. But if not, then he just might be able to pick up her trail.

He was passing the head of the stairs on his way back to his room when he heard voices in the hallway below. Recognizing the landlord's voice, he paused in the shadows to listen.

"At least the man is gone from the street," Josef was saying, his voice carrying up the stairs. "Now perhaps he'll stop hanging around here."

"Once he realizes she has gone, he will stop," Else said. It sounded as if they were moving out of the parlor and towards the kitchen and Herr Renner strained to make out the rest of the conversation. "I just hope he doesn't…gone…train station."

"And her room?"

"I told her…reserve…week…"

Renner scowled in frustration as Else's voice trailed off. They had gone into the kitchen and he heard the door close behind them.

Turning, he continued towards his own room. So the Englishwoman had someone else watching her. That in itself was interesting, but even more so was the fact that the landlord and his wife were aware of it. Whoever was watching the house was either sloppy or completely unconcerned with being seen. He was willing to bet on the latter. If someone else was aware of the Englishwoman's presence, then they had very good information and were most likely professionals, like himself. And that meant another government was interested as well.

Berlin wouldn't like that. In fact, he didn't like that. It made it all much more complicated.

Reaching his room, he unlocked the door and went inside. At least now he knew she had gone to a train station. He would hold off contacting Berlin until he'd determined where, in fact, Fraulein Maggie Richardson had gone. Once he knew that, he would know just what to report to his superior, and how he was going to proceed.

◉

Comrade Grigori watched from behind a stone pillar as the Englishwoman met a brunette in the lobby of the station. They were both carrying luggage and he pressed his lips together. The train station wasn't busy this time of night, but it also wasn't deserted. He had to keep his distance or the Englishwoman would see him, yet by doing so he ran the risk of losing them. If only he knew which train!

When she left the house earlier, she'd shown no sign of being aware of his surveillance. A taxi had pulled up to the curb outside the house and the landlord had carried out a suitcase, handing it to the driver. As the driver stowed the bag in the trunk, the Englishwoman had emerged from the house. She hadn't even glanced in his direction. In fact, she hadn't looked in either direction. She had gone straight to the taxi and got into the back, saying something to the landlord as she did so. He had nodded and closed the car door once she was inside, going back into the house as the taxi pulled away. The whole thing had taken less than a minute.

Even though she didn't appear to be aware of his presence in the street, Grigori knew she must be. It was the only explanation for the fact that she had managed to evade him for two days. Yesterday, he thought she had stayed in. However, when there was no sign of her today either, he knew he'd been blown.

Yet he'd been able to follow her to the station.

He puzzled over that as he watched the two women walk

The Oslo Affair

together towards the far stairs leading down to the tracks. If she was aware of his existence, why did she allow him to know where she was going? Or did she think he wouldn't follow her from the city?

He supposed it was possible that she assumed he would lose interest in her once she had left Oslo. In any other situation, he probably would have. But this wasn't any other situation and the loyalty of one of his own was in question. He had to know where she was going.

As soon as the women had disappeared through the far entrance, he emerged from his place behind the column and strode across the lobby to the ticket counter.

"Good evening," the man greeted him cheerfully. "How can I help?"

"Good evening. Could you tell me what trains are running tonight?" Grigori asked, pulling a wallet from inside his coat.

"There are three, sir. The line to Trondheim departs in an hour, the train to Bergen leaves at ten, and the Ostfold line to Stockholm leaves in ten minutes."

"That's the one I'm looking for," Grigori said. "Are there any sleepers left?"

"I'm afraid not, sir. I have a first class carriage available."

"That'll do."

A moment later, Comrade Grigori was striding across the lobby towards the far entrance. As soon as he was away from the ticket counter, a decidedly ugly look descended on his face.

Things weren't looking very good for Comrade Lyakhov. First he left for Stockholm, and now the English agent was doing the same. It could be a coincidence, but Grigori had been around long enough to know that the odds were rapidly deteriorating in Lyakhov's favor. There had been no sign of the two meeting in Oslo, but that didn't mean there wasn't a connection. It was possible that Comrade Lyakhov had realized he was being watched and arranged to meet the Englishwoman in Stockholm instead. He wouldn't have known that the English agent was also in surveillance.

Passing through the arches the two women had passed through moments before, Grigori started down the steps that led to the platform below. On the other hand, the Englishwoman could be a red herring and not connected to Comrade Lyakhov at all. Even now, knowing she was getting on a train to Stockholm, Grigori was inclined to think that this was all just a wild goose chase. But the fact that she was getting on the train was enough to make him follow.

If there truly was no connection with Lyakov, then all would be well. He would be in a perfect position to observe an English agent and see who she was meeting with and what she was doing, which Moscow would appreciate in any event, and Comrade Lyakhov would be cleared of any suspicion. It would be a good, successful mission.

But if a connection between the two was revealed, then things would get ugly.

Comrade Grigori reached the platform just as the conductors called the last boarding call. There was no sign of the two women and he moved towards the first class carriages quickly, his ticket in his hand.

For the Englishwoman's sake, he sincerely hoped there was no connection. She was a very beautiful young woman. It would be a shame to spoil that.

◉

Paris, France

Bill sipped his drink and glanced across the crowded drawing room at his wife. Marguerite was laughing at something one of the other women had said and, as he looked in her direction, her eyes met his almost beseechingly. She wanted to leave. Not surprising, really. He'd warned her that it was bound to be dreadfully dull for her. It was an evening for the diplomats and their wives, and she had absolutely nothing in common with most of the women here. He looked at his watch surreptitiously. In another half an hour, he could politely excuse them both and save her sanity.

"Monsieur Buckley?"

A voice spoke softly at his elbow and he turned to see a young footman standing there, looking very apologetic.

"Yes?"

"There is a messenger for you," he said softly, "from the embassy. He's waiting downstairs."

Bill raised his eyes in surprise and nodded. The man moved away as silently as he had come and Bill looked at the older man next to him.

"Pardon," he murmured. "I must go and see what this is all about."

The older man waved him away. "Of course, of course! We're always working, no?"

Bill laughed politely and nodded, turning towards the door of the drawing room. He looked back at Marguerite to find her with her

The Oslo Affair

head bent to listen as one of the wives whispered excitedly in her ear. Gossip. Heaven help them all. Marguerite couldn't abide what she called 'small-minded woman's talk.' His lips curved as he turned and left the room. Hopefully he would return before his wife had had enough.

He went down the stairs to the first floor where a clerk waited in the entry hall, just inside the door. He had an envelope in his hands and Bill felt his good humor fade.

"Hallo George," he said, reaching the hall. "You're working late."

"I was just leaving when a message came through for you, sir," George replied, meeting him halfway across the hall and handing him the envelope.

Bill took the envelope.

"I suppose we're all working longer hours than usual these days, eh?" he said, breaking the seal and unfolding the single sheet of paper.

"Yes, sir. If you need to send a reply, I can take it back for you before knocking off for the night."

Bill scanned the message swiftly. Other than a slight tightening of his lips, he showed no reaction to the message that had been deemed important enough to send a clerk over to Prime Minister Daladier's residence while an evening of entertainment was in progress.

"Thank you, George. I will send a reply. Would you mind waiting here a moment?"

"Of course, sir."

Bill turned and went back up the stairs, looking for the study, which he knew would be deserted at present. Once inside, he switched on a lamp and went to the desk, pulling a notepad towards him. He'd just torn off the top sheet and picked up a pencil when the door opened and one of Daladier's aids poked his head in.

"Oh! It's you, sir," he said with a grin. "I saw the light and thought I'd better check. Is everything all right?"

"Yes, thanks. The embassy sent over a message and I'm afraid I have to send an answer back. I hope it's all right. I won't be a minute."

"Of course! Take your time."

The aid withdrew and the congenial look on Bill's face disappeared. He pulled out the message again, reading it through once more. It wasn't any better on the second reading. A German SD agent by the name of Herr Renner had arrived two days before and Daniel Carew had had a man observing him. After checking into the Kolstad's boarding house that morning, he had now just booked a ticket on the first train out of Oslo in the morning, destination Stockholm.

He bent his head to scrawl a message to Jasper. It couldn't be a coincidence that now there was a German agent pursuing Evelyn. That was one agent too many. There was no doubt in his mind that they had a spy somewhere in London. Jasper had to be made aware of the situation.

He finished the message and folded the paper, looking around the top of the desk. Spotting a stack of envelopes in a pigeon hole, he extracted one and slid the paper inside. If there was any way he could warn Evelyn of the threat, he would, but there wasn't. She would be on a train to Stockholm herself by now. The most he could do was alert her when she checked in upon her arrival.

He turned to leave the study, uncomfortably aware that tomorrow could be too late. Her mission had been severely compromised, that much was clear, and the prudent thing to do now would be to recall her immediately.

A rush of irritation went through him. If Daniel Carew had informed them of this Herr Renner before now, they would never have approved her going to Stockholm. It was far too risky with two agents now aware of her presence. She hadn't been prepped for this. She had been prepped for a nice, easy fact-finding mission on friendly soil, and this had turned into anything but.

He went down the stairs to the hall again and handed the clerk the sealed envelope.

"Have this transmitted directly to Lord Montclair, in London," he told him briskly. "His eyes only."

"Yes, sir."

He watched the clerk hurry out the door and into the night before turning back to the stairs. His lips suddenly curved as he considered the situation. This was the second time that a simple, straight-forward mission had turned sideways on Evelyn. She really did appear to have the worst luck. The first time she had come through without a scratch, but that was before the war began.

The smile was gone as quickly as it appeared. Everything was different now. Both agents trailing her worked for countries that would not take kindly to a British agent in their midst. It was time to get her out of there.

He just hoped tomorrow would be in time.

Chapter Sixteen

The Strand Hotel, Stockholm
November 9

Evelyn signed the registry at the desk and waited while the man checking them in went to a cabinet to get the key to their room. It was early afternoon and the lobby was empty save for a few guests wandering through on their way to the door, heading for the sights and sounds of the harbor. Anna had stopped at a vendor outside on their way in, lured by the sight of newspapers and cigarettes, promising that she would be right in.

"Here you are, Miss Richardson." The man returned with the room key and a smile. "The lift is to the back. Would you like me to call a porter to carry your luggage?"

"Yes, thank you."

He nodded and motioned to a porter. "I hope you enjoy your stay with us. If you need anything at all, please don't hesitate to let us know."

"Oh! There is one thing. Can you have a message delivered to the British embassy for me?" she asked.

"Of course. Would you like some paper?"

"Yes, thank you."

He placed a pad of paper before her and handed her a pencil. "I'll ensure it is delivered immediately."

Picking up the pencil, Evelyn wrote a few lines on the paper and tore it off the pad. Then, folding the paper, she wrote a name across the front.

"Please have it delivered to Horace Manchester."

"Of course." He took the note and slipped it into an envelope, sealing it in front of her. "I'll send it over right away."

"Thank you very much." Evelyn picked up her gloves and purse and smiled brightly. "I appreciate it."

She turned from the desk as Anna came hurrying across the lobby, her heels clicking a rapid staccato on the tiled floor. She held a folded newspaper in her hand and her hair had partially slipped from under her hat in her haste.

"Maggie! You'll never guess what's happened!" she exclaimed breathlessly, coming up to the desk. She shoved the newspaper into Evelyn's hands. "Someone tried to kill Adolf Hitler!"

"What?!"

Evelyn grabbed the paper and opened it to the black and white headline. She didn't need to know Swedish to understand the headline: EXPLOSION MENADE FÖR HITLER.

"It says there was an explosion last night at the beer hall where he was speaking," Anna told her, looking at the paper with her. "He speaks there every year on the anniversary of the Putsch. Last night, not ten minutes after he left, a bomb exploded behind the podium where he had been speaking, bringing half the roof down. A bunch of people were killed, but it says that there's no doubt the bomb was meant for Hitler. His speech was supposed to be at nine, but they moved it up to eight so that the Führer could get back to Berlin. If he had started when originally planned, he would have been killed."

Evelyn stared at the paper for a moment, trying to decipher some of the words for herself, then looked at Anna.

"Does it say anything about the person responsible?"

Anna shook her head. "No. They're looking for them. They think the bomb was on a timer and put inside a stone column."

The porter cleared his throat apologetically and, when both women looked at him, he motioned to Anna's bags questioningly. She nodded and he picked them up along with Evelyn's.

"How extraordinary," Evelyn said, passing the paper back to Anna and turning to walk towards the lift. "I thought everyone loved him in Germany!"

"Not everyone, apparently." Anna fell into step beside her. "Could you imagine if it succeeded? It was so close! Hitler had just left!"

"If it had succeeded, it certainly would have taken care of this war," Evelyn said. "Pity. This could have all been over."

"I'm sure that's what the person who did this thought as well. I wonder if they'll catch him?"

"I'm sure they will. The Gestapo are nothing if not efficient."

Anna shot her a look as they stopped before the lift and the attendant opened the door and stood aside for them to step into the cage. The porter followed and once they were in, the attendant entered and pulled the grate closed. He said something in Swedish and Evelyn looked at Anna helplessly.

"He wants to know which floor," she said with a grin. "Where are we going?"

The Oslo Affair

"The fourth floor."

Anna told the attendant and he nodded, putting the lift in motion. The ride was a quiet one as Evelyn and Anna dropped the topic of Hitler for the moment, choosing instead to watch the floors of the hotel go slowly by. It was a small lift and between the boy with the luggage and the attendant, there was very little room. Evelyn stood still, watching the floors, her mind spinning.

Someone had really tried to kill Hitler! While it was completely unexpected, she supposed it shouldn't have been. Even though the press in Germany portrayed him as a beloved Führer, it stood to reason that there would be those who were less than enthusiastic. There always were. But to openly try to kill him? And the amazing thing was it would have worked! If he hadn't moved his speech up an hour, it would be a very different world today. It would be a world on its way back to peace.

The lift came to a stop and the attendant opened the gate, nodding to them with a smile. Evelyn stepped out and looked at the porter. He nodded and led the way to the left, saying something over his shoulder.

"He says to follow him," Anna said unnecessarily.

Evelyn looked at her. "I would never have guessed," she said dryly.

Anna grinned. "You wanted an interpreter. I'm simply doing my job."

"I wanted a companion as well," Evelyn retorted, tucking her arm through hers. "And you're doing that fabulously. Thank you."

"There's no need to thank me. I'm enjoying myself! This is a nice change from transcribing legal notes, I assure you."

The porter stopped before a door and set two of the bags down so he could unlock it. Once the door was opened, he handed the key to Evelyn and picked up the bags.

"Oh! How lovely!" Anna exclaimed, following Evelyn into the room and looking around.

They had stepped into a very modern sitting room with two arm chairs, a love seat, and a table in the center. A set of French doors opened onto a narrow balcony, and an ornate desk stood to the side of the doors. On either side of the sitting room was a door leading to a bedroom.

The porter set the bags down and turned to leave. Evelyn murmured thank you in Swedish as he passed and he bobbed his head. A moment later, the door was closing softly behind him.

"The view is outstanding!" Anna exclaimed from across the

room, opening the doors to step out onto the balcony. "Come and see!"

Evelyn smiled and walked across the room to where a cold breeze was blowing in.

"It's freezing!"

"It's not. It's lovely! You're just not used to it." Anna gazed out over the water. "Well, perhaps it's a bit brisk," she admitted a second later as a gust of wind caught them in the face and she reached up to hold her hat on her head.

Evelyn laughed, shivering. The hotel overlooked the harbor. Directly across the water stood the Royal Palace, imposing and elegant in all its timeless grandeur. The sun glistened off the surface, making the waves look like moving, glittering glass, and Evelyn breathed deeply. It truly was a wonderful view.

"Stunning," she said, turning to go back into the sitting room. "But too cold!"

Anna chuckled, shaking her head. After taking one last look across the water, she turned and went in, closing the doors behind her.

"I'll tell you this: if this is how you travel, I'll be your interpreter any time you like!" she said, taking off her hat and tossing it onto the table. "It's marvelous! We even have our own rooms!"

"You can thank Daniel Carew for that," Evelyn said, unbuttoning her coat and beginning to pull off her gloves. "He's the one who made the reservation."

"Perhaps I should take him up on his offer to come and work for him," she said with a grin, undoing her coat and shrugging out of it. "He's asked more than once."

Evelyn removed her coat and turned to pick up her bags, heading for the door on the right.

"I can't imagine this is the norm for embassy employees," she said over her shoulder. "Never mind. You can enjoy it while you're here."

Anna followed her to the door, leaning against it as she watched Evelyn set her suitcase down and turn to place her smaller travel case on the dressing table.

"What did you mean when you said that the Gestapo were nothing if not efficient?" she asked suddenly.

Evelyn looked at her in surprise. "What?"

"The way you said it, it sounded as if you had personal experience with them. Have you?"

"No, thank heavens. I've heard stories, that's all." Evelyn dropped her gloves next to her case and turned to face Anna. "They're the Nazi police. They must be good at it or they wouldn't have the reputation they do."

Anna made a face and straightened up from the door jam. "There's a difference between being good at something and being a bully," she muttered. "My brother says they're all thugs."

"Your brother?" Evelyn grasped at that, thankful to turn the conversation from herself and the Gestapo. "I didn't know you had a brother!"

"Yes. He's with the army up near Trondheim. His name is Erik." Anna turned to leave the bedroom. "He likes to think he knows everything."

"Don't all brothers?" Evelyn demanded with a laugh before she could stop herself.

Anna picked up her cases and looked back at her.

"You sound as if you have one of your own," she said. "Do you?"

"Yes. He's in the RAF." Evelyn glanced at her watch. "We just have time to get dressed for dinner," she said, turning back into her room. "Are you hungry?"

"I'm always hungry!" Anna went across the sitting room to the opposite door. "You don't have to tell me twice."

She disappeared into her room and the door closed behind her a moment later. Evelyn exhaled and closed her door, turning to lift her suitcase onto the bed. She didn't like to speak about herself at all with strangers, not wanting to inadvertently give too much information that could be used against her. It was something that had been drilled into her in Scotland. The less anyone knew about you, the better. The comment about brothers had slipped out before she could think, and now Anna knew she had a brother. She supposed it didn't really make a difference. Anna didn't know her real name, or even where she was from. It was unlikely that that particular piece of trivia would mean anything to the woman other than to present something they had in common.

That was something else her training had drilled into her. Always try to establish something in common with contacts, something they could relate to. Not that Anna was a mark for information, but she was still a contact. Perhaps it wouldn't hurt to build a relationship there. After all, who knew when she might have need of a friend in Norway?

Evelyn undid her case and opened it, pushing aside the nagging feeling of distaste at thinking of Anna in terms of how she could use her. The woman had come with her, miles from her home and into a different country, to act as an interpreter for her without question. If nothing else, she was certainly one of the most obliging females Evelyn had come across. She didn't like lying to her.

Pulling a blue dinner dress out of the case, her lips curved despite herself. She wasn't sure how much good the lying was actually doing with Anna, anyway. The woman already knew she wasn't the journalist she was pretending to be, and had figured out that Maggie Richardson was not her name. Because she worked with Daniel Carew, Anna knew that Evelyn was an agent of some kind. Hopefully, she didn't have a clear idea of exactly what kind.

The smile faded as she laid the dress on the bed next to the case. The story had to be maintained, but at this point both women knew the truth. The only question was why Anna had agreed to help her. Norway was a neutral country and, while England was their ally, they had made it clear that they wouldn't break their neutrality in favor of any of the combating nations. Why, then, was Anna so willing to assist? Was it simply because she was familiar with Carew and had acted as a courier for him on occasion? Or was it something more? Evelyn remembered the look on Anna's face that reminded her so forcibly of her feeling of uselessness just a short year ago, and she pressed her lips together thoughtfully.

With nothing to do until Vladimir made contact, she could focus on Anna. If she couldn't figure out her motives by the time she left Sweden then she had no business working for MI6 at all. Her job was to gather information from both friendly and enemy sources.

And that was exactly what she was going to do.

◉

London, England

The traffic was steady, streaming around Piccadilly just as it always had. If anything, the war had increased the congestion in the late afternoon as everyone tried to finish their errands before nightfall and the blackout. The man stepped out of a shop and looked around before turning and heading towards the corner. Looking over his shoulder to the street, he spotted an available taxi and raised his umbrella to summon it, stepping to the curb. While he waited for it to maneuver its way to the side of the road, he glanced at his watch. He had plenty of time before his meeting. There was no rush.

The taxi stopped beside him and he got into the back. "Whitehall, please."

The Oslo Affair

"Sir." The driver nodded and a moment later they were easing back into the flow of traffic.

The man looked out of the window, his lips tightening. He hadn't meant to be away from the office this long. It was supposed to be a quick trip to the tailor after lunch and then back to work. Things were hectic around the building these days, and he didn't like to be away for any longer than was necessary. This time, however, he'd had no choice. When the boy had pushed past him and shoved a grimy note into his hand, his return to the office had to be delayed. Which was why he was now in a cab, blocks away from the Foreign Ministry.

His face darkened as he watched the city go by. The message he retrieved at the shop in Piccadilly had been brief and to the point. They wanted the package; the package that he had assured them he would be able to deliver. They were getting impatient, and he really couldn't blame them. They wanted to know where it was.

And so did he.

He'd been to Ainsworth Manor and searched the study thoroughly. There was no sign of the package there. He'd even managed to get into the library and searched that as well, but it was useless. The package was nowhere to be found. It was as if it had simply disappeared.

Yet, he knew that wasn't the case. Robert Ainsworth would never have allowed it to be misplaced. He would have realized the value of what he'd come across, and he would have made sure it was secured. The most obvious place was his country seat, but he'd been unable to locate it there. So, when the man returned to London, he had searched the Ainsworth house in Brook Street. That, too, had proved fruitless. And now he was stymied.

Where on earth had the old man stashed it? The man had thought it unlikely that Ainsworth had carried it with him when he went on that last, fateful trip to Poland, but perhaps he had. And if that was the case, heaven only knew where it was now. The room in Bern had been searched thoroughly by more than one country's agency, and no one had found anything.

The man exhaled and peered through the front windshield as the cab slowed to a stop in traffic approaching Whitehall. After taking one look at the stopped traffic, he pulled some coins out of his pocket and passed one over the seat to the driver.

"Here. I'll walk the rest of the way."

"Are you sure? It'll get moving again in a moment."

"Yes. The fresh air will do me good. Thank you."

The man climbed out of the car and started up the sidewalk.

This whole situation was the result of him trying to make himself indispensable. Given the rash of failures lately, his standing was far from secure. He had thought presenting them with the package would be an easy way to cement himself as the perfect agent. Unfortunately, he hadn't taken into account Robert Ainsworth and his love of intrigue. It really was infuriating.

The man strode through the afternoon crowds, his lips pressed into a thin line and his umbrella tapping on the pavement imperiously. He had to find the package. The message today had been very clear. He could buy himself a little bit of time, but it would have to be found and passed on to them. The only way he was getting himself out of this without the package was if he managed to land something bigger and more important, and that wasn't looking very likely at this point. Not with the way things were going in the government at the moment.

No. It had to be the package. And it had to be sooner rather than later. If Ainsworth hadn't left it in either of his own residences, the only other possibility was that he'd entrusted it to someone else's care. While that had seemed impossible a few days ago, now the man considered the prospect with new eyes as he crossed a driveway. Who would the old man have left it with? Who on earth would he have trusted enough to leave a package that could have far reaching effects for the security of the British Commonwealth?

The man shook his head and a wave of something like irritation went through him. Who would have thought that, in death, Robert Ainsworth would have the last say? It was really quite ridiculous. The man had played at being a secret agent while maintaining a very successful diplomatic career. He was hardly what one would term a master of espionage.

The man's lips tightened. And yet, here he was, empty-handed because Ainsworth had taken the secret with him to the grave.

Perhaps Robert Ainsworth hadn't been such an amateur after all.

The Oslo Affair

Chapter Seventeen

Stockholm, Sweden

Evelyn stepped out of the lift with Anna and glanced at the busy desk in the lobby.

"I just have to speak with the concierge," she said. "I'll meet you in the restaurant."

Anna nodded cheerfully and went off towards the restaurant while Evelyn turned to cross the lobby. Her elegantly simple blue evening dress and shining blonde hair drew several appreciative glances from men as she went, but she ignored them as her eyes scanned the faces of everyone she passed. Oslo may be over two hundred miles away but she knew how easily she had got here. Others could do so just as easily, and that kept her eyes moving even as a smile curved her lips.

Walking up to the desk, she stood waiting for the concierge to finish with a customer. When he had, he promptly came over to her with a smile.

"How can I assist you?"

"I'd like to send a telegram, please."

"Of course." He turned to the back counter and opened a drawer, pulling out a pad. "We can send it over to the telegraph office. It's just around the corner. Is this urgent?"

"I'd like it sent as soon as possible, yes." Evelyn picked up a pencil and began to fill out the form. "It's to my editor in London and I'm afraid I forgot to do it earlier."

"I understand. I'll have it sent immediately."

Evelyn wrote out an innocuous message in her neat, precise hand informing the reader that she had arrived at the hotel and was looking forward to a successful stay. She would have the article ready for transmission soon. She kept it short and generic, handing it to the concierge a moment later.

"Thank you so much."

He nodded and raised a hand to summon an employee over. "Of course, miss. I'll send it right away. Enjoy your dinner."

"Thank you."

She turned away as he handed the telegram to the employee who joined him, speaking to him rapidly in Swedish. As she crossed the lobby to the restaurant, the telegram was on its way to being carried out the door.

A few moments later, she was shown through a very busy restaurant to a table where Anna was just being seated.

"That was quick," Anna said as Evelyn joined her. "Were you able to send it?"

"Yes. In fact, it's already on its way to the telegraph office." Evelyn accepted the menu from the attentive waiter and smiled. "I'm absolutely famished."

The waiter said something in Swedish and Anna replied before he turned to leave. Evelyn looked across the table.

"Something about drinks?" she asked.

"Very good! You're learning. I ordered us some wine."

"Very little, I'm afraid. Only bits, here and there. Some of the words are very similar to Norwegian, which I was starting to get used to."

Anna grinned. "You have a good ear. I suspect if you stayed for a few weeks, you wouldn't need me at all."

Evelyn smiled and lowered her eyes to the menu, scanning it before giving up and setting it aside.

"And that's where my cleverness ends," she said. "I can't make head or tail of it. Do they have any beef?"

"Yes. A beef tenderloin in what looks like a delicious wine and shallot sauce," Anna said after inspecting the menu for a moment.

"Perfect!"

Anna continued to look at the menu and, while her attention was occupied, Evelyn cast a slow look around at the neighboring tables while she removed her gloves. Their fellow diners seemed to be a mix of local residents out to enjoy the superior cuisine of the hotel restaurant and other foreign travelers like themselves. There were none that appeared suspicious in anyway and Evelyn laughed silently at herself as she realized she was looking for nefarious-looking Russians and Germans behind every menu.

"I think I'll gain a ton of weight while I'm with you," Anna finally announced, setting the menu down. "Everything looks so wonderful."

"Do you go out to dinner very much?" Evelyn asked, setting her gloves with her purse on the chair beside her.

"Not very, no. Drinks, yes! But it's expensive to eat out in Oslo, as I'm sure you noticed, so I don't do it very often. Unless, of

The Oslo Affair

course, I can talk a nice, good-looking man into paying for it," she added with a grin.

The waiter returned to set down a bottle of wine and poured them each a glass before Anna gave him their dinner order. He nodded and went away again and Anna looked across the table.

"Do you eat out often?"

"I don't know if I'd say it's often, but I do enjoy a good meal in town," Evelyn said evasively. "Of course, I also count a nice pub in that."

"I think I'd enjoy England if I ever got the opportunity to visit," Anna said thoughtfully. "Is it true that everyone carries an umbrella all the time?"

Evelyn blinked and chuckled. "Well, yes, for the most part. There's nothing worse than getting caught in the rain."

"Perhaps one day I'll get to see London."

Evelyn sipped her wine. "Have you ever traveled?"

"You mean aside from Sweden and Denmark? No, not really. We went to Finland once when I was very young, but I have no memory of it."

"Do you want to?"

"Oh yes. I've always wanted to see Europe. Now I don't suppose that will be possible, at least until after the war."

Evelyn smiled dryly. "No. I wouldn't advise it just now. France is safe enough at the moment, but if Hitler decides to move then that won't last for long."

"Erik wrote in his last letter that he thinks the Germans will try to take France in the Spring. What do you think?"

"I think your brother is right," she said slowly. "If Hitler plans to attack France, he will wait until the winter is over. He can use the time to reinforce his army and air force."

"If he does, Norway and Sweden may become the safest places for you," Anna said after a moment. "You should stay! I'm sure Daniel would love to have you in the embassy."

Evelyn laughed. "I don't know if I'd like that much. It's awfully cold here."

Anna waved that away. "You'd get used to it."

"I think I'd rather not find out. I enjoy my English weather, thank you." Evelyn watched as Anna sipped her wine. "You're bored with your work at the law firm, aren't you?" she asked suddenly.

Anna looked up in surprise, her eyebrows soaring into her forehead.

"What? How did you know?"

"It was something you said. You said it was a job, nothing more." Evelyn tilted her head and considered the other woman thoughtfully. "That's why you agreed to come with me, isn't it?"

After a second of hesitation, Anna nodded.

"You have no idea how unbelievably dull it is," she complained. "I feel as though I live for the times when Daniel asks for my help. At least with him I feel like what I'm doing is important. At the firm, all I do is translate boring documents into Norwegian and type memos. I don't even get to deliver the documents to the firms in Oslo. We have a courier boy who does that."

Evelyn smiled sympathetically. Her hunch had been right. Anna was desperate to do something meaningful with her life, and secretarial work was not it.

"I know exactly how you feel. I felt the same way last year."

"And now you're here."

Evelyn nodded slowly. "And now I'm here," she agreed.

Her eyes slid past Anna as something caught her attention. She wasn't sure what had drawn her eye, but something had and Evelyn felt a strange shiver go down her spine. In an instant, she recognized it as the same chill she had felt in the street when she first caught sight of her Soviet friend.

Her lips tightened and she looked past Anna at the tables filled with laughing guests. None of them were any different than they had been, and the waiters moving between them were unexceptional. To the right, midway between their table and the door, a white column was covered with mirrored glass, reflecting the restaurant back to itself. It was a stunning display, really, and Evelyn's gaze rested on it for a long moment. Had something in the reflection caught her attention? If so, whatever - or whoever – it was was gone now. All she saw reflected were the tables and waiters between them.

"Is everything all right?" Anna asked.

"What? Yes! Yes, everything's fine. I thought I saw someone I recognized," Evelyn said easily, reaching for her wine glass. "Perfectly ridiculous, of course. I don't know a soul in Sweden."

"Not even the person you're meeting?" Anna asked, raising an eyebrow. "You know them, surely."

She mentally bit her lip. Anna was very quick, and she had been very careless to make that slip.

"Yes, of course. I wasn't thinking."

Anna nodded, her dark eyes seeing more than Evelyn wanted, and she resisted the urge to squirm in her seat.

"When are you meeting them?"

The Oslo Affair

"I actually don't know." Evelyn forced a smile. "He's going to contact me."

"Is that how this usually works?" Anna asked, lowering her voice. "Do you usually just wait for someone to contact you?"

Evelyn swallowed. She had no idea how to answer that. This was the first time she'd done anything like this, but she wasn't about to share that with the woman sitting across from her.

"Not very exciting, is it? Are you regretting coming along now?"

Anna grinned. "Not in the least. I think it all sounds thrilling! I can't wait to see how everything unfolds. Oh look! Here's our dinner."

Evelyn looked up as the waiter approached bearing a platter with their dinner and breathed a silent sigh of relief as Anna turned her attention to the food. As he laid out their plates before them, Evelyn felt that same chill go down her spine again and she looked around, scanning the restaurant casually. She might be new to this whole business, but something wasn't right. She couldn't see anything, but she could feel it.

They were being watched.

⊙

The hotel lobby was quiet when they emerged from the restaurant after a delicious dinner and dessert. They had lingered over the latter, neither woman in a hurry to go back to their room, as spacious and comfortable as it was.

"Tomorrow I think I'd like to explore the city," Anna said as they walked towards the lift. "If you haven't heard from your friend, would you care to join me?"

"If I can, I'd love to."

Evelyn smiled at the lift attendant as they approached and he nodded back. He was just closing the gates when she saw a tall man move across the lobby from the direction of the restaurant. He was walking towards the front desk and, as he passed into her line of sight, Evelyn's stomach dropped and her gut clenched. Her breath caught in her throat as she watched the nameless Soviet agent from Oslo cross the hotel lobby. It was him! There was no doubt in her mind and, as the lift churned into action, he turned his head and looked directly at her.

Evelyn's heart pounded in her chest and the blood rushed in her ears as she stared at the man through the ornate metal gate. Within seconds, the lift had passed out of sight of the lobby and she exhaled silently, her heart still pounding.

Why? Why had he followed her? When she got into the taxi outside the boarding house, she knew he was watching. Yet, she assumed that when it was clear that she was leaving Oslo, that would be an end of it. Why would he pursue her beyond Norway? He had witnessed nothing to make her an object of interest. She had assured that by evading him for two days. And yet, here he was.

Who *was* he? And why was he so interested in her?

"Are you feeling all right?" Anna asked in concern, glancing at her. "You're suddenly very pale."

Evelyn swallowed painfully and forced a bright smile.

"Am I? How strange. I feel wonderful. Far too full of good food, but wonderful just the same."

Anna laughed and nodded, turning back to watching the floors roll slowly by. Evelyn gripped her purse in her hand, feeling the trembling in her fingers, and forced herself to take a deep, silent breath. Panicking was not going to accomplish anything. She had to find out who the man was and why he had followed her all the way to Stockholm.

And then she had to find a way to get rid of him before meeting with Risto Niva.

RAF Duxford

Miles opened the door unceremoniously without knocking and strolled into the bedroom with his hat in his hand and a cigarette in his mouth.

"What in blazes is taking you so long, Young Robbie?" he demanded. "We've finally got a night off and you're wasting it. We're supposed to have left half an hour ago!"

Rob looked up from the desk where he had the evening's post spread out, a letter in his hand.

"Good Lord, I'm sorry," he exclaimed, looking at the clock. "I lost all track of time! Are the others waiting?"

Miles tossed his hat on the bed and dropped onto the foot of it, lounging back on his elbow.

"They've gone on ahead. I told them we'd be along when you finally emerged from your closet. What's so interesting that you forgot

The Oslo Affair

all about dinner in London?"

Rob snorted and tossed the letter onto the desk with the others.

"Hardly interesting. It's all estate business. Well, except that one from my mother." His eyebrows came together in a sudden frown. "I wish I could get a few days leave to go check on her."

Miles raised an eyebrow and sat up. He leaned forward with his cigarette and Rob obligingly held out an ashtray for him to put it out.

"Everything all right? She's not ill, is she?"

"No, nothing like that. She's fine."

"It's not Evelyn?" Miles asked sharply, drawing a grin from Rob.

"Fear not. As far as I know, Evie's just fine as well." Miles visibly relaxed and Rob chuckled. "Lord, she's really got to you, hasn't she? Never thought I'd see the day Miles Lacey fell like a rock. Haven't you had a letter recently?"

"No."

"Never mind. She's insanely busy as well, by the sounds of things. My mother said she's only had one letter from her herself."

"If no one's ill, what has you so bothered?" Miles asked, returning to his lounging position across the foot of Rob's bed.

"It's probably nothing," Rob said, picking up the letter again. "She said there was a break-in at the house last week."

Miles' eyebrows soared into his head. "What?"

"Someone broke into the study," Rob said with a nod. "I don't know if you remember, but the study is on the ground floor."

"Yes. It faces the terrace at the back."

"That's right. Thomas, our butler y'know, saw a light in the middle of the night and went to investigate. It was some ungodly hour and he assumed someone had simply left a lamp on. He turned it off and went back to bed. The next morning he saw the window had been forced."

"Good Lord. Was anything missing?"

"That's the strange part. Nothing was taken. They've gone through all the rooms on the first floor and absolutely nothing is missing. Mother even checked her and Evie's jewelry upstairs and everything is accounted for." Rob dropped the letter on the desk again and shook his head. "I can't make head or tail of it."

"Could the window have been left open?"

"No. The lock was broken. She's had a locksmith out to replace it, and he replaced all the locks on the ground floor while he was at it. Most of them were older than all of us, so it's just as well.

Honestly, I think that's the only reason she even told me about the whole thing. She knew I'd see the bill."

Miles sat up with a frown. "Have the police been notified?"

"Yes, but they haven't had any other incidents in the county. It's all very strange. They're saying it was probably some kids for a prank."

"Are those the kinds of pranks they get up to in Lancashire?" Miles asked, raising an eyebrow.

"They never have before." Rob sighed and ran a hand through his hair. "I feel bloody responsible. With Dad gone, now it's all up to me. I mean, they're all alone there."

"It sounds as if this isn't the norm. I wouldn't worry too much unless it happens again. The police are probably right. It was probably just some kids on a prank. If the locks have been replaced and the servants are more mindful of keeping an eye on things, everything should be fine now."

"Mmmm." Rob nodded reluctantly. "I suppose you're right. I do wish Evie was still there, though."

Miles looked at him in surprise. "Evie? Why?"

Rob glanced at him and Miles was astonished to see his face turn a dull red. He shuffled the letters on his desk together, turning his face away, and Miles' curiosity grew.

"Oh, well, she'd be company for Mum, y'know," Rob muttered. "Kind of a moral support, if you know what I mean."

"How will that help against burglars?" Miles demanded bluntly.

The color on Rob's face increased and he shrugged, still avoiding Miles' gaze.

"She's a bloody good shot, you know. Once hit a pheasant at nearly two hundred feet!"

Miles pursed his lips skeptically but let the comment pass. While he had no doubt that Evelyn was a good shot, he had a hard time picturing her roaming the manor house with a rifle tucked under her arm. This was England, not the Wild West of America. But if Rob didn't want to tell him the real reason Evelyn would be useful against potential burglars, he wouldn't pry.

Miles felt his lips twitch. He'd just have to discover the truth from Evelyn herself.

"Well, are you coming to London or not? If not, I'm leaving and you can jolly well have beans on toast for your dinner," he announced, grabbing his hat and standing.

Rob choked back a laugh and turned to lift his coat off the back of his chair.

The Oslo Affair

"I'm coming!" he exclaimed, pulling it on and opening a desk drawer to pull out his wallet. "No need for threats."

Miles grinned and followed him to the door, noticing that the color in his friend's face had returned to normal. Evelyn was getting more and more fascinating by the day. What was the big, juicy secret that made her brother turn the color of beets?

And when the bloody hell was she going to answer his letters?

At least now he knew she was as busy as they were. He supposed it stood to reason, especially if she really *was* training plotters. If he'd had time to think on it properly, he would have realized that himself. Instead, he'd sent off three letters and a gift, and had heard crickets in reply. And that was something he hadn't been expecting.

Miles Lacey was not used to having to work for his female friends. Yet he had the sneaking suspicion that that was exactly what he was going to have to do with Assistant Section Officer Ainsworth. The prospect didn't bother him one bit, and he whistled jauntily as they went down the stairs and outside to his low-slung, two-seater Jaguar.

Evelyn Ainsworth didn't stand a chance.

Chapter Eighteen

Evelyn walked out of her room dressed in wide-legged trousers and a wrap blouse, her hair loose around her shoulders. Now that she'd changed from dinner and had had time to think, she felt calmer and more poised to take on this new challenge. There were ways around having a Soviet agent watch her every move. She just had to find them.

Anna was lounging in one of the chairs, smoking a cigarette and flipping through the pages of a glossy magazine. As Evelyn walked in, she glanced up.

"I wonder if the person who set that bomb in Germany was a communist," she said. "What do you think?"

Evelyn raised an eyebrow. "Why would you think that?"

"The paper said it might have been politically motivated, and I can't think of any other political party with the nerve to do it."

Evelyn dropped onto the love seat and thought for a minute.

"It's possible. If it was a communist, that won't bode well for continued good relations with the Soviet Union. More than likely, though, it was simply another German who opposes the Führer. I'd imagine there are enough of them about."

"Do you think so?" Anna laid the magazine in her lap and looked at Evelyn. "I received the impression from those two scientists the other night that most Germans are in agreement with the Nazis."

"Why? Because they won't do anything to oppose the unfair treatment of the Jews?" Evelyn shook her head. "I don't think that necessarily means they're in agreement. I think they've been conditioned against opposing the government, but that doesn't mean they all truly support it. Rather, I think it's just like anywhere else. There are those who are Nazis, and there are those who are not."

"Erik says that to be complacent is to be complicit. I'm starting to wonder if he's not onto something there."

"I think we should be careful not to hurry into judgment of people when we aren't in possession of the full story," Evelyn said with a frown. "For instance, Herr Mayer gave me the impression the other

The Oslo Affair

evening that he was disgusted by some of the things happening in his country. Yet he was frightened enough to cancel our dinner for fear of being caught speaking with a foreign correspondent. Does that make him complicit with what the Nazis are doing? Or does it simply make him fearful for his livelihood? Who are we to judge him?"

"He canceled your dinner?" Anna sat up. "I didn't know that. What do you mean he was afraid of being caught?"

Evelyn shrugged. "He left a note at the desk. He said that he'd thought about it and decided that it would be unwise for him to meet with me without the approval of the Ministry of Propaganda."

"How strange! How would they know?"

Evelyn thought of Herr Renner and his presence in Oslo, and the Hotel Bristol in particular.

"Perhaps he thought he was being watched by the Gestapo."

Anna got up and walked over to the table between them, stubbing out her cigarette in the cut glass ashtray.

"That's a shame. So you didn't get any information from the Germans after all."

Before she could answer, there was single knock on the door and a scraping noise. Both women started and turned to look at the door in surprise.

"Who on earth is that?" Anna wondered as Evelyn got to her feet.

Evelyn didn't answer. She couldn't. Her heart was pounding too hard in her chest. No one knew they were here, except the man who had crossed the lobby as they came up from dinner.

She walked across the living room towards the door apprehensively, wondering if she should open it. Then her step checked as her eyes fell on a white envelope on the floor. It hadn't been there a moment ago.

"What's that?" Anna asked behind her, pointing to the envelope.

"I don't know." Evelyn bent to pick it up. "It must have been shoved under the door."

She turned it over to see two initials scrawled across the front: M.R.

"Well, it's for you, whatever it is," Anna said, looking over her shoulder. "How strange. Why didn't they leave it at the front desk?"

Evelyn turned to carry the envelope over to the love seat, sinking down with it in her hands. Her heart was still beating fast and she wasn't sure she wanted to open it, but she resolutely turned it over to slide her finger under the sealed flap.

"Wait!" Anna went over to the desk and returned a moment later with a long letter opener. "You'll cut yourself."

Evelyn took the opener with an amused glance at her friend. "I tend not to worry about paper cuts, to be honest."

She used the letter opener anyway, sliding the blade under the flap and slicing the envelope open in one smooth motion. She handed the blade back to Anna and pulled out a single sheet of paper.

Den Gyldene Freden. Österlånggatan, Gamla Stan. 11:00 am.

Evelyn's brows came together as she stared at the message.

"Well?" Anna asked impatiently, perching on the arm of the love seat. "What does it say?"

"I think it might be a location, but I'm not sure. I don't understand it," Evelyn said, looking up at her. "Can you read it?"

Anna all but snatched the paper out of her hand, her excitement palpable.

"Den Gyldene Freden. Well, that translates into…golden peace. Can that be right?" she frowned, staring at the message. "It looks like an address, but I don't understand the bit about golden peace. What does that mean?"

Evelyn shrugged. "I have no idea!"

Anna studied the sheet for a long moment. "I really do think it's an address," she finally said.

"Could golden peace be the name of a tavern? Like a pub?" Evelyn asked. "Strange name, but I've heard even stranger."

"I suppose it could be," Anna said, passing the sheet back. "The one thing we can be sure of is the time. There's no doubt about that."

Evelyn nodded and slipped the paper back into the envelope, standing up.

"I'll ask at the desk in the morning. If it's an address, they should be able to point me in the right direction. Do you have a lighter?"

"On the table. Why?"

Evelyn walked over to the table and picked up the lighter. She lit the corner of the envelope and watched as flames licked along the edge hungrily before making their way along the paper, turning the envelope and its contents into charred ash. After tilting it to ensure that the flames were well and truly destroying the note, she dropped it into the ash tray and watched as what remained of the envelope curled and sizzled, devoured by the fire.

The Oslo Affair

"Are you sure you should have done that?" Anna asked, breaking the silence once the envelope had disappeared completely. "What if you don't remember the name?"

"I'll remember."

Anna stood and came over to stand beside her, staring down at the ash tray.

"This is all terribly exciting, isn't it?" she asked. "Secret messages pushed under doors, strange addresses, and destroying the evidence. How thrilling!"

Evelyn looked at her, a slow grin curving her lips. "You're not afraid?"

"Not in the least! I wish I could go with you! I suppose there's no possibility of that, is there?"

"I'm afraid not," Evelyn said, shaking her head. "It's far too dangerous. I have no idea what I'll be walking into."

Anna sighed. "Very well. I'll want to know absolutely everything when you get back!"

Evelyn laughed and turned to go to her room.

"I doubt it will make as exciting listening as you think," she said over her shoulder. "I'll be surprised if they even show up. Good night!"

She went into her room and closed the door, leaning on it for a moment. Contrary to what she'd just said, Evelyn had no doubt that Risto would be there at eleven in the morning. The question was why? And would her Soviet comrade from Oslo also be in attendance?

Evelyn moved away from the door and began to get ready for bed, trying to calm her jittery nerves. This was what she had been trained to do. There was no point in lamenting the fact now. She had to go tomorrow and meet this soviet agent and find out what he knew about Stalin's intentions towards Finland. It didn't matter that another agent had followed her to Stockholm, just as it didn't matter that she had absolutely no idea where Lyakhov was or whether or not he had been the one to slip the note under the door. All that mattered was that she get as much information as she could and get back to England, uncompromised. If she could do it without sacrificing Anna's safety, all the better, but her first priority was the meeting at eleven o'clock.

And the second was avoiding her old Soviet friend.

◉

A tall man dressed in a dark suit and darker coat walked into the lobby of The Strand Hotel and looked around. It was late and the only guest traffic was on the side where the entrance to the restaurant was located. He glanced at his watch and turned to walk across the tiled floor towards the concierge desk. A single suitcase was the only luggage he carried, clasped in a leather-gloved hand. The concierge looked up as he approached and smiled politely.

"Good evening, sir," he greeted him.

"Good evening," the man said, setting his case down and removing his hat. "Pratar du tyska?" he asked in heavily accented Swedish.

"Of course," the concierge replied in German. "How may I assist you?"

"I'd like a room, please."

"Of course. Will it be only you?"

"Yes." The man pulled a long passport case out of the inside pocket of his coat and extracted his passport. "If you have something overlooking the harbor, that would be preferred."

The concierge took the offered identification and opened the registry book, turning it around to face the man.

"I think I have something that will fit your needs," he said, opening the passport and glancing down at it. "And how long will you be with us, Herr Renner?"

"I'm not sure yet. Perhaps a few nights." Renner signed the registry and set the pen down. "I'm meeting a colleague. Could you tell me if she's arrived?"

The concierge finished copying the details from his passport onto his registry card and passed the identification back to him.

"Certainly. What's the name?"

"Richardson," Renner said, tucking the passport back into his holder and sliding it into his coat pocket again. "Margaret Richardson. She's a journalist for *The Daily Mail* in London."

The concierge nodded and turned to go to a drawer on the back wall. While he was looking, Renner turned to survey the lobby. He was tired and hungry and his patience was running thin.

When he arrived this afternoon, he'd been met at the station by one of their men from the embassy. In the car on the way to the embassy, he'd been informed that new orders had come in from Berlin. He was no longer simply to observe Fraulein Richardson. He was instructed to detain her for questioning. Someone in the Abwehr, the Wehrmacht's intelligence service, wanted to know everything she knew. They already had a location, he was told. Or at least, they believed they did. One of their plants in the British embassy reported that a message

The Oslo Affair

was hand delivered to Mr. Horace Manchester, a man known to be British Intelligence. The message had been delivered this afternoon from this hotel.

"Yes indeed, Herr Renner." The concierge was back and Renner turned back to the counter with a smile. "Miss Richardson arrived this afternoon. Would you like to leave a message for her?"

"No, that's quite all right. I'll undoubtedly see her tomorrow. I just wanted to know if I was the first one here."

"Very good, sir. Here is your room key. You're in room 305, on the third floor. I think you'll enjoy it. It has a beautiful view of the harbor and the palace."

"Thank you. Is the restaurant still open?" Renner accepted the key and picked up his hat.

"Yes." The concierge checked his watch. "We will be serving for another hour yet."

Renner nodded and picked up his case, turning away from the desk and walking towards the lift. He would go to his room and leave his case and his coat, then come back down for something to eat. He hadn't eaten since noon and he knew food would go a long way to improving his temper.

Then he could determine the best way to find and detain Fraulein Richardson.

◉

When Evelyn emerged from the lift the following morning, there was no sign of her friend from Oslo. The lobby was busy with guests checking out and both managers behind the front desk were occupied. Instead of going over to wait, she looked around the lobby for a porter or other employee. Everyone appeared to engaged.

Biting her lip, she gave an internal shrug and crossed the lobby to leave through the front doors. If she couldn't find anyone in the hotel who could point her in the right direction for her meeting with Risto Niva, she would simply ask a vendor or shop keeper in the city. Someone would be able to assist her.

Stepping into the brisk morning air, Evelyn shivered and turned to go towards the news vendor where Anna had purchased her paper yesterday. The morning had dawned overcast, but the clouds were dispersing now, sliced apart by the sunlight. If the sun had its way, it would turn into a beautiful day.

She approached the news vendor, catching him without any

customers, and smiled. He nodded respectfully and said something in Swedish. With an inward sigh, she shook her head and spoke in German. She wasn't sure how prevalent English would be in the streets, but German seemed to be more common as a second language. At least, she'd found that to be the case in Norway.

"Sprichen sie Deutsch?" she asked.

"Ja." He nodded and smiled widely.

"Oh good! I'm wondering if you can help me. I'm looking for something called Den Gyldene Freden? I believe it's located in Gamla Stan, is that right?"

He nodded and stroked his chin, staring at her consideringly.

"It is. It's a tavern in the old city. On Österlånggatan." He lowered his hand and shook his head. "Not a good neighborhood, Fraulein. Are you meeting someone there?"

"Yes." Evelyn frowned and bit her lip. "Is it very bad?"

"It's not terrible, but it's not for the likes of you," he said, scratching his wiry gray hair. "You'll attract a fair bit of notice, if you don't mind my saying."

She glanced down at her clothes and nodded in sudden understanding. "Would it help if I wore something different?"

"That might do it," he agreed. "And if you're meeting someone, you won't be completely alone. You'll want to be careful, though. As I said, it's not terrible, but it's not what you're used to, I'm sure."

"Thank you. I'll be very careful."

"Well then, you want to go along here," he said, turning and pointing in the direction she had been walking. "When you get up to that road there, you'll go straight and follow this until you reach the bridge. It crosses over the water. When you get to the other side, follow the road around to the left and take it down to Slottsbacken." Here he paused and frowned, then shook his head. "It will be easier with a map," he decided, bending down and rummaging behind the table of his booth. He straightened up with a folded map in his hands. "I'll mark it out for you on this."

"Thank you so much," Evelyn said, watching as he pulled out a pencil and opened the map of the city. "I'll pay for the map, of course."

He nodded and proceeded to draw a heavy line on the map, marking out exactly where she had to go.

"It's not far. Only about a fifteen-minute walk," he said, looking up from his task. "Quite pleasant, actually, until you reach the inner roads in Gamla Stan."

He finished and handed her the map. "Do be careful, miss."

The Oslo Affair

"I will. I'll change my clothes so I'm not quite so obvious," she promised him with a smile. "Can I have a newspaper as well, please?"

He nodded and she paid him for the map and the daily paper.

"Good luck," he said as she turned away.

Evelyn tucked the map inside the newspaper and carried it in one gloved hand as she went back the way she'd come. However, instead of going back into the hotel, she continued on to the next block and turned down the street, looking for clothing shops. It was a few blocks before she found what she was looking for and she went inside quickly, glancing at her watch. She didn't have very much time, but it had to be done. The last thing she wanted was to draw attention to herself.

She supposed she should be worried about going into an apparently seedy neighborhood, but she knew something the kindly gentleman at the newsstand didn't: it took a lot to bring her down. Many very skilled fighters had tried, and failed. It was an extremely useful thing to be trained in the martial art of Wing Chun.

After looking around for a moment, Evelyn headed to the back of the store where the heavily discounted and damaged items were located. With just a bit of luck and acting, she would blend in with the locals, minimizing the likelihood of any problems before they even began.

Chapter Nineteen

Comrade Grigori walked across the lobby towards the entrance of the hotel, his brows knit together in thought. The Englishwoman must have left her room already, but he hadn't seen it. A telegram had been delivered to her door personally by one of the hotel staff and the woman staying with her had accepted it. Listening from around the corner, he heard her tell the boy that the Englishwoman wasn't in but he could leave it with her and she'd make sure she got it. When had the woman left? He'd been watching the room all morning.

The concierge had been of no help. He didn't remember seeing the woman leave either. After checking the restaurant and determining that she wasn't there, Grigori was annoyed with himself. How did he manage to lose her in a hotel? He'd followed her all the way from Oslo easily enough!

He looked up as he approached the entrance to the hotel and his eyes widened as the object of his frustration strode by the door on the sidewalk outside.

She *had* slipped past him and out of the hotel! His pace increased and he exited the hotel just in time to see her disappear around the corner at the end of the block. At least now he had her again. He turned the collar of his coat up as a gust of wind blew off the water and went after her.

Last night he'd summoned Comrade Yakov to his room for a full report. There wasn't much. Vladimir Lyakhov had arrived in Stockholm early the day before and checked into a hotel halfway across the city. From there, Yakov had nothing but complaints about the amount of walking the man had done. It seemed Comrade Lyakhov had been sightseeing most of the day, ending up at the Royal Palace across from this very hotel. He did go into The Strand, but only to go to the restaurant where he had dinner, alone. He then returned to his room midway across the city. Yakov hadn't observed any contact with anyone.

The Oslo Affair

Grigori exhaled and turned the corner, spotting his quarry a block ahead. He slowed his pace, content to keep distance between them. He didn't want her to see him. It was bad enough that she'd caught sight of him last night when he was checking into the hotel. He'd managed to avoid being seen in the restaurant while she was eating, although there was one moment when he was convinced he'd been spotted. He'd purposefully waited until they were in the lift before crossing the lobby, but the lift had been much slower than he was expecting and so now she knew he was here. There was nothing to be done about it now. It made things more difficult, but not impossible.

Between the Englishwoman and Comrade Lyakhov, he felt like he was on a wild goose chase. He was growing more and more convinced with each passing hour that there was nothing here. Lyakhov hadn't been anywhere near her since she arrived, and she hadn't made any attempt to contact *him* that they could tell. Yakov had assured him that absolutely no messages had been delivered to Lyakhov's hotel the previous day, and Grigori himself had bribed one of the employees of the hotel to alert him to any messages the Englishwoman sent out. In an effort to make a good impression, his new friend had discovered that she had sent two messages out yesterday: one to her editor in London and one to the British embassy here in Stockholm. Neither of them could have made their way into Lyakhov's hands. No. Comrade Grigori was confident that there had been no contact initiated between them.

He crossed an intersection and continued to trail the elegant blonde woman ahead. Unless Yakov turned up something today, or he himself observed something irrefutable, Grigori was going to call this whole thing off. It was a waste of time and resources when he could be tracking down the real traitor.

He watched as the Englishwoman paused on the sidewalk and looked into a shop window before she continued on. This one may be slippery and may possibly even be a British agent, although he had his doubts, but she'd shown no interest at all in the Soviet comrades in Oslo. In fact, she seemed far more interested in the German scientists. That made perfect sense if she was indeed an agent, but Grigori would be impressed if that was the case. She was clearly from aristocratic breeding. She held herself in a manner that bespoke privilege, and her clothes looked as if they had been tailored just for her. He would place her more firmly in a category with rich, bored socialites than with intelligence agents.

He was still mulling over this two blocks later when she paused once again on the sidewalk before going into a shop. Glancing at the oncoming traffic, Grigori jogged across the wide road to the other side and moved along until he was parallel with the store. It was a woman's clothing store. He looked at his watch, then looked at the little bakery behind him. After one last glance at the store across the street, he turned and went into the bakery. It would be easier to watch from inside than out, and as he stepped into the shop the sweet, warm smell of freshly baked breads and pastry assaulted him.

Watching out of the corner of his eye through the front window, he turned to look at the rows of baked goods on display behind the counter. The Englishwoman would be a while. She would want to try clothes on. They always did. He had plenty of time to select something to ease his hunger while he waited.

After purchasing some pastry and half a loaf of brown bread that looked very similar to his favorite loaf in Moscow, he turned to leave the bakery. He had taken his time and spent over twenty minutes in the shop, but there was still no sign of her.

He stepped outside with the bag in his hand and frowned, looking at his watch again. He turned to walk to the next shop and went in, still keeping an eye on the store front across the road. Looking around, he found himself in a tobacconist. Ten minutes later, he emerged with a selection of cigarettes and one cigar, but still no sign of his quarry.

His lips tightened and he was debating the risk of going across the street and looking into the store window to see if he could see her when the door to the shop opened. He turned to walk a few steps, looking sideways under his hat. The customer exiting the shop was not the Englishwoman. She was a working girl, dressed in an ill-fitting skirt and shabby sweater with woolen stockings and very dull, sensible shoes. She carried a large handbag over her arm that looked as if it had seen better days, and clasped a newspaper in one hand. This woman was a far cry from the elegant, perfectly tailored woman he had been following for four days. After pausing outside the shop to straighten her hat, she turned to stride down the sidewalk. As she did so, Grigori noticed that the hand carrying the newspaper was covered with a soft leather glove.

His lips pursed and his brows snapped together as he turned to walk in the same direction, glancing at the shop once more as he did so. The woman who came out of the shop was about as far removed from Maggie Richardson as was possible, and yet something made Grigori turn his gaze back to her.

It was the gloves. The entire outfit was sensible, warm and completely unremarkable, but she was wearing leather gloves that were

The Oslo Affair

at complete odds with the rest of the clothing. Another gust of wind tore down the street and the woman raised her free hand to hold a plain brown hat on her head as she walked. The wind grabbed a lock of blonde hair and whipped it out from under the hat, and Grigori stared.

It couldn't be her. And yet…something told him that it was. The gloves, the hair, they both were compelling reasons to risk losing his quarry and follow her instead. And yet, that wasn't what made Comrade Grigori continue down the opposite side of the road, his eyes fixed on the woman. It was the clenching in his gut. Something wasn't right with this new development.

And Comrade Grigori had learned long ago not to dismiss that particular feeling.

⊙

Anna tossed the magazine she was looking at onto the table and sighed. Maggie had been gone for an hour and, in that time, she had checked her watch no less than twenty times. She couldn't concentrate on the store of magazines the hotel had provided. All she could think about was what her new friend was doing and whether or not she would find the address with the strange name. Something peace, wasn't it?

Shaking her head, she got up and went over to the French doors that lead out to the balcony. Maggie had left after a breakfast in their rooms just as calm as you please, as if she were merely going to the corner shop for a pack of cigarettes. Anna, on the other hand, had been brimming with pent-up excitement all morning. How could she be so calm? It was all so terribly exciting! First a secret note passed under the door, then leaving to go to an assigned meet. It was just like in the films!

Anna stared across the water at the Royal Palace in the distance. Not ten minutes after she left, a porter had knocked on the door with a telegram for Miss Margaret Richardson, marked urgent. She glanced over at the desk where the sealed message lay. Terrible luck that it had missed Maggie by a few minutes. Turning away from the doors, Anna went over to the table and picked up her cigarette case. She was opening it to take one out when the restlessness welling inside her got the better of her.

Dropping the case back on the table, she let out an impatient noise and turned to go into her bedroom. She couldn't do it. She couldn't stay cooped up in this room, as luxurious as it was, simply waiting. If she didn't get out and stretch her legs and get her mind off it, Anna was convinced she would go absolutely mad.

Grabbing her hat, she secured it on her head with a sturdy hat pin and turned to get her coat from the tall armoire. She would go out and look around the city, take in the sights, and by the time she returned, Maggie would be back.

She walked into the sitting room and her eye fell on the telegram sitting on the desk. She hesitated, looking at it consideringly. It didn't seem safe to leave it there, where a maid could see it. It *was* marked urgent, after all. She was probably being silly, but she thought of the spy novels she liked to read and an image of masked men ransacking the hotel room came to mind. Without another thought, she crossed the room and took the telegram, tucking it into her purse with her cigarettes.

Five minutes later, Anna emerged from the stairwell next to the lift, the stairs preferable to the lift due to the excess of nervous energy. She bent her head to button her coat as she began to walk across the lobby towards the door. When she lifted her head, she found herself staring straight at a tall man in a long black coat who had just come in from the street. Her step checked and she frowned. He was very familiar. She'd seen him before. But where?

Anna moved to the side and stepped behind a column, looking around it at the man. She didn't want to be caught staring, but she wanted to remember why he was so familiar. He hadn't noticed her and was crossing the floor, heading towards her side of the lobby. He turned his head in her direction, glancing towards the lift, and Anna gasped softly. She *did* know him! She'd seen him at the Hotel Bristol when she and Maggie were chatting with the two Germans. She'd noticed him because she thought he was terribly good-looking, and he'd somehow managed to be in their vicinity all evening. He'd never once looked in her direction, although she remembered she kept glancing at him all night. He'd been sitting with two other Germans, she recalled, and they had kept his attention.

What on earth was he doing here?

"Herr Renner!"

A short man came up behind Anna, walking towards the tall man. He passed her without a glance and joined the tall man on the other side of the wide column.

"Is everything in place?" Herr Renner asked in German, removing his gloves.

He looked towards the lift again and Anna moved unobtrusively to her right until she was completely concealed by the

The Oslo Affair

column. So his name was Renner, and he *was* German. But why was he *here*?

"Yes, just as we discussed. I have someone watching the back stairs and someone watching the lift. Otto is on the corner near the newspaper vendor. He has a clear view of the entrance. Franz is in the back alley, although I really don't think we need to worry about her going that way."

"You know as well as I do that it's better to have all the exits covered. Is she in her room?"

"No. There was a telegram delivered earlier and the boy had to leave it with her companion."

"Companion?" Renner's voice was sharp. "What companion?"

"Another woman. I haven't seen her yet." There was a hesitation and the rustling of paper as if the other man was looking through a notepad. "Tall with brown hair."

"That describes half the women in the hotel. See if you can get a better description or get a look at her yourself," Renner ordered. "Is she still in the room?"

"Yes."

"Take care of it, then. Deliver something for the Englishwoman. Perhaps some fruit, complements of the hotel? I'm sure you can think of something."

"Yes, Herr Renner." There was the distinct sound of a notebook snapping shut. "And when the Englishwoman returns?"

"Inform me immediately. I'll be in my room. Don't approach her. Let her go to her room. We can't afford a scene. I'll handle it once she's back."

"Understood."

The two men parted, the short one going towards the front desk and Herr Renner moving towards the lift. As he went past the column, Anna moved around it, keeping the column between them. She didn't know if he ever noticed her in the restaurant in Oslo, but she wasn't about to take any chances now.

When he had gone, she walked towards the entrance of the hotel, bending her head to pull on her gloves as she walked. Her heart was pounding and it took everything she had not to look back over her shoulder to see if someone was watching. Keeping her gaze on her hands, she finished buttoning her gloves and looked up to find herself at the door. With an exhale, she pushed it open and stepped out onto the street.

A gust of wind smacked her in her face and she shivered, burying her hands in her pockets. She glanced to the right and her eyes went to the vendor where she bought the paper yesterday. He had two customers buying papers and her gaze went beyond him, looking for the mysterious Otto. She was just turning to walk in the opposite direction when she spotted a man in a dark coat sitting on a bench across the street, near the water. He had a paper open before him, but he didn't seem very interested in the news. He was looking at the hotel.

Anna walked away, her head spinning and her breath coming short and fast. Who was Herr Renner? And what did he want with Maggie? It wasn't a good thing, that much she was sure of. The Germans weren't in the habit of following women over two hundred miles into another country unless that woman had something they wanted. And now they had the hotel surrounded! There was no way Maggie could get back in without being seen, and it was only luck and timing that had allowed her to get out when she did. She must have left the room while the short one was still arranging for it to be watched. Talk about a perfect window of opportunity! And she hadn't even been aware of any of it!

Biting her lip as she turned the corner, Anna forced herself to try to think clearly. Maggie was in serious trouble, and she didn't even know it yet. As far as Anna could see, she was the only person capable of standing between the Germans and Maggie right now. But how was she going to warn her when she didn't even know where she'd gone?

Her step checked and her lips parted on a quick inhale. Of course! She *did* know where she went. She didn't know the exact location, but she knew the street and the neighborhood. That would be enough to make it possible to head her off before she went back to the hotel and into the Nazi trap waiting for her.

Looking both ways, Anna spotted a break in the traffic and ran across the road quickly to a cafe. She would ask for directions to Gamla Stan and hope for a bit of luck.

◉

Vladimir looked at his watch and stifled a yawn. He'd been up and out of the hotel just as dawn was lightening the sky, leading his tail over half the city. Comrade Yakov really was slipping. He used to be invisible. He was the one they called when they absolutely could not let a subject know they were being watched. They called him The Ghost.

Well, he wasn't anymore. Now he was more like an ox.

He had spotted him on the first day in Oslo, almost as soon as he got off the train. It had been a few years, but he recognized him

The Oslo Affair

easily. Aside from more gray hair and a new set of jowls, Yakov looked the same as he always had. As soon as he saw him, Vladimir knew he was under investigation. He'd been waiting for it. It was inevitable. They would all be investigated until the traitor passing secrets to the British was found. It was a witch hunt, and the Soviets were very good at witch hunts.

Pulling a pack of cigarettes from his pocket, he gazed out of the window at the building across the street. Den Gyldene Freden, or The Golden Peace, was a tavern that had been serving food and drink to the people of Gamla Stan, or the old city, since the 1700s. Named for the Peace of Nystad between Sweden and Russia in 1721, it had withstood the tests of time, age, and the decline of the area around it. When Niva agreed to meet with the British agent to discuss the situation along the border of Finland, Vladimir had suggested the tavern as a possible meeting place. It was deep in the narrow, winding streets of the old part of the city where they were very unlikely to run across anyone from an embassy or consulate. The neighborhood was slowly rotting, the ancient buildings having fallen into decay over the centuries as the bustling medieval center turned into overcrowded streets and the noblemen moved their residences to other sections of the city.

Vladimir lit a cigarette and watched as Risto Niva approached the tavern. He looked around the street before disappearing inside and Vladimir blew a stream of smoke out of the side of his mouth. Niva was in place. Now he had to wait for the girl.

Evelyn Ainsworth was not what he had been expecting. He had seen photographs, presented by a proud father, and heard stories about the young woman, but he had somehow been expecting someone rather ordinary. Oh, not in appearance. Her beauty had been evident in every photo he looked at. But rather in demeanor. It was one thing for a proud father to expound on his daughter's intelligence and quickness of wit. It was to be expected. But the reality very rarely lived up to the accolades, at least in his experience. In Evelyn's case, though, it appeared that perhaps her doting father had been modest in his praise. Vladimir had been particularly impressed with how quickly she grasped the importance of meeting with Niva and learning what she could about the situation on the border between Finland and Soviet Russia. There had been no hesitation. For someone new to this game, she was very quick indeed.

He glanced at his watch again and settled back in the rickety old wooden chair that he'd dragged over to the window. He sat just out of sight from the street with a view of the entire corner building were the tavern was located. Studying the people in the street and the old building on the opposite corner that looked as if it had been a large and heavily fortified bank at one time, he looked for any signs that Niva had been followed and saw none. Sucking on his cigarette, he stared down thoughtfully. It didn't appear as if the witch hunt had expanded to the agents posted in other countries. Yet. Only the ones in Moscow were being watched.

He had to be very careful now. It wasn't like it was when Robert was still alive. Then he'd had an iron-clad reason for talking to a British agent, one that was beyond question. It had been ordered at the highest level. But now Robert was dead and, with him, his mission. He had to be very shrewd in how he went about his dealings with the daughter. Just one slip and he would end up in the Gulag, or worse.

Vladimir frowned suddenly and leaned forward, his eyes fixed on a slight figure moving through the crowded street. There was nothing remarkable about the woman. In fact, he wasn't even sure what it was that drew his attention to her instead of the twenty other women who looked just like her. After watching intently for a few moments as she made her way down the street, he realized what it was that had caught his eye. She was moving through the crowds with a very precise and confident stride, filled with assurance. It was the kind of assurance that could never be taught or imitated. It was the assurance inherent in knowing that one was able to defend oneself against most attacks. It was the assurance of knowing that she had complete and utter control over every movement her body made, and that that control had been tested repeatedly and not failed. It was the assurance of a woman who had been extensively trained in a fighting art.

He sat back and a small smile played on his lips. The daughter had many talents indeed. If he didn't know of her unusual background, she would never have drawn his attention. She blended in with the people around her so well that it was doubtful that anyone would ever look twice at her.

Robert's daughter had certainly adjusted to her new role with ease. He blew out smoke and watched as she crossed the street to the corner building across from his. She would do well in this war. And he now felt much more comfortable with her as his sole contact in the West.

For that was what she was now. He couldn't risk dealing with anyone else, nor was he about to let a talent like hers slip through his fingers.

The Oslo Affair

Chapter Twenty

Evelyn opened the heavy, old wooden door and went into the building. Immediately confronting her was a flight of stone steps leading down, and a narrow hallway to the left leading to the back of the building. She hesitated, unsure which path to take, but the smell of onions and the sound of voices wafting up from the stairs decided her. Taking a deep breath and trying to ignore the almost overwhelming feeling of apprehension that rolled over her, she started down the narrow steps. She was here and to back out now would be the height of cowardice. And she had never been accused of being a coward in her life.

Reaching the bottom, Evelyn stepped into a large cavern with low lighting and heavy, scarred wooden tables and benches. A bar ran along one side of the room and two serving girls moved through the tables, delivering plates of food. She was surprised at the amount of people in the underground tavern. Given the surrounding neighborhood, she hadn't expected much of a lunch crowd.

Looking around, Evelyn realized with a sinking heart that she had no idea who she was looking for. She didn't even have a general description. Her palms grew damp in her gloves as she stood there, her heart rate increasing in proportion with her sudden anxiety.

"Richardson?" a voice asked behind her and she turned sharply to see an older man with an apron wrapped around his waist.

"Yes?"

"Följ mig."

She had no idea what he said, but his actions made it clear that he wanted her to follow him. Walking behind him, Evelyn scanned the tables, looking for anything that would indicate she was being watched, and saw nothing. Aside from one or two curious looks as they passed, there was no sign of undue interest in her arrival. Exhaling silently, she breathed a little easier as the man led her through the tables to one in the far corner. There, partially concealed by the curve of the wall, sat a man with dark hair and a pencil mustache.

Waving her to the table, the man in the apron turned to leave, saying something in Swedish over his shoulder. The man at the table nodded and said something in return, standing as Evelyn approached.

"Miss Richardson?"

He spoke in Russian and Evelyn nodded, seating herself so that she was across from him but could still see the rest of the room.

"Yes."

"I'm Risto Niva. You can call me Niva. Everyone does." He took his seat and looked at her appreciatively. "I was beginning to think you weren't coming."

Evelyn smiled tentatively. "I'm sorry I'm a few minutes late. I had to make a stop on the way."

"Your Russian is very good. Have you spent time there?"

"No. I've not had the opportunity. I studied under a woman who lived in Moscow."

"You must be a very good student. The owner is bringing lunch. Have you eaten?"

"Yes, but please don't let that stop you."

Niva studied her across the table, his lips pursed together thoughtfully.

"You're not what I expected," he finally said. "Vladimir said I would be surprised. He was right."

"What were you expecting?"

"A man in a tweed coat with a pipe," he answered promptly, drawing a laugh from her. "I'm very pleased that you're not. I'd much rather have lunch with a beautiful young woman."

Evelyn murmured thanks for the compliment as a bar maid came to the table and set down two glasses filled with a berry colored liquid and large plate of dark brown, crusty bread. He said something to her in Swedish and she nodded before turning away. Once she'd gone, Niva motioned to the glass.

"I ordered a local drink. It's made from berries, I believe. I hope you like it. I find it refreshing."

Evelyn lifted the glass and sniffed the liquid inside. It smelled sweet and something like flowers. Sipping it, she was pleasantly surprised at the mildly sweet berry taste.

"It's good," she said, setting the glass down. "What is it?"

He shrugged with a grin. "I have no idea. There is something similar in Finland, but it is much stronger. I think this is made with lingonberries, but I am not sure. I'm glad you like it."

"I understand you live in Turku?" she asked after a moment. "That's on the coast, isn't it?"

The Oslo Affair

"Yes. It sits on the Aura River. It's an amazing city. It was once the capital of what is now Finland. The capital was moved to Helsinki in the 1800s. Now it is a major regional city in its own right."

"How long have you been there?"

"About five years now." Niva sipped his drink and shrugged. "It is nice there, but I fear that things are on the brink of changing."

"Things are changing everywhere," Evelyn said soberly. "The world is changing rapidly."

The barmaid returned then and set a bowl of thick stew down before Niva. She placed a thick wooden cutting board with cheese on it in the center of the table, then nodded and disappeared again.

"That's the truth," he said as if they hadn't been interrupted. "Did you see that someone tried to assassinate Hitler? We are living in unsettled times."

"Is that why you agreed to meet with me?" she asked softly.

He glanced up from his stew. "Among other reasons."

Evelyn considered him for a long moment. "Are you having second thoughts?"

"About meeting with you? No." Niva shook his head and reached for the bread, cutting a thick piece off with his knife. "About my country and the path our leaders have chosen? Yes."

Understanding dawned. "You're looking for a way out."

"You're very quick." He dipped his bread into his stew and took a bite. After a moment, he swallowed and met her gaze across the table. "I've become disillusioned with Stalin and his ministers. I don't see anything good coming from their policies. I'm a realistic man. I have no family to speak of, and I see no reason to remain in the Soviet Union."

He left the statement there and returned to his lunch, his meaning clear. Evelyn swallowed and reached for her drink.

"I have to contact my superiors," she said after a moment. "I can't promise anything. It would be better if I had something to give them in return."

"Of course." He picked up a napkin and wiped his mouth, reaching for his glass. After taking a long drink, he reached inside his coat to pull out what looked like several papers rolled into a tight tube. He set it on the table. "These are copies of orders that have come through over the past three weeks from Moscow," he told her in a low voice. "They tell the story on their own. Take them and give them to your handler."

Evelyn looked at the roll on the scarred table and shot a quick look around the tavern. All the other patrons were eating and drinking and no one was paying them the least amount of attention. After a moment's hesitation, she reached out and picked up the roll, putting it in her large bag. Niva nodded in approval.

"Moscow is getting tired of Kallio and his refusal to agree to their terms," he said, keeping his voice low. "They're making plans to force Finland into giving up the land in the Karelian Isthmus. The general feeling is that they tried to make an agreement and, since Kallio won't go along, they'll take it by force."

"How?"

"Do you know how the Germans justified their invasion of Poland?" Niva asked.

"They claimed the Polish attacked them first," she said. "Hitler said regular Polish troops attacked a transmitter in Gleiwitz, a town bordering Poland."

"That's what he said, yes." He reached for the bread again. "In actual fact, the attack was staged by the SS. They killed several prisoners and drove the bodies to Gleiwitz. SD men dressed in Polish uniforms then stormed the radio station there, supposedly killing the Germans in the attack."

Evelyn stared at him. This was something she hadn't been told when the frenzy of facts and misinformation flooded into England in those chaotic days immediately following Hitler's invasion of Poland. Although everyone knew that the supposed attack was an excuse to invade Poland, she had assumed the attack had still occurred as stated.

"The SS staged it?" she asked, stunned.

"Yes. Not just there, but also in several other locations," he said with a nod. "They were all staged by the SS and SD."

Evelyn sat back in her chair, her mind spinning. Through her astonishment, one thought came to the surface. She raised her eyes to his.

"Stalin is going to use the same tactic to invade Finland, isn't he?"

He met her gaze and said nothing. He didn't need to. They both knew the truth.

"Do you know a location?"

"No. It will be somewhere near to Leningrad, but the exact location is being closely guarded."

"When?"

"Soon. Planning is underway, as those transmissions I gave you will show. If I had to offer an educated guess, I'd say within the next few weeks."

The Oslo Affair

Evelyn exhaled. A few weeks? There was no way England could intervene in time. Chamberlain would never approve getting involved with an altercation against the Soviets without any provocation.

"Tell me, how is it that you are here?" Niva asked suddenly, sitting back in his chair and looking at her thoughtfully.

She raised an eyebrow and looked at him in surprise. "You know why I'm here."

"That's not what I mean. Why are you doing this?"

She was silent for a long moment. He was asking her why she was working for British secret intelligence, and she wasn't about to try to explain something she didn't quite understand herself, especially to a man who was so willing to defect from his own country.

"I don't think it matters why I'm here, does it?" she finally asked briskly.

He smiled faintly. "No, I suppose not," he agreed. "Tell me, what's it like in London now? Since the war began, I mean? Has it changed much?"

Evelyn thought for a moment, her brows coming together.

"Aside from the blackout? No, not really. It seems to be business as usual."

"No protests? No signs of disapproval with the war?"

"None," she said firmly.

"Interesting," he said thoughtfully, and she raised her eyebrow in reaction.

"Why do you say that?"

"We've been under the impression that the general feeling among the people in England is that they don't support the war."

Evelyn frowned. "What gave you that impression?"

The smile that crossed his face unnerved her. "The reports from our people in London."

She stared at him, feeling her skin grow cold.

"People?" she repeated, feeling very dumb.

He nodded calmly, his eyes on her face.

"Yes. You didn't think Moscow was operating blind as regards England, did you?" he asked softly. "Well, I can see that you did. You're surprised."

He leaned forward and pushed the bowl of stew out of his way.

"Let me give you one more piece of information that you might take to your superiors," he said, his voice low and his eyes serious. "Don't trust anyone in London. You have a rat in your ship, and it is very well hidden. I would hate to see a lovely thing like you fall into the hands of the SS, or the NKVD. They would destroy you, and what a waste that would be."

Evelyn swallowed, her mouth suddenly dry. "Am I in danger?"

He sat back again.

"Everyone is in danger," he told her. "The question isn't whether or not you are at risk. It is who you are at risk from, and whether or not you are prepared for what may come."

Oslo, Norway

Daniel Carew looked up from his desk when a short knock was immediately followed by the door swinging open. He raised his brows in surprise at the sight of a clerk who seemed to be very out of breath.

"Excuse me, sir," he gasped, coming quickly into the office. "This arrived a few minutes ago. I was told to bring it straight to you."

He held in his hands a rather thick package wrapped in brown paper and Daniel frowned, standing. He came around from behind the desk and took the package from the clerk.

"Who delivered it?"

"I don't know, sir. Someone banged on the door and when I opened it, they shoved it at me and ran away again." The clerk shrugged. "It was a man, but I didn't get a good look at him."

Daniel turned the package over and found his name scrawled across the front.

"All right. Thank you. You may go."

He turned to go back to his desk as the clerk left the office, closing the door softly behind him. Daniel set the parcel on his desk and slowly sank down into his chair.

So it had happened. The message from the unknown sender had been fulfilled.

He sat back in his chair and stared at the package. When he received the message almost a week ago now, he'd thought it might be some kind of prank. It had been mailed through the post with no indication as to the author. Typed on plain paper, the text had been short and to the point. If he arranged for a slight change in the BBC's German broadcast, he would receive a report on German military and scientific advancements. Although skeptical, the requested change was so minor that Daniel had contacted MI6 in London and they had

The Oslo Affair

arranged for it to be done. Changing the introduction of the broadcast to "Hullo, hier ist London" for one broadcast seemed a simple enough task in return for the possibility of gaining valuable information.

Now, apparently, here was the result.

He leaned forward and picked up the parcel, feeling the contents through the wrapping. There was more than just paper inside. A lump indicated something small and hard was included. Tearing open the brown covering, he extracted several typed sheets of paper and discovered that the hard lump appeared to be a mechanical or electrical tube of some sort. Holding it up, he examined it carefully, his lips pressed together. It looked very similar to a vacuum tube.

Setting it on the desk, he sat back with the typed pages and began to read through them. As he read, his interest grew. This wasn't some vague account from a disgruntled factory worker. The pages contained specific details in several different areas, including airplanes, ships, bombs and rockets. The information included was so specialized that he strongly suspected it was, in fact, written by a scientist.

Daniel went back to the beginning of the report and began to read through it again, this time slowly and more carefully. With each page, his excitement grew as he realized that the information in his hands was something that came directly from Berlin. Reaching the last section of the report, he read about electric fuses and how they were being used in artillery shells and bombs instead of mechanical fuses.

Lifting his eyes, he picked up the tube and looked at it consideringly. Could it be an electric fuse? Or was is part of something else? The report described several different technologies that were being tested in Germany for use in their weapons. This could be an example of a component of any of them.

Daniel set the tube down again and dropped the report on the desk next to it. What an amazing stroke of luck! He had no idea who the anonymous benefactor was, but it was clear that they were well-versed in science and technology. In fact, the understanding they revealed regarding the use of radar alone was outstanding. The author had included details in their report which would enable them to develop countermeasures, showing his knowledge of how such countermeasures could be developed. In addition, he included several locations which could, if targeted, deliver crippling blows to the military production of the Reich.

In all, the report was filled with information that Daniel felt was highly valuable. And it had been given to them freely.

He leaned forward and took a cigarette from the box on his desk, fishing in his pocket for a lighter. It didn't escape his notice that this report had been delivered in the midst of a scientific convention in Oslo. Nor did he think that it was simply coincidence. Somewhere in the city was a German citizen who opposed the Nazis enough to risk what was probably a very good scientific career to pass information on to England. They had done so knowing that the consequences of being caught included death.

Lighting his cigarette, Daniel sat back and stared at the pile on his desk. Who would have thought that Oslo would have turned into such a hotbed of activity in a mere few days? Not only had this golden egg landed on his desk, but the agent from London was actively pursuing a viable Soviet lead which she gained right here in the city. In the past two months, none of the agents sent over from London had uncovered so much as a stray code. Now, in the course of a few days, they had gathered more intelligence than they had in months.

What a turn of events!

The Oslo Affair

Chapter Twenty-One

Evelyn walked along the street with her hands in the pockets of the short, shabby coat she had purchased from the damaged rack. What it lacked in style, it barely made up for in warmth. While blocking the worst of the gusts of icy wind, the fabric was thin and, after repeated onslaught, the cold seeped through until she was shivering. Missing her warm English wool coat with the soft warm lining, she reflected on how ridiculous it was that she was walking along freezing when the means to be comfortable was contained in the large bag over her arm. She briefly debated stopping and exchanging the cheap coat for her real thing, but another look at her surroundings convinced her not to. Once she was across the bridge and back in more gentile surroundings she could go somewhere and change back into her clothes. Until then, she would have to shiver.

All the chills coursing through her weren't necessarily the result of the frigid temperatures. Some of them were caused by Niva's statement that the Soviets had a spy entrenched in London. He had told her almost as an after-thought, as if it was a well-known fact. Obviously for them it was, but for her it was not. And she was willing to wager that Jasper Montclair was unaware of any moles in the government.

The most natural thing for her to do would have been to dismiss the statement as untrue. Yet, it actually made sense. The Soviet agent in Oslo had known she was there almost immediately. How else could that be? She and Daniel had thought as much when he sent the first message to London, informing them that she was being followed. They assumed the fault was in Oslo, but what if it were in London?

Then there was the issue of Herr Renner. How had *he* known she was in Oslo? Evelyn frowned as she walked along the road that would bring her to the bridge and back to the hotel. If the spy Niva referred to was a Soviet agent, how did Renner know about her? Was there another one? A German? Or had he discovered her through chance once she was already in Norway?

So many questions without answers, and now there was the question of who could be trusted and who might be working for either the Soviets or the Germans. She shook her head and tried not to let a feeling of helplessness overwhelm her. She may not know who in London could be trusted, but she at least knew she could trust Bill. Of that she had no doubt. The rest? Well, that was a problem to be addressed when she arrived back in England. Right now, she had more pressing matters to be concerned with.

Like how her Soviet friend had followed her from Oslo, and why.

Evelyn exhaled and glanced up at the bridge ahead. Once she was across it, she would search out a cafe with a restroom where she could change back into her own clothes. While these had served their purpose beautifully, the coarse fabric was rubbing her skin, and she wanted to scratch the back of her neck where the rough label was cutting into her. With that in mind, she quickened her pace.

What about Anna? The thought popped into her head without warning and Evelyn pressed her lips together. Where did Anna fit into all this? Was she simply bored, just as she had said? Or was *she* the reason Renner knew she was in Norway? As much as she liked the woman, did she know that she could really trust her? Daniel Carew trusted her, but was that enough?

Evelyn looked up as she approached the bridge and her step checked as Anna herself stepped away from the railing at the foot of the bridge. Her eyes were on Evelyn and she hurried forward quickly.

"Oh thank God!" she exclaimed, reaching her. "I've been standing here for over half an hour and I don't think I can feel my feet!"

Evelyn blinked and automatically looked down at the woman's fashionable, but not very sensible, shoes.

"Why are you here?" she asked, bringing her gaze back to Anna's face. "What are you doing?"

"I've come to warn you," Anna said, tucking her arm through Evelyn's and guiding her to the side of the walkway leading to the bridge. "I didn't know where else to try to intercept you. I remembered the name of the street from the message and asked at a cafe. They told me this bridge was really the only way in and out of the old city, without going miles in another direction. So I decided to wait here, knowing you'd have to come back this way. Wasn't that clever of me?"

"Very. But why?"

"Why, to stop you from walking into a trap, of course!"

The Oslo Affair

Evelyn felt like she was trapped in some kind of practical joke. "Oh, well, of course," she muttered sarcastically, drawing a laugh from Anna.

"I suppose that did sound rather silly," she admitted. "Let me start from the beginning."

"That would be good."

"After you left, I tried to read a magazine but just couldn't concentrate. I was too excited."

Evelyn raised her eyebrows and Anna shrugged defensively.

"This might be normal for you, but I've never been part of anything so clandestine before! It's all terribly exciting to me. I couldn't settle down and finally decided that I would go mad if I stayed in the room. So I left to get some air and do some sightseeing."

"That sounds reasonable."

"Well, when I got to the lobby I saw someone I recognized."

Evelyn looked at her sharply. "What? Who?"

"A man I saw at the Hotel Bristol when we had dinner that night. Remember when we were having drinks with those scientists? There was a man a few tables away. I noticed him because, well, I thought he was attractive." Anna paused for a moment, then made a face. "I was a little put out because he didn't take any notice of me, but now I'm glad he didn't."

"Who is he?"

"His name is Herr Renner, and he's a German," Anna said. "I think he might be Gestapo."

Evelyn stared at her, taken aback, and felt the color draining from her face. She had been expecting to hear a description of her soviet companion. Hearing instead that the tall German had also followed her sent a streak of fear through her.

"Renner?"

Anna nodded, frowning at the look on Evelyn's face. "You know him?"

"No, not really," she said, shaking her head. "I bumped into him at the Hotel Bristol the night Herr Mayer canceled dinner. I didn't think anything of it, until he turned up at the boarding house the night we left Oslo."

Anna's mouth dropped open. "He was there? At the Kolstad's?"

"Yes. I ran into him at the top of the stairs. He was staying there."

"That's terrifying," Anna said decidedly.

"I don't know about terrifying," Evelyn said dryly. "Unnerving, perhaps."

"That's because you don't know the rest!" Anna grabbed her arm. "Listen to me! I overheard him talking in the lobby. He was talking to someone, a short little man, and they were talking about how they were going to trap 'the Englishwoman.'"

Evelyn's blood ran cold and her mouth went dry. "The Englishwoman? That's what he said?"

"Yes. It can't be a coincidence. He *must* have been talking about you."

"Trap? What kind of trap?"

"They've got people watching all the entrances of the hotel, looking for you. As soon as you go back, they'll notify Herr Renner and he said that he would take it from there." Anna bit her lip, her forehead creased in worry. "I don't know what they're planning, but I'm frightened. I think they mean to take you."

Evelyn leaned against the railing along the water and tried to think clearly. The cold wind suddenly felt good on her face, cooling her flushed cheeks and acting as a cold compress. If Renner had all the exits covered in the hotel, she couldn't go back. At least, not as it stood right now. She would have to be invisible. Yet, she had to go back. She needed her toiletry bag!

A wave of panic rolled over her. The microfilm! What if they had searched her room and found it?

Turning, she grabbed Anna's arm. "Do they know you left?" she demanded.

Anna looked startled. "I don't know. Possibly. Herr Renner told the short man to go to the room and try to get a better description of me. He wanted to know what I look like."

"If he did, they know you went out as well." Evelyn dropped her hand and turned her attention to stare over the water. "Damn!"

"Why? What is it?"

"Nothing. I need to get back into the hotel."

"Yes, but how? They'll see you and that's what they're waiting for." Anna stopped and looked at her. "Even dressed as you are, you're still recognizable. Why *are* you wearing those ridiculous clothes?"

Evelyn glanced down at herself and laughed shortly. "To fit in with the locals. I was told the neighborhood I was going to wasn't a place someone of my stature would frequent."

Anna nodded. "I was told it was a slum," she said bluntly. "Was it?"

"It certainly wasn't what I'm used to."

The Oslo Affair

Anna was silent for a moment, then she shook her head. "What are we going to do? Perhaps I can go back and get everything from the room?"

Evelyn was shaking her head before she had even finished.

"He'll have got a description from one of the hotel employees by now. They'll be looking for you as well. If you try to clean the room out, they'll stop you."

"Then we go without our things. That's the only other option."

"That's not an option. I need my bags. There's...something important in them."

"What's so important that—" Anna broke off suddenly with a gasp. "Å gud! I completely forgot! A telegram came for you not ten minutes after you left!"

Evelyn's head snapped around. "What?"

"Yes. I have it here." Anna opened her purse and pulled out the telegram. "I didn't want to leave it in the hotel. I thought I was being silly at the time, but now I don't think I was."

Evelyn took the telegram and tore it open, scanning the message.

Upon consideration, story not worth expense. Return to London ASAP by all means available. Repeat: LEAVE STOCKHOLM.

She stared at the message, her blood going cold. Did he know about the two agents? Or was there something else? He'd used the code that only the two of them knew, warning her that her life was in danger. But then he'd followed it with very clear instructions to get out of the city. He wanted there to be no misunderstanding. She was to get out of there.

Through the blood pounding in her ears, she heard Anna talking and struggled to focus on what she was saying.

"If they know I'm not in the room, will they break in and search it?" she was asking. "That's what they do in the books. If they do, I'm even more glad I didn't leave that in the sitting room. What does it say? It's not good, is it? Is it from Daniel?"

"No. It's from London." Evelyn took a deep breath and turned away from the water, shoving the telegram into her absurdly large handbag. "It says to leave Stockholm and get back to London."

"Well, I agree with that, but how are you going to do it?" she demanded. "How are we going to get our things from the hotel and arrange a train back to Oslo without them finding you?"

Evelyn was silent for a long time, then she lifted blue eyes to Anna's face.

"We're not," she said. "*You* are."

Anna stared at her. "What?"

"I can't go back to Oslo, but you have to. You'll take a train home."

"But what about you?"

"I'll find a way back to England."

Anna shook her head vehemently. "Oh no. I'm not leaving you. You don't speak Swedish, you're all alone and you have the Gestapo on your heels. I can't just leave you!"

"It's too dangerous for you not to," Evelyn argued. "It was wrong for me to ask you to come. Now you're in as much danger as I am."

"You warned me it was dangerous, and I agreed to come anyway. Now we're in this together. We'll find a way out of it, but we'll do it together."

Evelyn looked at her thoughtfully for a moment, then she pursed her lips.

"Actually," she said slowly, "there might be a way."

"Well?" Anna demanded when she didn't continue right away.

Evelyn was silent, then her lips curved into a slow smile.

"How's your acting?"

◉

Paris, France

Bill walked down the hall quickly, his shoes echoing on the tiled floor. His brows were creased into a furrow as he went, his lips pressed tightly together. It was past noon and he still hadn't received word from the radio room regarding the telegram he sent to Jian. He didn't even know if it had been delivered.

When he'd received the message from Daniel the night before, Bill realized immediately that somehow, somewhere, Evelyn's carefully constructed cover had been blown. Whether it was here in London or there in Oslo was immaterial. The fact remained that this Herr Renner not only knew of her, but had found her in Oslo. There could be no doubt that he was an SS or SD agent. The only question was how he knew about Evelyn.

Bill frowned thoughtfully. It was possible that her run in with Hans Voss last year had made more of an impression than they had originally realized. They had moved quickly at the time to minimize the

The Oslo Affair

damage and create a back story for Evelyn that would pass even the rigorous SD and Gestapo checks. Even so, Bill admitted now that it was entirely possible that the Germans had realized who, and what, she really was. But how on earth could they have known that she was going to Norway, of all places? It was hardly a hotbed of intelligence activity at the moment. Yet something had clearly drawn the German agent to Oslo.

Bill thought for a moment. He supposed it could simply be that this Herr Renner was in Oslo to keep an eye on the German scientists from Berlin. After all, the Nazis were known to keep a strict watch on their people. They were kept on a very tight rein when they ventured outside Germany. He supposed that would go double for the scientists. If that was the case, it could just be that Renner had been in Oslo and recognized Evelyn from the description given by Hans Voss last year. They hadn't bothered to change her appearance. There had seemed to be no need. Perhaps this whole situation was simply something as innocuous as being recognized in the wrong place at the wrong time.

As wonderful as that might be, Bill had a sinking suspicion that it wasn't the case at all. There were two agents in Oslo now, who had not only recognized Jian, but had proceeded to make their pursuit known. That couldn't be a coincidence.

Someone was feeding information to both the Soviets and the Germans.

Bill came to a door at the far end of the corridor and reached for the handle. He stepped inside a small room and looked around. There were four desks, two of which were occupied by men with headphones over their heads, wired into large square radios. The only sound in the room was the hum of the radios themselves, and the occasional tapping noise as the radio operators decoded new incoming messages.

Bill closed the door behind him softly and moved forward to lay his hand on the shoulder of one of the radio operators. The man turned his head in surprise and removed the headset from his head.

"Any word yet?" Bill asked softly.

"No, sir. I did receive confirmation that the telegram was received, but no reply as of yet."

Bill frowned but nodded, patting the man's shoulder.

"Let me know as soon as you hear something," he instructed. "I don't care what time it is. Come and find me."

The operator nodded and reached for his headset again as Bill turned to leave, the frown on his face growing.

CW Browning

He headed for the door to the stairwell a few feet away. They should've heard something by now, but there was nothing he could do until he received word back from Evelyn. He had to trust that she had received the telegram in time and was taking all available precautions. If not, then they very well could be on the brink of losing potentially the best agent they had so far in this Phony War.

He was jogging down the steps to the first floor when a thought occurred to him. She wasn't alone in Stockholm. The translator was with her, the one called Anna. The thought cheered him a bit. With two of them working together, Evelyn had a greater chance of avoiding Renner. But if the mysterious Soviet agent was also in play, then things were a lot more complicated, and a lot more dangerous, than he'd at first supposed.

The frown returned to his face. In fact, this whole situation had become more complicated than it was supposed to be. If the Soviet agent *had* followed her to Sweden, how on earth was she going to avoid two enemy agents and get out of Stockholm?

Her first line of communication would have to be their man at the embassy, Horace Manchester. Daniel had been very clear that he had instructed her to contact him as soon as she arrived in Stockholm. Accordingly, Carew had received confirmation from Horace that she had done so. Jasper had already authorized Horace to use all available means to get her out of Sweden and back to England as soon as possible.

There was still a chance that she could make it out without any confrontations. It was a slim chance, but there was a chance.

Bill opened the door at the bottom of the stairwell and crossed the tiled hall of the embassy in Paris. Although he was now regretting giving his approval for the unscheduled trip to Stockholm, Bill couldn't help but wonder what information Evelyn might be bringing back. Would it be worth all this worry? Or would this whole trip turn out to be a wild goose chase? There was no way of knowing until she returned with whatever information she had managed to gather. That is, if she hadn't been forced to destroy it in her flight.

As he stepped out onto the busy Paris street, the sun was shining and Parisians were cheerfully going about their daily lives around him. Setting his hat on his head, he turned to walk down the street towards his favorite restaurant. While Paris was still eating and drinking with abandon, he was desperately trying to assemble and organize his agents before the war actually got going. And it would. They all knew that. Hitler was not about to stop now.

And when it did get started in earnest, he was going to need

The Oslo Affair
every available agent, including Evelyn. She had to make it back.

Chapter Twenty-Two

Gamla Stan, Stockholm

Comrade Grigori stood in the mouth of the alley, watching the building on the corner. He had followed the Englishwoman and watched her go inside, but had chosen not to follow. It was getting too risky now. She knew he was here but, so far, he'd been able to avoid her noticing that he was following her. He knew that wouldn't last for long, though. As she'd shown in Oslo, she was very adept at watching her back.

He reached into his pocket to pull out a pack of cigarettes. It had been over twenty minutes since she entered the building and he'd now concluded that she was, in fact, meeting someone for lunch. He wished he could go in to get a glimpse of them and see if it was Lyakhov, but he couldn't. He must wait until she left. With a bit of luck, they would exit the building together and he would see who it was that had drawn her into this disreputable neighborhood.

After lighting a cigarette, Grigori looked around his surroundings distastefully. The buildings quite possibly had been beautiful at one time, but now they were ancient. Time and decay had taken their toll, and the once proud structures had fallen into disrepair that appeared to be beyond restoration. The best thing Stockholm could do, in his opinion, was to raze the lot and rebuild. But if the government in Sweden was anything like his own in Moscow, that would not happen. As much as Stalin liked to consider himself modern in his outlook and policies, Grigori believed he was really a traditionalist at heart. Most of the buildings in Moscow had been preserved after their great revolution, and when Stalin took power, he made no attempt to alter them.

He returned his gaze to the corner across the street. He rather hoped that it wouldn't be Lyakhov that walked out of the door. So far he'd found no evidence of treasonous behavior. It would be a shame for that to change now. He'd always liked Vladimir Lyakhov. The man was astute in his work and unbending in his convictions, two characteristics that Grigori admired, especially in their profession.

The Oslo Affair

He was on his second cigarette when the door to the building finally opened and the Englishwoman emerged. Dropping the cigarette, he put it out with his shoe as his body tensed in expectation. The door remained open after she stepped outside. Someone was coming out with her.

The man that followed her out of the tavern was not Comrade Lyakhov and Grigori stared in surprise. It was a face he hadn't been expecting to see. In fact, it was a face that, as far as he knew, was not under suspicion yet.

He pressed his lips together and watched as the Englishwoman turned to say something to the man. He answered and held out his hand. Watching the Englishwoman shake it and turn to walk away, Grigori felt a surge of anger. There could be no doubt that Comrade Risto Niva had been meeting with the British agent.

They had found their intelligence leak.

He watched as the Englishwoman walked back the way she had come and Comrade Niva turned to walk in the opposite direction. With a final glance at the Englishwoman, Grigori stepped out of the alleyway and turned to his right. He strode to the end of the block, where Comrade Yakov lurked in the shadows.

"Where is Lyakhov?" he demanded shortly.

"I followed him as far as the bridge. I lost him when he came into this neighborhood."

"I want you to follow Comrade Niva," Grigori told him. "Leave Lyakhov for now."

Yakov nodded and prepared to head in the opposite direction. After a few steps, he paused and turned back.

"And the girl?"

"Don't worry about her. She'll head back to the hotel and I'll apprehend her there. By the end of the day, we'll know everything we need to know about the Englishwoman and Comrade Niva. Don't lose him. I'll take care of him when I'm finished with her."

Yakov nodded and turned away to go after Niva. Turning, Grigori continued up the street. He could still see the Englishwoman ahead, moving through the crowds quickly as she headed out of Gamla Stan.

While he hadn't wanted to believe that Lyakhov was, in fact, a traitor, he was still surprised at who the leak was. Niva was based in Finland, of all places. How on earth had the British got to him? As far as he knew, the British had no presence in Finland outside Helsinki. Yet clearly they had managed to get to Comrade Niva.

The frown on his face grew. And what about Oslo? Niva had never been there. He remained firmly in Finland, with occasional forays into Stockholm. After thinking for a moment, Comrade Grigori pressed his lips together thoughtfully. Niva didn't have to be in Oslo. The Germans were in Oslo. What if the Englishwoman was there for the Germans, then she moved on to Stockholm? There was nothing to stop an agent from pursuing two contacts in the same trip. He'd done it himself many times. And if that was the case, it was only pure luck that he was able to track down her meeting with Niva today.

But Comrade Grigori didn't believe in luck. In a bizarre twist of convictions, he actually did believe in fate. Many of his successes could only be attributed to that very thing.

It was fate that had brought him to Oslo, he decided as he walked through the old streets of Gamla Stan. Just as it was fate that led him to Stockholm. He looked at the woman ahead of him thoughtfully.

It could be that it was fate that brought the Englishwoman into his sphere. Comrade Niva spoke only Russian, Finnish and Swedish, so she had to speak one of those three languages. The fact that she was traveling with an obvious translator indicated that the language she had in common with Niva was Russian or Finnish. Personally, his wager was on Russian, and if the Englishwoman spoke Russian well enough to be understood, that was no small feat. In fact, it made her a rarity as far as British agents went.

And that made her a perfect target to be turned as a double agent.

◉

Herr Renner looked up as the door to his room opened. He set down his pen and sat back, watching as the shorter man closed the door and turned to cross the sitting room.

"Well?"

"No one is in the room. The other woman must have left sometime after the Englishwoman." The man seated himself in one of the chairs and crossed his legs comfortably. "I went through the rooms. I found nothing that could be of use to us."

Renner frowned. "Nothing at all?"

The man shook his head. "No. All that's there is clothing and some magazines."

"What about the telegram that was delivered?"

The Oslo Affair

"There was no sign of it."

Renner cursed. "The other woman must have taken it with her. Do we know for certain it was meant for the Englishwoman?"

"Oh yes. I spoke with the boy who hand delivered it myself. It was for Miss Margaret Richardson."

Getting to his feet, Renner walked over to the window overlooking the harbor and stared out silently for a moment.

"Any idea who it was from?" he asked over his shoulder.

"Her editor in London, or so I was told."

Renner nodded. That made sense. The British Secret Service would hardly send instructions from their own agency. They would use something in line with their agents cover story.

"There is one thing that might help us," the man said slowly from the chair. "She will have to contact the British embassy if she suspects that she's been compromised. We have a man there already. If she sends anything to Mr. Manchester, we'll know about it."

Renner turned from the window. "I don't see how that helps us. If she suspects she's been compromised, she won't come back to the hotel. Especially if there's nothing in her room worth saving."

"There isn't."

Silence fell over the sitting room and the man in the chair leaned his head back, staring at the ceiling while Renner paced before the window.

"I don't think it will come to any of that," he finally said, breaking the silence. "She doesn't know we're here. You arrived after she left, so she hasn't seen you. The woman with her is nobody, just a Norwegian girl from what the concierge said. She's probably here to translate for her, so she knows nothing. There's no reason for either of them to suspect anything."

Herr Renner looked at him consideringly. The other man was right. He'd been careful not to be seen by Maggie Richardson. She had no idea he was here. As far as she knew, he was still in Oslo.

"Has Franz seen anything in the back?" he asked, going back to his chair at the desk and seating himself again.

"No. Everything is quiet. The only people going into the alley are the hotel staff."

He nodded and picked up his pen, twirling it absently between his long fingers.

"We'll use the alley," he decided after a moment. "Is Helmut still at the consulate with the car?"

"Yes."

"Tell him to be prepared to come when I call for him. When

Fraulein Richardson returns to the hotel, we'll allow her to go to her room. Once she's there, I'll pay her a visit."

"We can take her from the room," the man suggested. "There's a stairwell that goes down to the back of hotel, near the back entrance. It would be quick and easy to get her down the stairs."

Renner shook his head.

"No. We can't take her from inside the hotel," he said firmly. "We can't risk causing an incident that will be protested, as it surely would. Sweden will not take kindly to us breaching her neutrality in such a fashion. Remember, we are under orders to be discreet. Himmler doesn't want anyone to know about the Fraulein."

The man frowned and lifted his head, looking at Renner.

"If we can't take her from inside the hotel, what do you suggest?"

"I'll get her to leave the hotel with me. Once we're downstairs, I'll take her into the alley where Helmut will be waiting with the car."

The man's brow cleared and he nodded slowly.

"There's less risk in the alley," he agreed. "Less likelihood of being seen."

"Precisely." Renner laid his pen down on the desk and leaned forward. "Once she's in the car, we have her. Then I'll find out what Obersturmbannführer Voss wants to know."

The man glanced at him. "What *does* he want to know?"

Renner waved his hand dismissively. "That's none of your concern. Just be sure to alert me as soon as she enters the hotel again."

"What about the other woman? I have a description now. What if she returns?"

"Let her through. The only way she interests me is if Fraulein Richardson doesn't return. Then we'll use the woman to draw her out."

The man nodded and pushed himself out of the chair.

"I'll go let the others know," he said, turning towards the door. "We should have something for you soon."

Renner nodded and watched as the other man left, closing the door silently behind him. He returned his attention to the letter he was composing to send to Berlin. He was confident that he would have Fraulein Richardson in hand by the evening at the latest.

And once they had what they needed, he had instructions to bring her back to Germany. Fraulein Richardson was about to be removed from the theatre of operations.

The Oslo Affair

When the tall, dark-haired woman breezed through the doors of The Strand with a dull-looking companion trailing behind, the only immediate person to notice was the porter standing just inside. After a brief glance, he returned his attention to the conversation he was holding in a low voice with one of the other hotel employees, uninterested. Later, however, he would claim that he knew there was something excitable about the woman as soon he laid eyes on her. After all, all Spaniards were high-strung, weren't they? It was because of their hot climate, he would say confidently. When challenged by another porter, he offered his uncle as a point of reference. He'd worked in Madrid for a summer and was well acquainted with the Spanish. While this was highly suspect, by that point two things were beyond dispute: the dark-haired woman was, indeed, Spanish, and, as it turned out, was also very high-strung and excitable.

At that present moment, though, the lobby of the hotel was quiet and no one was really paying any attention to the two women entering from the street. The morning and early afternoon flurry of check-ins and outs was over and a quiet calm had descended over the lobby, broken only by the occasional whir of the lift. The man sitting in a chair on the far side of the lobby with an unrestricted view of both the entrance and the lift stifled a yawn and looked up from his newspaper as the two women came through the door. After a very brief glance, he dismissed them and went back to his paper. They were not who he was waiting for.

He'd just returned to the half-hearted pretense of reading a newspaper that he couldn't understand when a shrill voice made its way to his corner of the lobby. He looked up in astonishment as the dark-haired woman stopped a few feet into the lobby and swung around to face her companion. She appeared to be berating the other woman, but as she was speaking in Spanish, it was very hard to know for sure. The man lowered his paper, his attention well and truly caught as the well-dressed Spaniard laid into her companion, her voice carrying across the lobby.

The sudden outburst stunned the few people scattered around and a shocked silence fell as one and all stared at the women, trying to understand what on earth was happening. Instead of appearing embarrassed by the public tongue-lashing she was getting, the companion looked resigned. Her clothes were good, but not of the same high quality as the woman in the process of losing her temper, indicating her status of a personal secretary or paid companion. She had dark hair pulled into a tight bun and a sensible, brown hat covered the lot. The man looked at her, noting the black-rimmed spectacles perched on her nose and the woolen stockings that covered her legs under a plain woolen skirt. Not even the faintest flicker of surprise crossed her face at the outburst, showing plainly that this was a common enough occurrence.

"…… completo imbécil! ¿Cómo puedes olvidar recoger el vestido? ¡¿Qué se supone que debo usar esta noche ?!"

The woman was rattling on in Spanish, her voice increasing in volume with each word. When she paused for breath, her companion murmured something unintelligible that only seemed to enrage her further.

"Bah!" she exclaimed in disgust, turning to continue across the lobby with swift, angry strides. "Eres una idiota!"

The hotel manager appeared then, moving across the tiled floor to intercept them smoothly, and the man with the paper felt a wave of amusement wash over him. Ah. Here was the manager to try to diffuse the situation and quiet her down. The scene, as diverting as it was, would be over in a minute.

Every eye in the lobby was on the trio in the middle of the floor, midway between the entrance and the lift. The man imagined that if someone pulled out a pistol and fired it, no one would take any notice. Everyone was straining to hear what the manager was saying in a low, quiet voice.

"I am Senora Damita Huerta Lucero," the woman responded to his low tone in heavily accented English that carried to every ear in the lobby. "I have come to see the Condesa de Carilla for tea. She is expecting me."

The manager nodded and said something again in a low voice at which the dark-haired woman seemed to calm slightly.

"Thank you. This is my secretary. She will be accompanying me, although I should not allow her anywhere near the Condesa. Her incompetence is outstanding." The woman turned to continue towards the lift, the manager beside her. "I should discharge her but it is very difficult to find good help in my country since the civil war."

The man watched as the trio moved towards the lift, the secretary trailing behind. Just when it appeared that the excitement was over, the dark-haired woman turned her head and snapped at the other woman.

"¡Darse prisa! ¡Te mueves como una cerda preñada!"

The man had no idea what the woman had said, but a snicker

The Oslo Affair

came from the direction of the front desk. The manager shot a look over his shoulder and the guilty party flushed and promptly lowered his head to become suddenly engrossed in paperwork.

"Do you see what I must deal with?" the woman demanded of the manager, drawing his attention back to her. "Just look at her dawdling! If she had her way, we would miss tea altogether! She does it on purpose, you know. Her family is socialist. They fought with the Republicans and she doesn't approve of the aristocracy. I notice it doesn't stop her from taking her salary from us, though."

The lift attendant had the door open before the trio even reached it and the manager handed her into the cage quickly, saying something in a low voice to the attendant. A moment later, the gate was closed and the lift churned into action, carrying the woman and her hapless companion out of sight.

Shaking his head, the man in the chair glanced once more at the entrance and raised his newspaper again. That was the most interesting thing to happen so far today. If the Englishwoman didn't show up soon, he was going to fall asleep in this chair.

Stifling another yawn, he looked at his watch. Herr Renner would be down in half an hour to relieve him. He just had to make it another half hour. With any luck, the Englishwoman would return before then and the tedious wait would be over. He was growing weary of doing nothing but watch the door. The sooner she came and they got to work, the better for all of them.

Chapter Twenty-Three

As soon as the lift began its ponderous upward journey, Evelyn exhaled silently and glanced at Anna. The woman really *did* look the part of a harassed and weary personal secretary. Her glasses had slipped to the end of her nose and her hat had tilted sideways sometime in their walk from the entrance to the lift. She kept her gaze downcast and Evelyn really was impressed. She hadn't been sure that Anna would be able to pull off her small part, but no one had suspected that she was anything other than what she appeared to be. Even the man with the newspaper hadn't looked twice at either of them until Evelyn started her performance.

When they entered the lobby, he was the first one she noticed. Despite holding a newspaper, he'd been more interested in the entrance of the hotel than what was typed on the pages before him. She had recognized the cut of the dark suit as soon as she saw it. It was undoubtedly German, as was the hat on the chair next to him.

There was no sign of Herr Renner, but she knew that he would appear eventually. When he did, she wanted to be nowhere in sight. While she had obviously been able to get past everyone else in the lobby just now, Evelyn wasn't so sure that Renner would be as easily fooled. He had eyes that seemed to see everything, and he had an uncanny way of appearing just when she was least expecting him.

She looked at the back of the attendant's head and then looked at Anna again. Meeting her gaze, she smiled faintly. Then, tossing her head, she began speaking rapidly in Spanish once again. The attendant started at the harsh tone but, to his credit, failed to turn and stare. Instead, he stood stoically with his face turned forward while Evelyn proceeded to reprimand her 'secretary' once again, alternating between Spanish and English.

"Nunca he tenido una empleada tan estúpida!" she exclaimed, waving her hands. "And now, now we are late to tea. Es inaceptable! Your very presence offends me! Informaré a la condesa que es tu culpa. Siempre es tu culpa. I'm not putting up with it! I refuse to stay in your company one more minuto!"

The Oslo Affair

Evelyn turned her attention to the attendant.

"Stop the lift," she commanded imperiously.

The attendant turned to look at her, startled. He rattled something off in Swedish and Evelyn sighed loudly, turning to her companion expectantly. Anna pushed her glasses up on her nose.

"He said but you are going to the fifth floor. This is only the fourth," she said in English.

"Stop it, I say! I will not ride another floor with this...this...nincompoop!"

Anna obligingly translated, only the faintest tremor in her voice.

The attendant swallowed and obediently pushed the lever, bringing the lift to a stop at the fourth floor. He opened the gate, expecting to see the companion disembark. Instead, Evelyn strode out and turned to glare at the companion with a dramatic flourish.

"I will take the stairs rather than look at your face!" she announced, tossing her head. "You will go on and wait for me." Then, just as the attendant was sliding the gate closed again, her eyes met Anna's. "Godspeed, my friend," she said, keeping the berating tone in her voice.

The faintest smile crossed Anna's lips and she nodded, pushing her glasses up on her nose.

"And you," she murmured.

The lift started up again and Evelyn turned away with an exaggerated huff, her eyes darting around the wide hallway. She was just in time to see a blond head retreat behind the corner at the far end of the corridor. From that spot, the man could see not only the lift, but the door to her and Anna's room.

After glancing at the other end of the corridor and seeing nothing, she took a deep breath and started down the hallway, muttering to herself in Spanish. Just in case the man watching their room happened to know Spanish, she kept her complaints in the same vein as the reprimanding she'd been engaged in for the past ten minutes.

"Stupid, incompetent girl! She doesn't have much to do, but she still manages to get it all wrong. And she looks like a depressed cow half the time. No wonder I'm going out of my mind. It's like having Job for a secretary. Worse! At least *he* was Catholic!"

Glancing at her watch, Evelyn waited a beat, then increased her pace, all the while still complaining under her breath. When she reached the corner, she rounded it at full speed and plowed right into a solid mass.

"Oof!"

She grunted as her nose came into contact with a shoulder and she fell backwards, stumbling.

"For the love of St Mary herself!" she exploded, staring at the blond man furiously. "What do you think you're doing?!"

Evelyn spoke in Spanish and received a blank stare back. The man clearly didn't understand a word.

"Es tut mir leid, Fräulein," he apologized stiffly. "Ich habe dich nicht gesehen."

Evelyn tossed her head and gave him an assessing look.

"Oh, you are German," she said haltingly in German. She formed her words awkwardly, giving them a Spanish sound and wincing in her mind as she heard them come out. Lord, that sounded awful! "It is Frau. I am Senor Antonio Lucera's wife."

The man bowed politely. "Again, my apologies."

"I will accept them," she decided graciously. "I have had enough of stupidity today. Tell me, are you staying on this floor?"

"I...yes."

"Where are the stairs? I am late for tea with the Condesa de Carilla, but I cannot find the way to the fifth floor."

"The lift is back there," he said, drawing an exasperated sigh from her.

"The lift is currently occupied by the biggest imbecile this side of the Atlantic," she said roundly. Then she frowned as a thought suddenly occurred to her. "Are we near the Atlantic here? I do not think we are. I suppose I should say 'this side of the North Sea', eh?"

The man blinked and seemed to be wrestling between the urge to laugh and a desire to remain aloof.

"The stairs are on the other end of that hallway," he finally said, motioning back the way she'd just come. "If you go to the end, you'll see them."

"They are that way?" She looked over her shoulder and peered down the hallway. As she did, she saw a dark head appear at the far end. "Of course they are! My secretary has already made me late, and now I see I was already near them when I went the wrong way. Typical! Thank you for telling me."

Evelyn moved to turn around and caught her heel in the plush carpet on the floor. Before the man could catch her, she tumbled forward and her purse opened, spilling its contents across the hall.

"Oh!" she exclaimed, falling to her knees.

With a muffled exclamation, the man knelt beside her. "Are you hurt?"

The Oslo Affair

Shaking her head, she began to reach for the tube of lipstick near her on the floor.

"No, no, I am quite all right. I caught my heel, that is all. Oh look! Everything is everywhere!"

The man turned to reach for a compact mirror and a small notebook. While he was gathering up items behind him, Evelyn shot a look out of the corner of her eye. Anna was just disappearing into the hotel room halfway between them and the lift. The door closed silently behind her and Evelyn turned back to accept the handful of items from the man on his knees with her.

"Thank you so much," she said, shoving them all back into her purse.

He got to his feet and offered her his hand, pulling her up.

"Are you sure you're not hurt?"

"Yes, thank you." She brushed herself off and smiled at him before turning away. "The stairs are this way?"

He nodded and walked a few steps with her to point to the other end of the hallway.

"You can just see them from here," he told her. "There, at the end."

"I see them now," she said nodding. "Thank you again!"

Evelyn strode down the hallway towards the stairwell, her back straight and her head high. Her pace was steady but her heart was pounding. He had looked right into her face. Anything could have gone wrong. If he'd been shown a photo, he could have recognized her. He could have looked up and realized that someone was crossing the hallway behind her while he was helping her pick up the contents of the purse. At the very least, he should have been leery of the fact that a member of the Spanish nobility had condescended to strike up a conversation with him in the hallway of a hotel in Sweden.

The numerous scenarios of what could have gone awry continued to play their way through her head and, when Evelyn reached the stairs and started up them to the fifth floor, her heart was still in her mouth.

What if he came after her? What if Renner was on the fifth floor? Evelyn's step checked as that thought occurred to her and she glanced up at the next floor apprehensively. What if he had someone watching the fifth floor?

She shook her head and continued on resolutely. No. Anna had got off the lift on the fifth floor and came down these very stairs without issue not five minutes before. Everything was going to be fine. She had to get a hold of herself.

Evelyn emerged on to the fifth floor and cast a swift look up and down the wide hallway. There wasn't another soul in sight. Exhaling in relief, she passed the empty lift shaft and walked to the end of the hall, turning the corner. There, she leaned against the wall and checked at her watch. She just had to stay out of sight here for thirty minutes. There was no fear that the Condesa would emerge from her room and go to the lobby when they were supposed to be having tea. The Condesa de Carilla was notoriously reticent, preferring to entertain privately and rarely venturing beyond the comfort of her rooms. It had been a marvelous stroke of luck, seeing her check into the hotel the evening before when she was on her way to dinner. The Condesa hadn't seen her, which was fortunate. Evelyn had had the privilege of meeting her on two separate occasions, once in London and again in Paris. The woman could talk for hours. She was fascinating, but exceedingly annoying. However, her presence here had played beautifully into Evelyn's plans.

Looking around, she spied an alcove in the wall further down where the laundry chute was partially hidden by a potted fern. A moment later, she was concealed by the fern, settling down to wait. The timing was most important. Too many pieces were in play now. It was imperative that she wait the half hour before proceeding.

Her mind went back to the German on the floor below her. It really was a miracle that he hadn't suspected a thing, and most especially hadn't realized that he had been run down by the very person he was waiting for. Instead, he helped her pick up her belongings while Anna went into their room undetected, and then he was even obliging enough to show her where to go to get to the stairs.

Her lips curved and Evelyn felt the urge to chuckle. He'd done exactly what she wanted him to do. He'd seen exactly what she hoped he'd see, and it had all worked perfectly. Her role in the charade was now almost over.

The rest was up to Anna.

◉

When Evelyn finally moved out of the little alcove she'd had plenty of time to calm down from the excitement of her lively performance. Her heart rate was back to normal and her step was light as she moved around the corner towards the lift. She glanced at the ornate dial above the shaft, smiling when she saw that the lift was

The Oslo Affair

engaged on the floor below her. Perfect. Everything was still going according to plan.

She continued to the stairs and entered the art nouveau inspired stairwell, starting down the steps quickly. Her heels echoed on the tiled floor, but she was unconcerned at the sound. There was no one on the stairs to notice, and even if there were, they wouldn't think twice at the sight of a well-dressed woman taking the stairs rather than the lift. After all, the lift was engaged.

Keeping one gloved hand on the shiny railing, Evelyn moved quickly down the flights until she was nearing the bottom. There she slowed, her eyes on the opening that led to the lobby. The stairs emerged next to the lift, and she knew they would be watching the lift.

She could see people moving through the lobby as she came closer to the last step and she hesitated. Had she beat the lift down? As the thought entered her head, Evelyn heard the whirring of the gears and then a muffled clank as the lift settled on the ground floor. She exhaled and waited on the last step, listening. There was the creak of the gate opening. It was almost time.

Stepping off the last step, Evelyn moved over to the wall and stood against it, her eyes fixed on the path to the front desk in the lobby. Voices echoed down the stairs from high above and then the sound of footsteps heralded the advent of guests who didn't want to wait for the lift. Biting her bottom lip, she glanced up swiftly. She had to move out of the stairwell before the people coming down saw her. Upon entering the hotel, her goal had been to have as many people see and notice her as possible, but now it was the complete opposite. The last thing in the world that she wanted was to have other guests see her lurking at the bottom of the stairs. There could be no good explanation for it and, worse, it would cause them to notice her.

Movement out of the corner of her eye drew her attention back to the lobby and she watched as Anna strode by in her own clothing, her head high, while the porter followed with all their luggage. She was right on time.

Good girl, she thought, watching as the woman went towards the concierge desk. Then she scanned the rest of the lobby, looking for the man who had been reading the newspaper when they came in. Her breath caught in her throat as, instead of him, a tall man moved across the lobby towards the front desk, his eyes fixed on Anna.

Renner!

Casting a frantic look around for the other one, Evelyn knew she had to move. The footsteps were drawing closer and any minute one of the guests on the stairs could look down and see her standing there.

After a second of panicked hesitation, Evelyn moved out of the stairwell, glancing towards the desk. Anna was talking to the manager, waving her hand airily, a bright smile on her face. Herr Renner was standing a few feet behind, listening to every word, and Evelyn bit back a smile of her own. His focus was on the woman at the desk in front of him, not the lift or the stairs beside it.

She turned and moved quickly towards the back of the hotel and the long, narrow corridor that went past the porter's lounge and out to the alley behind the hotel. While Anna was drawing the attention of Herr Renner and all his minions in the front of the hotel, the back alley would be empty except for the one man Anna heard them say was posted there.

And that was Renner's tactical blunder. There was only one exit to the hotel that was secluded and out of sight from the harbor, leading straight to the busy street at the side of the hotel. And he'd left it attended by only one man. While she didn't relish the idea of a run-in with a Gestapo agent in the alley, she liked her odds better there than in the lobby of the hotel.

A moment later, she emerged into the narrow alley. The height of the hotel and the building behind it combined to block what was left of the late afternoon sun and the narrow lane was cloaked in shadows. Glancing to her left, she saw the street ahead. Between her and the busy road lay half the length of the hotel. After looking to her right and finding a row of trash cans, Evelyn blanched at the smell of rotting vegetables and bad fish. She turned hurriedly towards the road, holding her breath as she moved away from the noxious fumes.

She was halfway down the alley when she saw him. He was leaning against the adjoining building in the shadows, dressed in dark clothes with a long black coat to protect him from the cold. Evelyn felt a shudder go through her, though whether from the sight of the man or from the sudden gust of wind that whipped between the buildings she wasn't sure. He hadn't seen her yet. He was watching the cars on the road ahead. But he would see her any moment. There was no avoiding it.

Evelyn began to mutter angrily in Spanish as she walked. Perhaps he would think she was a crazy foreigner and leave her alone. But one swift look from under her eyelashes disabused her of that hopeful thought. He had straightened up and was staring at her, trying to see her clearly in the gloom. Increasing her pace, she also increased the volume of her muttering, her voice carrying through the alley. If he

The Oslo Affair

knew Spanish, he was listening to a diatribe on the curse of having incompetent employees who couldn't even have the car brought round to the right entrance of a hotel. If he didn't know Spanish, he heard only anger in her tone. Either way, the man was watching the same performance that had fooled his counterparts inside earlier.

Lifting her head, Evelyn looked at him and pretended to have spotted him for the first time. Her step checked in surprise, then her anger increased as if she was offended by him staring at her.

"¿Quién crees que eres?" she demanded, tossing her head.

The man didn't answer. Instead, he continued to watch her with a heavy frown on his face. His lack of response made her nervous and she took a closer look at him as she strode down the alley. He had both his hands in his coat pockets and his hat was pulled low over his forehead, casting his face into shadow. As she drew closer, he moved suddenly away from the side of the building, partially blocking her path to the road.

"Why are you back here?" he demanded in German, his voice deep and gravelly. "You shouldn't be back here. This is no place for a lady."

By the time he'd finished speaking, he'd blocked her path completely, pulling his hands from his pockets. Evelyn's eyes narrowed sharply. So much for slipping by without any unpleasantness. She waited until she was within reach of him before answering softly in his own language.

"Who says I'm a lady?"

His eyes widened in surprise, but it was too late. Evelyn moved swiftly, grabbing one of his wrists and twisting it sharply. He gasped in pain, but the sound quickly turned into a cry when she used the painful angle of his wrist as leverage to spin him around, twisting his arm up behind his back. Before the cry could escalate into a full roar, she used her other hand to smash his head into the side of the hotel. A sickening crunch sounded as his nose made contact with stone and he grunted in agony. He tried to push himself back, using the wall in an attempt to turn himself towards her, but Evelyn drove her fist into his kidney, robbing him of the ability to make any noise at all. As he fell forward against the building, she released his mangled arm and sliced the edge of her palm down into the side of his neck. She stepped back as his eyes closed and he slid down the building, unconscious.

By the time he came to, or someone found him, she would be long gone.

After shooting a swift glance down the alley towards the rear door, she turned to hurry away from the prone figure in the shadows. A moment later she reached the busy street and emerged from the alley. Shoving her hands deep in her pockets, Evelyn strode away from The Strand, blending into the throngs of other well-dressed pedestrians and disappearing into the growing shadows.

The Oslo Affair

Chapter Twenty-Four

As the lift attendant opened the latticed gate, Anna took a deep, silent breath before stepping out into the lobby. When she'd opened the door to the porter upstairs, she'd caught sight of a man hurriedly disappearing around the corner at the end of the corridor. Even though she knew the Germans were watching the room, she had still felt a surge of fear at the visual confirmation. When she left the room with the porter a few minutes later, there was no sign of him, but she knew he was still there.

Just as his companions were all over the lobby and outside.

Squaring her shoulders, she walked across the large, tiled lobby towards the desk. Out of the corner of her eye, she saw Herr Renner step out from behind the very column she had stood behind this morning. Ignoring the sudden trembling in her legs, she went to the front desk, trying desperately to act as if everything was completely normal. Her heart was pounding in her chest, and by the time she reached the support of the smooth wood counter, she was convinced that her entire body was shaking. The concierge didn't appear to notice anything the matter, however, as he came over with a ready smile.

"Ah, Miss Salvesen," he greeted her. "I understand you're leaving us."

"Yes." Anna set her purse down, relieved when her voice came out clear and steady. "Miss Richardson ran into an old friend this afternoon. She has a house in the city and invited us to stay with her. Miss Richardson felt it would be impolite to refuse."

"I understand completely." The concierge turned to retrieve the registration card from the drawer on the wall behind him. "Shall I forward the bill to her new address?"

"No. I'll settle it now."

"Very good." He returned with the card and handed it to her. "If you could just sign under Miss Richardson's signature there."

Anna picked up the pen and signed her name, conscious of the pair of dark eyes watching her every move and listening to the conversation. Herr Renner had moved close by, apparently waiting patiently for the concierge to finish with her. When she finished, she opened her purse and extracted the money Maggie had given her earlier. She carefully counted out the correct amount, passing it to the man, then added a rather large addition for him.

"Miss Richardson extends her gratitude for a delightful stay," she told him with a smile.

He inclined his head and pocketed the extra smoothly. "It was our pleasure. Shall I call a car for you?"

"That's not necessary. Her friend is having one sent round." Anna picked up her purse and glanced towards the entrance. "It should be here now. Thank you very much for everything."

"Our pleasure. I sincerely hope you'll visit The Strand again."

Anna smiled and turned away from the desk, motioning for the porter to follow. As she turned, her eyes met Herr Renner's and a shock went through her. There was nothing but polite disinterest in his face, however, and she turned to walk towards the entrance, exhaling silently. His eyes had been cold and impersonal, but there was no doubt that he had been watching her very closely.

Resisting the urge to look back over her shoulder, she continued across the lobby, forcing her stride to remain unhurried. She mustn't appear to be rushing. Maggie had been very clear about that.

Maggie had been very clear about a lot of things in the few hours they had spent rushing around the city, preparing for their elaborate charade. While they hurriedly gathered appropriate clothing and accessories to aid in their performance, Maggie had gone over her plan in detail, stressing the importance of both timing and calm. She should never appear hesitant or unsure. The best disguise was confidence. Anna's lips twitched at the corners as she remembered that particular instruction. She had laughed, but Maggie had been deadly serious. It was human nature, she explained. Present a confident appearance and very few will challenge that image. And she had been right. Herr Renner was watching, but he was making no move to stop her. He couldn't afford to. She was a respected guest until she walked out that door.

She just had to make it past the short man whom she'd seen earlier and who was standing just inside the entrance, talking to another gentleman.

Maggie had been right about it all. The man in the hallway, the men in the lobby, and even Herr Renner. As soon as she stepped out of the hotel room, all eyes were on her. They wanted to know where she was going. In the absence of their true target, she was the next best

The Oslo Affair

thing. Maggie had assured her they would swarm to her like bees, and that was just what they were doing.

"Excuse me, Miss!"

A deep voice called suddenly behind her. He spoke in Norwegian and Anna knew without turning that it was Renner. Her breath caught in her throat and her stomach clenched as she turned, pausing a few feet from the door. Renner was striding towards her quickly, something in his hand.

"I believe you dropped this," he said, holding out his hand.

Anna stopped just short of letting out a gasp. He held a handkerchief that was most definitely hers. She had left it on the table in the sitting room earlier this morning. She'd completely forgotten about it, but now she stared at it in bemusement. It hadn't been there when she was hastily gathering everything a few moments before.

"Oh!" she said, realizing that he was waiting for an answer. "Thank you!"

She reached out to take it but as her fingers touched it, it drifted to the floor.

"I'm so sorry," he apologized, bending at the same time as her to retrieve it. As he did so, she felt her purse begin to slip. Moving her arm quickly, she turned sideways as she reached for the slip of fabric on the floor. The swift movement prevented the bag from falling and spilling out all over the floor and she felt a measure of satisfaction at the very brief tightening of his lips. Of all the nerve! He was trying to get something from her purse!

Anna plucked the handkerchief off the floor and straightened up, a smile plastered across her face.

"It's quite all right," she told him, tucking it into her purse and snapping the bag closed with a firm click. "Thank you for returning it."

She turned on her heel and continued to the door, leaving Renner standing in the middle of lobby watching her go. The two men inside the door looked at him for a moment, then resumed their conversation as she passed. She breathed a sigh of relief as she stepped outside into the gathering dusk a moment later.

A black sedan sat at the curb, and as she exited the hotel, the driver got out and went to the back to open the trunk. He nodded to her politely as the porter went around her to load the bags into the car. Anna watched and smiled as the porter turned to return to the hotel.

"Tak," she murmured.

He touched his cap in acknowledgment and Anna waited for the driver to open the door for her.

"The train station, please," she told him as she got in, making sure her voice carried to the man lurking in the shadows a few feet away. "Quickly."

"Yes miss."

The driver closed the door and Anna glanced out the window as he got behind the wheel again. As they pulled away from the hotel, she saw the man rush from the shadows into the hotel and she sat back in the seat. A smile curved her lips. They would take the bait. They had no choice. She was their only link to Maggie. They would have to follow her.

Anna looked at her watch in the fading light. Timing. It was everything. She waited a few blocks then, when the hand on her watch ticked to the quarter hour, she looked up.

"Could you stop just up here for a moment?" she asked cheerfully. "I need to drop something off. I won't be a minute."

"Of course."

The driver turned the corner where she indicated, pulling up behind a gray sedan already parked by the side of the road. As he eased to a stop, the back door of the other car opened and tall, young man emerged. Anna opened her door and got out, walking forward to meet him while her driver climbed out from behind the steering wheel again.

"Mr. Manchester?" she asked in surprise.

He shook his head. "No. I'm Collins, his assistant. He sent me to collect the baggage."

She nodded and turned to the driver who was standing discreetly at slight distance.

"Could you open the back, please?"

He nodded and went to the back of the car, opening the truck. Collins joined him and motioned to Anna.

"Which ones?" he asked.

"The two on the right, and the small toiletries case."

He collected the bags and transferred them to the gray sedan, then walked back to hold out his hand.

"Mr. Manchester extends his deepest gratitude," he told her quietly. "He hopes you didn't find it all too unpleasant."

Anna laughed and took his hand. "On the contrary! I'm enjoying myself immensely!"

He looked startled at that, then a slow smile crossed his face.

"Have a safe trip home, Miss Salvesen," he said, dropping his hand and touching his hat. "Please take all care. Daniel Carew will have all of us on a rack if anything happens to you. He's threatening all sorts of reprisals if you don't return safely."

The Oslo Affair

"I'll be careful," she assured him, turning to get back into her car. "Send him a message and tell him I said to stop being an old woman. I'll be just fine."

⊙

Comrade Grigori looked up when the lift opened and a tall, dark-haired woman walked out. A porter followed, carrying multiple bags, and Grigori was just lowering his eyes back to his newspaper when something made him look again. He frowned, watching the woman thoughtfully. She looked familiar, but he really couldn't place why. Had he seen her earlier? In the restaurant perhaps? Whoever she was, she was obviously checking out of the hotel.

The woman was halfway across the lobby now and, as she walked, she tossed her head in a peculiar sideways motion. Grigori inhaled sharply. He'd seen her in another hotel, in Oslo! It was that strange toss of the head that brought the memory back. She had been with the Englishwoman that night in the restaurant!

Folding the paper, he got up and started to cross the lobby towards her just as another tall man moved out from behind one of the columns. Grigori's step checked and he raised an eyebrow as the man followed the woman to the desk, stopping a few feet away. At first glance, he appeared to be just another guest awaiting service at the busy concierge desk, but Comrade Grigori knew a German SD agent when he saw one. This was no ordinary guest.

He turned his eyes back to the woman, his frown deepening. If the SD were watching her, there could only be one explanation: they were watching the Englishwoman as well.

Moving closer, he listened as the woman spoke to the concierge in clear, carrying tones. She was speaking in Swedish, which wasn't one of Grigori's stronger languages. Yet he was able to make out enough to realize that the Englishwoman wouldn't be returning to the hotel.

Irritation rolled through him and he glanced at the German listening a few feet away. He supposed he had the SD to thank for this. As usual, they had blundered into something they knew nothing about and, in the process, alerted the English spy to the danger of returning to the hotel. She'd already been on her guard because he himself was staying there. The SD would have clinched the matter. Only a fool would return to their room under these circumstances.

Grigori changed direction and moved towards the entrance of

the hotel, his lips pressed together in displeasure. The question was, where had she gone, and the only one who knew the answer to that was the woman currently standing at the desk. He looked up and saw two men standing inside the front entrance talking. His eyes narrowed and he pulled on his gloves, pausing to do up the buttons on his coat. The men paid him no attention, focused instead on the woman at the desk. Once his coat was buttoned, Grigori continued to the door, passing outside without drawing any attention.

How many of them were there? The irritation had now turned into full-fledged anger. What did they think they were doing? They couldn't take a British subject in the middle of a neutral city! If it were possible, Grigori would have detained her long before now. Yet if there were three of them in the lobby, that meant there were even more outside. They probably had all the exits covered, and someone watching her room. That all pointed to an attempt to kidnap her right from the hotel.

Pulling the collar of his coat up against the chill, Grigori turned and walked a few feet to his right. He pulled out a cigarette and lit it, raising his eyes as he did so to study the man lounging on the opposite side of the entrance in the shadows. There was another one. The Germans were definitely up to no good.

And because of it, he'd lost his chance to question the spy himself.

He flicked his lighter closed and lifted his head, nodding pleasantly to the doorman. The doorman nodded back and he moved closer to the hotel, just another guest stepping outside for a smoke and some fresh air. A few moments later, a black sedan rolled up to the curb in front of the door and stopped, idling in the growing dusk.

The woman strode out with the porter following and, as she did, the driver of the black sedan got out and went to the back of the car to open the trunk. Grigori watched as the bags were loaded in and the porter departed.

"The train station, please. Quickly!"

The driver nodded and the woman got into the car. Grigori waited until the driver got behind the wheel before dropping his cigarette onto the pavement and putting it out with his shoe. By the time the black sedan was pulling away from the curb, he was already moving towards the corner to hail a taxi.

The Oslo Affair

Renner watched through the doors as the car pulled away from the curb and Otto rushed in from the street. He skidded to a stop and looked disconcerted at finding Renner standing so close to the entrance. As he opened his mouth to speak, Renner made an impatient sound and motioned for him to follow him. Swallowing, Otto glanced at the two men inside the door, who shrugged and followed with him as Renner led them across the lobby to a quiet section on the other side where they wouldn't be overheard.

"Well?" he asked, his voice short and clipped.

"She's going to the train station," Otto announced breathlessly. "She told the driver to be quick."

Renner let out a low curse and turned to stride over to the desk against the wall that held the lobby telephone. He picked up the receiver and dialed quickly, a scowl on his face. The three men behind him looked at each other, then shamelessly moved forward a few steps to listen.

"This is Sturmbannführer Wilhelm Renner. Send Helmut to The Strand immediately. I'll meet him in the back."

He hung up and turned to the others.

"Gather everyone except Kurt and bring them to the alley," he commanded. "Tell Kurt to remain behind in case the Englishwoman comes back. Otto, come with me."

The other two nodded and immediately split up as Otto joined Renner in striding across the lobby towards the back of the hotel.

"Did you hear anything else?"

"No. Just to go to the train station and to be quick."

"Did the driver seem surprised?"

Otto thought for a moment, then shook his head. "No, actually. He seemed to be expecting it."

Renner offered no response to that, his lips pressed together in a thin line. His strides were measured and controlled, but he was furious. How did the other woman, this Miss Salvesen, get back into hotel without any of his men seeing? She should never have had the opportunity to call the porter, or to leave at all. If he'd known she'd returned to the room, he would have gone himself to see her. Renner had no doubt that in ten minutes he would have found out where the Richardson woman was. Instead, he had no idea where she was and he'd been forced to watch as their one link to her drove away.

He cursed again and felt Otto stare at him in surprise. Let him look. Somehow that woman had got past all of them, and Renner held each of them responsible. There was no excuse for their incompetence. This simple operation had turned into a debacle, and now he was going to have to explain to Obersturmbannführer Hans Voss how they had allowed her to slip through their fingers.

Renner reached the door to the alley and pushed it open, stepping outside. A stiff, cold wind smacked him in the face and he quickly began buttoning his coat while he looked around the narrow lane.

"Where's Franz?" he demanded after a second. "Dammit, is everyone incompetent today?!"

"Oh my God!" Otto suddenly exclaimed, running forward. "He's here!"

Renner followed, his cold gaze falling on the prone figure laying on the ground halfway up the alley. Otto reached him and dropped down beside him, feeling on his neck for a pulse.

"He's still breathing," he announced, glancing up at Renner. "Looks like his nose was broken."

Renner stared down at the man, then raised his gaze to look around the dark alley. The anger intensified.

"I think we now know how Miss Salvesen got into the hotel," he said, his voice harsh.

"But who did this?" Otto demanded, standing. "A woman couldn't do this."

Renner looked down at Franz consideringly. "So you'd think," he murmured.

"What?"

Headlights illuminated the mouth of the alley as a black car pulled into the narrow lane.

"Nothing." Renner turned to look back at the door as the others emerged into the alley. "Get Franz into the car. We can't leave him here. He'll have to go with you."

"Where are we going?"

"To the train station," Renner said shortly, walking towards the car. "I'll instruct Helmut. Get Franz up. Have one of them help you."

"What about you? We all won't fit in the car."

"I'll follow in my own," he said over his shoulder. "Schnell! She already has a five-minute head start!"

Otto started to lift Franz off the ground and one of the others came forward quickly to help him. While they struggled with the dead weight, the others hurried to the car. Renner watched them, then bent down to speak to the driver.

"Go to the train station. You're looking for a black sedan, number AB-504. Otto can help. He was standing right next to it."

The man nodded. "And when I find it?"

The Oslo Affair

"Don't let it out of your sight."

Chapter Twenty-Five

Paris, France

Bill looked up as a knock fell on the door. Calling for them to come in, he slid the sheet of paper he was reading smoothing under a folder. He watched as Wesley Fitch, his assistant, entered carrying a tray with a teapot, two teacups, and a stack of correspondence.

"Afternoon," he said cheerfully, closing the door behind him. "I have good news, sir."

Bill sat back in his chair and stretched.

"Good. I could use some," he said. "What is it?"

"Topper made it out of Poland at last and is in Zürich," Wesley told him, carrying the tray over and setting it down on a side table near the desk. "He should be in London in two days, at the latest."

"That *is* good news!" Bill stood up and walked over to where Wesley was pouring tea into the cups. "Any word on whether or not he's injured?"

"No. The message was only that he made it out and arrived in Zürich this morning." Wesley turned to hand him a full cup of tea. "I've already sent a message to London to let them know."

"Thank you." Bill took the cup and turned to go back to his seat. "I'll need to go back to London. Make the arrangements, will you? The first available flight in the morning, I think."

"Shall I book for Mrs. Buckley as well?"

Bill sipped his tea before setting the cup and saucer down. "Not this time. I think she's enjoying being back in France. She won't want to leave again so soon."

Wesley nodded and picked up the stack of correspondence, carrying it over to him.

"Here are today's transmissions and briefings," he said. "There's one from Sir Jasper there. You may want to look at that first."

Bill took the stack and began sorting through it as Wesley went back to pour tea into the other cup. The brief silence in the office was broken by another knock at the door and Bill looked up in surprise.

The Oslo Affair

"Come in!"

The door opened and one of the radio operators rushed in breathlessly.

"Excuse me, sir, but you wanted to know as soon as I received word from Stockholm," he gasped.

Bill raised his eyebrows sharply and nodded, taking in the operators disheveled appearance. It looked as though he had run all the way from the radio room three floors above.

"Take a minute and catch your breath, Corporal. Another thirty seconds won't make much difference, now will it?"

Wesley turned with his tea and sipped it, leaning against the side table and watching the radio operator curiously. The air of barely controlled excitement was palpable and he glanced at his boss to find him sitting back in his chair, waiting patiently for the young man to catch his breath.

"Sorry, sir," the young man said after a moment. "I just wanted to get the news to you as quickly as possible. Horace Manchester sent a message from the embassy."

He walked over to the desk and handed Bill a sealed communication, then returned to his place a few feet away as Bill opened it and quickly scanned the contents.

RECEIVED MESSAGE FROM JIAN. NEEDS EMERGENCY EVACUATION. ARRANGED PASSAGE ON MERCHANT SHIP SS STORRA LEAVING TONIGHT FOR DENMARK.

Bill exhaled, relief pouring through him.

"Excellent. Thank you, Corporal. Was there anything else?"

"No, sir."

"Very well. Let me know if anything else comes through."

Bill watched the radio operator leave the room, closing the door again, and looked at Wesley.

"Manchester's arranged passage for Jian on a merchant ship leaving Stockholm tonight," he said. "The *SS Storra*. It sails for Denmark. Find out where she docks and when she'll get in."

Wesley nodded and set down his cup and saucer, but Bill made a clucking noise and waved his hand.

"Finish your tea," he said. "Ten minutes won't make any difference. Who do we have in Copenhagen?"

Wesley thought for a moment. "Isn't that Pierson, sir?"

Bill frowned. "Is it? Good Lord. Well, he'll have to do. Once you find out when the ship will arrive, contact him and arrange for him to meet Jian. He'll have to get her from Copenhagen to...God, where's the most accessible port for one of our ships to retrieve her?"

Wesley smiled and turned to walk over to a wall map currently displaying Poland.

"Don't you remember your geography, sir?" he asked over his shoulder with a chuckle. "You really should. You run agents all over Europe."

"Don't get cheeky with me," Bill said without heat, reaching for his cup. "When you reach my age, you'll realize some trivia isn't worth holding on to when there are perfectly serviceable maps to be used."

Wesley chuckled again and began pulling down maps, searching for one of Scandinavia and Denmark. When he found it, he clipped it up and stepped back to study it thoughtfully.

"Well?"

"It looks like it might be Esbjerg, sir," Wesley said slowly, "but it's clear across the country from Copenhagen, not to mention quite a bit of water in between."

Bill got up and carried his cup over to study the map. While he stared at it, Wesley drank his tea, knowing what was coming. He'd worked with William Buckley for over a year now. He knew him well.

"You'd better go find out where the ship will dock," he finally grunted. "If it's not Copenhagen, we need to arrange addition transport. And contact the base in Scotland while you're at it. Make sure there's no reason for us to get her back sooner."

Wesley nodded and set his empty cup down, turning towards the door. Once he'd gone, Bill continued studying the map with a frown. Once Evelyn was on the western side of Denmark, he had a few different options to get her home. The most straight-forward would be by ship across the North Sea. If that wasn't feasible in their unexpected time table, then he could move her down through the Netherlands and Belgium, then across from France. That option would take significantly longer.

With a sigh, he turned away from the map and went back to his desk. It all hinged on where the ship would dock, and whether or not she was on it.

He sank down into his chair and stared at the message on his desk. When this was sent, she was obviously still safe. But he knew how quickly that could change, especially with both German and Soviet agents on her tail. Even with the Norwegian helping, it was still damn tricky. There was no guarantee that Evelyn would make that ship, and

The Oslo Affair

every minute she was still in Stockholm was another minute she was in danger.

He hoped to God she'd found a way out of this mess.

Stockholm, Sweden

The more blocks Evelyn put between herself and The Strand Hotel, the more her pounding heart slowed and began to return to normal. The sun was almost gone now and long shadows covered the city as she moved through the crowds, her hands buried in her coat pockets and her head bowed against the frigid wind.

The trembling in her hands and legs had finally eased and she knew that the after-effects of her run-in with the man in the alley were fading. Sifu had tried to warn her of the effects of adrenaline and how it would affect her movements in a hostile setting, but she hadn't fully understood. After all, she had trained with other students and they had sparred together daily. Wasn't that the same thing?

Evelyn shook her head and glanced behind her as she turned to cross the road. It wasn't the same thing at all. She'd had her first taste of it last summer in France, and now she'd had another rush of it. Her Wing Chun master had been right. The adrenaline made her movements sloppy and impaired her thinking. Her breathing had been more labored than it should have been and, when it was all over and she walked away, her legs had almost given away completely. Sifu had tried to prepare her, but now she knew that there was no way anyone could have truly prepared her for the rush of nerves and energy that flooded through her. Only experience could be her teacher now.

It was her rigorous training and repetitive practice of the basics that had saved her in that alley. Her movements had been sloppy, yes, but they had been made on instinct and without thought. She had reverted back to the long hours of training in the balmy gardens of Hong Kong, and that was the only thing that had kept her from making a costly mistake.

Biting her lip, Evelyn reached the other side of the road and turned down a street, following the map she had memorized earlier that day. She had walked away the victor in that battle, but she knew that with each Gestapo agent she touched, her anonymity and safety were compromised. The man in the alley was the second one of their agents that she'd knocked unconscious. The first was last summer, and Herr

Untersturmführer Hans Voss was well aware that she'd been the one responsible then. But where that incident could be explained away as a lucky shot, the man in the alley tonight would not be. One woman would not be that lucky twice. They would realize she had special training, and that would make her more of a threat to them. Maggie Richardson was about to become a woman whom the SD would stop at nothing to catch.

Evelyn paused under a street light and looked at her watch. Anna should be well on her way to the train station now, and Herr Renner would have discovered his agent in the alley. She had to keep moving. Lifting her head, she strode down the sidewalk until she came to the entrance of a small cafe on the corner. With a last furtive look behind her, she opened the door and went inside.

The warmth and smell of good coffee and simple food enveloped her, welcoming her in from the cold outside, and she breathed deeply, looking around. Her stomach rumbled, reminding her that she hadn't eaten since that morning, but there was no time now. Every minute she remained in the city was another minute one, or both, of the enemy agents could find her. Anna was drawing Renner and his men away from her, but she had no idea where her Soviet friend was, or how long Renner would be distracted.

A tall man at one of the tables near the back raised his hand, and Evelyn moved towards him. He was younger than she had expected, unless it wasn't Horace Manchester who was standing politely as she approached.

"Miss Richardson?" he asked, moving to pull out a chair for her. "I'm Collins, Mr. Manchester's assistant. He sends his apologies that he couldn't be here personally. He believes he is being watched, you see. He didn't want to expose you any further."

She nodded and seated herself in the offered chair, unbuttoning her coat.

"I understand, and appreciate his caution," she said. "It's a pleasure to meet you."

Collins seated himself again and smiled at her, his face open and friendly.

"I wish it were under better circumstances," he said, reaching into the inside pocket of his coat. He pulled out a thick envelope and passed it to her. "Everything you need is inside. We've arranged passage for you on a merchant ship leaving for Denmark tonight. It will take you to Copenhagen. From there, it is up to you to find your way back to England."

Evelyn took the envelope and tucked it into her purse. "Thank

The Oslo Affair

you."

"London has been alerted to the arrangements," he continued. "The passage is booked under the name of Clare Billadeau, a French national."

"Did Anna get away?"

"Yes. I saw her not ten minutes ago. She's on her way to the station." He glanced at his watch. "You have to leave now if you're to make the ship. There is a gray sedan outside that will take you to the docks. Your baggage is inside."

Evelyn nodded and stood, holding her hand out to him.

"Thank you for everything, Mr. Collins," she said. "Please extend my thanks to Mr. Manchester as well."

"Of course," he shook her hand with a smile. "Have a safe journey, Miss Richardson."

She nodded and turned to leave, trying not to feel as if she was leaving behind the last friendly face she'd see for a while. It had been daunting to sail from Scotland for Norway with no idea what awaited her, but that was nothing compared to the prospect of sailing to Copenhagen with no idea how she would get from there back to England. She didn't speak Danish, nor did she know if there was even a train that would take her from Copenhagen to the western coast of Denmark.

Before an overwhelming sense of panic could consume her, Evelyn took a deep breath and focused on the next few minutes. She'd get to the car before she worried about anything else, then worry about boarding the ship. Once she was away from Sweden there would be time enough to worry about Denmark. She could only worry about one thing at a time, and had to tackle each moment as it happened. Otherwise, she wouldn't make it out of here.

She stepped out into the night again and looked around. A gray sedan was parked a few feet away and, as she walked towards it, the driver got out and moved to open the back door.

"Miss Richardson?"

She nodded and got into the car. As the door closed and the driver got behind the wheel again, Collins emerged from the cafe. The car pulled away from the curb as he turned to walk in the opposite direction.

◉

Herr Renner strode across the sidewalk towards the entrance

of the train station, his eyes on the two men waiting for him.

"Where are the others?" he demanded, joining them.

"Already inside," Otto said, turning to walk with him through the wide doors.

"And the woman?"

"Disappeared."

Renner looked at him sharply, his eyes narrowing. "What do you mean, disappeared?"

"She came in here, but there's no sign of her yet. The others split up and are checking the waiting areas."

Renner scowled and looked around the large lobby of the station. The ticket booth had one person waiting, an older gentleman carrying a briefcase, and the woman at the counter weighed at least three times what the woman who left the hotel did. He looked around slowly, scanning the crowds. It was the height of rush hour as people were catching trains out of the city at the end of the work day, and men and women swarmed around, hurrying to catch their train.

"There couldn't be a worse time for this," he muttered. "How many trains to Norway?"

"Two. But there are five more that go to other stations in Sweden where a connecting train can be caught to Oslo," Otto told him.

"So seven altogether?" Renner looked at his watch. "What time does the next one leave?"

When there was no answer immediately forthcoming, he shot a look at Otto. That man looked uncomfortable.

"I...I don't know." As storm clouds formed on his superior's brow, he turned hurriedly towards the ticket booth. "I'll find out now."

Renner watched him go in disbelief. They had taken the time at least to find out what trains went to Norway, but none of them had thought to get the times? Unbelievable! After glancing at his watch again, he started to make his way through the crowds, searching for a tall, dark-haired woman. There were any number of them, but none were the one from the hotel. And looking for a blonde woman was out of the question, he decided after a few moments. He was standing in a sea of light-haired women, all about the right height. It would be impossible to examine them all.

"Herr Sturmbannführer Renner!"

He swung around, watching as Otto pushed through the crowds towards him.

"It's leaving now!" he gasped, joining him. "From track seven. Direct to Oslo."

The Oslo Affair

Renner turned and scanned the platform entrances, searching for the one that led to track seven.

"This way!" Otto said, motioning for him to follow. "It's on this side."

Renner followed him quickly as he pushed his way through the crowds, leaving exclamations of anger in his wake. Ignoring them, the two men half-ran to the entrance. Wide, shallow steps led down to the platform and Renner bolted ahead of him, his coat flaring out around his legs as he descended rapidly to the underground platform. He was halfway down when he heard the conductor call the last boarding call.

"Schnell!" He threw over his shoulder as Otto huffed after him, his face turning red from the exertion. "It's the last boarding call!"

He reached the bottom of the stairs and ran along the short, wide corridor towards the platform ahead. The whistle blew just as he emerged onto the empty platform and he let out a string of curses at the sight of the train pulling away from the platform.

"Too late!" Otto gasped, stopping next to him and staring at the train pulling away. "Did you see her?"

"Nein." Renner turned away as the train began to pick up speed.

"Perhaps she's not on it," Otto suggested breathlessly. "There are other trains."

Herr Renner nodded and began to walk back towards the stairs. Suddenly he felt the hair on the back of his neck raise and he swung around, nearly plowing into Otto as he did so. With a scowl, he pushed him out of the way and took a few steps towards the departing train. The front had already left the station and the back was just sliding by when he saw her.

She was in the second-to-last car, staring at them. As the car flew by them, she raised a hand to her lips and blew him a kiss, her lips curving in what could only be described as an impish grin.

Chapter Twenty-Six

Evelyn stood on the deck, her hands deep in her pockets, with a strong, bitter wind whipping at her hair. The sun had set and the sky was clear, sparkling with thousands of bright stars. If it weren't for the cold, it would be a lovely night on the water. A fierce shudder went through her and she burrowed her chin into her coat as she watched the coast, glittering with lights, slip by. They were moving through what looked to be a sound now, with small, coastal islands on either side. If she looked to her left, she could see the port in the distance with the lights of Stockholm shining brightly. When she looked to the right, she saw more lights dotting the horizon as the ship made its way towards the Baltic Sea.

Another shudder went through her, but Evelyn ignored it. She couldn't go back to her cabin until she knew she was safely away. The city was still just too close for comfort.

A young sailor stood a few feet away and he kept glancing at her as she stood at the railing, watching the land slide by. He must have thought she was absolutely insane. She was the only passenger on the deck. The cold, frigid wind had already driven the others inside to where it was warm and they had access to a light supper. Her stomach had ceased rumbling long ago, but she supposed she would have to go in and eat something soon.

"Ursäkta mig, är du inte kall?"

She turned in surprise as the young sailor addressed her, a friendly smile on his face.

"I'm sorry. I don't speak Swedish," Evelyn said in French, shrugging apologetically.

Instead of looking confused at the language, the young man visibly brightened.

"You're French!" he exclaimed in kind, a grin breaking across his face. "So am I! I'm from Marseilles!"

Evelyn smiled. "My family is from Paris."

The Oslo Affair

"I haven't spoken to another Frenchman in over six months," the young man said, moving closer. "My name is Lucas," he added, shoving his hand out.

"I'm Clare." She pulled her hand out of her pocket to shake the offered hand, then shoved it back in quickly as another violent shudder went through her.

"You're cold," he said unnecessarily. "It's very cold tonight. Why don't you go inside where it's warm? You'll get sick out here."

"I just want to watch until we get to the sea," she said, nodding to the passing coastline. "I love to watch the lights go by."

"I suppose I'm used to it," Lucas said, following her gaze. "How long were you in Sweden?"

"A few weeks. I was visiting an old school friend," Evelyn lied smoothly. "I wasn't due to leave until next week, but I received word that my grand-mère is ill."

"And so you grabbed passage on the first ship you could," he said with a nod. "We dock at Copenhagen, but there are always liners coming in and out of port. You should be able to get passage relatively quickly."

"That's what I'm hoping."

"You really shouldn't be out here without at least a scarf. Do you have one?"

"I'm afraid not."

He clucked his tongue and shook his head. Then, after a moment of thought, he patted her arm.

"Wait here," he told her. "I'll be right back."

Evelyn watched her new acquaintance turn and hurry along the deck to a door, disappearing inside. She smiled faintly and turned back to look at the lights. They were getting more sporadic now and further away as the ship got closer to the sea. It was nice to talk to someone in a civilized language, she reflected. Anna had been lovely, of course, but it was comforting to hear French again.

The smile faded as she thought of Anna. Had she reached the train in time? Had she managed to lose Herr Renner and his thugs? Evelyn hadn't liked leaving her to play the part of the decoy alone, but Anna had insisted. As soon as she found out that Evelyn could contact the embassy and get out of Stockholm, there had been no swaying her. She had quite logically pointed out that the Germans could hardly detain her. She was Norwegian and, not only was Norway neutral in the war, but she had done nothing except accompany a new friend to Sweden. There was absolutely nothing they could do except threaten her. And, Anna had said with a martial glint in her eyes, she'd just like to see them try.

In the end, Evelyn had agreed, knowing that it was paramount that she get out of Sweden with her intelligence. She never mentioned the Soviet agent to Anna. Her new friend had enough to worry about with Herr Renner. The other one would just complicate things needlessly. After all, her Russian Comrade had never seen Anna. He was no threat to her.

As they ran around the city gathering the supplies they needed to stage a performance for the SD, Anna had been a great help to her. She was able to procure almost everything Evelyn needed to change her appearance while Evelyn sent a telegram to Horace Manchester at the embassy and another one to Daniel Carew in Oslo. Then, while Evelyn was closeted in a restroom at the back of a cafe darkening her blonde hair until it was almost black, she went to purchase appropriate clothing. When she returned, Evelyn couldn't have been happier. Everything the other woman had selected was perfect, right down to the black-rimmed spectacles she'd got for herself. In fact, Evelyn admitted now, she couldn't have done it without Anna.

"Here. Take this."

Lucas was back beside her, holding out a long, thick scarf. Evelyn looked at him in surprise.

"I couldn't!"

"Yes, please do! I have two, and you need this more than I do. It's long, so you can wrap it around your head, and it's very warm. Take it."

"Thank you very much. It's very kind of you!" She took it and began to wrap it around her neck and head. "You must let me give you some money for it!"

"No, no. I don't need money for it. Just think of me when you wear it and offer up a prayer for my safe return to our beloved France," he said with a grin.

Evelyn finished wrapping it around herself and sighed in relief. The heavy wool was very warm indeed, and it blocked the harsh wind from whipping down inside her coat.

"Oh, that's wonderful," she breathed with a smile. "Thank you so much!"

He nodded and grinned, then turned to leave again.

"I have to get back to my station. Don't stay out here too much longer. Even with that scarf, you'll be frozen soon!"

Evelyn nodded and turned to look at the coastline in the distance as Lucas left, her hands back in her pockets. Anna had to be

The Oslo Affair

on the train by now. She should be on her way back to Oslo, where she would once again be safe. Evelyn wished there was a way to know if she made it safely back, but she would have to wait until she reached England to know for sure. In the meantime, all she could do was hope and pray that everything had gone according to their hastily conceived plan.

As the last stretch of coastline slid by, Evelyn finally turned away from the railing and turned to go inside. She had made it safely away. She could get something to eat and then go to her room and sleep in relative peace. Tomorrow would be soon enough to worry about how she was going to make it back to England.

Tonight it was enough that she had escaped.

◉

Comrade Grigori strode through the lobby of The Strand, his face folded into a scowl. The Englishwoman was gone, and so was her companion. He'd followed the other woman to the station, where he watched as she joined the crowds of commuters. He'd been able to keep track of her easily enough until she went into the ladies' washroom. While he waited for her to come out again, he had ample time to examine his options. He would follow her to the train in case the Englishwoman was waiting for her there, but he knew it was unlikely. The Englishwoman would have realized that the Germans would follow the other woman. In fact, that was probably the reasoning behind this whole trip to the station. The other woman was probably a decoy, distracting the SD agents while the Englishwoman made her escape by a different route. Unfortunately, he couldn't take the chance that it wasn't.

And so he'd still been there when the dark-haired woman emerged from the washroom several minutes later. She had looked around cautiously, then moved quickly into the crowds. A few minutes later, they emerged onto a train platform just as the conductor was calling for the last passengers. She boarded the train alone, with no sign of the Englishwoman anywhere in sight.

Grigori was ascending the stairs again when the tall SD agent from the hotel lobby had come tearing down them, a shorter man huffing to keep pace. The two hadn't paid any attention to the other people on the stairs and certainly hadn't noticed himself as they ran for the train. He'd gone to the top of the stairs and waited off to the side, watching. Not five minutes later, they were coming back and the tall one looked furious.

A small smile pulled at his lips now, lightening the scowl as he strode, not to the lift, but to the stairwell. At least the Germans had come up empty-handed as well.

Except he wasn't empty-handed, he reminded himself as he started up the stairs. He may not have had to opportunity to question the British agent as he wanted, but he wasn't returning to Moscow with nothing to show for his efforts. Moscow had sent him to find a traitor, and that was just what he'd done. He might not know how the Englishwoman had turned Comrade Niva, or even how she'd become acquainted with him, but now they knew who the leak was and could stop the flow.

The frown returned. What bothered him was how Niva had managed to access some of the information that had been released to the British. Much of it he could have obtained easily, but some would have been impossible for him get his hands on.

Grigori shook his head. He wished he could have interrogated the Englishwoman. She could have cleared up all these niggling little details that he knew would keep him awake for many nights to come.

Reaching the third floor, he went down the corridor to his room and unlocked the door, stepping inside. The door closed behind him and he slid the bolt home, then turned to cross the sitting room to a window overlooking the harbor. The lights of the palace glittered across the water and he sighed in contentment. It was a beautiful view, even if the palace itself was symbolic of everything decadent and corrupt in the West. After enjoying the view for a moment, he turned to switch on the lamp on the desk and froze.

"Good evening, Comrade Grigori," Vladimir said calmly. He was seated in one of the armchairs with his legs crossed and his gloves laying across his knee. He'd unbuttoned his overcoat and looked completely at home. "You look well."

"As do you, Comrade Lyakhov." Grigori found his voice and began to remove his gloves. "I had no idea you were in Stockholm."

Vladimir raised one eyebrow just a bit and a faint smile toyed with his lips.

"Didn't you?" he asked, watching as Grigori tossed his gloves on the table and began removing his coat. "I'd have thought Comrade Yakov would have told you. You do know he's here, yes?"

"Yes." Grigori pulled off his coat and tossed it over the back of the love seat. "Please. Remove your coat and make yourself comfortable, my old friend. If you took the time to break into my room, you might as well take the time to remove your coat."

The Oslo Affair

Vladimir smiled and stood up to shrug out of the heavy garment.

"I'm afraid Yakov is getting sloppy in his aging years," he said, carefully laying his coat over the back of his chair. "He's not the ghost that he once was."

Grigori shot him a glance under his brows and walked to a long console on the other side of the room where a bottle of schnapps sat with two glasses.

"No, he's not," he agreed. "When did you know he was there?"

"The first night in Oslo." Vladimir seated himself again. "It wasn't until the third night that I realized you were there as well."

Grigori grunted and held up the bottle questioningly. "It's not vodka, but it's tolerable."

"Thank you."

He poured schnapps into both glasses and turned to carry them over to Vladimir, offering him a choice of glass. Vladimir took one and Grigori carried the other over to a chair and sat down.

"It wasn't anything personal, you understand," he said, sitting back.

"If I thought it was personal, we wouldn't be having this conversation," Vladimir replied dryly. "You would have disappeared in Norway."

That drew a smile from the other man and he chuckled.

"You haven't lost your fire, have you Vlad?"

Vladimir held up his glass. "I hope I never will."

Grigori sipped his drink, then sighed and stretched his legs out. "Why are you here?"

Vladimir looked at him, surprised. "Why, to help you catch a traitor, of course."

"And how do you propose to do that?"

"I don't propose anything. I have done it already."

Grigori frowned and stared hard at him. "What do you mean?"

"You were in Gamla Stan this morning," Vladimir said, crossing his legs again and sitting back comfortably. "You saw him with your own eyes. Comrade Niva met with a British agent. Now, unless he was authorized to do so by Moscow, I believe that's grounds for treason, don't you?"

"You were there?" Grigori asked quickly. "How do you know this?"

Vladimir shrugged. "Because I, also, have been trying to find the traitor in our midst."

"You?" Grigori scowled. "Impossible."

The smile that crossed Vladimir's face was chilling. "Is it?"

"I would have been informed."

"Would you?"

Grigori stared at him for a long moment in silence, then sipped his drink. It was true that the left hand often did not know what the right was doing. It was like that in Moscow, especially when suspicion mounted within their own ranks. Vladimir could very well have been instructed to hunt for the traitor while he was going about his own work. Furthermore, Grigori would not be surprised to find that he had been told to observe Vladimir as a fail-safe.

"We have no way of knowing that Comrade Niva arranged that meeting today," he said finally. "We only have the evidence that he was in the same tavern as a British agent. We didn't see them talking, unless you were inside. Were you inside?"

Vladimir shook his head. "No. I was in the building across the street."

"There. Then all we have is that Niva was in the same place as a British agent. It is enough to allocate more manpower to watch him, but not enough to bring him back to Moscow. However, it will make Moscow happy that progress has been made."

Vladimir reached into his suit jacket and pulled a folded piece paper out of the pocket. Leaning forward, he tossed it onto the table between them.

"Take a look at that, and then tell me if you don't have enough to bring him in."

Grigori frowned and leaned forward to set his drink down and reach for the paper.

"I retrieved that before it could be destroyed," Vladimir continued, sitting back in his chair again.

Grigori unfolded the paper and read the short, handwritten message, his face impassive.

Instruct agent to meet at Den Gyldene Freden in Gamla Stan at eleven o'clock.

"As you can see, it is handwritten. I believe you'll find it matches Comrade Niva's handwriting perfectly."

"Where did you get this?" Grigori finally asked.

"Where the facilitator left it, in a trash receptacle across from the hotel where Niva is staying."

"And the facilitator?"

"I never saw his face. He had his back to me. Niva passed him the paper in the street and continued into the hotel." Vladimir

The Oslo Affair

shrugged. "I can tell you he is of medium height and was wearing a long, dark coat and a hat."

"Which is unhelpful."

"Precisely."

Grigori folded the paper and slid it into his pocket.

"Do you know anything about this Englishwoman?" he asked. "Did you see her before this morning?"

Vladimir sipped his drink, his eyes resting on Grigori's face thoughtfully.

"I would think you know more about her than I do at this point," he said. "It's unlike you not to observe an enemy agent when you have the chance."

Grigori was surprised into a short laugh.

"You know me well, Vlad."

"I should. We've known each other for years."

"Ah, we've seen some things, haven't we?" Grigori said with smile. "And we'll see some more before this war is over."

"One can only hope."

"I have been observing her, yes. I haven't learned very much, though. She doesn't go about very much. Only to dinner, really. She seems to enjoy finer foods and wine, but she never indulges beyond what is reasonable. No vices that I've been able to ascertain. She keeps herself to herself, for the most part, which confuses me. She doesn't display any of the usual traits of an agent that we're used to seeing. It makes it very difficult."

"Have you found how she communicates with her contacts?" Vladimir asked after a moment.

Grigori shook his head.

"No. If she uses a facilitator, as you suggested, that could be why."

"I assumed it was Niva who insisted on that arrangement," Vladimir said slowly, "but I suppose it could be her way of doing things. I wouldn't have thought the English were that intelligent."

"They were intelligent enough to find and turn Niva," Grigori muttered, getting up to refill his glass. He motioned to Vladimir's, who shook his head. "I wish I knew how they did that."

"Perhaps they didn't. Perhaps he approached them."

Grigori refilled his glass and turned from the sideboard, sipping it thoughtfully.

"Perhaps."

"How did you find out about the Englishwoman, anyway?" Vladimir asked, tilting his head curiously. "I didn't know about her until

I saw her check into this hotel."

"The Nazis were kind enough to share the information," Grigori said, going back to his chair. "For once, they appear to be right."

"The Abwehr?" Vladimir's eyebrows soared into his forehead. "They're useless!"

"Yes, they are," Grigori agreed with a nod. "It was the SD, I believe. One of Himmler's black boots. They learned of her last year."

"Interesting. I wonder what they know of her."

Grigori scoffed. "Not much, I don't think. They're here, in Stockholm, and they managed to scare her right off."

"What? Here?"

He nodded glumly. "Yes. They were in the hotel, spread out and watching her room and all the exits. The fools. Did they think she wouldn't notice?"

"They're too arrogant to think anything," Vladimir muttered. "I assume she's gone?"

"Yes, and so is her companion. I followed the other woman to the train station. That's where I've just come from. She's on her way back to Oslo, but there was no sign of the Englishwoman."

"And the Germans?"

"Missed the train. At least they're empty-handed as well."

Vladimir was quiet for a moment, then he looked over to his old friend and smiled slowly.

"Ah, but you're not empty-handed, comrade," he said. "You have handwritten proof of Niva's deceit, and you return to Moscow successful. You'll undoubtedly get a promotion out of this."

Grigori grunted and looked across the table at Vladimir.

"And you? I won't forget my old comrade. Would you like a promotion?"

"I'm quite willing to be guided by the ministry. You know I've never sought to advance."

"And yet you have. Consistently." Grigori raised his glass to him. "To the future!"

Vladimir raised his glass.

"To the future!"

The Oslo Affair

Chapter Twenty-Seven

London, England
November 23, 1939

Evelyn got out of the taxi and looked up at the familiar facade of the house on Brook Street. She didn't think there would ever be a time when it looked more welcoming than it did right this minute. It stood tall and elegant over the street, like an old retainer waiting to be of service once again. She found comfort in the knowledge that the house had withstood several wars over the course of the years, and remained stoically solid through them all. With a deep sigh of contentment, she turned to take her bags from the driver as he pulled them out of the boot of the car.

" 'Ere ye are, miss," he said cheerfully, his cockney accent rolling over her. "Do you need me to carry them up?"

"No, that's quite all right, thank you," she said with a smile, passing him the fare. "I can manage."

She turned to go up the steps to the glossy black door, setting the bags down while she fished in her purse for the key. The taxi pulled away, the driver giving a friendly wave, and she smiled. It was nice to be back in England and to hear the welcoming accent of home. Even if it was from the East End, she thought with a grin.

Pulling out the key, she unlocked the door and pushed it open, picking up her bags again. The Ainsworth House had been in her family longer than anyone cared to remember. It was their residence when they were in London for the season, and her father had used it during the rest of the year when he was working and couldn't make the long trip back to Lancashire. Since his death, it had seen much less use, and would probably see even less as the war dragged on. The servants were at Ainsworth Manor with her mother and there were dust covers over the furniture, but she didn't care. Evelyn closed the door and exhaled in relief.

She was home.

She dropped her bags in the long, wide hallway and looked around, an overwhelming sense of calm coming over her. She moved across the hallway to the first door on her left and opened it, stepping into the front drawing room. The chairs and sofas were covered with dust covers, as were the tables and the piano in the corner. Evelyn looked around slowly. She knew Robbie came to stay here when he was in London, but the drawing room looked as if it hadn't been touched since the house was closed at the end of the summer. She walked over to the front window and opened the thick blackout curtains, staring out at Brook Street. She watched the traffic for a moment, enjoying the familiar sound of the busy London street.

Her journey through Denmark, while uneventful, had been fraught with an anxious desire to reach home. As she went from train to connecting train, arriving ultimately on the west coast of Denmark, she had stared at the strange countryside and suddenly become very homesick. Her guide, a man by the name of Frederick, had been very friendly and had taken great pleasure in pointing out landmarks and imparting history as they went through his country, but it had done very little to alleviate her longing for home.

When Pierson, the MI6 contact who had met her off the ship in Copenhagen, told her that he'd arranged for a guide to take her across Denmark, she had protested that it was unnecessary. However, as the journey extended into days, she was very grateful for the company. Frederick was a wealth of interesting information about Denmark and her people. He was also well-versed in European politics, and they spent many hours discussing the events unfolding around them. When they reached Esbjerg, she'd said goodbye with a sense of parting from an old friend.

Evelyn turned away from the window and went to the door, returning to the hallway and going towards the back of the house. After spending two days in the coastal town of Esbjerg, she had boarded a ship at last, bound for London.

Even though it was an English ship, she still hadn't relaxed until they docked in London. The very fact that it *was* an English ship made crossing the North Sea particularly dangerous. The Germans had mines in the waters, and she had been told by the captain that their U-boats were sinking a growing number of merchant ships both in the North Sea and in the Atlantic. As if realizing that perhaps he shouldn't have told her that, the captain then hastened to assure her that he had never had any problems yet. It didn't go very far to alleviating her discomfort, and she spent the voyage in a state of nervous anxiety.

When the ship sailed up the Thames estuary, Evelyn had never been so pleased to see the London landscape. But even as she stood on the deck to take in her first sight of England after a particularly trying journey, her joy was tempered by the knowledge that this feeling of

The Oslo Affair

relief at being home was just the beginning. She had the disquieting feeling that as this war continued, the likelihood of her coming home safely would become less and less.

Putting the dark thought out of her head, she made her way to the kitchen. While she had no expectation of finding an ounce of food in the house, Evelyn sincerely hoped that Rob had at least stocked the kitchen with tea the last time he was here. Stepping into the large square room, she was pleasantly surprised to find sun streaming through the windows and not a dust cover in sight. At least now she knew where Rob spent most of his time when he *did* come to stay.

Crossing the old tiled floor, Evelyn started opening cabinets, looking for tea. On the third try, she found it. And Rob, it seemed, had outdone himself. Not only where there two different types of tea, but there was also a can of coffee. She lifted it out and looked at it curiously. While she drank coffee extensively on the continent, it was rare for it to make an appearance at home. She set it back in the cabinet and reached for the tea. Whatever the reason, she was grateful for the foresight that had led Rob to buy the coffee. It would be a welcome treat in the next few days.

She was just filling the kettle from the faucet in the sink when the bells above the kitchen door chimed. She started, then finished filling the kettle and set it on the stove top. After lighting the burner, she turned to leave the kitchen. Someone was at the front door, and only one person knew that she was in London.

A moment later she opened the door to find Bill standing on the top step, a large paper bag in his arms.

"Welcome back," he said.

"How on earth did you know I'd arrived?" Evelyn demanded, opening the door wider and motioning him in. "I just got here!"

"I had someone at the dock watching for the ship. I would've gone myself to meet you but we weren't sure when you were coming in. Here. These are for you. I can't imagine there's a thing in the house to eat."

Evelyn took the bag from him and looked inside. It was filled with groceries.

"Oh! This is wonderful! You're right. There's absolutely nothing in the way of food. In fact, I was just relieved to find that Robbie left some tea here the last time he stayed." She turned to lead the way down the hallway to the back of the house. "I've put the kettle on, so I can offer you some tea. I'm afraid we'll have to drink it in the kitchen, though. I haven't had time to remove the dust covers from any of the other rooms."

"How was your trip through Denmark?" Bill asked, following her into the kitchen. "Did Pierson take care of you?"

"Yes, he did. Thank you for arranging for him to meet me. I'll admit I was feeling somewhat overwhelmed by the time we reached Copenhagen." She set the bag of groceries down on the counter and began to empty it as Bill seated himself at the kitchen table. "All I could think was that I didn't speak a word of Danish and how on earth was I going to navigate my way to the North Sea," she added with a laugh.

"Which is precisely why I arranged for Pierson to meet you," he said with a smile. "He can be a bit much at times, but I've always had the impression that he was a very kind man."

Evelyn thought of the eccentric agent with the shocking red hair that had met her off the ship and grinned.

"He certainly isn't what I would have expected," she admitted. "But he was very helpful, and yes, he was very kind. He showed me to a good, clean hotel and then met me the next morning with a guide to escort me through Denmark."

"And the journey was uneventful?"

"Very much so."

Evelyn finished emptying the bag and surveyed the goodies that Bill had picked up. There was a loaf of bread, cheese, a bottle of milk, some eggs, and a pack of sausages. He'd also included some tea and a package of biscuits.

"This is lovely, Bill. Thank you!"

"It will do for a day or two," he said with a nod. "Tomorrow you'll come to Broadway for a full debriefing. Montclair wants to have dinner with you tomorrow night. You should be able to return to your station in Scotland the following day, barring any unforeseen delays. I thought this would be enough to get you through, but of course if you need anything else, you can go out to the shops. I thought you'd be tired today."

Evelyn turned to look at him. "You're a good man, Mr. Buckley. I *am* tired, and this is just what I needed."

He smiled faintly. "I can hardly let one of my best agents go hungry on her first night back in London, can I?" he asked, sitting back and crossing his legs. "Marguerite would have my head!"

"How is she?" She turned to get a teapot and two cups and saucers as the kettle began to whistle. "Is she still in France?"

"Yes. She's getting the house ready to close. She's decided to come back to England next month for Christmas and, given the increased tensions, she'll be remaining in England. If it is still safe to travel, she may go back to Paris for a short trip in the spring, but I

The Oslo Affair

don't think it will remain safe for long. The Germans will make a move towards France soon."

"Will she stay in London or go to your estate? It's in Hertfordshire, isn't it?"

"Yes. She'll go to the estate, although how long I can keep her there, I don't know," he said with a short laugh. "You know how restless she gets."

"My mother would enjoy seeing her," Evelyn said over her shoulder as she fixed the tea. "She's welcome to visit Ainsworth Manor at any time, I'm sure."

"And she will. We're coming for Christmas, as a matter of fact."

"Oh good! I was hoping that would be the case." Evelyn lifted the kettle with a towel and poured boiling water into the teapot. "This first Christmas without Dad will be hard. I think it will help to retain as many of the traditions as we can."

"That's what your mother said," Bill said, amused. "I've arranged for you to take two-days leave. You'll have Christmas Eve and Christmas Day. I couldn't do more, I'm afraid."

Evelyn turned to carry the teapot over to the table.

"I understand. Thank you! I hope Rob can get away, and..." She stopped abruptly and turned to get the cups.

"And?" Bill prompted when she didn't continue.

"It's nothing." She set the cups down and turned to grab the packet of biscuits off the counter. "Just someone Rob flies with. There was talk that he might join us for Christmas."

Bill raised an eyebrow and watched as she set a bowl of sugar on table.

"Oh? Does this someone have a name?"

Evelyn grabbed the bottle of milk and turned to seat herself across from him.

"Lacey," she said, reaching for his cup. "Miles Lacey. Do you take milk?"

"Yes, thank you." Bill studied her face interestedly. "You look rather flushed. Are you quite all right?"

She poured milk into his cup and handed it to him. "Do I? How strange. It must be the heat from the water. I'm fine."

Bill spooned some sugar into his cup, his lips twitching.

"You know, for someone who just recently learned to lie, you're developing a real talent for it," he murmured. Then, after a second, "Tell me about Vladimir Lyakhov," he said, changing the subject. "Did you meet with him?"

"Yes." Evelyn poured tea into his cup then her own. "He's not what I expected. He's really quite interesting, if a little brusque. I'm still not sure why he refuses to deal with anyone but myself, but he gave me the microfilm. I haven't looked to see what's on it."

She got up and left the kitchen, coming back a moment later with a small traveling case. Bill watched as she opened it and lifted out the insert.

"That's how you carried it back?" he asked, leaning forward to examine the case more closely. "That's very good. Did you make this yourself, or did they give it to you in Scotland?"

"A bit of both, actually. The case is mine. One of the instructors there was able to show me how to modify it." Evelyn lifted out the microfilm and the tightly wound roll of paper that Risto Niva had handed over. "This is the microfilm from Shustov," she said, handing it to him. "And this is from the other Soviet agent, Risto Niva. He said that they are copies of transmissions."

"Transmissions?" Bill glanced up from the microfilm he was examining against the light. "Transmissions from what?"

"I've no idea. Coded transmissions, I believe, but he never actually said." She replaced the insert in the case and closed it, setting it aside before retaking her seat. "He says that Stalin is planning to invade Finland. He thinks it will be soon."

Bill set down the microfilm and reached for his tea. "Did he say why?"

"He said it was in those transmissions. I read through them on the crossing from Denmark. It certainly appears that they're planning something, but it gives no indication of where. In fact, it doesn't even mention a country, just a code phrase. It could be anywhere."

"Why did Niva think it was Finland?"

"Because Stalin is very unhappy that they've refused to concede the territory that he wants."

Bill was quiet for a moment, drinking his tea thoughtfully.

"What were your impressions of him?" he asked suddenly. "What did you think of him?"

Evelyn thought for a moment.

"I think he's getting tired of the Soviet regime," she said slowly. "I think he's looking for a way out. Perhaps Vladimir suggested to him that England could be a route out of the Soviet Union. I do think he has information he's willing to give, but I'm not sure how useful or relevant that information may be."

"Did he mention the possibility of being extracted?"

"Yes. He wants asylum in England."

The Oslo Affair

Bill nodded, seeming to be unsurprised. Obviously this wasn't the first time he'd heard that particular request.

"He did say something that has me worried," she said after a moment, looking down at her tea.

"Oh?"

"Yes. I'm telling you, but I'd rather not mention it tomorrow at the debriefing." Evelyn looked up, her eyes meeting his. "He mentioned it in a personal conversation, and it wasn't meant to be forwarded with the rest of the information."

Bill frowned. "What did he say?"

"That we have a leak in our ship," she said bluntly. "He said the Soviets have agents embedded in London, and that I was to trust no one here."

Bill sat back and studied her face. "Do you believe him?"

"Someone knew I was in Oslo as soon as I landed, and it wasn't because of something I did," she said with a shrug. "Not only that, but the German SD knew I was there as well. Someone is talking, and that person could very well be here in London. Niva gave me the impression that he knows specifically of men who are well entrenched here, and possibly above suspicion."

"And you don't know who you can trust," Bill finished.

She nodded.

"I've not been doing this long enough to know anyone or to have formed opinions, so it's very difficult for me. As it stands right now, you're the only one I can honestly say I trust without hesitation. That's why I'm telling you. I don't know what I should do with the information."

"Don't mention it to anyone else, for starters," Bill said, leaning forward. "You've been frank with me, so I'll return the favor. I'd already realized there's a leak here somewhere. When you sent word that you were followed by a Soviet agent in Oslo, I took it to Montclair. He wasn't entirely convinced. However, when the SD showed up, I think that clinched things. He and I are making inquiries, but it's a very delicate business. It will take time. We can't risk alerting the spy to our investigation and losing him altogether. We need to exercise utter discretion."

"What do you need me to do?" she asked simply.

"Continue as you are. We're moving you from Scotland to somewhere closer to London after Christmas. The alias of Maggie Richardson is, I think you'll agree, completely blown. We're working up a new one, but I am handling it myself. My assistant, whom I trust implicitly, is helping with the details. We're not going through the usual channels, so when we're finished, the only people who will have any knowledge of your new cover identity will be ourselves."

"Not even Montclair?"

"Not even Montclair. That was his idea, by the way. We'll have a specific code name for you and that is the only name that will be used within the section. He wants to ensure that no more damage is done."

"What about the others?" Evelyn asked after a moment.

"Just worry about yourself," Bill advised. "As this war goes on, and it *will* go on, that will be quite enough. It will be hard enough for you to take care of yourself without worrying about other agents as well."

She looked at him, tilting her head.

"Is there something wrong?" she asked. "Something I should know about?"

Bill hesitated, then sighed.

"I shouldn't be telling you this, but I think it will only create a false sense of security for you by hiding it. We received news yesterday that two of our agents were captured in Holland and taken into Germany."

"What?" Evelyn gasped, her eyes wide.

"It occurred weeks ago, on the 9th, but Himmler just released the information yesterday. They were taken at a small border town, Venlo, just five meters from the border with Germany. A Dutch intelligence officer with them was shot and killed."

"But...how?"

"They had arranged a meeting with a supposed major in the Wehrmacht who was part of a group of conspirators against Hitler. Of course, now we know that he wasn't, and that the whole thing was a ruse to lure two of our agents to the border. The German press are claiming they were behind the attempt on Hitler's life earlier this month. Total bollocks, of course." Bill made a disgusted sound in the back of his throat. "Montclair believes the network in the Netherlands has been infiltrated, but Chamberlain is having none of it, even after this. There's quite a bit of blame going round, but in the meantime, two of our agents have no doubt been being interrogated for the past few weeks. Lord only knows what they've revealed under torture. It's a complete shambles."

Evelyn sat back, stunned. "And no one knew? How is that possible?"

"The SD continued to send messages as the conspirators. The other members of the network didn't communicate that the agents were even missing. It's doubtful that they even knew. The entire

The Oslo Affair

meeting was so closely guarded that only a handful here in London knew about it, and the only ones in Holland who knew about it were the agents themselves."

"And just like that, they're in Nazi Germany." She rubbed her forehead, her skin cold. "And that could have happened to me in Stockholm."

He nodded soberly.

"And so, you see, you'll need to be very focused. If anything feels off, go with your gut feelings. Himmler has his spies everywhere, and they are not playing by the rules. Neither should you."

She nodded and sipped her tea. Reaching for the biscuits, she opened the package and offered him one. He took one with a nod of thanks and she selected one for herself with a hand that was only slightly trembling.

"Did Anna make it back to Oslo?" she asked after a moment.

"She didn't go back to Oslo." Bill dunked his biscuit in his tea and took a bite. "She got off the train at the first stop in Norway. Carew had someone meet her and they drove her into the north. She'll stay there until it's safe to return to the city."

Evelyn exhaled. "That's a relief. I was worried that Renner would pursue her when he couldn't find me."

"As far as we can tell, he did. When Anna's train arrived in Oslo, there were three SD men waiting. Herr Renner arrived by train a few hours later. When he could find no sign of Anna, he left Norway. Carew believes he returned to Germany."

"I suppose he won't want me back in Norway any time soon," she said sheepishly. "I seem to have a caused a good deal of commotion."

Bill grinned. "I think he rather enjoyed it," he said. "That's the most excitement Oslo's seen in a long while. And you weren't the only cause."

Evelyn raised an eyebrow questioningly. "Oh?"

"I shouldn't be telling you this either, but Daniel told me you were trying to get information from a couple of scientists there, so I think you'll find this interesting. He received an anonymous report after you left. It was written by, we believe, a German scientist. We're calling it the Oslo Report, for lack of a more imaginative name. If the information checks out, it may very well be a God-send for us."

Evelyn thought of the nervous scientist she'd met who had backed out of their dinner date and smiled.

"It's amazing that someone had the courage to do it," she said. "I was to have dinner with a scientist, but when I went, he'd left a note crying off. He was very afraid of the Gestapo and thought having dinner with a reporter without the permission of the Propaganda Ministry could lead to reprisals. I got the impression that most of them were of the same mind."

"Well, someone went through some lengths to get the information to us. We have people going over the information. At least one if the items has since been proven to be true, so it's looking quite hopeful. Anyway, as you see, you're not the only source of excitement for Carew."

Evelyn grinned. "Even though I cost him one of his best translators?"

Bill chuckled. "I don't think you cost him anything, my dear. I believe he has plans for Anna, and you facilitated them."

She thought of the young woman who had been such a great help to her.

"She will make someone an amazing agent," she said slowly. "I'm glad she's safe."

"And I'm glad you're safe." Bill finished his tea and picked up the microfilm and roll of papers, tucking them into the inside pocket of his overcoat. "It seems that once again I must extend my apologies. This was supposed to an easy assignment to get your feet wet. It turned out to be anything but."

Evelyn stood with him and gave him a twisted smile.

"That's hardly your fault. I'm considering it as on-the-job training," she told him. "The things I'm learning now may very well save my life another day, so I shan't complain."

He nodded and turned to walk with her out of the kitchen and down the hallway to the front door.

"I'll see you tomorrow, bright and early at nine o'clock. Don't be late," he said as they reached the door.

She nodded and reached for the handle.

"Thank you for the groceries. They are very much appreciated."

"As are you, Jian. Welcome home."

The Oslo Affair

Chapter Twenty-Eight

4th December, 1939

Dear Evelyn,
It was wonderful to finally hear from you. Have things calmed down a bit now? I can't imagine being stuck in the highlands for three weeks. I hope the training was worth it. Glad you're back at your station and able to catch up on the important things - such as writing to me.

Things have been fairly uneventful around here. Flying every day and some nights, waiting for things to get started. All the action in this war seems to be happening everywhere but here. Now Finland is in the thick of it. Did you see that Stalin attacked them? Rather surprising, that. I suppose that means that Norway or Sweden will be next. Somehow, I don't think this war will be over by Christmas as everyone said, do you?

We did have one bit of excitement the other day. The American had a bit of trouble with his landing gear and was forced to land his plane on its belly. It was rather hair-raising, and I don't think any of us thought he'd actually pull it off without blowing himself to kingdom come, but the blighter actually managed it! Fantastic flying, or rather landing. The whole thing did make me think that half of flying is really just plain luck. Sobering thought, really.

I'm so glad you're able to take leave over Christmas. I'm looking forward to seeing you. It's a shame you and Rob have to be back on station on Boxing Day. He's put out that the traditional hunt won't happen, but at least we'll have Christmas Eve and Christmas Day. I was lucky enough to get Boxing Day as well, so I'll be able to drop in on the pile up in Yorkshire and do the duty to the elders before heading back to the squadron.

You know, when this war does get going, it will be harder to manage meetings like this. If you were closer, we could perhaps meet for dinner occasionally. What are your thoughts on trying for a posting closer to London? It must be tiresome to be so far away.

Yours,

FO Miles Lacey

Christmas Eve, 1939

The train rocked to a stop in the station as Evelyn made her way down the aisle to the door, a single case in her hand. The conductor nodded to her with a smile.

"Happy Christmas, miss," he said, touching his cap. "Watch your step now."

"Thank you. Enjoy your Christmas!"

She held onto the vertical railing on the side of the door with one hand while she looked out over the platform, searching for Rob. After missing her original train from Scotland, she'd had to catch a later one, and she was a full four hours later than anyone expected. Rob had been going to pick her up from the earlier train, but she had no idea if anyone had come to meet this one.

Not seeing her brother in the crowds waiting on the platform, Evelyn moved down to the last step above the platform. Just before stepping off the train, she looked up again and her breath caught in her throat. A little flutter of butterflies stirred in her belly as a rush of excitement went through her.

Miles was making his way through the throng, standing a full head over those around him. He was dressed in his RAF blues with a spotted blue silk neckerchief tied carelessly around his throat, looking rakishly elegant despite being in uniform. He caught sight of her just as she looked up and a smile curved his full lips.

"Ahem!"

Evelyn started as a woman cleared her throat behind her. Murmuring an apology over her shoulder, she stepped off the train quickly and moved towards Miles.

"Hallo!" he greeted her, reaching for her suitcase. "You finally made it!"

The Oslo Affair

"At last!" she agreed with a laugh, looking up into his sparkling green eyes. "I wasn't expecting to see you here. Where's Robbie?"

"I offered to come collect you," he said, turning to walk beside her. "I hope you don't mind."

"Of course not! It's lovely to see you. When did you arrive?"

"Rob and I drove up from London and got here just in time for lunch." He glanced down at her. "We all thought you were getting in earlier. When you weren't on the train, Rob decided you'd missed it. Did you?"

Evelyn laughed sheepishly. "Yes, I'm afraid so. I got caught up with work and had to wait for the next one. I thought I'd never get here."

"Never mind. You're here now."

His voice rolled over her warmly and Evelyn felt a rush of warmth go through her as she realized that this was what she'd been looking forward to all week. It wasn't spending Christmas with her family, although she was happy to do that as well, but it was the anticipation of seeing the sparkling green eyes that had haunted her for two months. And the reality was far better than she'd expected.

They walked out of the station and a blast of icy wind greeted them. Evelyn gasped and tucked her arm through his, leaning closer to him with a shiver.

"Please tell me you have a car here," she said, hunching her shoulders.

"I have a car here," he replied promptly, steering her to the parking area to the right. "And it has a heater."

"Thank goodness!"

He looked down at her and pulled her closer as another shiver went through her.

"Perhaps next time you'll remember your coat," he said with a grin.

She shot him a disgruntled look. "You're not wearing one," she pointed out.

"I'm not the one shivering with cold."

"I did bring it, actually, but it's in my case. It was unbearably warm on the train. Tell me, am I the last one to arrive?"

"I'm afraid so. Your mother was starting to fret that you weren't coming." Miles grinned. "Your brother didn't help matters when he offered the theory that your train had derailed."

"He didn't!"

"He did. Don't worry. Mr. Buckley managed to convince her that you weren't laying in a ditch somewhere."

"Bill and Marguerite are there too? Oh wonderful! It's just like…" Evelyn's voice trailed off suddenly and Miles looked at her.

"Like what?"

She shrugged and shook her head. "I was going to say it's just like last year, but of course it's not," she said. "I don't think I'll ever get used to coming home and Dad not being here."

He squeezed her arm gently. "Perhaps not, but it will get easier," he said softly. "Or so I'm told."

"I do hope so." Evelyn raised her eyebrows as they approached a low, green two-seater Jaguar SS100. "Is this yours?"

"Yes."

"It's beautiful!"

"Do you like it?" He opened the passenger door for her. "That's right. I forgot you said you like fast cars."

She laughed and got in, twinkling up at him. "And reckless pilots."

He grinned and winked. "*That* I didn't forget."

He closed the door and walked around the back to set her case in the small luggage boot. When he got behind the wheel, Evelyn smiled at him.

"I'm glad you came to fetch me."

He looked at her. "Because I drive a fast sports car?"

"Because I really didn't fancy walking all the way home."

Miles laughed and the engine started with a low growl. Evelyn rubbed her hands together in the dark briskly, a smile playing with her lips. She'd forgotten how easy it was to banter with him, and how comfortable it felt to do so. It was as if they'd known each other all their lives, rather than just a few months. It was so strange, this connection that they seemed to have with each other. It was like nothing she'd ever felt before, but she wasn't about to question it.

She relaxed in the expensive leather seat as he reversed out of the parking spot and pulled out of the lot. His broad shoulders seemed to fill the car, making it seem much smaller inside. Leather mixed with the musky smell of him and she felt the tension flow out of her.

"And how have you been, Assistant Section Officer?" Miles asked after a moment of silence.

"I'm doing much better now that I'm here," she answered, turning her head on the seat to look at his profile in the moonlight. Heat was pouring out of the vents now and her shivering had stopped. In its place was languid contentment. "How are you faring up in the great blue?"

The Oslo Affair

"Piece of cake," was the flippant answer, drawing a smile from her.

"No more landings without wheels?"

He shook his head. "No, thank God."

"How is that possible? To land without wheels?" she asked, her brows knit together thoughtfully. "It doesn't seem like it would work very well."

"It usually doesn't," Miles said bluntly, glancing at her. "The Yank was bloody lucky. His fuel was low and Bertie thinks that's what saved him. When you come in without landing gear, you see, you have to land completely on your belly. If you tilt one way or the other, the wing goes into the ground and, well, then it's all over, isn't it? It's jolly difficult to do."

"Have you ever had to do that?"

"No, and I hope to God I never do. Chris said it was terrifying. He doesn't even know how he did it and says he couldn't do it again if his life depended on it."

"It sounds like his life *will* depend on it if it ever happens again," Evelyn murmured, turning her gaze out her window. "I'm glad he made it."

"So were we all, but let's not talk about that anymore. How are you getting on with your training?"

"It's going well, actually. The girls are doing well." Evelyn said, swallowing the pang of guilt at the ongoing lie.

"Any possibility of getting out of Scotland?"

"You know, if I didn't know better, I'd think you were psychic. I'm getting reassigned after Christmas."

He looked at her in surprise. "No! Are you?"

She laughed at the look on his face and nodded. "Yes."

"Where?"

"I don't know yet, but somewhere closer to London. So, you just might get to meet me for dinner once in a while after all."

The smile on his face went straight through her and she felt it right down to her toes.

"Do you know, Assistant Section Officer Ainsworth, I think you've just made my Christmas."

She leaned her head back on the seat again, smiling.

"You might regret that," she warned. "For all you know, I might be nothing but trouble."

He glanced at her, his lips curved and his eyes warm.

"I'm a fighter pilot, m'dear. I live for trouble."

"Evelyn! At last!" Mrs. Ainsworth got out of her chair and moved across the drawing room quickly to wrap Evelyn in a scented, warm embrace. "I thought you'd never get here!"

"So did I, Mum," Evelyn said with a laugh, returning the hug. "It's so good to see you!"

"Miles got you here in one piece, I see," Rob said with a grin, setting his drink down and coming over to take his turn embracing her. "Miracle, that."

"This coming from the man who rolled into a ditch last week," Miles drawled from the doorway.

"Rolled into a ditch? You didn't!" Evelyn pulled away from her brother and stared at him. "Tell me he's joking."

"Afraid not," Rob said cheerfully. "Can't see a damn thing on the ground when you're in the cockpit. How was I to know they'd dug a trench there while I was up?"

She burst out laughing. "Oh Robbie, it's so good to see you again!"

Her brother grinned and looked down at her fondly. "I'm glad to see you too, Evie," he said. "I'm glad you finally made it. Did you miss the train?"

Evelyn shot Miles a glance over shoulder and he winked.

"Yes, as you well knew because you ratted me out to Miles," she said. "But I'm here now."

"Yes, and you'll want to change and freshen up," Mrs. Ainsworth said. "Bill and Marguerite are here as well. They're just dressing for dinner."

Evelyn looked at her watch and kissed her mother on the cheek. "I'll be as quick as I can," she said, turning towards the door. "Robbie, have a drink waiting, will you?"

She smiled at Miles as she passed him and ran lightly across the large, square hallway to the wide stairs. It was lovely to be home, even if it was only for a short time. The house she grew up in was like a welcoming port in choppy seas, and she truly felt as if the war couldn't touch them here. It was absolute nonsense, of course. The effects of the war were already beginning show, even this far away from London. At the station, she'd noticed the increased number of military uniforms crowding the platform, and on the drive out to the Ainsworth Manor many of the homes were observing the blackout. Even in this remote part of Lancashire, the world was beginning to change.

The Oslo Affair

Evelyn started up the stairs, her hand on the banister, and resolutely put thoughts of the war out of her head. For the next twenty-four hours, she didn't have to think about it. She would simply enjoy her mother and brother and forget the shadows that she was beginning to accept as her new reality.

A small flash of excitement surged through her and she couldn't stop the small smile that crossed across her face. And for the next twenty-four hours, she had Flying Officer Miles Lacey all to herself.

"Evelyn! My dear!"

A voice interrupted her thoughts and she looked up to see Bill and his wife, Marguerite, approaching the top of the stairs. Marguerite moved forward, her hands outstretched.

"Hallo Mrs. Buckley!" Evelyn said with a smile, running up the remainder of the steps and grasping her hands. "It's wonderful to see you again!"

"You look so official in your uniform!" Marguerite said with a laugh, kissing her cheek. "Your father would be very proud. Did you just arrive?"

"Yes. I'm afraid I missed my train and had to catch a later one." Evelyn turned to Bill with a smile and held out her hands to him. "It's so nice to see you again! It's been absolute ages!"

Bill grinned and took her hands, leaning down to kiss her cheek affectionately. As far as his wife, and indeed anyone else in the house, was concerned, he hadn't seen her since the funeral.

"How are the WAAFs treating you, Evelyn?" he asked cheerfully, releasing her hands. "Not working you too hard, I hope?"

"Not in the slightest," she assured him with a twinkle. "I spend most of my day trying to make sense of regulations that contradict each other."

"And the rest of your day?"

"Spent stopping my girls from sneaking out to the pub with pilots," she returned promptly, drawing a laugh from both of them. "I must go and get changed before Rob wastes away to nothing. You know he's always starving."

"Go, my dear. We'll see you downstairs," Marguerite said, waving her away.

With a final smile at both of them, Evelyn hurried down the carpeted hallway to her room. It was lovely to see Marguerite again, but trying to keep a straight face while pretending not to have seen Bill in months was a challenge. He hadn't shown by even the slightest flicker that he had just seen her last week in London following the completion of a short, weekend training course in the city. Shaking her head, she reached for the handle of her bedroom door. It was easy to lie to strangers, but something entirely different to act a part in your own house. That might end up being her biggest challenge.

Evelyn went into her room quickly, startling the maid who was in the process of unpacking her bag. As she entered, the young woman turned in surprise.

"Oh, hello miss!"

"Hello, Fran," Evelyn said, crossing over to the wardrobe. "How are you?"

"Doing well, miss, thank you," she answered, flushing slightly in pleasure. "It's nice to have you back."

"Thank you! It's nice to be back, even if it's only for a few hours." Evelyn threw open the wardrobe door and examined the evening gowns hanging there. "How's your family? Everyone well?"

"Yes, thank you for asking, miss." Fran watched as Evelyn selected a gown of mauve silk. "Would you like me to help you dress?"

"No, that's all right, Fran," Evelyn said, carrying the gown over to lay it across the coverlet on the bed. "I can manage. When I've finished, could you take this uniform and clean it? I'm afraid it has soot all down it from the train. I'll need it again to travel on Boxing Day."

"Of course, miss. I'll just take this case away and store it for you."

Fran closed the empty suitcase and lifted it off the chair, turning to go quietly out of the room. Evelyn watched her go, wondering how long the maid would remain at Ainsworth Manor. She'd been with them for a few years, but Evelyn knew that many servants were joining up to do their part in the war. It was inevitable that Fran would want to do the same. While she would miss her attention to detail, Evelyn wouldn't be surprised to see her go.

She changed quickly, stepping into the elegant evening dress and pulling it up over her shoulders before reaching behind to do up the zipper. The dress was one she had purchased in Paris over the summer. She'd only worn it twice, but it was one of her favorites. On both occasions, Evelyn had received multiple compliments, which is precisely why she'd chosen it tonight. She wanted to look her best for Miles. If she only had a short time to make an impression, she had to start immediately.

Turning to look at herself critically in the full length mirror, Evelyn smoothed the shimmering fabric over her hips and tilted her head. The dress fell to the floor in graceful lines, clinging to her figure and transforming her from a WAAF into the wealthy heiress that she

The Oslo Affair

was. In an instant, she went from the intelligence agent posing as an Assistant Section Officer to a socialite about to join her family for dinner. Once she added her jewels and ran a brush through her hair, the image would be complete.

Her lips twisted as she surveyed herself for a moment. Which one was the real Evelyn Ainsworth? The woman in a false uniform? Or the heiress in a gown?

Turning away from the glass, she went over to the tall chest that held her jewelry. The question a silly one. She was both, but tonight she would embrace the heiress. That was what was expected of her, and it was who she was as soon as she stepped into her family home. As she selected a necklace, a brief and unusual flash of clarity sharpened that thought and made her pause.

She had to separate the two, the intelligence agent and the heiress, and keep them separate if she were to survive this war without losing herself completely. It really was that simple.

Evelyn lifted a diamond necklace from the jewelry chest and turned to cross over to her dressing table. She seated herself before the mirror and fastened the glittering strand around her neck. When she was in England, she would cling to the life she'd always known and set aside the stranger she'd become overseas. Perhaps then she would remember why she'd embarked on this road to begin with. For, though she couldn't pretend to know what the future held for her, Evelyn was sure of one thing: it wasn't going to be easy, and she knew without a doubt that she would need something to hold onto in the months to come.

And that something was going to have to be herself.

Chapter Twenty-Nine

Evelyn sipped her tea in the bright sunlight, squinting as she looked out over the south lawn. It was brisk and cold, but the sun was beginning to share its warmth across the countryside as the new day stirred. Rob wasn't down yet, and neither was her mother, leaving her to enjoy the start of Christmas in quiet solitude.

She shivered and burrowed deeper into her coat. The wind blew and whisked at her hair, pulling strands from her pins and causing her ears and nose to turn red with cold. She didn't mind. She needed to feel the crisp cold air and listen to the wonderful silence. No sound of military trucks heading out to airfields, or chatter of enlisted men and women hurrying to the mess for breakfast, marred the peace as she sipped her tea. No sound of footsteps following her down a dark, city street as she made her way back to her lodgings.

Evelyn stared out over the frost covered lawns. Was she even strong enough to make it through this war? She had committed herself to her country, and thousands of young men and women were counting on her to bring back information that would help them defeat the enemy. Hundreds of pilots like Rob and Miles were depending on advance warning of attack to give them an edge in the inevitable air battle that would precede any invasion attempt by Hitler. They may not know it, but the intelligence she gathered could save their lives.

And it could make her forfeit hers if she was ever caught. And, if they failed and England lost this war, she would be one of the first ones executed by the Germans.

"Good morning," a voice said behind her and Evelyn turned in surprise to watch Miles step out onto the terrace.

"Good morning!"

"You look surprised to see me," he said with a grin, crossing the flagged stones towards her with a steaming cup of tea in his hands.

"I suppose I thought you'd sleep the morning away like Robbie," she said with a sheepish laugh. "God knows you deserve to."

The Oslo Affair

"The training isn't as stressful as you think," he said with a shrug, joining her at the balustrade. "We're used to it now. And I've always been an early riser."

"So have I." She smiled at him. "Happy Christmas."

He looked down at her and smiled warmly, his eyes creasing at the edges and his green eyes glinting in the sunlight.

"Happy Christmas."

They were quiet, sipping their tea and looking out over the morning in companionable silence.

"It hardly seems possible that it's Christmas already," he said suddenly. "I feel as though it was just yesterday that I crashed your dinner with Rob at the Savoy."

Evelyn thought over the two months since that night and marveled herself at how quickly the time had gone by. It seemed like just yesterday that she was fleeing Herr Renner in Sweden, yet it had been over a month since she'd returned to England.

"And are you glad you crashed dinner?" she asked, glancing up at him with a grin.

His eyes met hers. "Every day."

She laughed and his eyes dropped to the scarf tied carelessly around her throat. The sunlight caught a silver piece of metal in its folds and his lips curved into a smile.

"I see you got my present."

Evelyn lifted her hand to touch the small brooch and smiled. The silver had been twisted into a reproduction of a Spitfire, creating a unique and charming piece of jewelry.

"I did, and I believe I wrote a very nice thank you letter at the time," she said.

Miles grinned. "So you did. An air sergeant at the base makes those for all the pilot's girls. He's very talented. He did an exceptionally nice job on that one."

"Yes, he did. It's lovely."

"I'm glad you like it."

Their eyes met and Evelyn felt something stir deep inside her, a feeling of contentment. She dropped her eyes away from his in consternation and swallowed the last bit of tea left in her cup.

"I think I'm off for a walk," she said, turning towards the house with her empty cup.

"A walk?" he repeated, gulping down the last of his tea and following.

"Yes. There's nothing better than a nice, brisk walk in the morning to start the day."

Miles nodded wisely, his eyes twinkling.

"You sound just like my nanny when I was a boy. Only her walks consisted of near hikes around the countryside until I thought I should die."

Evelyn laughed. "I don't hike."

"In that case, then I think I'll join you," he said as they went through the parlor. "If you don't mind, of course."

"I'd like that."

They crossed the hall and left their cups in the dining room where breakfast would be set out, then went out the front door, walking in silence until they reached the west meadow. Finally, Evelyn glanced at Miles.

"How's the Polish coming along?"

He burst out laughing. "HQ gave up on that venture, thank God. It really was a bit much."

"I wouldn't have known Swedish from Polish," she admitted. "I'm surprised you did."

He looked at her, surprised. "I thought you were a linguistic prodigy." He grinned when she looked surprised. "Rob told me. He said you speak just about every language there is."

"That's a gross exaggeration. I only speak a handful, and Polish and Swedish are not among them."

"What *do* you speak then?"

"Oh, the usual. French, Italian, German…some Russian."

He choked. "The usual? Russian is usual?"

She twinkled up at him. "No. That was just for fun."

"Oh, of course. For fun." He was laughing at her, and she couldn't help laughing with him. "But you don't know Swedish from Polish?"

"Well, since you're making such a point of it, I'll learn both just to make you happy."

He laughed. "It doesn't make a bit of difference to me," he told her. "I think you're fascinating as you are. And I, happily, *do* know some Swedish, so I can translate for you should the need ever arise."

Evelyn swallowed. "I'll remember that," she said in a choked voice. "If you're no longer being made to learn Swedish, whatever do you do to keep busy when you're not flying?"

"Oh, we're learning aircraft recognition now. Too many pilots can't tell the difference between ours and theirs."

"And you?"

The Oslo Affair

"Of course I can tell the difference," he retorted. "But it's downright depressing how many of our pilots will be shooting down Blenheims and Hurricanes if they don't crack down and learn."

They walked in silence for a moment, then Evelyn sighed.

"It's funny how this Phony War is acting to our advantage," she said thoughtfully. "It's giving us time to train and prepare. Perhaps it's Hitler's biggest mistake yet."

"Hitler's biggest mistake was invading Poland," Miles said. "He's got to be barmy to think he can take on Britain and France like this."

Evelyn frowned thoughtfully. "I'm not dismissing him that quickly. He wouldn't have done it if he didn't think he could win."

Miles raised an eyebrow. "You think he's more prepared than we've been led to believe?"

She thought of the latest reports of Luftwaffe aircraft production that she'd seen last week and her lips tightened.

"I'm just saying it's possible," she said. Then, catching his sharp look, she smiled. "But enough talk about that. Tell me about the American."

He blinked. "The Yank?"

"Yes. I think it's fantastic that you have an American in the squadron. How's he getting on?"

"Cool as you please," Miles said with a shrug. "He gets quite a lot of ribbing thrown his way, but he takes it all in part. Jolly good flier."

"I suppose he must be to land his plane with no wheels. I hope I can meet him one day. I've never met an American before."

"Oh, they're very much like us, you know," he drawled. "Two legs, two arms…only one head."

She laughed. "Imagine that! I was expecting at least two."

"He's actually keen to meet you as well," he said after a moment. At her look of surprise, he grinned. "He was with me when I was reading one of your letters. Asked who it was from. Now he wants to see you for himself. He's convinced you have three chins with a wart on every one."

Evelyn gaped at him, horrified. "What on earth did you tell him?!"

"It's the name, you see," he told her apologetically. "Assistant Section Officer Ainsworth does sound a trifle militant."

"Well I hope you set him straight."

He nodded complacently.

"I did. I told him that you had four chins, but only two warts. He was quite impressed."

"You're horrid!"

"And you're beautiful," he countered with a wink. "I'll race you to the next hedgerow."

"Pardon?"

Evelyn was surprised out of her calm, but it was too late. Miles was already running towards the line of hedges in the distance. After a second of stunned disbelief, a laugh bubbled out of her and she took off after him in the morning mist, catching up with him a moment later. He turned and grabbed her hand and Evelyn found herself tearing through the grass, his fingers firmly around hers. The war faded behind them and, in that moment, she felt free.

It was an exhilarating feeling.

⊙

Evelyn looked up as a knock preceded her bedroom door opening. Rob poked his head in and, upon spotting her seated at the writing desk near her window, his shoulders and torso followed.

"Here you are," he said, closing the door. "I've been searching for you. I haven't had two minutes alone with you since you arrived."

She set down her pen and turned to face him, her lips curving.

"I didn't know you wanted two minutes alone with me. You're not going to bore me with warnings about Miles, are you?"

Rob laughed and threw himself across the foot of her bed.

"Good Lord no. You can take care of yourself. Besides, Miles is a good old egg." He lounged on his elbow and tilted his head to look at her. "Do you like him?"

"Of course I do. What's not to like?"

"You know what I mean, Evie. Don't play dumb."

She hesitated for a second, then sighed. "It doesn't matter who I like or don't like, Robbie. It's impossible to think about anything other than the war right now."

"That's a load of nonsense and you know it," he said without heat. "What's the war got to do with anything?"

"Well I can't very well make plans for a future when I don't know what that future holds, can I?" she protested.

Her brother rolled his eyes and then flopped onto his back, staring up at the ceiling.

"I never can understand the way your mind works," he

The Oslo Affair

muttered. "Everyone's rushing to get married precisely because they don't know what the future holds. You're the only one thinking the other way. You've always been like this."

"Like what?"

"Marching to the beat of your own drum." He paused and turned his head to look at her. "I'll tell you this, though: Miles is a good choice if you ever do decide to stop breaking hearts all over Europe. He comes from good stock, and he's not bad looking either."

"You make him sound like a horse."

He grinned. "I'm just pointing out facts. You can't just settle for anyone, y'know. There are standards we have the maintain."

"And Miles is acceptable," she finished. "You know Robbie, you're really starting to sound like a pompous old man."

"Well as the head of this family now," he began, attempting to lower his voice condescendingly. He caught sight of her face and burst out laughing. "Good God, I can't even say that with a straight face."

He sat up and swung his legs over the foot of the bed to face her.

"I just want you to be happy, Evie, and I can see that Miles does that."

Evelyn smiled at him fondly. "I know you do, dearest. But you really must stay out of it. I don't know how I feel, and I'm sure he doesn't either. This is only the third time we've seen each other, really. Let us get to know each other before you have me married and pushing out babies."

Rob looked horrified. "Who said anything about babies?"

She laughed at the look on his face. "They do tend to happen, Robbie."

He shuddered dramatically. "Horrible thought!" Then, sobering, he cleared his throat. "I actually didn't intend to talk about Miles at all."

She raised an eyebrow. "Oh? What then?"

"I'm worried," he said seriously, leaning his elbows on his knees and dangling his hands between them. "I don't like both of us being so far away from Mum."

"Because of Dad, you mean?" Evelyn asked, her brows creasing in a frown. "I think she's doing all right. It's difficult, I'm sure, but she seems in good spirits."

"It's not Dad, although that did worry me at first," he said slowly. "It's the fact that this house is so far away from everything. If anything were to happen…"

Her frown grew as his voice trailed off and her eyes narrowed.

"What is it, Robbie? *Has* something happened?"

"Something has, yes." He got up restlessly and felt about his pockets. "You haven't got any cigarettes in here, have you?"

She got up and went to her purse, pulling out a case and tossing it to him.

"Cheers." He pulled out a cigarette. "There was a break-in last month."

Evelyn stared at him, a surge of shock going through her. "What?!"

He nodded glumly and looked around. "Any matches? I seem to have left my lighter somewhere."

She shook her head and crossed to the desk, opening the drawer and extracting a box of matches.

"When? What happened?" she demanded, handing him the matches.

"Someone forced the window in the study. Thomas saw a light in the middle of night and went to turn it off. The next day he saw the window had been forced."

Evelyn dropped into her seat, staring at him.

"Why didn't anyone tell me?" she asked. "When did this happen? What was taken?"

"I suppose Mum didn't want to worry you," he said, lighting his cigarette. He shook out the match and walked over to open the bedroom window. He tossed it out and blew smoke outside. "I didn't think to write you about it, to be honest. It happened in the beginning of November. Nothing was taken. In fact, Thomas and the servants couldn't find anything out of place anywhere."

"Is he sure the window wasn't just left off the latch?" she asked after a moment of silence.

"Oh, it was definitely forced. He had to call a locksmith to come out and replace the lock. While he was at it, he replaced all the locks on the ground floor." Rob leaned against the window sill and looked at her. "Everything seemed fine and the local police put it down to kids. But it did get me thinking that perhaps Mum shouldn't be here all alone."

"She's not all alone, though. She has the servants."

"But for how long? Thomas won't go anywhere. He's too old to join up, bless him, and so is his wife. And I suppose Jones will stay on with the horses, and Samuel to take care of the cars and drive her. But the others will probably go, and then Mum will be in this old house alone, with only the older servants."

Evelyn pressed her lips together thoughtfully. "Auntie Agatha

The Oslo Affair

is coming in January," she said slowly. "She's going to stay indefinitely. Mum said that she doesn't want to stay in London while there's a war on. Can't say I blame her. If Hitler does attack, London will be hit hard. So Mum will at least have her."

"That's true." Rob brightened. "And I defy anyone to try to break in while she's around. The woman's terrifying."

Evelyn was surprised into a laugh. "She's hardly terrifying. She's just rather blunt."

They were both quiet for a moment, Rob smoking at the window and Evelyn staring at the wall, lost in thought.

"It was the study, you said?" she asked suddenly, turning her eyes back to him.

He nodded and leaned out the window to put out the cigarettes on the bricks before tossing the butt away.

"Yes, why?"

"I don't know. I suppose it's just disconcerting. I mean, that was Dad's domain. The thought of a stranger breaking in there…"

He nodded and closed the window again.

"I know what you mean. That's how I felt when I heard. It's almost like a desecration somehow." He looked down at her. "I wish you weren't stuck up in Scotland. I'd feel better if you were stationed somewhere closer. Not that you could be of any help from an air field, but at least you wouldn't be hours away."

"Actually, I'm being reassigned after Christmas," she told him. "I don't know where yet, but I think it will be closer to London."

His face lit up. "Really? That's fantastic news! Why didn't you say anything last night?"

"I didn't think of it," she said with a shrug. "But being closer to London won't help Mum at all. It's a four-hour drive."

"Still better than Scotland," he said, turning to go towards the door. "That makes me feel heaps better. And we can meet in London once in a while!"

Evelyn grinned. "Yes, so I've been told," she murmured. "Don't get your hopes up, though. I don't know where I'll be yet."

"Doesn't matter where you are if you're closer to London." He reached for the door handle. "And I'm sure I'm just making a mountain out of a mole hill with the study window. It was probably just some kids on a dare, as the police said. Nothing's happened since, and Thomas has been vigilant about ensuring all the windows are secured every night. With Auntie Agatha here, I'm sure everything will be just fine. I'm going to hunt out Miles and see if he fancies a game of billiards before luncheon. Care to join us?"

"I'm going to finish writing this letter, but I may join you later," she said absently.

"Right-o."

And with that, he went out the door. Evelyn stared at it for a long moment, deep in thought, then her eyes slowly shifted to look at the wardrobe consideringly. Getting up, she crossed the room and opened the doors, pushing dresses and skirts out of the way to reveal shelves built into the back. She reached up to the top shelf and pulled down a wooden box, turning to carry it over to the desk. Setting it down, she stared at it thoughtfully.

The smallish box was made out of smooth wood with several panels connecting together seamlessly. It was a Chinese puzzle box, and ever since their stint in Hong Kong, her father had delighted in giving her a new one every year on her birthday. Each year they got progressively more difficult, and this one she hadn't figured out yet.

Evelyn sat down and stared at the box. Instead of giving it to her on her birthday, her father had surprised her with it in August, a week before he left on that fateful trip. He'd called her to his study to give it to her. When she entered, he'd just been sliding a panel into place on the box. It was their little game. He always left something inside the boxes for her to find.

Why would someone break into a house and not take anything? And what kind of vandal didn't make a mess? Robbie said that Thomas found nothing out of place. As soon as she heard that, warning bells had gone off in her head. Something would have been knocked over, or moved, or been put back where it didn't belong. Especially if it were kids on a dare. They would have taken something, even if it was just an ashtray, to prove they'd done it. If it was any kind of standard break in, there would have been obvious signs of an intruder. The very fact that there weren't made Evelyn's skin go cold.

Rob had no idea that their father was anything other than what they had always thought he was: a diplomat on whom very powerful men counted to keep the precarious balance between ambassadors and politicians. Rob, her mother, Thomas…even the police had no reason to believe there could be anything more to this break in. But she knew differently. And she knew that if she mentioned it to Bill, he would realize the same thing she had.

Someone had been searching for something specific, and they were careful enough not to leave a trace of their search. Too careful, as it turned out.

Evelyn eyed the box in front of her. When he gave it to her, her father had said it was a special box. She'd thought it a strange thing

The Oslo Affair

to say at the time. Weren't all puzzle boxes special? What if it wasn't the box that was special, but what was inside it?

She reached for it.

Chapter Thirty

Evelyn laughed as Rob threw his cards down disgustedly. "I swear I don't know how you do it," he complained. "That's the third straight hand you've won."

"Well if you insist on broadcasting your every move, how am I not to?" she asked, gathering up the cards.

"Are you having difficulties, Rob?" Bill asked, looking over from where he was pouring himself a drink. "Never say your sister is trouncing you."

"I am, and she is." Rob got up to walk over to the mantel to retrieve his forgotten cigarette case. "Miles, come and even the field, will you?"

Miles looked up from where he was playing dance tunes on the piano in the corner.

"And ruin the fun watching you squirm? Not a chance, old boy."

"Well I'm not playing another hand with this shark. She'll have me bankrupt before I go to bed."

"I'm sure your luck will change," Evelyn said with a twinkle. "It's bound to."

"Aha! See? That's what all the sharks say! The next thing you know, you're wandering home at dawn without a farthing left!"

Evelyn stood up and stretched, then moved across the drawing room to join Bill by the drinks.

"I do think you're being a bit dramatic, Robbie dear," Mrs. Ainsworth said from the couch where she and Marguerite had been happily ensconced together since they all moved in from dinner.

"Is he?" Bill asked Evelyn, setting down the brandy decanter.

"I did take him for quite a bit that last hand," she admitted with a grin. "I couldn't resist. It was too easy!"

Bill chuckled. "That's my girl," he said under his breath. "What would you like, my dear?"

The Oslo Affair

"I'll have some of that wine, thank you." She watched as he poured it into a glass. "Did you know that the study here was broken into last month?"

They were far enough away from the others that they wouldn't be overheard, but she lowered her voice anyway. Bill glanced at her sharply.

"No. When?"

"The beginning of November. Robbie told me earlier today." She took the glass from him. "The window was forced in the middle of night. Thomas saw the light on and went to turn it off. It was the next morning that he saw the broken latch."

"What was taken?"

"That's the interesting part. Absolutely nothing. And nothing was out of place."

Bill's brows snapped together in a scowl. "Nothing at all?"

"No. The police think it was a couple of kids. Mum's had all the locks on the first floor replaced and nothing's happened since."

"Then they may have found what they were looking for," he murmured. "Damn! Robert was always careful never to bring anything here that would expose him, or any of us. But last summer he told me he'd come across something that was too important to leave anywhere. I never did find out what it was."

"He didn't tell you anything?"

Bill shook his head.

"No. He said he needed to confirm the information and that was the last I heard of it." He lifted his brandy glass to his lips. "I completely forgot about it until after we received word of his death."

Evelyn frowned. "What made you remember?"

He hesitated for a moment, then sighed.

"I suppose there's no point in keeping it from you now. His office in London was ransacked a few days after he died. His assistant was blamed and discharged, but I wondered at the time if it was something more ominous. Now you're telling me that a few weeks later, someone went through his study here."

Evelyn's heart sank. Her suspicions were correct, then. It hadn't been a simple break in. While she'd known it couldn't be, a small part of her had been hoping that Bill would have another explanation. Instead, all he'd done was confirm it.

"Well, there was nothing for them to find," she finally said, sipping her wine. "I can assure you of that."

"How can you be sure?"

"Because I'm fairly confident that whatever my father may have had in there was given to me a week before he left for Poland."

Bill stared at her. "What?"

She shrugged. "I can't get to it at the moment, but I will eventually."

"What do you mean you can't get to it?"

"It's inside a puzzle box."

The confusion on Bill's brow cleared and a slow smile crossed his face.

"The sneaky old devil. He was still finding new boxes for you every year? I thought that had stopped."

She shook her head. "No. The last few have been near impossible to figure out," she admitted.

"And he gave you one before he left for Poland?"

"Yes. I worked on it for three days after he left, but then I went back to Scotland and left it here. After Rob told me what happened, I pulled it out and started again. It will take time, but I'll figure it out. I'll take it with me when I leave."

Bill pursed his lips together and slowly shook his head.

"No," he said softly. "Leave it here for now. It will be safer here. If it really does have something inside, this is the best place for it."

"Unless they come back," she argued. "I can't leave it here and put my mother at risk."

They both glanced over to the sofa where Madeleine and Marguerite had their heads together, laughing over something they were looking at in a magazine.

"She won't be at risk," Bill said after a moment. "I'll send someone to keep an eye on things."

Evelyn gaped at him. "What?"

"Don't look so shocked. I'll arrange for a footman or gardener, or something. Someone who will keep an eye out and alert us to anything. We can't wait almost two months to find out something happened again."

She chewed her lip for a minute, then nodded slowly.

"That would certainly set my mind at ease," she admitted. "I know Rob is worried. He said as much this afternoon. When the servants start to join up, he's worried that Mum will only be left with the older ones who won't be much use against an intruder. I know he's wishing I wasn't away from home now."

The Oslo Affair

"I'll make the arrangements," Bill said with a quick nod. "In the meantime, leave the box here and work on it when you come to visit."

"What if it's time sensitive?"

"I'd rather risk that than have it lost or destroyed by moving it around." Bill finished his brandy and set the glass down. "And given your penchant for getting yourself into sticky situations, I think it's safer here."

Evelyn made a face at him but couldn't argue. The box would be safer in her wardrobe than in a room on a RAF base where people came and went practically at will.

"Evie!" Rob called from across the room. "Come tell Miles about the time you made it to London in the Lagonda in two hours and twenty minutes. He doesn't believe me!"

Bill smiled and winked at her.

"Go and enjoy yourself," he said. "Forget about work for a while. It's Christmas, after all."

Evelyn nodded and turned walk towards her brother and Miles. It was easy for him to say that. He wasn't the one who had a box with a secret in it, a secret that was apparently worth breaking into a country manor over.

A secret that she had no idea how to get to.

◉

Evelyn sighed and tucked her feet up beside her comfortably. A large, cheerful fire crackled in the hearth, casting a comfortable glow over the study. She smiled as Miles handed her a glass of sherry before taking the chair across from her. After her mother had gone to bed, they had come into the study with Rob. But after smoking a cigarette, he'd cast Evelyn a sly grin and taken himself off, leaving her alone with Miles.

"Your brother isn't very subtle, is he?" Miles asked, sitting back and crossing his legs.

"Not very, no," she agreed with a laugh. "Do you mind?"

He smiled slowly. "Not a bit."

"I hope this wasn't all too strange for you," she said after a moment. "It's been a very odd Christmas. We're usually much more lively than this."

"I imagine it's not easy, being the first holiday without your father."

"It's not," she said frankly, shaking her head. "I don't think I was fully prepared for how difficult it would be. One realizes, of course, that things will be different, but I suppose I didn't think of the little things."

"Like the goose?"

Evelyn nodded. When they sat down to dinner and the roast goose was set on the table, there was a moment sheer panic as Mrs. Ainsworth and her children all stared at each other. None of them had even considered who would carve it. It was always her father's pride and joy to do it.

"Thank goodness for B—Mr. Buckley," she said. "If he hadn't stepped in, I don't know what would have happened. Robbie can't cut anything to save his life."

Miles grinned.

"I expect he would have just torn it apart with his hands and chucked it onto our plates like a cricket ball."

Evelyn choked on her sherry as she laughed.

"That's probably exactly what he would have done!" she gasped, her eyes watering. "Good heavens. Here's to Mr. Buckley!"

Mile raised his glass and sipped his brandy.

"I wish I'd got the opportunity to meet your father," he said slowly. "Rob's told me some stories. I think I would have liked him."

Evelyn smiled. "He would have liked you."

"Do you think so?"

"Yes."

They were quiet for a moment and then Evelyn shook her head.

"We're in danger of being thrust into a maudlin silence," she announced, "and that will never do. Tell me why you became a pilot."

"I've always loved flying. I talked your brother into taking lessons down at the auxiliary flying club near university. Never looked back after the first day."

"What about your father? What did he say?"

Miles shrugged. "Not much, actually. He knew I wasn't cut out for a career in politics. I think by that point he was just hoping I wouldn't bankrupt him before I finished university."

Evelyn grinned. "Was that a possibility?"

"Me? Not a chance. I'm an angel, m'dear, the perfect son." He winked. "After it became clear that the flying wasn't just a passing phase, he warmed up to the idea. I think he's rather proud to have a son in the RAF now."

"What will you do when the war's over? Will you continue with

The Oslo Affair

the Air Force?"

"That depends on my father. Eventually I'll have to take over the estate." He shrugged. "I'll cross that bridge when I come to it. What about you?"

"What about me?"

"Before you joined the WAAFs and started training young things to work in the grid stations, there must have been something you wanted to do. Come on. Fess up. What was it?"

"I love how you assume to know what it is that I train my girls to do," she said with a grin.

"I thought we'd already established that I know all your dirty secrets," he retorted teasingly. "There's no point in pretending now."

Evelyn swallowed as guilt washed over her. If he had even an inkling of her dirty secrets, he would run as fast and as far as he could. And who would blame him?

"And you still haven't answered the question," he continued, oblivious to her discomfort.

"I was still trying to figure that out," she said honestly. Here, at least, she could be truthful with him. "I didn't really know what I wanted to do. My mother wanted me to get married and set up house with a respectable and suitable peer, of course."

A faint smile played on his lips. "But that didn't suit you?"

She shook her head. "Not much, no."

"What about your father? What did he have to say?"

"He suggested a career, actually. He said I should go to university and find a use for my talent for language. I toyed with the idea of journalism, but then all this happened and, well, here we are."

Miles sipped his brandy, studying her over the rim.

"Would you have enjoyed journalism?" he asked.

"I've always enjoyed world politics and events, so perhaps," she said thoughtfully.

"Will you try it after the war, do you think?"

"I don't know. I'll cross that bridge when I come to it."

He chuckled and held up his glass in a silent toast. "Touché."

"This war certainly isn't turning out to be what everyone expected, is it?" she asked after a moment of silence. "Here it is, Christmas, and things seem to be getting worse."

"You're talking about what's happening in Scandinavia?"

She nodded.

"Finland will fall," he predicted. "Although, they're putting up a much stronger fight than I think the Soviets expected."

"Let's hope they hold out."

"Chamberlain sold thirty of our fighters to them," Miles said with a shrug. "With any luck, they'll help."

Evelyn glanced at him. "But you don't think they will."

He shook his head.

"No. And eventually Hitler will turn his attention to France. We'll need our fighters then, and Chamberlain is selling them all off."

She sipped her drink, thinking once again of the reports of aircraft production coming out of Germany. Hitler was also ordering an increase in ammunition and mine production. Miles was closer to the truth than he knew.

"What does he think thirty fighters are going to accomplish against the entire Soviet force?" he continued. "Finland needs troops and support, not a handful of planes that we'll soon be needing."

"They're England's ally," she reminded him. "Chamberlain had to send them something."

"Yes, but not planes. We have precious few to spare. Do you have any idea how many fighters we have ready to defend England right now? Less than a thousand. Do you know how many fighters Goering has under his command? Round about two thousand." Miles got up restlessly and went over to the desk to open the cigarette case there. "And those are just the fighters!" he added over his shoulder. "We should be keeping our fighters for our own defense."

He opened the box and took out a cigarette. Turning, he offered the box to her and she leaned forward to take one.

"How do you know those figures are accurate?" she asked, inwardly shaken at how close his numbers were to the truth.

"My CO and I were discussing it earlier this week." Miles looked at her sheepishly. "I'm not supposed to know the numbers, but I do. He let it slip."

He flicked open his lighter, holding it out for her.

"And I'm bloody angry that Chamberlain is selling the few planes we do have to other countries."

Evelyn watched as he lit his cigarette and began pacing in front of the fire. He knew entirely too much, but she couldn't say anything without revealing her own knowledge on the subject. She decided to change the direction of the conversation instead.

"Do you think the war will really continue into France then?" she asked. "A lot of people don't think it will."

"Everyone said Hitler wouldn't go past the Sudetenland. Then they said he wouldn't go into Poland. Then they said the war would be over by Christmas. Now they're saying he won't go into France." Miles paused to flick ash into the fire. "I think you'll agree that we can't assume anything anymore when it comes to Herr Hitler."

"I think he'll try as well," Evelyn said with a sigh. "Why wouldn't he? Look at how quickly his forces went through Poland. France was already invaded once this century, and he was there. He knows it can be done."

"Have you read his book?" Miles asked suddenly, glancing at her.

She swallowed hard. Not only had she read it, but it was that book that had convinced Bill to approach her on that long ago day in Paris.

"No. Did he write one?" She managed a feigned look of surprise.

He nodded. "I plowed my way through it this summer. It's a monstrosity of a thing, not well written at all, and makes almost no sense."

"Hm. Sounds like the man himself."

Miles flashed her a grin, then sobered again.

"It's a rambling mess, jumping from one soap box to another, but there are some rather disturbing things in it. If he's able to implement even half of what he discusses in there, it will be Hell on earth."

Evelyn was silent, thinking of Karl in Strasbourg and what he'd told her of the concentration camps. Since then, she'd learned more. Not only was Hitler making good on what he'd written in *Mein Kampf*, but it seemed he was doing it on a much grander scale than anyone chose to acknowledge. Anyone except those who lived daily under the threat of it. They were well aware of the dangers of ending up in Dachau.

"So much for lightening the mood, eh?" he suddenly asked, looking at her guiltily. "I'm terribly sorry. I don't suppose this is the conversation you want to be having on Christmas night."

Evelyn summoned a smile and got up to throw her cigarette in the fire.

"I don't mind," she said. "Honestly. I told you I've always enjoyed world affairs. This is part of our world now. I don't have to like it, but it doesn't mean I won't discuss it."

Miles tossed his butt into the fire as well and looked down at her, a strange glint in his eyes.

"You really are the most extraordinary girl," he murmured. "I'm not really sure what to do with you. I don't know if I should put you in the bluestocking category, or chalk you up as a wealthy eccentric."

She tossed her head, her eyes twinkling up at him.

"Why don't you withhold judgment for a bit longer and kiss me instead?"

A laugh leapt into his eyes and he followed her gaze upwards. There, hanging from the ceiling, was a bunch of mistletoe tied with a pretty white ribbon.

"How long has that been there?" he demanded, dropping his eyes back to her face.

"All day," she said with a laugh. "It's one of Millie, the housekeeper's, favorite things to do. Every year she hangs a bunch of them, then moves them throughout the day to catch unsuspecting people like you."

Miles grinned and slid his arms around her waist, pulling her close.

"Then we mustn't disappoint Millie," he murmured, lowering his lips to hers.

Evelyn felt a shock go through her as his lips touched hers. His arms were strong and warm around her and she suddenly forgot all about the war and fighter planes and concentration camps. He smelled like musk mixed with brandy and a rush of heat rolled over her that had nothing to do with the fire. She lifted her hands to hold on to his shoulders, clinging to his solid strength as her world slipped sideways. This was what she'd been waiting for. All the stolen kisses in the gardens of Paris, and all the flirtations in the drawing rooms in London had never come close to this feeling of exhilaration.

When Miles lifted his head a few moments later, they stared at each other for a long moment before he exhaled and laughed a little ruefully.

"I'm not quite sure that that's what dear Millie had in mind when she hung that piece of greenery, but I don't regret it."

"Neither do I."

He was making no move to pull away, so Evelyn took the opportunity to trace the scar at the corner of his eyebrow.

"How did this happen?"

"I was over confident when I was a boy and tried to take a fence that was too high. My horse had more sense than I did and threw me. The fence added its disapproval for good measure."

Her eyes shifted to his and she smiled slowly, gazing into the sparkling green depths.

"I see the recklessness isn't new, then," she said. "You're lucky you weren't killed."

"Would you be sad if I had been?"

The Oslo Affair

"Of course! Then who would be here kissing me under the mistletoe?" she demanded playfully.

The smile that curved his lips was wicked and he dropped his eyes to her lips again.

"Speaking of..." he murmured, lowering his head again.

This time when he lifted his head, they were both breathless and Evelyn took a deep, steadying gulp of air.

"Definitely not what Millie had in mind," she agreed breathlessly.

"Perhaps not, but I've been wanting to do that since the Savoy," he confessed with a rueful smile.

Evelyn felt her pulse leap again and swallowed before sliding her hands off his shoulders.

"I wish we didn't have to leave tomorrow," she said, her voice low.

Miles sighed and reluctantly pulled away from her.

"At least you'll be moving closer to London," he said, moving back to the desk to pick up his abandoned brandy. "We'll see each other again soon."

She nodded and watched as he finished his brandy, one hand tucked carelessly in his pocket. He was the image of idle peerage, but she knew he was anything but idle right now. He was training day and night to defend England from the storm that was coming; a storm that could very well take his life.

A stab of panicked fear shot through her and a lump took over her throat, making her catch her breath. Neither of them knew what was coming, but they knew it wasn't going to be good for anyone. While he would be defending the skies against the inevitable onslaught from the full might of the Luftwaffe, she would be God knew where trying to gather the information that would give England an edge in this war. Both of them would be fighting for survival, with not much hope of success.

Miles looked over and frowned in concern, setting his empty glass down and crossing to her in two strides.

"What's wrong?"

Evelyn lifted her face to his and she knew he could see the tears shimmering in her eyes. Any other time, she would be absolutely mortified at the thought of anyone seeing her so vulnerable, but this wasn't any other time. And she suddenly found that she didn't care if he saw the tears.

"How do we say goodbye when we don't even know where we'll be in a few months?" she whispered around the lump in her throat. "We could be…"

Her throat closed on the words and she couldn't finish the thought, but it was unnecessary. They both knew what she was trying to say. Miles lifted his hands to cup her face and brushed his lips against hers softly.

"We don't," he said. "We don't say goodbye. There's nothing that says we have to, after all. Goodbyes are over-rated anyway. They're so damn final. And there's nothing final about this. I fully intend to see you again."

She swallowed and stared into his eyes. Hearing the confidence in his voice and seeing the determination in his eyes gave her strength, and she nodded slowly.

"You're right," she agreed softly. "All right. We won't say goodbye."

He smiled pulled her close into a warm hug. "That's my girl."

Evelyn smiled at the endearment and rested her cheek on his shoulder for a second before pulling away.

"Now I've gone and made things maudlin anyway," she said, forcing a lightness to her voice that she didn't feel. "Say something diverting."

"Did you really relieve your brother of fifty quid tonight?" Miles asked promptly.

She blinked, then gurgled with laughter.

"I did," she confessed, "but he makes it far too easy."

He grinned. "Remind me never to play cards with you."

She tilted her head and considered him, a smile playing on her lips.

"Somehow I don't think you would be as easy to read."

"Why do I get the distinct impression that you could read hieroglyphics if you so chose?" he drawled.

Evelyn smiled, not answering. She raised a hand to his cheek and stood on tiptoe to press a soft kiss on his lips.

"Take care of your Spitfire, Flying Officer Lacey," she whispered.

"And you take care of your WAAFs, Assistant Section Officer Ainsworth," he replied just as softly.

Evelyn smiled and turned to leave the study. As she opened the door, she glanced back to find him leaning against the desk, watching her with an unreadable look on his face. When she met his gaze, he smiled slowly and winked.

As she crossed the hallway to the stairs, Evelyn felt a rush of emotion that she couldn't understand. She didn't know what the future

The Oslo Affair

held, or what the next few months would bring, but that suddenly didn't seem to matter. No matter what happened, she knew that she wasn't alone. Miles would be fighting the same war against the same odds. While he went back to his Spits and training, she would go back to her classified missions, knowing that they always had tonight.

And she would carry the memory of that slow, sexy wink with her into the shadows.

Epilogue

**Berlin, Germany
December, 1939**

Herr Renner sat upright with his hands on his knees, waiting. He was dressed in full uniform, not a crease or speck of lint in sight, with his hat placed carefully beside him on the bench. He stared across the entryway at a portrait of the Führer hanging opposite, his face void of any expression. Silence reigned in the waiting area, broken only occasionally by the sound of a telephone in a distant office.

A tall door opened suddenly to his left and a man in the black uniform of the SD emerged. He looked at Renner and stood to attention.

"Herr Obersturmbannführer Voss will see you now," he announced.

Herr Renner rose to his feet and placed his hat under his arm, turning precisely to go through the door without a word. Once inside, he stopped and clicked his heels together smartly as he raised his arm in salute.

"Heil Hitler!"

A tall blond officer turned from the window, casting a swift glance over him. After a moment of silence, he motioned him to stand at ease and crossed the room to the desk. He took his seat and opened a folder.

"Sturmbannführer Renner, you're aware that a determination has been made in the investigation of the events that took place in Stockholm on the tenth of November?" he asked, glancing up from the paper in front of him.

Herr Renner didn't look away from his superior's face. "Yes, Herr Obersturmbannführer Voss."

"And you're aware that you have been found guilty of negligence of duty in allowing an enemy of the Reich to evade capture?"

"Yes, Herr Obersturmbannführer."

The Oslo Affair

Hans Voss sat back in his chair and studied the other man for a long moment.

"What have you to say for yourself?" he finally asked.

"There's nothing to say, Herr Obersturmbannführer. I allowed the English agent to slip through my fingers."

There was another long silence, then Hans Voss stood up and went around the desk to lean against it, facing him.

"You knew how important it was that we detain her?"

"Yes, Herr Obersturmbannführer. I am sorry."

"So am I, Sturmbannführer Renner." He was quiet for a moment. "That was our only chance. We won't get another."

"With respect, Herr Obersturmbannführer, I disagree," Renner objected. "The other woman, the Norwegian, she will surface eventually. She can be made to talk. She will lead us to the English agent."

"No doubt she would," Hans agreed, "but you misunderstand me. We won't get another chance because the whole case has been removed from our jurisdiction."

Herr Renner stared at him. "Excuse me?"

"The SD no longer has any involvement in the affairs of the English agent known as Maggie Richardson. The Abwehr will be taking complete control of the case."

Renner's mouth dropped open. "The Abwehr!" he exclaimed. "Why?"

"Because, Herr Sturmbannführer, by your own admission you allowed a girl to slip through your fingers!" Hans' voice sharpened. "If I thought for one moment you would allow such a thing to happen, I would never have sent you to Oslo. I had all confidence that you could detain her, but I was mistaken. And this is the result. The Abwehr is turning it over to Eisenjager."

Renner's face drained of color and he stared at Hans in shock.

"Eisenjager?" he whispered. "The man's a myth, a legend. He doesn't exist, surely?"

"He exists, just as you and I do."

"And he's going to hunt down the English agent?"

"Yes. So you understand the position you've put me in. Himmler is furious." Hans straightened up and turned to return to his seat behind the desk, the informal portion of the interview over. "You will return to your quarters and remain there for the rest of the day. Tomorrow, a car will arrive to take you to the station. You are being reassigned to Warsaw."

"Poland!" Renner exclaimed. He immediately stopped his protest when Hans lifted cold blue eyes to his. "Yes, Herr Obersturmbannführer."

"Do you have any questions?" Hans asked, lowering his eyes again to the paper before him and picking up a pen.

"Just one, if you would indulge me, Herr Obersturmbannführer."

"Yes?"

"What is so important about this particular English agent?"

The pen paused in its journey to sign the order and Hans looked up slowly.

"I wish I knew."

The Oslo Affair

Author's Notes

1. Oslo Report: Hans Ferdinand Mayer was a German mathematician and physicist who approached the British Naval Attaché, Captain Hector Boyes, in Oslo Station in late October 1939. He sent instructions which arrived by post, offering technical information on German military projects. He instructed for the BBC German broadcast to be altered to say "Hullo, hier ist London" and, if it was, then a package would be delivered. Boyes arranged it and on November 3, a packet was hand-delivered to the embassy. It contained 10 pages of technical information ranging from the development of experimental pilotless aircraft at Peenemunde to the introduction of radar along the German coasts, as well as advances made in the manufacture of bomb fuses, an example of which was included with the report. The package was sent to SIS Headquarters on Broadway in London, where it was received by Section IV on the basis that the air section was the only SIS section with any technical knowledge. However, they did not have the scientific knowledge to evaluate the report. They called in a scientist working for the Air Ministry's Directorate of Scientific Research, Dr. R.V. Jones, who confirmed that all the information was genuine and that the Report was of the highest importance. Unfortunately, no one else agreed. At the time, all scientific research was so compartmentalized in England and other countries that SIS felt that no one scientist would ever have access to such a variety of information. What they didn't realize was that Germany did not compartmentalize their research in the same way. Therefore, Mayer did indeed have access to the research he provided. But SIS concluded that the Oslo Report was a plant sent by the Germans to mislead them. Therefore, Mayer was never pursued as an asset. In time, the Oslo Report proved to be genuine as more and more things within it were confirmed and discovered, but SIS lost the opportunity to learn more by utilizing Mayer. (MI6 British Secret Intelligence Service Operations 1909-1945 by Nigel West, pg 111-112. Weidenfeld and Nicolson - London. 1983)

CW Browning

- Hans Ferdinand Mayer was born October 23, 1895 in Pforzheim, Germany; and died October 18, 1980 in Munich, West Germany. In 1936 Mayer became the Director of the Siemens Research Laboratory in Berlin. Unhappy with the Nazi regime, he arranged a business trip to Scandinavia in late Oct 1939. He arrived in Oslo, his first scheduled stop, on Oct 30 and checked into the Hotel Bristol. Borrowing a typewriter from the hotel, he typed the Oslo Report in the form of two letters over the course of two days, delivering it to the embassy himself. He returned to Germany and continued his scientific work until 1943, when he was arrested by the Gestapo for listening to British broadcasts on the radio and criticizing the Nazi party. He was imprisoned in Nazi concentration camps until the war ended. Because of the intervention of his mentor, a devout Nazi Socialist and Nobel prize winner, he wasn't executed. The Germans never knew of the Oslo Report, or he would undoubtedly have been killed. As it was, he survived the war and went back to science. At his request, no one knew he was the author of the Oslo Report until after his death. (Wikipedia) (https://ethw.org/Hans_Ferdinand_Mayer)

- While Hans Mayer was in Oslo at the time indicated in this book, there was no scientific convention in Oslo at the time. For the sake of the story, I invented the convention as well as his associate and the meeting between him and Evelyn. Everything else relating to the Oslo Report, however, is historically accurate as portrayed.

2. **English roundup of German spies:** In Sept, 1939, MI5 knew of six agents working in England for the Hamburg Station (German Intelligence). Four of them were interned at once, it being unlikely that they would provide leads to other agents. One was a Swedish woman, suspected of working as a courier and local banker for German intelligence. She was left with her freedom and watched until December, 1939, when she was arrested for giving false details on an exit visa. The last was a Welsh engineer - codenamed Snow - who had been briefly employed by SIS in 1936 until it was discovered that he was in contact with the Germans. After that, he remained in contact with SIS and, on Sept 4, 1939, offered his services to them again as a double agent. (British Intelligence in the Second World War, Vol 4, pg. 41 by F H Hinsley and C A Simkins. Cambridge University Press 1990)
- That was the extent of the officially documented German spies in London at the start of the war. The spy present in London in the book

The Oslo Affair

is a fictional character. To my knowledge, there is no record of any spies in London leaking SIS agent identities during the war.

3. **Battle of Barking Creek:** On Sept 6, 1939, three days after war was declared, a radar fault led to a false alarm that unidentified aircraft were approaching from the east at high altitude over West Mersea, on the Essex coast. Six Hurricane fighter planes were scrambled from North Weald Airfield in Essex. However, two additional Hurricanes were also sent up in reserve. The two reserves were identified as enemy aircraft and Spitfires from Hornchurch were ordered to attack them. Both Hurricanes were shot down. One pilot, Montague Hulton-Harrop was killed, while the other pilot, Frank Rose, survived. Hulton-Harrop was the first fighter pilot to die in the war, and the Hurricane shot down in the Battle of Barking Creek was the first plane ever shot down by a Spitfire. (Wikipedia)
(https://www.bbc.co.uk/history/ww2peopleswar/stories/70/a5781170.shtml)

- The friendly-fire incident Miles writes about in his letter to Evelyn was loosely based on the real incident of the Battle of Barking Creek. However, I moved the incident to November and used bombers instead of fighters to fit the story better. As far as I'm aware, there was no such incident involving bombers in the fall and winter of 1939.

4. **Gamla Stan:** Gamla Stan is also known as the Old City in Stockholm. It dates back to the 13th Century and consists of medieval alleys and cobbled streets. Many of the original buildings are still present, but many have also been destroyed over time. From the mid-19th century to the early-mid 20th century, Gamla stan was considered a slum. Many of its historical buildings were left in disrepair and, just after World War II, several blocks were demolished. Now, it has been restored and is a tourist attraction consisting of shops and restaurants.

- I was privileged to spend some time in Stockholm in 1995, when I fell in love with the old city. The restaurant Den gyldene freden (The Golden Peace) is a real restaurant located on Österlånggatan. It has been in business, continuously, since 1722 and, according to the Guinness Book of Records, is the longest operated restaurant with an unchanged environment and is one of the oldest restaurants in the world. (Wikipedia)

5. **The Venlo Incident:** A covert German SD operation on November 9, 1939 that took place 5 meters from the German border in Venlo, Netherlands. Two British SIS agents, Capt. Payne Best and Maj. Richard Stevens, believed they were meeting with a German officer who was working with a resistance group in the German Army to overthrow Hitler. In reality, the 'officer' was an SD agent and the plan was orchestrated by Himmler and approved by Hitler himself. Upon arriving at the appointed meeting place in Venlo, the two SIS agents were captured and taken across the border to Germany, where they were interrogated. Goebbels used them as a propaganda stunt and pinned the November 8th assassination attempt on Hitler to them, broadcasting that they had been the brains and money behind the attempt. They were imprisoned in concentration camps for the entirety of the war, but survived. The entire affair was a humiliating intelligence defeat that decimated Britain's entire European intelligence network. (Wikipedia) (https://www.historynet.com/unveiling-venlo.htm)

6. **General Note:** SIS, or the Secret Intelligence Service, was known throughout the war as MI6 for the sake of expediency and clarity. Before and after the war, it reverted back to its title of SIS. For the sake of continuity, and because of its more recognizable connotation, I refer to it as MI6 throughout the Shadows of War series. Though it had several different sections, the main headquarters was located on Broadway, across from St. James Park Underground Station.

7. **66 Squadron:** 66 Squadron was a real Spitfire squadron during the war. They were stationed in Duxford before moving to Horsham in May, and then on to Coltishall from May-Sept, 1940. In September, they went to Kenley, then on to Gravesend from Sept-Oct, 1940. As was common during the war, the squadrons were constantly moving around as they rotated through the busier sections. For example, a fighter squadron in the southern section known as 11 Group would have been in the heaviest fighting during the Battle of Britain. They would be rotated to the north of England where they could get a break from the constant stress of battle while another squadron took their place in the south. 66 Squadron was no different in that regard. Once the war began in earnest, they moved frequently throughout the war. While Miles and Rob's squadron is named 66 Squadron, and is loosely

The Oslo Affair

based on the real squadron, all the scenarios and references specific to it in these books are fictional. While I have come across multiple references to a squadron that was referred to as the Corinthian Squadron due to the large number of wealthy pilots, there is no indication that it was the 66 Squadron. None of the pilots included in the books based in any way on any of the incredibly brave pilots that really were part of 66 squadron.

Other Titles in the Shadows of War Series by CW Browning:

The Courier

Night Falls on Norway

The Iron Storm

Into the Iron Shadows

Other Titles by CW Browning:

Next Exit, Three Miles (Exit Series #1)

Next Exit, Pay Toll (Exit Series #2)

Next Exit, Dead Ahead (Exit Series #3)

Next Exit, Quarter Mile (Exit Series #4)

Next Exit, Use Caution (Exit Series #5)

Next Exit, One Way (Exit Series #6)

Next Exit, No Outlet (Exit Series #7)

Games of Deceit (Kai Corbyn #1)

About the Author

CW Browning was writing before she could spell. Making up stories with her childhood best friend in the backyard in Olathe, Kansas, imagination ran wild from the very beginning. At the age of eight, she printed out her first full-length novel on a dot-matrix printer. All eighteen chapters of it. Through the years, the writing took a backseat to the mechanics of life as she pursued other avenues of interest. Those mechanics, however, have a great way of underlining what truly lifts a spirt and makes the soul sing. After attending Rutgers University and studying History, her love for writing was rekindled. It became apparent where her heart lay. Picking up an old manuscript, she dusted it off and went back to what made her whole. CW still makes up stories in her backyard, but now she crafts them for her readers to enjoy. She makes her home in Southern New Jersey, where she loves to grill steak and sip red wine on the patio.

Visit her at: www.cwbrowning.com
Also find her on Facebook, Instagram and Twitter!

Printed in Great Britain
by Amazon